GARDEN of MADNESS

Center Point
Large Print

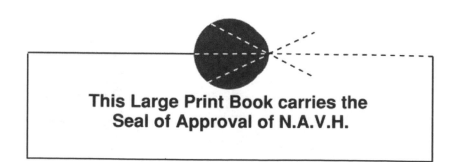

**This Large Print Book carries the
Seal of Approval of N.A.V.H.**

GARDEN *of* MADNESS

Tracy L. Higley

CENTER POINT LARGE PRINT
THORNDIKE, MAINE

The text of this Large Print edition is unabridged.
In other aspects, this book may
vary from the original edition.
Printed in the United States of America
on permanent paper.
Set in 16-point Times New Roman type.

ISBN: 978-1-61173-487-4

Library of Congress Cataloging-in-Publication Data

Higley, T. L.
Garden of madness / Tracy L. Higley.
pages ; cm
ISBN 978-1-61173-487-4 (library binding : alk. paper)
1. Large type books. I. Title.
PS3608.I375G37 2012b
813'.6—dc23

2012007329

To my fantastic "Ffrinds"—
Randy, John, Jim, Rick, Tosca,
Meredith, Camy, and Mary
This book has bounced along a road
with lows and highs,
and through the ride you have offered
encouragement, support, advice, and hugs.
I am honored by, and grateful for,
your friendship.

Word List

ashipu—a member of the Babylonian clergy with both healing and cultic responsibilities

ashlû—measurement equivalent to about fifty yards

asû—a Babylonian physician

bêru—measurement equivalent to about five miles

haruspicy—a form of divination, often using the entrails of animals

heptascopy—examination of the liver, specifically, as a method of divination

kalû—priests employed as singers and chanters in ritual worship

kanû—measurement equivalent to about eight feet

tanbûr—a fretted, stringed instrument, similar to a lute

There is a God in heaven
who reveals secrets . . .
—DANIEL 2:28

Prologue

Babylon, 570 BC

My name is Nebuchadnezzar. Let the nations hear it!
I am ruler of Babylon, greatest empire on earth.
Here in its capital city, I am like a god.

Tonight, as the sun falls to its death in the western desert, I walk along the balconies I have built, overlooking the city I have built, and know there is none like me.

I inhale the twilight air and catch the scent of a dozen sacrifices. Across the city, the smoke and flames lift from Etemenanki, the House of the Platform of Heaven and Earth. The priests sacrifice tonight in honor of Tiamat, for tomorrow she will be wed. Though I have questioned the wisdom of a marriage with the captive Judaeans, tomorrow will not be a day for questions. It will be a day of celebration, such as befits a princess.

Tiamat comes to me now on the balcony, those dark eyes wide with entreaty. "Please, Father."

I encircle her shoulders in a warm embrace and turn her to the city.

"There, Tia. There is our glorious Babylon. Do you not wish to serve her?"

She leans her head against my chest, her voice

thick. "Yes, of course. But I do not wish to marry."

I pat her shoulder, kiss the top of her head. My sweet Tia. Who would have foretold that she would become such a part of me?

"Have no fear, dear one. Nothing shall change. Husband or not, I shall always love you. Always protect you."

She clutches me, a desperate grip around my waist.

I release her arms and look into her eyes. "Go now. Your mother will be searching for you. Tomorrow will be a grand day, for you are the daughter of the greatest king Babylon has ever seen."

I use my thumb to rub a tear from her eye, give her a gentle push, and she is gone with a last look of grief that breaks my heart.

The greatest king Babylon has ever seen. The words echo like raindrops plunking on stones. I try to ignore a tickling at the back of my thoughts. Something Belteshazzar told me, many months ago. A dream.

I shake my head, willing my mind to be free of the memory. My longtime Jewish advisor, part of my kingdom since we were both youths, often troubles me with his advice. I keep him close because he has become a friend. I keep him close because he is too often right.

But I do not want to think of Belteshazzar.

Tonight is for me alone. For my pleasure, as I gaze across all that I have built, all that I have accomplished. This great Babylon, this royal residence with its Gardens to rival those created by the gods. Built by my mighty power. For the glory of my majesty. I grip the balcony wall, inhale the smoky sweetness again, and smile. It is good.

I hear a voice and think perhaps Belteshazzar has found me after all, for the words sound like something he would say, and yet the voice . . . The voice is of another.

"There is a decree gone out for you, Nebuchadnezzar. Your kingship has been stripped from you."

I turn to the traitorous words, but no one is there. And yet the voice continues, rumbling in my own chest, echoing in my head.

"You will be driven from men to dwell with beasts. You will eat the herbs of oxen and seven times will pass over you, until you know that the Most High is ruler in the kingdom of men. To whom He wills power, He gives power."

The tickling is there again, in my mind. I roll my shoulders to ease the discomfort, but it grows. It grows to a scratching, a clawing at the inside of my head, until I fear I shall bleed within.

The fear swells in me and I am frantic now. I rub my eyes, swat my ears, and still the scratching and scraping goes on, digging away at my memories, at my sense of self, of who I am and what I have done, and I stare at the sky above and the stones below and bend my waist and fall upon the ground where it is better, better to be on the ground, and I want only to find food, food, food. And a two-legged one comes and makes noises with her mouth and clutches at me but I understand none of it, and even this knowledge that I do not understand is slipping, slipping from me as the sun slips into the desert.

And in the darkness, I am no more.

Chapter 1

Seven years later

The night her husband died, Tia ran with abandon.

The city wall, wide enough for chariots to race upon its baked bricks, absorbed the slap of her bare feet and cooled her skin. She flew past the Ishtar Gate as though chased by demons, knowing the night guard in his stone tower would be watching. Leering. Tia ignored his attention.

Tonight, this night, she wanted only to run.

A lone trickle of sweat chased down her backbone. The desert chill soaked into her bones and somewhere in the vast sands beyond the city walls, a jackal shrieked over its kill. Her exhalation clouded the air and the quiet huffs of her breath kept time with her feet.

Breathe, slap, slap, slap.

They would be waiting. Expecting her. A tremor disturbed her rhythm. Her tears for Shealtiel were long spent, stolen by the desert air before they fell.

Flames surged from the Tower and snagged her attention. Priests and their nightly sacrifices, promising to ensure the health of the city. For all of Babylon's riches, the districts encircled by the double city walls smelled of poverty, disease, and hopelessness. But the palace was an oasis in a desert.

She would not run the entire three bêru around the city. Not tonight. Only to the Marduk Gate and back to the Southern Palace, where her mother would be glaring her displeasure at both her absence and her choice of pastime. Tia had spent long days at Shealtiel's bedside, waiting for the end. Could her mother not wait an hour?

Too soon, the Marduk Gate loomed and Tia slowed. The guard leaned over the waist-high crenellation, thrust a torch above his head, and hailed the trespasser.

"Only Tiamat." She panted and lifted a hand. "Running."

He shrugged and shook his head, then turned back to his post, as though a princess running the city wall at night in the trousers of a Persian were a curiosity, nothing more. Perhaps he'd already seen her run. More likely, her reputation ran ahead of her. The night hid her flush of shame.

13

But she could delay no longer. The guilt had solidified, a stone in her belly she could not ignore.

She pivoted, sucked in a deep breath, and shot forward, legs and arms pounding for home.

Home. *Do I still call it such?* When all that was precious had been taken? Married at fourteen. A widow by twenty-one. And every year a lie.

"I shall always love you, always protect you."

He had spoken the words on the night he had been lost to her. And where was love? Where was protection? Not with Shealtiel.

The night sky deepened above her head, and a crescent moon hung crooked against the blackness. Sataran and Aya rose in the east, overlapping in false union.

"The brightest light in your lifetime's sky," an elderly mage had said of the merged stars. The scholar's lessons on the workings of the cosmos interested her, and she paid attention. As a princess already married for treaty, she was fortunate to retain tutors.

Ahead, the Ishtar Gate's blue-glazed mosaics, splashed with yellow lions, surged against the purpling sky, and to its left the false wooded mountain built atop the palace for her mother, Amytis, equaled its height. Tia chose the east wall of the gate for a focal point and ignored the Gardens. Tonight the palace had already seen death. She needn't also dwell on madness.

Breathe, slap, slap, slap. Chest on fire, almost there.

She reached the palace's northeast corner, where it nearly brushed the city wall, and slowed to a stop, bent at the waist. Hands braced against her knees, she sucked in cold air. Her heartbeat quieted.

When she turned back toward the palace, she saw what her mother had done.

A distance of one kanû separated the wide inner city wall from the lip of the palace roof, slightly lower. Tia kept a length of cedar wood there on the roof, a plank narrow enough to discourage most, and braced it across the chasm for her nightly runs. When she returned, she would pull it back to the roof, where anyone who might venture past the guards on the wall would not gain access. Only during her run did this plank bridge the gap, awaiting her return.

Amytis had removed it.

Something like heat lightning snapped across Tia's vision and left a bitter, metallic taste in her mouth. Her mother thought to teach her a lesson. Punish her for her manifold breaches of etiquette by forcing her to take the long way down, humiliate herself to the sentinel guard.

She would not succeed.

With a practiced eye Tia measured the distance from the ledge to the palace roof. She would have the advantage of going from a higher to a lower level. A controlled fall, really. Nothing more.

But she made the mistake of looking over to the street level far below. Her senses spun and she gripped the wall.

She scrambled onto the ledge, wide enough to take the stance needed for a long jump, and bent into position, one leg extended behind. The palace rooftop garden held only a small temple in its center, lit with three torches. Nothing to break her fall, or her legs, when she hit. She counted, steadying mind and body.

The wind caught her hair, loosened during her run, and blew it across her eyes. She flicked her head to sweep it away, rocked twice on the balls of her feet, and leaped.

The night air *whooshed* against her ears, and her legs cycled through the void as though she ran on air itself. The flimsy trousers whipped against her skin, and for one exhilarating moment Tia flew like an egret wheeling above the city and knew sweet freedom.

This was how it should always be. *My life. My choice. I alone control my destiny.*

She hit the stone roof grinning like a trick monkey, and it took five running steps to capture her balance.

Glorious.

Across the rooftop, a whisper of white fluttered. A swish of silk and a pinched expression disappeared through the opening to the stairs. Amytis

16

had been waiting to see her stranded on the city wall, and Tia had soured her pleasure. The moment of victory faded, and Tia straightened her hair, smoothed her clothing.

"Your skill is improving." The eerie voice drifted to Tia across the dark roof and she flinched. A chill rippled through her skin.

Shadir stood at the far end of the roof wall, where the platform ended and the palace wall rose higher to support the Gardens. His attention was pinned to the stars, and a scroll lay on the ledge before him, weighted with amulets.

"You startled me, Shadir. Lurking there in the shadows."

The mage turned, slid his gaze down the length of her in sharp appraisal. "It would seem I am not the only one who prefers the night."

Long ago, Shadir had been one of her father's chief advisors. Before—before the day of which they never spoke. Since that monstrous day, he held amorphous power over court and kingdom, power that few questioned and even fewer defied. His oiled hair hung in tight curls to his shoulders and the full beard and mustache concealed too much of his face, leaving hollow eyes that seemed to follow even when he did not turn his head.

Tia shifted on her feet and eyed the door. "It is cooler to run at night."

The mage held himself unnaturally still. Did he even breathe?

As a child Tia had believed Shadir could scan her thoughts like the night sky and read her secrets. Little relief had come with age. Another shudder ran its cold finger down her back.

Tia lowered her chin, all the obeisance she would give, and escaped the rooftop. Behind her, he spoke in a tone more hiss than speech. "The night holds many dangers."

She shook off the unpleasant encounter. Better to ready herself for the unpleasantness she yet faced tonight.

Her husband's family would have arrived by this time, but sweating like a soldier and dressed like a Persian, she was in no state to make an appearance in the death chamber. Instead, she went to her own rooms, where her two slave women, Omarsa and Gula, sat vigil as though they were the grieving widows. They both jumped when Tia entered and busied themselves with lighting more oil lamps and fetching bathwater.

In spite of her marriage to the eldest son of the captive Judaean king, Tia's chambers were her own. She had gone to Shealtiel when it was required, and only then. The other nights she spent here among her own possessions—silk fabrics purchased from merchants who traveled east of Babylon, copper bowls hammered smooth by city jewelers, golden statues of the gods, rare carved woods from fertile lands in the west. A room of luxury. One that Shealtiel disdained and

18

she adored. She was born a Babylonian princess. Let him have his austerity, his righteous self-denial. It had done him little good.

One of her women stripped her trousers, then unwound the damp sash that bound her lean upper body. Tia stood in the center of the bath chamber, its slight floor depression poked with drainage holes under her feet, and tried to be still as they doused her with tepid water and scrubbed with a scented paste of plant ash and animal fat until her skin stung.

When they had dressed her appropriately, her ladies escorted her through the palace corridors to the chamber where her husband of nearly seven years lay cold.

Seven years since she lost herself and her father on the same day. Neither of them had met death, but all the same, they were lost. Seven years of emptiness where shelter had been, of longing instead of love.

But much had ended today—Shealtiel's long illness and Tia's long imprisonment.

She paused outside the chamber door. Could she harden herself for the inevitable? The wails of women's laments drifted under the door and wrapped around her heart, squeezing pity from her. A wave of sorrow, for the evil that took those who are loved, tightened her throat. But her grief was more for his family than herself. He had been harsh and unloving and narrow-minded, and now she was free. Tia would enter, give the family her respect, and escape to peace.

She nodded to one of her women, and Gula tapped the door twice and pushed it open.

Shealtiel's body lay across a pallet, skin already graying. The chamber smelled of death and frankincense. Three women attended her husband— Shealtiel's sister, his mother, and Tia's own. His mother, Marta, sat in a chair close to the body. Her mourning clothes, donned over her large frame, were ashy and torn. She lifted her head briefly, saw that it was only Tia, and returned to her keening. Her shoulders rocked and her hands clutched at a knot of clothing, perhaps belonging to Shealtiel. His sister, Rachel, stood against the wall and gave her a shy smile, a smile that melded sorrow and admiration. She was younger than Tia by five years, still unmarried, a sweet girl.

"Good of you to join us, Tia." Her mother's eyes slitted and traveled the length of Tia's robes. Tia expected some comment about her earlier dress, but Amytis held her tongue.

"I was . . . detained." Their gazes clashed over Shealtiel's body and Tia challenged her with a silent smile. The tension held for a moment, then Tia bent her head.

She was exquisite, Amytis. No amount of resentment on Tia's part could blind her to this truth. Though Amytis had made it clear that Tia's sisters held her affections, and though Tia had long ago given up calling her *Mother* in her heart, she could not deny that her charms still held sway in Babylon. From old men to children, Amytis was adored. Her lustrous hair fell to her waist, still black though she was nearly fifty, and her obsidian eyes over marble cheekbones were a favorite of the city's best sculptors. Some said Tia favored her, but if she did, the likeness did nothing to stir a motherly affection.

Tia went to Shealtiel's mother and whispered over her, "May the gods show kindness to you today, Marta. It is a difficult day for us all." The woman's grief broke Tia's heart, and she placed a hand on Marta's wide shoulder to share in it.

Marta sniffed and pulled away. "Do not call upon your false gods for me, girl."

Amytis sucked in a breath, her lips taut.

Tia's jaw tightened. "He was a good man, Marta. He will be missed." Both of these statements Tia made without falsehood. Shealtiel was the most pious man she had ever known, fully committed to following the exacting requirements of his God.

Marta seemed to soften. She reached a plump hand to pat Tia's own, still on her shoulder. "But how could the Holy One have taken him before he saw any children born?"

Tia stiffened and brought her hand to her side, forcing the fingers to relax. Marta rocked and moaned on, muttering about Tia's inhospitable

21

womb. Tia dared not point out that perhaps her son was to blame.

"But there is still a chance." Marta looked to Amytis, then to Tia. "It is our way. When the husband dies without an heir, his brother—"

"No."

The single word came from both her mother's and her own lips as one. Marta blinked and looked between them.

"It is our way." Marta glanced at Rachel against the wall, as though seeking an ally. "My second son, Pedaiah, is unmarried yet. Perhaps Tia could still bear a son for Shealtiel—"

"You have had your treaty marriage with Babylon." Amytis drew herself up, accentuating her lean height. "There will not be another."

Tia remained silent. Her mother and she, in agreement? Had Amytis watched her languish these seven years and regretted flinging her like day-old meat to the Judaean dogs? Did she also hope for a life with more purpose for Tia now that she had been released? Tia lifted a smile, ever hopeful that Amytis's heart had somehow softened toward her youngest daughter.

"Jeconiah shall hear of your refusal!" Marta stood, her chin puckering.

Amytis huffed. "Take the news to your imprisoned husband, then. I shall not wait for his retribution." She seemed to sense the unfairness of the moment and regret her calloused words.

"Come, Tia. Let us leave these women to grieve." She meant it kindly but it was yet another insult, the implication that Tia need not remain for any personal grief.

Tia followed Amytis from the chamber into the hall, her strong perfume trailing. Amytis spun on her, and her heavy red robe whirled and settled. Her nostrils flared and she spoke through clenched teeth.

"By all the gods, Tiamat! For how long will you make our family a mockery?"

Chapter 2

Tia choked down the first words that came to her at Amytis's accusation—words that would slash at her hypocrisy—and instead lifted a verbal shield. "Mother, you presume attention I do not command."

Amytis twirled and stalked down the corridor, requiring Tia to follow on her heels. The vermillion robe she wore over her white tunic flowed backward like a scarlet river. "Why can you not confine yourself to the chamber I built for you? For your activities?" Disdain poured over the final word. Amytis did not, could not understand the frustration that compelled Tia to run.

"You have built me nothing, Mother. You

directed slaves to outfit a room, then called it a 'gift,' as though it were not designed to keep me hidden." An extension of the rooms where through childhood you kept me trapped. "And I cannot run in a single chamber."

Amytis thrust an arm into the air but did not turn. "It is the size of the throne room! Run in circles if you must! And those ridiculous trousers. You look like a traveling merchant."

The palace halls held ears, so Tia held her tongue.

Amytis glanced back. "Why are you lingering back there? Come to my chambers. We have much to discuss."

Weariness fell like a weight, but Tia followed Amytis through the hall of the harem. Curious eyes appeared above veiled faces. Amytis often swept through this corridor. To remind them all that she still reigned as queen?

Around a corner, past the representative of the harem, who maintained his stoic post, they reached Amytis's personal chambers. At her approach a guard opened the door. Amytis entered, flung her outer robe across the over-cushioned bed, and turned on Tia.

Tia remained at the threshold of her mother's chamber, but the door closed against her back.

The room was Amytis personified. As though she had come into a naked chamber and simply *lived* until it had become an extension of her very self, everything sparkling in the firelight, from gold-tasseled bed cushions to embroidered tapestries hung from bedposts. Even after a lifetime, the room left Tia dazzled.

Amytis crossed the chamber and poured wine from an amphora into a jewel-encrusted cup. "We must talk of your future." She sipped the wine, her glittering eyes studying Tia over the cup's rim.

"But Shealtiel's mourning days will not be finished until—"

Amytis waved away the words with a dismissive hand and lowered herself to a carved chair. "After that, after that. Of course his death was anticipated, so messages have been prepared for days and already dispatched."

"Messages?" The repetition sounded dull in her ears, the question of an ignorant child. Tia's lips and tongue felt thick, useless.

Amytis raised her eyes to the painted ceiling and sighed. "To my family, in Media, of course."

"Why—?"

Amytis clunked the cup onto a cedarwood side table. "Did you think I would allow you to remain unmarried, to run around the city like a street urchin?"

"But you told Marta—"

Amytis relaxed against the back of her chair, crossed her legs, and smoothed the white silk over her thighs. "No more Jews. Of course not.

That woman's next son is a brooding beast of a man, and marriage to him would benefit only their family, not ours." Her voice was as smooth as the silk, unruffled by the harsh prospect of Tia's future. "No, I have someone far better in mind."

Tia should have anticipated this, and yet the information flattened her against the door, her hands worrying the rough wood as though it could absorb her. Memories of years with Shealtiel fluttered like moths. Her throat convulsed against her words and they emerged half strangled. "So, once again, a commodity to be traded?"

Amytis lifted her chin and those hard, hard eyes under half-lowered lids were terrifying. "This time will be different. He is a Mede. An older cousin of mine and a prince."

"I would not care if he were king of all the world! I do not wish to again be under a man's thumb." *Within his embrace, perhaps, but no more.*

"Do not be foolish, Tia. It is the way of all royalty. We do what we must." She used her own thumb to rub the palm of her other hand with focused attention. "The gods know I have done what was necessary."

Amytis had been royalty herself, a Median princess, when her father brought her to Babylon for treaty and gave her to Tia's father. Such marriages, like her own, were more political contract than loving relationship, with the wife fulfilling her duty of bearing children to link two nations, but little more.

Amytis brought her gaze back to Tia, but it was the vacant look of one who stared into the past. "And it does not have to be wretched." Her voice had softened, and a stranger would have thought her tone consoling. Tia had learned the sound of manipulation.

"Look at me, Tia." She spread her arms to the abundant luxuries of her chamber, then lifted a hand toward the ceiling, indicating all that lay above them—the king's living, growing tribute of the Gardens. "You will find joy in it. The children will bring happiness."

The words lit a flame in Tia's belly. The same lies Amytis had spoken nearly seven years ago. Did she believe her own words? Clearly Tia did not bring *her* any happiness. But of course there were her sisters, married to Babylonian nobles and dutifully producing children.

"I will not marry again." Her voice was tight.

Amytis laughed, that soft musical laugh her father claimed was the first part of her he loved. "If all goes as planned, he will be here in less than two months. When your thirty days of mourning are finished, you will be given to Zagros."

Amytis would say that all her life Tia had been rebellious. But they had been insignificant mutinies, small refusals to bow to silly customs. In this, as in all that mattered, she had always been controlled.

The flame in her gut was an ancient, slow burn with an abundant source of fuel. *Would that it were a raging fire to purify my life.* She crossed the vine-choked carpet and fell to her knees at Amytis's chair, cursed tears stinging her eyes.

"It is not too late, Mother." The white silk twisted between her pleading fingers. "If the messages have only just been sent, you can send another to overtake the first, retrieve the scrolls." Her voice faltered, the whimper of a child begging for reprieve. "Please, Mother. Do not give me away again."

She bent her head to Amytis's knee, held the tenuous connection. She almost dared to hope her mother would lay a pitying hand on her head. Stroke her hair. Whisper assurances of love. *One touch, Mother. One touch.*

Instead, when Amytis shifted, it was to reach for her wine.

Tia pulled away and went to the square-cut window. The chest-high opening looked south, and at this height there was no need for a safety grid, leaving the view unobstructed. She leaned her head against the opening, blinking away emotion.

"You are unreasonable, Tia." Amytis joined her to look over the city. The fires of a thousand hearths glinted through the streets like watchful eyes. Amytis studied Tia's face and lifted her cup. "And you are distraught. Take some wine."

Tia wanted to grab the cup and toss it through the window but took it from Amytis's hand and sipped obediently.

Amytis watched her through calculating eyes, then turned back to the city.

"You are a princess, Tia. You have a responsibility to your kingdom. Marriage treaties ensure its peace." She jutted her chin toward the city, the fires. "If you will not fulfill your duty to them, then you might as well be a peasant yourself." She leaned through the opening and peered into the darkness below. Her voice deepened. "And I wonder how you would fare in the streets of Babylon."

Heat flooded from Tia's toes to her hairline. Subtle, as always, and yet clear. Do as she was told, or she would be as a commoner, thrust from her home and her position, unburdened of her possessions and left with nothing.

"Is there not some other way to serve, Mother? Can I not find ways to help—?"

"This is the way, Tia. I will hear no more."

The flush receded, leaving Tia chilled. She set the cup on the sill and left the chamber, silent, feeling Amytis's hard stare against her back. There was only one place she wished to be, and Amytis would not approve of her destination.

● ● ●

The hour was late but typical for Tia's secret errand.

She crossed three torch-lit courtyards to reach the wide stairs that led into the underbelly of the palace. Slaves tasked with second watch toiled on their knees to keep the flowers watered and mulched. Their listless eyes followed her steps, but what did she have to fear from slaves?

Once, years ago, a guard had caught her and dragged her to her mother's feet. Amytis called for an explanation, then slapped Tia when she gave it. Since then, she had only gone at night.

The stairs plunged downward, turned once. Two lonely torches burned in wall sockets as she descended, and at the bottom twin tunnels diverged in shadows, their vaulted ceilings lost in darkness. Tia shot a glance in each direction and held her breath, listening for a scrape of sandal on stone or a sword unsheathed. Nothing.

The vast tunnels and passageways of the palace could hide a thousand villainies. Though it had always been her home, still she felt its treachery. Wherever power resides, there is always evil.

Seven barrel-vaulted chambers lay in succession, but she need only reach the third. Here her preferred entrance, unused by anyone else, climbed upward. Within moments she regained the palace level, but no doorway led to a courtyard. Instead, the stairs spiraled toward the sky—a narrow shaft, a tunnel turned vertical.

First tier. Second. Her hand trailed the cold stones to her right and she twisted upward, upward.

Five. Six.

Tia paused at the seventh and topmost tier of her father's beloved Gardens, only lightly winded. *All that running has done some good.*

The door was locked, for she was always careful. What lay beyond must never escape. Her fingers fumbled at the leather-strung key at her throat and she fitted it to the socket. For one last breath she clung to the security of the landing. She had come many times but still held no illusion of safety. Heart thrumming, she nudged the door inward, a whisper of wood against the bricks.

Night air rushed through the open door, a cold greeting. Tia crossed the threshold and perched at the summit.

Viewed from the streets, the mountain built above the palace astounded citizen and traveler alike, a forest of trees and flowers, suspended above the city. Tonight, fronds of lofty palms scraped the dark sky and blotted out starlight. Sharp, jutted trunks bristled like angry soldiers standing guard over the Gardens. Tia darted to the first set of steps and descended one tier, moving with caution and a listening ear, her senses sparking with cold awareness.

A throaty growl reached her, the threatened

sound of a beast with eyes on an interloper. Tia halted, hand extended to the blood-red petals of a rose. Glossy-green leaves shone black in the darkness, and the smell of earth and moss mingled with another smell, neither animal nor human, but something frighteningly in between.

No need to call out. He understood nothing.

She lowered herself to the bottom step and waited. He would come.

The buzz of night insects kept her lonely company for some minutes. But then a shadow shifted, there came a scraping sound, nails dragged across stone, and he was there.

"Hello, Father," Tia whispered, her voice as tremulous as an old woman's. She held out a hand, palm downward, fingers forced to relax.

He inched toward her, feet and hands tapping the stones, then stopped. Stared from under bushy eyebrows and hair grown long and matted. His beard, too, had been uncut for nearly seven years and dragged over the ground. Tattered scraps of clothing, the last clinging vestige of humanity, hung from him in ribbons. His skin was caked with the mud of years. She had tried, those first few years, to make him comfortable, to care for his body, but the collapse of his mind prevented her ministrations.

What little light reached them here reflected in the whites of his eyes, and as always Tia fell into their empty depths, willing herself to see some flicker of awareness, some perception of who he was, of who she was to him.

There was nothing but the wet softness of animal eyes.

He scrabbled forward and sniffed her outstretched hand.

Tia lifted it to touch his cheek, but he jerked away and she grabbed her own hand. After all these years, his rejection still burned.

"Shealtiel is dead, Father." She spoke as though he understood, her seven-year defense against her crushing despair of what he had become.

He skittered a few paces, to a clump of blooming lavender at the base of a fig tree, and settled. His gaze never left her face.

"I know you wanted me to marry Shealtiel, and I sorrow for his family, but I am not much grieved for my own loss. Is that wrong?" Tia drew her legs up in front of her chest and wrapped her arms around them to ward off the night chill. She confessed her guilt to the only one who would ever listen.

"Mother plans to give me again. To the Median prince from her home."

At this last, he lifted himself from the dirt and paced the stones, a jackal waiting for prey. A chill breeze irritated the palms. Surely he was unhappy with the news? Her self-deception was all that kept her soul from shattering.

He had once been a magnificent man, her

father. Regal in bearing, a superior mind. A gift for the long-range planning it took to build such a city, and a skilled politician. Tia had adored him, and he had loved her. Perhaps the only one who ever would.

Sweet memories intruded, thoughts of his laughter at her childish joys.

"Faster, Father, faster!" Twirling her in these very Gardens, his head thrown back with delight, arms tight about her waist.

Had he given up on having sons, embracing instead this last daughter who loved to run and jump and sneak into the courtyard fountain on scorching days? He had indulged her and lavished her with his attention. "You are beautiful, Tia. Smart as a mage, strong enough to change the world." And then he gave her away and left her fatherless. How had they come to this?

"I do not know what to do, Father. Mother will thrust me from the palace if I refuse to marry again, I know she will." Tia plucked a rose leaf from its thorny branch and ripped it into green shreds. "I am not afraid of the city, but I do not wish to be a peasant, mucking in the dirt for a pitiful living. If I am not a princess, what am I?"

She waited for his answer. It was her way.

He still paced, like one of his caged panthers kept for the hunt. His blackened nails clicked against the stones. Around his mouth the gore of food crusted his beard.

Tia shuddered. A deep sadness welled up within her, sadness for how far her father had fallen and for how the loss of him had left her stranded. She swiped at hot tears with the back of her hand.

"When will you return to me, Father?"

She had always linked her marriage with her father's exile. Would her change in status bring about another change, one for which she had prayed to the gods but dared not hope? Her words were a whisper, and he did not slow his tread.

A hard determination flowed into her veins.

She could not, would not marry the Median prince.

But neither could she leave the palace. Her position and her possessions defined her life.

And she could not leave her father.

"I will find another way," she swore to the king and to the gods of the night if they listened, her voice dangerously loud.

"My destiny is my own."

Chapter 3

Pedaiah laid aside the scroll he'd been studying these many hours, rubbed his burning eyes, and yawned.

A low laugh filtered across the lamp-lit court-yard from a reed chair beside the fountain. "Quitting so early, Pedaiah?"

Pedaiah turned to the beloved voice and squinted to make out the lean form. Daniel held his own scroll to the lamp beside him on a narrow stone column, and Pedaiah smiled. "I'll not be looking for my bed before you, old man."

Daniel laughed again but set aside his writings and stood. "Perhaps it is time for a break. For us both." He looked to the wing of the courtyard, inclined his head to a young man who stood against the wall. The servant hurried forward, eyes on Daniel.

"Melchi, would you be so kind as to bring us some bread and cheese? A little wine, perhaps?" The boy bobbed his head and hurried from the courtyard.

Pedaiah stood and stretched his back, his neck, cramped from so many hours poring over the writings and from the tension of waiting for news of his brother.

Daniel pointed to his scroll. "You are studying Jeremiah's letters again?"

"Yes. I—I understand what the prophet tells us, but some of our brothers warp his encouragement to be content here, twist it into a defense of their flirtation with Babylon's detestable idolatry. I desire to find a way to show them their error."

A clearing of the throat near the front entrance of the courtyard turned their attention to the doorkeeper, a Jew even older than Daniel. He had been installed in his post since Pedaiah was a boy. "A visitor, Chief."

Daniel waved a beckoning hand and the door-keeper turned to invite the visitor to the inner courtyard. Pedaiah waited to see who came at this late hour, though it was a common occurrence for Daniel, still sought for his wisdom by the Jews, if not by the Babylonian rulers for years.

A middle-aged man, clearly Babylonian, entered a moment later, head bowed and fingers pressed together in respect. Pedaiah watched with narrowed eyes. He did not care for this type who sometimes came to Daniel at night, their oiled curls and beaded headbands signifying they were magi in Nebuchadnezzar's court.

"Enlil, is it?" Daniel crossed the courtyard swiftly, hands outstretched in greeting. "Come in, sit. We were about to take some food. Please, join us."

Enlil's eyes darted to Pedaiah, and he seemed to sense his animosity. "I cannot stay. I—I have only a question for you."

Daniel smiled and nodded once.

Pedaiah exhaled, his jaw tight. *This is how it always begins. With questions.*

"Some are saying, in the palace, I mean, I have heard—"

"Speak your question, Enlil. You have only friends here."

With a look of doubt at Pedaiah, the man took a

37

deep breath. "Do you still teach magi in the ways of the Judaean's One God?"

Daniel's answer was solemn, like an oath. "I do."

"I would like—if I may—I would like to join you."

The servant returned with food and wine, and Pedaiah thanked him, then busied himself at a small table, pouring two cups and tearing apart the bread. Even with his back to Daniel and the mage, he could feel the warmth of Daniel's response.

"You may certainly join us, Enlil, if your heart is seeking truth and not simply the satisfaction of curiosity."

"I want to know more of your One God. I—I have doubts—"

"Then you will come."

Daniel gave the mage the day and time of their meeting, and instructed him in secrecy.

Pedaiah tore a piece of bread with his teeth, the movement jerky and tense.

The mage fled moments later and Daniel joined him at the table. "You do not approve, son?"

Pedaiah thawed a bit at the term. With his own father in prison these many years, it always warmed him to hear Daniel call him *son*.

"I fear that one day you will welcome the wrong man, one bent on exposing your work, on bringing you to destruction."

Daniel shrugged. "Perhaps I shall. But it is more than my safety that troubles you, eh?"

Pedaiah dropped to a reed chair, cup in hand. "You are a wonder, Daniel. We all see that. So many years in the king's court and yet you have not compromised, not allowed yourself to become tainted by this place. But we do not all have your strength." He set the cup down with a thud. "We must remain separate to remain pure. If we are to survive this chastising, this exile, and return to our land as followers of Yahweh still, we cannot comingle our lives with theirs!" Pedaiah reclined against the chair, a bit winded.

Daniel sipped from his cup and studied Pedaiah. When he spoke, the words were slow, deliberate. "I wish you had been there when they walked from that furnace."

Pedaiah shook his head, smiling. The story had become legend among the Jews. Daniel's brash young friends, defying the king's edict. Thrown into one of the city's many brick-making furnaces, then walking out unsinged. "How does that—?"

"I saw the king and more than one mage fall on his knees before our One God that day."

"And one day *all* our enemies will bow the knee! But what is that to us? *We* are His people and must remain true to Him."

Daniel's brow furrowed. "And you believe Yahweh loves only the Jews?"

Pedaiah sighed. It was an old argument. One in which he was never the victor. "He loves all people. I know."

"Loves them. Calls them to Himself. Gives us to them, even. As a lamp stand of truth."

"And still they grovel before their wooden idols and commit every indecent act of which man is capable."

"Yes."

Pedaiah paced, fueled by agitation over his people's casual attitude toward idolatry, even now. And by the inevitable sacrifice to Babylon that his family would soon make—his own brother. "Would you have me accept their ways, join myself to them?"

"As your brother has?"

"I do not wish to talk of Shealtiel."

"I am still praying for his recovery."

Pedaiah kicked a chair from the path of his pacing. "He will not recover. Someone has made certain of that."

"And you believe Shealtiel's marriage to the king's daughter has brought this about?"

"Yes! What else?"

Daniel shrugged. "I have seen you on a few occasions with Tiamat. I would not think you found her so detestable—"

"Stop. Stop, Daniel." Pedaiah fell into his chair, dropped his face to his hands. "How can you even say such things?"

Daniel edged forward, gripped Pedaiah's shoulder. "You have acted with honor, Pedaiah. You have no cause for shame. I have watched you remove yourself from the palace, keep yourself distant even when speaking with her. You have hardened a cold shell around your heart, even as you sensed Shealtiel did not appreciate the gift he had been given."

Pedaiah lifted his face, found it damp. "Shealtiel has been like a blind man all these years, Daniel. It is as though he cannot even see how strong she is, how beautiful and compassionate. How intelligent and driven." He returned to his pacing. "But how *could* it be a gift? Marriage to one of these pagans?"

Another shuffling at the doorkeeper's entry. They turned, but there was no need for him to speak. Beside him stood one of the palace messengers, oft employed by Pedaiah's family in the palace to bring him news. The boy's face was downcast, his shoulders slumped.

Pedaiah clutched Daniel's arm but spoke to the messenger. "He is gone?"

The boy nodded.

My brother is dead.

The news shattered his heart and rocked his senses. It was more than the loss of his elder brother. They were sons of a king, he and Shealtiel. And now Pedaiah was next in the line of David. His father languished in a Babylonian prison and might not live long. When Jeconiah went to his fathers, Pedaiah would be the exiled, but rightful, king of Judah.

He reached for the neckline of his tunic, yanked until the fabric ripped.

Daniel whispered at his side, "Do you want me to accompany you?"

"No. No, I don't want you to take risks in the palace. I will go." They stood and Daniel embraced him, which was nearly Pedaiah's undoing.

He reached the palace before an hour had passed, found the chamber that held his brother's body, and breathed deeply at its door. Two terrible things he would see in this chamber—Shealtiel lying cold and Princess Tiamat with all her fiery warmth. Pedaiah strengthened his heart for both and pushed open the chamber door.

His mother and Rachel fell upon him immediately, their tears washing his neck. He wrapped an arm around each and they wept together.

Tiamat was not present, thanks be to Yahweh. Pedaiah led his mother and sister to chairs, and they sat with hands clasped, speaking in low tones of Shealtiel, his life, his last days, and the preparations to come.

Behind all of this, a current of thought gushed like a swollen river through Pedaiah's mind—sometimes cold, sometimes boiling.

Tiamat is now a widow. Tiamat is now free.

A hard shell, Daniel had called him. Well, he would let nothing penetrate that shell even now.

Nothing.

Chapter 4

In the chill of the Gardens, Tia's limbs deadened with cold. And yet she stayed. The night was birthing a plan.

Her father disappeared to roam the lower tiers. His elite guards manned the entrances at the base of the Gardens, so Tia raced upward. A flush of hope warmed her clammy skin. She descended the spiraling shaft, barely aware of her own steps.

She must return to the death chamber, to Shealtiel.

Marta would still be sitting with his body. She must be.

In the upper corridors she slowed her pace. No need to garner the attention of slaves and attendants. Her mother must not hear of Tia running the halls.

She shoved open the door to the chamber, too eager, for it crashed against the broad back of a man just inside. He turned, taller than her by a head, and frowned.

He had been speaking. She had interrupted.

The next brother in line, the condescending Pedaiah.

His tunic was excessively torn, a peculiarity of Judaean mourning. Tia dipped her head in mute apology and slipped into the room.

"Marta"—she kept her voice low in respect and did not look at her husband, covered now and awaiting his ritual purification—"we must speak together."

Marta stood with head bowed, a solid wall of grief.

Pedaiah resumed his speech, reciting some sort of prayer in his native tongue. *"Barukh atah Adonai Eloheinu melekh ha'olam, dayan ha-emet."*

Tia stepped away, embarrassed to have intruded. Rachel was no longer present. Tia had no allies in the room.

Pedaiah lifted his eyes to her and translated, with a tilt of his head and a tone that seemed to indicate she was too ignorant to understand the language of his homeland. "Blessed are You, Lord, our God, King of the universe, the *True* Judge."

He stressed the *true,* slight enough to go unnoticed, but she understood.

In a land where the king served as ultimate judge, these Jews, captives for over forty years, still insisted that their One God ruled over all. It would be ludicrous if they weren't so serious.

Yes, *serious.* One of the few traits Pedaiah shared with his dead brother. Both so pious, so formal. So cold.

Pedaiah appeared to finish his recitation, so Tia turned to Marta. "I have been thinking about—about my unfortunate childlessness." She spoke quietly, to exclude Pedaiah from the conversation.

Marta's eyes went immediately to her son, however, with a flicker of hope. "Yes?"

Tia bit her lip and turned so her back was to him. "I believe you are right. I should do all I can to give Shealtiel an heir."

Marta grasped her arm, her eyes glassy.

"But not Pedaiah."

Confusion swept Marta's features. Her eyes shifted to Tia's left, to the presence of the brother at her back.

Tia swallowed her discomfort, the humiliation.

"Tell us, Princess." Pedaiah's voice was shot through with sarcasm. "Please, enlighten us as to why you will not have me."

She forced her stance open to include him. He stood close, too close, and she had to angle her head to see into his dark eyes. The thin white scar on his chin that had always piqued her curiosity glowed in the lamplight.

Pedaiah was nothing like his brother. Tall and lean where Shealtiel had been shorter than Tia and too wide. Thick dark hair, trimmed short, instead of his brother's thinning hairline. All that Shealtiel lacked in attractiveness, Pedaiah had gained. But his bearing always seemed prideful, conceited. Shealtiel had tended to bow and scrape.

Pedaiah's gaze roamed her clothing, obviously troubled by the skin she left exposed, compared to his Judaean mother and sister.

Tia leaned back on her heels. "Let us not play games, Pedaiah. You hate me. You always have. A marriage between us would be an affront, and I doubt you could even bring yourself to give Shealtiel an heir."

He said nothing, but she did not miss the cringe —that tiny squint of the eyes, the creased brow.

Marta interjected. "I do not understand. You will not marry Pedaiah?"

Tia dragged her gaze from the brother, gave him her shoulder. "Nedabiah," she said to Marta.

"Nedabiah!" Both mother and son repeated the name with equal outrage.

Marta's hands flew to her cheeks. "He—he is ten years old!"

Exactly.

"It is done all the time." Tia swung her hair over her shoulder and grasped Marta's arm. "Treaty marriages between children."

Pedaiah's voice was low in her ear. "You are no child."

She turned on him. "And you are no fool. This arrangement is best for all concerned." Desperation hardened her tone. "The bride-price your family paid was inconsequential. To receive it back would be nothing. Far better for you to keep me in the family."

Marta pinched her son's forearms, her eyes wild. "Say you will marry her, Pedaiah. Do not keep refusing."

So, he has rejected me already. She should not have been surprised, but still it stung.

"Look at her, Pedaiah." Marta was pleading now. "She is beautiful. So beautiful."

But he refused to look at her. "Too long our people have been seduced away from principles by beauty."

Tia snorted to cover the shame. "Principles. Just like your brother."

"I am nothing like my brother."

Ah, the first bit of ire she had seen in him. Had she struck a nerve? Could she follow it, find the place where more hurt could be inflicted? But to do so would be to appear petty, to admit offense. She would not hand him such a prize.

"Stop!" Marta covered her ears. "Your brother lies dead beside you and still you cannot respect his choices."

There was more here than Tia understood. Pedaiah trembled, still unwilling to face her.

Her Garden-born plan was in danger. The fear that had lodged like a brick in her chest since Amytis's announcement threatened to suffocate. "Marta, you must see that I am right. Wed me to Nedabiah, and in due time I shall perhaps bear a son in Shealtiel's name."

In truth, the very thought was repugnant, but she had decided in the Gardens that this was her best alternative. To escape the control of a husband, she must find one whom she could command.

Never mind that Nedabiah will eventually become a man. Tia would worry about that later.

Marta sighed, a sound so weighted with sorrow and resignation that compassion nearly drove Tia to retract her hasty plan.

"Your mother will never agree."

Marta was weakening, and she must push forward. Tia waved away her concern. "We will do it quietly, before she can interfere. I will handle my mother. Appeal to my father's advisors. She will listen."

Marta looked to Pedaiah, a question in her eyes.

So, Pedaiah had become the decision maker with his father in prison these many years.

Tia sidled closer to him. He inhaled sharply and turned his head, as though he could not bear the sight nor the scent of her. She watched him swallow hard, saw his breathing shallow. Was she so repulsive?

"Take this to your father, Pedaiah. You know it is best." Her voice shook and Tia willed it to remain steady. "You know it is best."

He spoke to her but looked only to his mother, his face pale. "Any association our family, our nation, has had with yours, Princess Tiamat, has brought nothing but death. What reason would we have to continue such madness?"

Marta's quick intake of breath spoke more than words. They did not speak of madness in the

48

palace. Not ever. The secret that roamed the tiered Gardens was closely guarded.

But Pedaiah did not regret his comment, Tia could see it. He was like one of the well-bred stallions she kept for chariot racing. Haughty and arrogant but given his head far too often until he believed he was master rather than beast. All these years she had seen his eyes follow her whenever he came to the palace. Yes, he was finer looking than his brother, but she preferred Shealtiel's apathy and neglect to Pedaiah's disdain.

She studied his profile, the tiny muscle pulsing in his jaw, then drew so close he leaned his upper body backward. "You forget yourself, Pedaiah. You would do well to remember who is the vassal and who is the victor."

He met her eyes then, with such coldness her pulse stuttered.

"It is time for the ritual washing of my brother's body." He held an arm toward the door, indicating that she was dismissed. "Family only."

Chapter 5

Tia stormed from the death chamber and halfway down the dark corridor before she slowed to chastise her own timidity.

Pedaiah has no right to dismiss me.

Should she return? She was not wanted. In this, there was humiliation.

But I must make them want me again. They must agree to let her marry Nedabiah.

Her pace quickened with her thoughts, and she sped through the hall with no destination in mind, only to keep moving. Her mind worked best with her body active.

She rounded a corner in the southeast wing, smacked against a solid surface, and reeled.

Hands shot out, grabbed her arms, and held tight.

"My lady." The voice was smooth as warm oil.

Tia looked up into eyes that stole her breath.

She had seen him before, twice, but only from a distance. Her father's court of advisors were a muddled mix of magi, sorcerer, diviner, and priest, each playing a different role and each with a bevy of protégés. The man who held her studied privately under Shadir.

She smiled too widely, blinked too rapidly. "My apologies." Her voice sounded shrill in her ears. "I was not paying attention."

He still held her arms and smoothed the fabric before releasing her. "You are more accustomed to *being* watched than watching, I am certain."

She searched his slight smile for mockery but could see he intended to flatter. He bowed, and she took in the wavy hair, falling to narrow shoulders in the magi way.

"I am Amel-Marduk."

He wore the clothes of a mage. His flowing and

heavily embroidered robe hung open, and the thin fabric of his tunic revealed a lean but muscular physique. But it was his eyes that dragged her in, smoky gray with lashes that seemed to brush his cheeks.

"I am Tiamat."

He smiled, lips tugged downward as if amused that she gave her name. Of course, he knew it already. "Strange name for so beautiful a creature." He tilted his head, studied her. "But perhaps you have inherited a bit of the goddess. A little of her fire, her energy?"

Tia licked her lips and looked down to hide her pleasure. It had long been a matter of shame to her that Amytis named her for the dragon goddess—the hideous monster of chaos, Tiamat. That Amel would create something complimentary from her mother's choice sent a warmth to her cheeks.

"I am sorry to hear of your loss today, Tia."

His familiarity should have outraged her. It did not.

"It has been a difficult day for you, no doubt. You look flushed." He lifted his chin and peered over her head, to the end of the hall. "Would you like to take some air?"

What could it harm? "Yes. The air always brings relief."

He invited her to walk ahead with a guiding hand, the slightest touch at the base of her back.

The gesture seemed protective and brought again a flash of warmth.

The entrance to the small rooftop garden where earlier Tia crossed to the city wall lay at the end of the corridor, and they passed into the night air, silent. Tia's heart raced, as it had when she'd returned from her run hours earlier. Roses she always ignored smelled sweeter than she remembered.

Why had she come to the garden with this man she'd never met, on the day her husband died? The crescent moon soared higher than when she'd run under it, and that running hour felt part of another night, another time.

Amel let her wander ahead, along the walkway banked with jasmine and roses. She turned a corner toward the outer wall and paused. Ahead, something lay across the walk. Half-hidden in shadows, it was a mystery. Amel stepped beside her and followed her gaze.

"Someone has left their cloak?"

Tia shook her head. Too large for that.

It was absurd to hesitate, to not simply walk forward for a closer look. But something in her chest held her back, some strange premonition, a fluttering fear.

She glanced at Amel and he merely smiled. "Let us see what has been left behind, then." She stepped forward with a pretense of boldness.

Three paces from the shadow, she saw it was a body.

She dashed the last few paces and bent to the prone form. "Amel, bring a torch!"

It was a man, unconscious or dead, she could not tell. Even in the starlight she could see blood.

Amel returned with a torch and lowered it to Tia's shoulder. She gasped and fell back, braced her hand against stones behind her, and found her palm slick. Amel lifted her to her feet and she wiped her bloody hand on her tunic, then stepped out of the dark pool surrounding the body.

The body had been mutilated, but his face had only been scratched. She recognized the distinguished features of the nobleman, one of her father's longtime friends.

"It is Kaldu." The connection to her father brought a wave of sadness.

Amel's gaze was on her, not the tragedy at their feet, but he nodded.

Kaldu's upper body lay in a bed of flowers. She stepped around bloody stones to get a closer look. She bent again to examine him, aware that Amel still held the torch and kept a safer distance.

The length of the torso had been ripped open, like a sacrificial bull. But instead of a priest collecting Kaldu's blood, it had seeped across the stones. Lacerations crisscrossed his arms and legs at random angles. Whatever had cut his body had shredded his tunic and the fabric clung to ragged wounds. His fingers were bloody. Long fingers that once played the lyre.

He played at my wedding. Her fingers trembled at the injustice of his death. *Oh, Kaldu, who has done this to you?*

Tia studied his face again. Why had it been spared? The preponderance of gashes on his forearms were a clue. He had shielded his face from his attacker.

But what kind of attack? Cuts too irregular for knife wounds. Some deep, others shallow. One particular cut across his calf had slashed so deeply the bone was visible. She studied the fibrous muscles that had been exposed and ran a hand over her own calf to compare.

"Tia, we should summon the court asû."

"Kaldu is dead."

"Still—"

"Yes, and his family." Her heart tightened at the thought of Kaldu's wife and daughter. She looked up from the body. "Will you go?"

"Whoever—whatever—killed him may still be close—"

She gestured to the garden. "It is not so large, Amel. You can see we are alone. Go quickly."

Her tone indicated it was a command, and he bowed his head and backed away, though with a hesitancy that pleased her.

"Leave the torch."

He set it into a wall socket and disappeared.

She took the opportunity to make a closer inspection of the area. The position of the body was odd. Crumpled, like he'd been tossed here.

But with all this blood, this must be where he died. And no marks to indicate he'd been dragged.

Around her were indications of a furious struggle. Plants ripped up at the roots, flowers crushed, dirt spread over stones. He was missing a sandal, which Tia found paces from his bare foot.

She saw no knife, no weapon.

Who may have witnessed this attack?

It was a small, private garden, kept for royal use alone and accessible by a single door. Her eyes strayed to the cedar plank she kept propped against the stone wall and she bit her lip. Could someone have crossed from the city wall while she had been running? She needed to find the slave who tended the flowers.

Amel returned within minutes, with the asû, the court physician. Shadir and her mother followed.

She glanced at Amytis. What brought her?

Amytis lifted her eyes to Tia with an expression Tia could not decipher. Kaldu had been a family friend. Yet Amytis did not seem distraught.

The asû set about his examinations. Kaldu's wife and daughter arrived within minutes, and the sadness of the event swept over Tia afresh. Although a puzzle, this death was primarily a great tragedy.

Kaldu's wife kneeled in his blood, her cries muted but heartbreaking, and took his whiskered face in her hands.

Tia fought back her own tears at the woman's pain. She, too, had lost a husband today, but would she ever love enough to feel this keen a loss?

Amel remained in the shadows. He slipped to her side and touched her arm in sympathy. The wind rose, rustling garden shrubbery and whistling over the stone wall. For the second time that night she heard a jackal howl, and the sound raised the hair on her arms.

"Who did this?" Kaldu's daughter moaned. "Who killed my father?"

The asû had little to do but proffer his opinion. "He has been mauled. I have only seen this in the desert or among the animals kept for the hunt." His voice dropped in pitch, as though he feared his own words. "Some kind of predator has done this killing."

Tia did not react. Nor did anyone else on the rooftop, to their credit. But the words hung in the air like a pronouncement of guilt, and every one of them must have had the same thought.

True fear clutched Tia's heart, and her own blood seemed to drain to the stones. All these years, all these years they had kept the secrets . . . A coldness slithered through her and she fought to keep from shaking.

Shadir's eyes were on her. Amytis looked over the northern city wall, across desert sand to places unknown.

"We should give the family their privacy."

Amytis turned to the asû. "You will take care of the body?" He nodded.

With that, they were ushered from the rooftop by the force of Amytis's personality.

In the palace hall Shadir pulled Amel toward the east wing. The younger mage turned once, a lingering look and cool smile for Tia. Amytis saw it, raised her eyebrows, then left Tia standing alone.

Just as well that she had been abandoned. She had a single thought and must pursue it.

When she had left the Gardens earlier, her thoughts had been wrapped around her plan to avoid the Median prince and safely marry Shealtiel's youngest brother, Nedabiah. One question now scorched her thoughts.

Had she left the door to the upper tier of the Gardens unlocked?

For the second time that night, Tia trekked through courtyards, down steps, across underground chambers, and up the shaft to the small door that was her private entrance.

She found it ajar.

Heart pounding, Tia slammed it shut, yanked the key from under her tunic, and secured the door. Then she turned, leaned her back against the splintered wood, and tried to breathe.

One way or another, whether unlocked door or cedar plank, Tia feared Kaldu's blood was on her trembling hands.

There was more at stake here than her freedom. She would not forsake her plan to marry Nedabiah and keep herself safe.

But she must find out what happened to Kaldu.

Chapter 6

Dreams clung to the long night.

A jackal with my father's eyes roams the Gardens, the palace balconies, the courtyards. I follow, my feet bare, slipping from columned arch to leafy palm, watching the jackal prowl. The beast slows, lifts its gray snout, sniffs the air. Turns its eyes to me. My heart beats like a bull's-hide drum, hollow and deep, and those eyes, those eyes take me in and study me as though they would dissect soul from body. A numbing cold spreads like a wave from my eyes to my feet and out to my fingers, and I grasp the rough palm trunk and burrow cold fingers into its jagged bark.

Tia woke, breathing hard and fingers tangled in bedcoverings.

Gula was at her bedside a moment later, holding a palm-sized oil lamp that etched her face with shadows. She reached for the cup of warmed wine she'd given Tia before she retired.

Tia shoved Gula's arm from her vision and clawed at the coverings. "I am well, Gula. Only a dream." But the dry rasp of her tone betrayed the pretense.

Gula ran a narrow-eyed gaze over her, then returned to her pallet in the adjoining room.

Tia sought sleep again, though it had been an oppressor.

In the morning her first thought was of Kaldu's mutilated body and that unlocked door. Questions tightened the muscles of her neck and shoulders, and the night's pent-up tension left her with the urge to strike. Or scream.

I must run.

"Gula, make ready my training chamber."

She appeared in the doorway at Tia's call. "But your husband's burial—"

"Not until tonight. It is the Jews' Shabbat."

"Still, your mother—"

"Gula! The chamber!"

She bowed out of the room, and when Omarsa had her dressed, Tia left, keeping to the back corridors.

As always, guards crawled the halls. One of these, a wide-chested soldier, joined her as she rounded the final corner. He accompanied Tia to the double-wide door of the chamber, standing too close.

Will no one let me breathe?

The guard assumed his post outside the door, and she entered alone.

Finally. This need she had to run, to strive, to

sweat—her training chamber was all she had to ease the pressure of a life too idle, too indulgent.

The four windowless walls were hung with braziers, lit by Gula. It was an inner room formerly used for storage, enclosed by other rooms. Shadows played on the undecorated baked brick walls. *"The ugliest room in the palace,"* Amytis had sneered. Perhaps to her. To Tia, it was her sanctuary, her temple. She did not utter such thoughts aloud, for fear the gods would be jealous, but in this room she controlled her own life.

And that control had become her religion.

Tia had chosen every item herself, from the straw-stuffed mats to hemp ropes and rigged pulleys. But the piece she loved most, the one that most angered Amytis, was the hide-covered wooden bull in the center of the room.

Tia crossed to the beast and stroked its back. "Greetings, old friend."

Its marble-chip eyes stared into the dark corners. It had stubbed horns, long enough for handholds, but not as sharp as a real bull's.

Tia had never taken part in bull-leaping outside this room, but it was a favorite dream. The annual festival gave the city's best athletes the chance to flaunt their talent. She could race chariots with the best of them, but she was not yet ready for the bulls.

She bent to the animal's carved ear. "Someday." And what would Mother say on that day?

In spite of her complaint to Amytis, Tia often ran here, and she began this morning by chasing shadows around the circuit of the cavernous room until her skin glowed in the firelight and her lungs burned.

After a swig of water from the jug at the head of the chamber, Tia stretched her muscles, then faced the bull with undivided focus. Her limbs twitched, a prickling pain that craved action. She looked into the bull's marble eyes, readied her stance, then shot forward at full speed. *One, two, three, LEAP!*

Her hands clasped the horns. A grunt escaped her chest. Back leg kicked upward, up, higher, and she was inverted on the bull's head, balanced. *Hold, hold.* A thrust with her lower body and she completed the flip, soared over the bull's body, and landed with a shout of triumph.

A bit unsteady. Needed to work on that. But her lips curved with pleasure and her pulse beat a satisfied rhythm through her veins.

"You are an acrobat."

She spun to the shadows that held the smooth voice. "Who is there?"

She knew the answer before he stepped into the torchlight. Had his voice already become so familiar?

Panting, Tia used her forearm to wipe dampness from her brow, conscious of her strange attire and strands of hair affixed to her cheeks

61

with sweat. "How did you get past the guard?"

Amel-Marduk's smile boasted flawless teeth, perfection unnoticed in the solemn moments beside Kaldu. His full lips held amusement at her expense and his arms were crossed over his strong chest. He was no stranger to training either, it was clear. He shrugged a shoulder, as if accustomed to the world giving way at his touch. "You are not the only one who enjoys taking risks."

Tia swiped hair from her face. "Is there news of Kaldu's killer?"

Amel strolled to her, hooked a finger around an errant strand of hair, and shook his head, slowly. His hand brushed her cheek and felt like summer lightning.

Her mouth had gone dry. From exertion, no doubt. She pulled away, fetched the water jug, and drank directly from its lip. Too late she realized her usual method was less than feminine. She set the jug down too hard and turned, eyes on his feet.

But Amel-Marduk laughed, still amused by her, it seemed. He tipped his chin upward. "You are like a soldier in combat, Tia. But who is your enemy?"

Who, indeed?

She met his gaze. "Why did you come?" Her voice scratched, a little hitch of nervousness.

He was by her side again, those eyes drawing her in. Did he have some secret knowledge imparted by magi? Secrets that left her swaying on her feet as though wrapped in a spell, with only his eyes to keep her upright?

"I came to see you."

"Why?"

He spoke the answer against her ear. "Because you are the goddess Tiamat. And from you the whole world is formed."

He spoke of creation, of all land and sea that came from the chaos of Tiamat.

She turned her head away, thoughts jumbled, and answered with a whisper. "But it was *Marduk* who slew her."

His laugh was a low rumble in his throat, dangerous and predatory. He traced her jawline with a cool finger. "Fear me, Princess?"

He smelled of smoke and incense. *Yes, and he is trained in ways more mysterious than I understand.*

Tia grabbed at a pulley fixed to the ceiling. All of this was not right, not what it should be. "You will forgive me, Amel, if I continue alone. I have a full day ahead."

His eyes never left hers. As though they still spoke, even in silence. At last she broke the heady connection and turned her eyes to the mats.

The door whispered closed a moment later.

Her breath escaped her chest and she leaned against the pulley. It gave way and she stumbled and cursed. She had sought to release her anxiety, but Amel's visit had sharpened it with the hint of the desirable, the forbidden, until the very air made her skin itch. Shaking, she bound her hands with strips of cloth, then attacked the hide-covered bull, beating her fists against its cushioned surface. She pounded with a fury she had not known, all the guilt and frustration and loss of the past day building, building and coursing through her arms like a river surge.

Her husband—dead. Another foreign prince summoned to take what remained of her.

While she maneuvered to marry herself to a child, a mage not permitted to even speak to her invaded her chamber, her thoughts, and crawled under her very skin.

To all this, add Kaldu's strange death. And the fear that the one person to whom she still clung, perhaps without reason, might be slipping away. Too much for even her.

The surge of emotion swelled, then spent itself against the unforgiving hides.

She fell against the bull and wept.

Chapter 7

Tia had never entered slave chambers. The floor of the single room, much smaller than her own, was littered with no less than a dozen pallets. The bare walls bore no tapestries, no furniture stole floor space, not a single item of indulgence graced the room.

Amytis was wrong. Her training chamber was not the ugliest room in the palace.

A few well-placed questions of other slaves led her to the chambers of Ying, the slave who tended the rooftop garden. She had not expected to find so many slaves—six of the pallets held sleeping women. Were their slaves permitted to sleep so late? One of them lifted her head, focused on Tia, then scrambled to her feet. She was younger than Tia, with the darker skin of Upper Egypt. Did she remember her home? Still cling to former freedom?

Tia mustered a cool look, trying to convey an obligatory disapproval of the slave's laziness. "I am looking for Ying."

The girl raked fingers through tangled hair and blinked rapidly. "Ying works in the day."

Her voice was high and light, like a wisp of cloud, and the way she leaned into the word *day* unraveled Tia's mistake. These women were not neglecting their duties. They worked all night and slept in daylight. She had never considered that slaves worked whilst she slept. She fought to keep a flush of shame at bay. "Where would I find her?"

"She keeps gardens. Mostly the outermost courtyard, closest to the palace's east gate."

Tia nodded her thanks, a quick bob of her head

more dismissive than grateful. Slave relations were complicated. They could not be treated as equals. Even if the injustice nagged her conscience.

Amytis loved the east courtyard. Would Tia find her there? She would not approve of her daughter's questions.

She found Ying kneeling alongside another slave woman, clipping back the stems of anemones. Her gaze followed Tia's entrance and she spoke to her companion, too softly for Tia to make out the words. At Tia's bidding, she rose and wiped dirt from her hands.

She was from the East, the land of silk and ivory. Small-framed and strong, with the lovely almond eyes and delicate fingers of her people. Babylon's conquests extended far. Tia sensed resentment at her intrusion, though Ying's expression quickly shifted to a mask of deference.

The resentment puzzled Tia, and when she spoke, her words sounded clipped, harsh. "You tend the rooftop garden off the northwest wing?"

"Yes, my lady. Is something amiss?"

So the news had not yet traveled through the palace. Had Shadir's influence kept it quiet? "You worked there yesterday?"

Her eyes shifted to the right, then back to Tia, unreadable. "Yes, into the evening."

Tia stepped across a paving stone and lowered her voice. "Did you see anyone there?"

Ying tilted her head, studying Tia like a diviner trying to read a sheep's liver. "Yes . . ." She drew the word out until it sounded more like a question.

"Tell me"—she resisted the desire to shake the truth from her—"who was in the garden last night?"

Ying's eyes fixed on hers, suddenly cold and accusing. "You were, my lady."

Those eyes. Did Ying know what had happened to Kaldu? A flutter of apprehension tickled Tia's stomach. "Before me. Or perhaps after. Someone else."

"I saw you enter and cross to the wall in your usual way."

The flutter became a crawling up her back. How many nights had Ying watched her from silent shadows?

Ying squinted into the sun, rising above the courtyard wall. "I finished before you returned. There was no one else."

But there *had* been someone else. "You may return to your work." Again, that little flame of resentment flared behind Ying's eyes. Tia dismissed her with a wave of her hand and left the courtyard.

Ying had seen no one before her, including Kaldu. Shadir had been there when she jumped from the city wall. Tia recalled his words, his tone. Had he known Kaldu's body lay mangled nearby? Had he tried to keep her from it? She had seen no blood on Shadir's clothing. Would not such a struggle leave signs?

She must find the asû who had been summoned to the garden to examine the body.

A twinge of uncertainty dogged Tia's steps. Should she be so preoccupied with the death of a nobleman when her own husband also lay dead in the palace?

But Shealtiel's death was expected, the culmination of a long illness, and she could not quash her curiosity nor her fear to sit in mourning. Not when her father might be in danger.

The asû assigned to the palace did not spend his time in a temple, as was customary for the profession. Instead he had his own chambers in the palace and was expected to care for any and all in need, from slave to king. Tia had long desired to help care for his suffering patients, to ease their pain, but Shealtiel did not approve of what he called her "gruesome interests." He preferred her to keep to her studies and leisure.

She found the asû bent over his latest patient, a court official's wife. Seluku's short, wide build was a source of amusement for children and adults, earning him the nickname "Mouse." Indeed, his pointed nose and two prominent front teeth did not help.

Seluku barely acknowledged her, so intent was he on his procedure. Tia should have been offended, but instead his work drew her to the bedside.

The woman was not conscious—whether intentional or not, Tia did not know—and her breathing was labored, with a strange warbling on the intake.

Seluku glanced at Tia, then indicated a thin lead tubing at the foot of the bed. She placed it in his extended hand.

"Her chest is filling with a death demon." He held a flint knife in his small right hand. "We make an incision here, in the fourth rib."

He spoke like one of her tutors and she watched, unflinching. The knife slit the woman's skin easily. A trail of blood followed the incision. The woman's body twitched, and Tia stepped forward to lay a calming hand on her shoulder. She seemed insensible to Tia's touch, and Tia longed to relieve her discomfort.

"We insert the tube." He angled it downward, watched the patient's face as he twisted it into position. "And let it drain."

Indeed, it did drain. A foul, yellowish fluid that must certainly be deadly. Tia stroked the woman's hair, spoke softly. "And she will live?"

He pulled two amulets from a pouch that lay across a chair and began to swing them over her body. "If the hand of the god wills it." A gentle chant escaped his lips and Tia did not interrupt his prayers. Did the gods truly intervene on behalf of man? She found a cloth and jug of water and bathed the woman's fever-flushed forehead.

After Seluku finished and dressed the incision, he mixed a paste of some sort of powder and water and placed a small amount against the inside of her cheek. "For the pain." He gathered his supplies, then asked, "You have come about Kaldu?"

Perceptive little mouse. "Two questions."

His lips twitched in amusement and he secreted the amulets in his pouch.

With her hand still on the woman's brow, Tia plunged forward. "How long do you believe the body lay before it was found?"

"And the next question?"

"What kind of weapon did such damage?"

Seluku watched the woman for a long moment, then turned and pushed past Tia, out of the chamber. Tia whispered a few words of comfort in the woman's ear, then followed.

He waddled along the darkened corridor and spoke without turning. "You have a healer's heart and strength of stomach, Princess."

She glowed under his praise. "I am very interested in seeing those in pain healed. I do not care to see harm come to the body."

"Yes, and one body in particular."

She caught up with him as they emerged from the corridor into a courtyard and touched his arm. He slowed and turned. "Seluku, what can you tell me?"

He worried his bottom lip with those two teeth and scanned the courtyard, as if to ensure their privacy. "No more than I told you last night. The wounds were inflicted by something other than any blade I have seen. The skin was torn, such as wounds from an animal. As to the time of his death . . ." He squinted up at the sky as though reading the hour. "I would say he was not long dead when you found him. The evening was cool but the body was warm. The blood had not yet dried. Certainly he had not lain more than an hour or two."

Tia took this information and fitted it into the facts she already knew. But Seluku was not finished.

He drew close, his head reaching only to her chin, and his eyes darted right and left. "I have never seen an animal capable of this attack in the palace."

Was he probing for information, or did he have a theory of his own? The family secret was so well kept, she did not even know who was privy to it.

Tia chose to misinterpret his comment. "I will be careful, Seluku, thank you."

Bony fingers gripped her wrist. "If this—animal—is loose, it will kill again. And it must be stopped."

He knows. By Marduk, he knew and he was serving Tia a warning. The words spawned a nausea his procedure had not. She extricated her wrist from his web of fingers, her own hand shaking. "Yes. Indeed." All she could think to say, but the words held no meaning.

He straightened, as if they had been talking of nothing but potions and charms. "You will accompany me again, to visit the sick?"

She smiled. *If the desire to heal ever overcomes my fear of the queen.* "Perhaps."

His glance at the sky reminded her of how far the day was already spent. Shealtiel's burial would occur at sundown, and she could not afford to offend his family, not with her marriage request still unanswered.

Tia took her leave of Seluku, stretching neck muscles grown tense. Her questioning had yielded little information, and it would not be long before news of Kaldu's death would spread. She was her father's only protection.

And she was running out of time.

Chapter 8

Darkness fell upon the Jews' Shabbat, and Tia hurried to join the family assembled in the first courtyard inside the palace arch. Twelve chariots and their horses circled and waited for passengers. An evening burial was odd, but the Judaean vassals insisted on burying their dead within twenty-four hours. Shealtiel had been piously faithful in life; of course he would be in death.

That Tia had been excluded from all preparations was not surprising. His family had accepted her only as a token of good faith between families, a relationship long since degenerated. She had never been a daughter to Marta, nor a sister to Shealtiel's siblings. Now she belonged to no one.

Amytis joined her at once, clutched her arm, and dragged her toward the lead chariot.

"Tia, you are his wife." Her tone was like a slap. "You should have been among the first to arrive."

Amytis's perfume lay heavy and Tia's eyes teared. "I had some business to—"

"Your business is here. Acting the part of a royal daughter."

Marta glared from the second chariot at her wayward daughter-in-law. Did she wish Tia had not attended? Beside Marta, Pedaiah's gaze fixed beyond the palace arch, as though nothing here was worth his attention. She would not wait to catch his eye.

It was a strange relationship, her father's hold on the world, this forced alliance between the vast Babylonian empire and the tiny province of Judaea. Nebuchadnezzar subjected entire nations to his reign, turned kings into vassals, but somehow those he trampled retained his respect. The Jews had been decimated in their own land, with even their great temple destroyed, over forty years ago. Her father had brought the best of them here to Babylon to ensure the cooperation of those left behind in their ruined land. Though captives, many held positions of prominence, like Nebuchadnezzar's own chief advisor, the Judaean Belteshazzar, though Tia had seen little of him these seven years. And the family of King Jeconiah enjoyed special privileges, despite their father languishing in prison, for some reason known only to her father, or known to him once, when his mind was whole.

Still, the Jews resisted assimilation into Babylonian culture. They kept their holidays, their feasts, their rituals. They refused to eat certain foods, dressed according to their old ways, and most significantly, held tightly to their "One God," as though they had brought him here from Judaea and the Babylonian gods were nothing.

All the same, Tia had been wed to Shealtiel, and the family had been invited to reside in the palace. Such connection made today's burial procession a royal event.

Tia climbed into the foremost chariot alongside Amytis. Sitting within, wrapped in heavy robes, was the peasant whose life had become one of deceit, simply because he strongly resembled the king. Tia bent to give him the obligatory kiss but did not meet his eyes. They had never spoken, and his presence was reserved for the occasional public wave from the palace balcony. Or a funeral procession. Compared with her father, he was like an empty shell.

Another chariot held Tia's two sisters and their husbands. An assortment of officials followed Marta and Pedaiah, in honor of the Jewish royal death, along with Shealtiel's sister, Rachel, and younger brothers. Tia peered across the courtyard for a glimpse of Nedabiah, who would soon be her next husband, and gripped the edge of the chariot.

"You are not ill?" Her mother's eyes narrowed, more disapproving than concerned. "I have told you that your ridiculous nighttime excursions are not healthy—"

"I am well, Mother."

In truth, something like sickness did seem to hover. Was it only the upheaval of her new widowhood? Worry for her father and Kaldu's strange palace death? It seemed something more, an oppression begun last night after the dream, and had not yet lifted.

They started off down the ramp, and the chariot lurched over an uneven paving stone, knocking Tia against Amytis. She pushed Tia upright and Tia again gripped the chariot wall.

In the street a six-wheeled wagon drawn by a team of brown workhorses held the huge terracotta burial urn. Tia turned her face from it, unwilling to dwell on Shealtiel's body secreted inside. Two slaves stood on either side of the

75

urn, holding it upright as the wagon wheeled through the still-crowded Processional Way. They followed, and in the chariots behind them, laments began.

Tia's nightly run afforded her only the barest glimpse into its streets. To be on the ground, among the people, assaulted her senses in ways unaccustomed. She bit her lip to maintain her solemnity but felt the stares of the people and wished she could stare in return. The Processional Way, the massive thoroughfare built by her father, began at the Ishtar Gate and continued through the city, past the soaring tower of Etemenanki, with its seven tiers to match the Gardens, then stretched to the hazy horizon where it met the outer wall.

They rolled through the crowds, who made way for their convoy with their own laments, to honor the dead. Tia gazed on citizens, both rich and poor with their dirty tunics, and merchants with their wagons loaded with timber and wine. A cart of oranges caught her eye and she could almost taste the tang of the juicy fruit. It was all so . . . *real*. So different from the palace. But so removed, she might as well have been only the statue of Ishtar paraded in the annual Akitu Festival procession.

Though Tia would have tarried, would have reached her hands to the outstretched fingers of those they passed, still she wished the moon would rise faster in the east to hurry them along. A goat pranced back and forth on the end of a rope, and Tia felt a restless kinship with the animal. She shifted in the chariot and drummed her fingers along its walls. Amytis jabbed her with an elbow, then bowed her head. *Too interested in my surroundings for a properly grieving widow.* She stilled her body and stared ahead.

At last they reached the burial ground, a collection of royal tombs at the southern edge of the city, and alighted to stand at its edge.

The crowd formed around the tomb given to the royal family. Marta and Pedaiah joined her, and Amytis dropped back to stand with the Babylonian officials, as was fitting. Behind them, Rachel and Nedabiah held hands. But Tia did not belong with either group, not the family, nor the Babylonians, and she held herself apart.

They waited for slaves to complete the laborious process of removing the heavy urn from the wagon and transporting it to the tomb. The night air was damp and heavy, and Tia lifted the hair from her neck. Pedaiah stepped to her side. She could feel his tense anger, strung tight beside her. Would he welcome her sympathy?

"I am sorry for the loss of your brother." She said it quietly, as it was meant only for him.

He glanced at her and then away. "Are you?"

Perhaps he guessed her small measure of relief in her freedom. Tears stung her eyes at her own callousness. She formed her words slowly, thoughtfully. "I know that you loved him. And he spoke often of you."

At this, Pedaiah let out a small breath. "Did he?"

"He wished for you to live in the palace with the rest of your family."

Pedaiah studied the slaves, sweating over their cargo as they dragged it toward the brick tomb. "He knew that could never happen." The declaration was like a judgment, a sentence that brooked no argument.

Is the great Pedaiah too proud for that?

Tia kicked at the dirt with the toe of her sandal. "Shealtiel also knew what you thought of him."

He did not respond. Since the day she met Pedaiah seven years ago, he had seemed intent on infuriating her.

"You felt our marriage signified compromise. That he displeased your God."

His attention was still only on the slaves, but at least he spoke. "My people do their best to live under the thumb of your family. They do not always choose wisely."

"So I was a foolish choice? That is what you believe?" Tia fought the rise in pitch.

"I believe we grow complacent after too many years in your desert. I would see rebellion as a better choice than compromise."

She laughed, a quiet chuckle that drew Marta's

scowl. "In that, Pedaiah, we are agreed." She felt his sideways glance and smiled. "Yes, I am as surprised as you."

The burial urn was ready at last to be placed inside the tomb. As a family, they approached and each laid a hand on its side. She followed, unsure of the Judaean practice and wanting to show respect. Though the wailing that had accompanied them from the palace had largely been simulated, there was true grief here in this little group. Pedaiah's lips moved silently, his eyes closed, and the moment seemed holy. Different than Babylonian burials. Marta and Rachel huddled beside Pedaiah and cried.

Tia felt their sadness deep in her own heart, joined them in it, and became more family in that moment than she yet had. And in the end, Tia wept as well, for what she'd lost and what she'd never had.

She embraced Marta and Rachel. Pedaiah watched her with narrowed eyes. Did he believe she pretended grief to win their favor, to win Nedabiah as her child-husband? Pedaiah seemed eager to always think the worst.

They returned to the chariots, and Pedaiah took Tia's hand to assist her upward. She clutched the gilded wall with one hand, but he retained the other, longer than necessary. She met his eyes and found him still watchful, as though he saw something in her no one else could see.

Something passed between them as they studied each other for that long moment. Something strange and wholly perplexing, a current like a trail of flame. She felt a protectiveness from him, a desire to keep her safe. Tia pulled her fingers from his grip and held her hand to her belly. He dropped his own and turned. As he walked through the night toward his chariot, he held his arm from his body as if his hand were unclean. And yet it had not been revulsion she had seen in his eyes. Her breath grew shallow, and she barely heard Amytis's barked instructions to the charioteer.

Pedaiah's look followed her all the way to the palace, her mind forming an unintentional comparison between the mage Amel-Marduk and the prince Pedaiah. One was all charm and beauty and danger. The other—all gruff anger, resentment, and piety.

And yet, for those few moments at Pedaiah's side, the oppression that had fallen over Tia these past two days had seemed to lift.

Amytis was speaking low and harsh. "Still you draw undue attention, Tiamat."

Tia scanned the Processional Way. "What have I done?"

Amytis followed her gaze. "Not here! In the palace. I have spent the time at the burial ground hearing gossip from court officials."

Tia sighed and watched the city slide past.

"We must now deal with the next problem you have created." Amytis shifted in the chariot and set her face toward the palace. "Pedaiah, it would seem, believes you murdered your husband."

Chapter 9

Tia entered the rooftop garden, intent on her errand, and crossed to the site of Kaldu's death to scan stones and dirt for anything she might have missed. The stones had been scrubbed clean by Ying and the crushed plants cut back or removed. One would never know such a gruesome death had occurred. There was nothing more to be seen, so Tia retrieved her plank, bridged the gap to the city wall, and hurried across.

Tonight's run would be abbreviated. Only a short distance to the next gate, where she would descend through the sentry tower and make her way to the home she sought.

Despite her determination, two days had passed before she had an opportunity to pursue her questions. Two days of worry over palace gossip, knowing she could do nothing. While she'd concerned herself with one killing, she was suspected of another. But since she had done nothing wrong and Shealtiel's body had been interred, nothing could be proven.

Though proof matters little. My reputation will be tainted.

Tia cared little for norms and conventions, but her honor was another matter. In truth, it galled her to think Pedaiah had yet another reason to think her inferior. To clear herself, tonight she sought answers.

Two guards manned the tower at the Sin Gate. She approached slowly to show she was no threat. They watched her from their elevated post and laughed when she crossed the threshold of the tower entrance. A narrow set of stone steps spiraled downward, and the rough wall scratched her arm as she descended. In the street below, a tiny thrill shot through her body. Alone in the city!

The streets held secrets, clasped between alleys and mud-brick houses, buried under piles of refuse, hidden in shrines that littered the way. But tonight she sought truth in one particular household, sought some explanation for the brutal murder of Kaldu—an explanation that did not include her family. The night flickered with torches, sinister and shadowy. She did not linger.

As a court official, Kaldu retained his own residence rather than occupy the palace, but it lay only an ashlû away, and within minutes she was rousing the doorkeeper. He was a portly slave and moved too slowly for her taste.

She waved him closer. "Tiamat, royal daughter, to see the wife of Kaldu."

His eyes widened and he looked over her head, then leaned to search behind her.

"I am alone."

At this, his heavy lips parted and his eyebrows arched, creasing his forehead. She pushed past him. If he would not invite her, she would enter alone.

"I am coming, I am coming." He scurried ahead, up the few steps that led to the main level. "You may wait here. I will announce you."

Tia heard the tapping of sandals across the inner courtyard long before Kaldu's wife rounded the corner, lips parted and eyes wide.

"My lady!" She extended an arm. "Please, please come."

She wore the dark tunic of mourning, and Tia did not miss the woman's second glance at her own clothing. She wished she had not masked her intentions by dressing "like a Persian merchant."

Kaldu's home was nothing so grand as the palace but still richly appointed, with a central courtyard of leafy palms, a small pool, and stone benches for reclining. Braziers burned on each side of the courtyard, bathing the space in warmth and light. A welcome respite from the menacing darkness of the streets. From this courtyard branched all the rooms of the house, and Tia saw no one but Kaldu's wife. Gemeti, she remembered. The home smelled of bread and onions.

Gemeti inclined her head to a nearby slave. "Bring wine. The finest."

"That is not necessary, Gemeti. I have no wish to impose. I only wanted to see how you are."

Gemeti smiled—a quick, obligatory smile—and invited Tia to one of two benches facing each other. She took the other and picked at her robe where it lay across her knee. "My husband's death leaves us bereft."

Tia could hear the tears hovering below the surface. "I am sure the palace will provide—"

"But you lost a husband recently as well."

Too much curiosity in her voice. Tia lowered her head. "Yes, in that we have become sisters."

Gemeti came to sit beside Tia and patted her hand. "We will both survive. Women always do."

"True." Tia clasped the woman's hand, warming it with her own. "But I should think your loss more difficult. I knew for some time that Shealtiel would be taken from me. Kaldu's death was— terrible." An awkward finish. How had she thought it right to come with such a selfish objective?

Gemeti pulled her hand from Tia's and smoothed her robes with shaky fingers. She looked across the garden to a room at the back of the house. "There are more ways than sickness to watch one's husband be taken slowly." Her voice was taut with emotion, and her eyes found Tia's and spoke more than words. She must have felt kinship.

The slave brought wine in earthenware cups. Tia accepted one for the sake of courtesy and took a slow sip. Gemeti's confession opened a door Tia could not ignore. Her reason for coming. "I remember Kaldu as quite devoted to his family. To you."

Gemeti drew in a deep breath before answering and leaned against her slightly. "Once, perhaps. But these last months . . ."

Tia whispered her question. No need for slave ears to hear everything. "You believe there was someone else?"

"Someone. Some . . . thing. I cannot say." Gemeti ceased her constant fidgeting and wound her fingers together. Tia covered the woman's hand with her own. "He spent all of his time at the palace. Grew melancholy here at home. And I—I heard things."

"I heard nothing."

Gemeti smiled into the distance as though grateful for Tia's attempt at denial. "Other court officials. Wives invited to dine at the palace on occasion. Even merchants. Everyone eager to tell me that Kaldu seemed enamored with a particular slave girl in the palace and was seen with her often, even more than he attached himself to the magi."

Tia's heart pounded. "Do you know this slave? I shall question her!"

Gemeti wrapped an arm around her shoulder

and squeezed. "No need, Princess. No need. He is gone now, so what does it accomplish? And no, I do not know who she was and do not care."

"But, Gemeti, do you not wish to know who killed Kaldu?"

Her features darkened, a veil of suspicion dropping over her eyes. She released Tia and stood. "That is for the gods to know. I pray to Anu every day for justice." She crossed to the other bench but did not sit. "Why does a princess leave the palace alone to concern herself with such questions?" A sudden coldness struck the room, a coldness the flaming braziers did nothing to dispel.

Tia rose and inclined her head in respect. "I only desired to wish you peace, Gemeti."

Her features were closed yet composed, as though she willed her eyes and mouth into stone. "And you, my lady." The tone was flat, the words lifeless.

Ignoring her coldness, Tia embraced her quickly before leaving.

Gemeti did not escort her to the door. Tia felt the woman's eyes at her back as she crossed the courtyard and turned into the entryway. The doorkeeper had vanished.

The night had advanced while she followed her questions. Her run should have taken her home long ago. Tia slogged toward the palace, her energy sapped. She tried to run, to make up the time lost, but her muscles were sluggish, chilled.

What use was any of her questioning? Did she truly believe she could find answers here in the city or in the palace? Should she not be more concerned with her own situation? She must ensure her marriage to Nedabiah to prevent Amytis from giving her to her cousin.

Tia crossed the shadowy streets one after another, her gaze darting in and out of doorways and corners. Was she watched? Did the suspicion that she had murdered her husband follow her? Were those whispers of unseen enemies who lay in wait, plotting against her?

What was this paranoia? This sudden, oppressive fear?

No, it was not sudden. The weight of it had been with her for days, only now exaggerated as she pushed herself toward the palace, all her senses slowed and lethargic.

She slipped upward through the sentry tower with only a nod from the guard, crossed back to the palace and returned her escape plank, then fled to her chambers.

And yet when she entered, her chambers felt no safer.

Someone has been here.

Someone other than her personal attendants. Tia stood in the center, gaze roaming. What was different? What was amiss?

Her furniture—carved chairs and cedar tables—

lay unmoved. She examined the small chest where her jewels were kept, but it was untouched.

The smell of incense filtered to her senses, as though a ritual or incantation had been performed here. She drummed fingers against her thigh in a nervous rhythm. A slow suspicion rooted her to the floor and kept her searching the room for something added, not taken. Something small yet lethal.

There. Strewn across her bed, both a warning and an attack. Tiny charms belonging to demons and one preventative amulet, broken in two jagged pieces. She stared at the broken demon Labartu, her chest expanding in a mix of fury and fear.

"Gula! Omarsa!" Only Gula appeared. "Who has been here?" Tia pointed to the evil on the bed.

Gula's eyes widened. "No one, my lady."

"Is it because they think I killed my husband?" Or did someone know she asked questions about Kaldu and think to frighten her into silence? She snatched the charms from her bed, crossed the chamber, and tossed them through the open window.

Let them threaten. It only reveals there is something to hide.

She would not neglect to make sure Shealtiel's family agreed to her plan.

But first she intended to find the truth.

Chapter 10

From the doorway Tia watched the slaves in the palace kitchen at their morning work. The large room in the corner of the palace complex had direct access to the city street for deliveries and felt open, airy. Slaves laughed and chatted in groups of mixed races around wooden tables where they chopped and sliced and butchered today's meals.

Tia had never frequented the cooking rooms. She had cared little for what she ate and even less for how it was prepared. But gossip ruled the palace, and it was no more prevalent than around the worktables of the kitchen slaves.

The camaraderie ceased the moment Tia's presence was noted. More than a dozen pairs of eyes fixed on her, knives in midair and cook fires unattended. She leaned against a roughened worktable near the door, grabbed a handful of figs from a wooden dish, and chewed.

"I am looking for someone."

They waited, all of them silent.

"Kaldu's slave."

At this, a few stolen side looks. She turned to those who reacted.

"Who is she?"

A dark-skinned man, slightly built with the look

of a Nubian, stepped forward. "Kaldu kept no personal slaves here in the palace, my lady. Perhaps in his home—"

"You know of whom I speak. I need to find her. No harm will come to her. I only have some questions."

More glances between several. Did they protect someone? Or merely question why the princess had entered their domain with odd questions? Tia set down the figs and crossed her arms.

At last the Nubian spoke. "Perhaps my lady inquires after Ying. Kaldu often sought her out for various tasks."

Interest sparked through Tia's veins. "Ying? Who tends the rooftop garden?"

More guilty faces. "Yes, my lady."

Ying. Tia's thoughts rushed her from the kitchens. At last something she could pursue. It could not be a coincidence.

Tia shook off the feeling that she should not be pursuing any of this, crossed two courtyards and then the back halls of the palace, her robes billowing behind in her haste. Two flights of stairs led her to the entrance to the rooftop garden. She pushed open the door with care, as though a murderer might await.

Ying knelt, attacking the soil, with her back to Tia. She worked the ground around a bed of red roses. She was clearly strong. Tia watched her for a moment, watched her arm swing down again and again to rip the sun-baked dirt. She used a handheld tool, something Tia had never seen. Something like an iron claw. Her heart thudded.

As though she heard the sound of it, Ying turned. Her eyes flashed with something Tia could not name, but then Ying was all deference again, as she had been the first time they spoke. She stood and dusted the dirt from her hands. "My lady." She delivered a slight bow. "Would you like me to place the cedar plank?"

Tia crossed the garden and ran her hand over some green shrubbery. "I came to speak with you."

"How can I serve you?" The words, though proper, seemed to come from a far-off place, a place of mystery, like her homeland.

"You can tell me why you were seen often with Kaldu."

Ying's face blanched and her skin grew even lighter than the pale shade of her race. "I was assigned to assist him with his needs while in the palace."

"Assigned by whom?"

She turned away, a risk in the presence of royalty, and bent again to her flowers. Somehow in this Ying stole power from Tia, challenged her, because she knew more than Tia.

"Why does the command of slaves concern you, Princess?"

It is my father's safety that concerns me. Tia frowned. "Assigned by whom?"

The answer, when it came, was soft, spoken toward the soil. Tia stood close enough to hear the whisper. "Your mother."

When does my mother ever concern herself with slave assignments? "Why?"

Ying shrugged one small shoulder, her back still to Tia. "They spoke often. I saw them together on the night that he was—the night he died."

This was a revelation to ponder later. For now, Tia needed more information. She asked the question that nudged her heart the moment she saw Ying assault the soil. "Did Kaldu mistreat you?"

Ying snatched a hand from the flowers and turned it, palm upward. A drop of blood beaded on the tip of her index finger and swelled.

The oppression that had dogged Tia also swelled, a hand squeezing her heart. The blood on Ying's pale, pale skin was an awful thing, and somehow all the dread of the evil charms in her chambers, of the whisperings in the dark streets, of the threat to her father, all focused on that single drop of blood. She backed away, washed in revulsion.

Ying stood and stared, her finger held outward like an offering but her face tight with a flinching fear, like one who'd been bled as a target to circling birds of prey.

The moment broke, and Ying pressed the bloody finger against her breast. It left an imprint on her white tunic. Her voice was a harsh whisper. "He did not mistreat me."

Tia would press further, but still the dread wrapped her in silence. Ying pushed past her and escaped the garden.

Tia exhaled the moment she was gone, as though released from a vicious hold, reached to steady herself, and found nothing but flowering plants.

She would not let go. She would go where the information led. And next must be her mother.

"The shipments from Nubia must be unloaded the moment they arrive, and the sailors penalized for the delay."

Tia stood at the rear of the throne room for several minutes, her back to the wall, watching Amytis instruct her officials. The queen dealt with her advisors with all the authority of a king, her voice ringing with imperial strength across the room. Amazing, the way Amytis emanated power and charm wrapped together.

The king's top advisors, Rabi and Dagan, bowed to her command. As always, they sought her favor and acceded to her in matters of state. In the seven years since her father's illness, Amytis had grown to a position of prominence she had not known when he ruled. Still, it was the magi who held the ultimate power.

And all of us conspire together. Magi and royals

alike, to ensure the city and the world believed Nebuchadnezzar ruled from his sickbed. It was a testament to the cleverness of the men in this room that the citizens of Babylon, and more important their enemies, had not learned the truth.

But it could not last forever. Men at all times grasped for power. And a king gone mad left a void someone would eventually attempt to fill. He was vulnerable, her father. In more ways than one.

Amytis saw Tia at last and motioned her forward, the next petitioner in line, come to ask for favors. Tia crossed to the base of the platform and stood on her toes, forcing a respectful smile.

"I would speak to you alone, Mother."

Amytis sighed and lifted her eyes to the vaulted ceiling. "In my chambers."

Tia followed her through the back corridor to her rooms, which smelled of her dizzying perfume. Amytis seated herself and directed a slave to brush her hair.

"Mother, why did you assign a slave to Kaldu?"

Amytis stretched her neck, and the slave followed the movement of her head with the comb. "What nonsense are you talking, Tia?"

"Kaldu. The slave Ying says you gave her to Kaldu while he visited the palace."

Amytis fingered the emeralds around her neck and studied herself in the polished bronze, a blurry reflection. In that pause, that hesitation, Tia realized her mistake.

In all her years her mother had never told her the truth. She lied without remorse whenever it suited her needs. Or her wants. Why should today be different?

When she was younger, Tia had tried to keep count of the lies, of the deceit and trickery Amytis had used against her. She had given up years ago. Tia had asked her once why she loved her older sisters and scorned her. "You have your father's love," Amytis said. As if that were enough for anyone, and Tia should not need the love of a mother.

Amytis turned to her and waved away the slave. "Kaldu was a busy man. Besides his official duties, he studied under the magi. I approved this tutelage and offered him Ying for his needs."

"Are you not concerned about his death? About how it might have occurred?"

"Kaldu's death will no doubt be explained somehow. Or perhaps whatever killed him will act again and this time be observed."

Tia watched her mother's hazy reflection in the bronze. Did her thoughts run along the same path as Tia's own?

Amytis slapped her hands against her thighs and stood. "It is time to leave off useless questions, Tia." She ran a hand along Tia's hair, correcting whatever flaws she perceived. "You have been scurrying about the palace like the wayward child of a slave, and it is time to act as a princess. There is much to do in preparation for your marriage."

Tia bowed her head briefly and escaped her mother's chamber without speaking. What was there to say? Would she beg at her knee again? Plead with her to show some affection, some pity? Never.

Once a wayward child, always a wayward child.

Chapter 11

A few well-placed questions after the morning meal gave Tia her next objective. Nearby, but she would have to escape the palace once more. She would not wait for nightfall and her evening run. Instead, Tia directed her chamber slaves to dress her for an excursion, in a long tunic and embroidered woolen robes, with a wrapped head scarf to cover her unruly hair.

She would go quietly, without attendants or even a chariot. Amytis was in the throne room at this hour, as were her advisors, and Tia found the palace halls quiet. She slipped through the series of fountained courtyards, watching for Ying.

Tia had played the foolish princess, uncaring about matters of city and kingdom, heedless to the true workings of power. While her father prowled the Gardens, others made decisions in the throne room and in whispered, unseen enclaves. At the center, as it had always been, were the magi. The magi who interested Kaldu.

Now she must find answers outside their secretive circle. Someone with knowledge of their activities, yet not a colleague. Belteshazzar.

She had not thought of Belteshazzar in years. The name brought pleasant childhood memories, of better days when her father was whole, when he was the laughing, generous man she remembered, whose chief advisor had been a strange but affectionate Jew he kept close at hand. What had become of Belteshazzar in the years since her father's confinement? Did he still live?

Guards at the palace entry arch slowed Tia's progress, recognized her, and let her pass. She did not miss their amusement. Was she a joke among them all?

At the base of the wide palace steps, a sudden voice at her side startled her.

"Running away, are you?"

The ever-present Pedaiah, with his ever-mocking tone. Why am I surprised?

"But what am I saying?" He indicated her embroidered robes. "You are not dressed for running."

Tia bristled and kept walking, but he fell into step beside her. Had he been waiting for her? "What do you know of it?"

Pedaiah shrugged and nodded to a group of Jews they passed.

That was all the answer Tia was to receive, so she answered his implied question. "I needed to breathe air outside the palace."

"Hmm. Yes, I know how that feels."

"You have never lived in the palace."

Silence met her statement, so she pushed along the Processional Way.

When would he fall back? Tia felt his gaze on her profile. "Your mother and sister came to live in the palace when I married Shealtiel. But not you."

"No. Not me."

She needed to rid herself of him before finding Belteshazzar, but her curiosity bested her. "Why not?"

"Some of us prefer to remain untainted."

The words were like a slap against her cheek. She halted and turned on him. "The foul Babylonians, is that it? You fear we would defile you?"

He raised his chin and looked down on her. "You have that power. Indeed."

"You speak as though we brought you to the uncultured wilderness rather than the most splendid city on earth. Of what can your home country boast?"

He lowered his eyes and inhaled as if in pain.

Tia waved a hand. "Why do you not return to whatever it is you do, *outside* the palace?" She shoved through the crowd, leaving him behind.

But he was not to be shaken. Moments later, when she had weaved through a group of merchants bearing wagons of millet, he was there again beside her.

She elbowed him aside. "Stop following me!"

"Perhaps I am only going the same direction."

Tia growled, her fingers tightening to a fist. "Then, please, tell me where you are headed so I can choose another route."

He pulled at her arm and Tia whirled on him. "Do not touch me!"

"You are not safe outside the palace unaccompanied."

"So you would be my protector?"

He bowed in deference, unsmiling. "Pleased to oblige."

"I—I did not ask—" The words sputtered out, barely intelligible.

They drew attention. Merchants and shoppers passed, eyes shifted to their argument. He stepped closer and lowered his voice. "Princess, you are happily naive of those who would take advantage of finding you in the city alone. I will not force you back to the palace, but I do insist upon joining your adventure."

He said *adventure* as though Tia were a little girl out for a jaunt in the frightening city. "Very well."

He nodded once and walked at her side. "Where are we going?"

"To visit a childhood friend."

They did not have to travel far through the squalor of the city. Belteshazzar's house lay in the shadow of the great palace. Surprising for a Judaean captive, and yet he had been a favorite of her father's and lived in the palace when she was a child.

The streets here, so close to the royal family, were kept pristine, with well-tended rooftop gardens and smooth-facing stones hiding mud bricks. The children of nobles and court officials played in the streets, and the occasional merchant delivering grains and fruit to wives within hollered warnings to clear the way.

Tia and Pedaiah reached the last home on the left of the Street of Marduk, and Tia slowed at the single door facing the street.

Pedaiah scowled. "This is your childhood friend? Belteshazzar?"

"You do not approve?"

He huffed. "I should not have thought you would have any respect—"

"For a Jew?"

His gaze found hers and bore into her thoughts. "It would be a first."

Tia looked away, shame warming her face.

Pedaiah slapped the door and the doorkeeper appeared a moment later. The older man's eyes lit with pleasure, but it was not Tia's visit that delighted.

"Pedaiah!" He bowed low. "He will be most happy to see you." To Tia, he gave only a passing glance.

Pedaiah allowed her to enter first. Surprisingly, the unimposing door led to a spacious house with a beautifully tended courtyard. It would seem her father's chief advisor still enjoyed some benefits of his former position, though he could have lived more lavishly in the palace.

The doorkeeper bustled off to find Belteshazzar, and Pedaiah led her across the courtyard to a stone bench, recalling to her the earlier visit with Kaldu's wife.

I have gotten out of the palace more in the week since becoming a widow than in the year prior. She chose to remain standing.

He came at once, her father's old friend, and looked unchanged from Tia's memory, save perhaps a bit more gray. Tall, with a lean build and trimmed beard. A quick smile and eyes that sparkled with some unknown amusement. He crossed the courtyard, arms extended.

"Pedaiah. I did not expect you for another few days—" His eyes caught Tia's and he slowed, forgetting the intended embrace. "Is it the princess?" He looked to her protector, his brow furrowed. "You have brought me his daughter?"

Pedaiah held up a palm. "She has come of her own accord, Daniel. I only followed."

Tia had his full attention now, this *Daniel* as

she now remembered his Judaean name. It had been a point of good-natured contention between her father and him, the way he refused to substitute their god's name for his own, as was custom.

"Come, sit." He indicated the benches and Tia obliged. "You are much grown." His gaze traveled the length of her. "But still, I would know that hair, those eyes, anywhere."

"And I, you, Belteshazzar."

He shook his head. "*Tsk,* child. It is Daniel."

She smiled with warmth at having taken up her father's argument. "You are unchanged, *Daniel,* though I have not seen you in the palace for years."

His smile disappeared. "Your father? Something has happened?"

Tia sensed true concern. "No. Well, perhaps—" She glanced at Pedaiah.

Daniel waved an eager hand. "Continue, continue, child. You can speak in front of Pedaiah. He is like my own son."

Pedaiah's nod of approval was for Daniel alone.

"There has been a death in the palace."

"Two deaths." He nodded. "Your husband and Kaldu."

"Yes, of course. Two deaths." Tia looked to Pedaiah again, but his attention had moved across the courtyard to a girl entering with a tray. Her fleeting look toward Pedaiah spoke much. "My husband's illness was long and unfortunate. But it is Kaldu's death that brings me today."

Daniel noticed Pedaiah's glance and signaled the young woman forward. "I know little of it, I fear."

The servant set her tray on a low table between them with a glance at Tia that held some hostility. Tia paused to let her complete her task. She was clearly another Jew, about Tia's age. Her robes were a pale yellow, setting off her flawless skin. Though dressed in the modest way of the Jews, with her hair nearly covered, the fashion did nothing to obscure her beauty—the kind of womanly innocence men appreciated. She bent over the table, pouring wine and cutting crusty bread. The scent of the fresh-baked bread reached Tia's nose and her stomach growled. The three laughed, and a flush crept across her neck and face.

The girl lifted a plate. "Please, my lady, take some food." Her tone was pleasant, if a bit mocking.

"Thank you. I shall." Tia bit into the yeasty loaf and watched the unspoken communication between the girl and Pedaiah. Tia could not decipher its meaning, but it made her uneasy, she knew not why.

Daniel patted the girl's shoulder but spoke to Tia. "It has been some time since I was part of the everyday affairs of the palace. These days, I do not know much of its intrigue."

"My father relied on you, I remember."

Daniel lowered his head. "We did not always agree, the king and I, but our conversation was always interesting. Several times I believed he would finally bow the knee to the Most High, especially after . . ." He sighed. "I had hoped this present humiliation should not be necessary. But he is a proud man."

Troubling words. As though her father had brought upon himself his present state. *And are not all kings to be proud?* This idea of only One God, it both mystified and intrigued.

The girl would not leave. She fussed with the food, the cups, the plants. She hovered around Pedaiah like a bee drawn to a sticky sweetness, and he in turn seemed interested in all she did.

Tia tried to focus on Daniel. "Kaldu had taken up with the magi. Do you know why?"

His look turned dark. "Why does any man seek them out? For power, and power alone."

"You were one of them."

Daniel pulled at his beard and seemed to debate within himself how best to answer. "It is complicated, the position in which I found myself in your father's court, Tiamat."

She nodded.

"The Most High gave me to know certain things, to interpret your father's dreams, to advise him in important matters. For many years there was much jealousy among the other wise men and magi who would have my position. Their power and knowledge, when it is authentic, comes from elsewhere."

"They feared you."

He smiled, a brief flash of a smile, that was part amusement, part melancholy. "They fear the Source of true power. Hate it, even."

"And Kaldu?"

He leaned forward and patted her hand. "Be careful, young Tiamat. There is much at work that you do not understand. Much that is better left alone."

His tone was fatherly in its condescension, but Tia resisted. "If I recall, you were never afraid to challenge those who opposed you."

His eyebrows arched. "And you are ready for such a challenge?"

"I must know the truth. For the sake of my father."

Daniel twined his fingers together, pressed his index fingers to his lips, and studied her. When he spoke, lowering his hands, the words were deep and intense with eyes to match. "Then question everything, dear girl. Question everything you have been taught, everything you have been told." He slanted forward, eyes haunted, and his next words were a mere whisper. "The time of the prophecy is upon us."

A chill shuddered through Tia, a portent of evil to come, of substantial change and the dangerous unknown. She looked to Pedaiah, whose attention was on the conversation at last. His expression was unreadable but fierce.

Her icy fingers bit into the lip of the bench, searching for steadiness, but her skin crawled and the edges of her sight went dark, as though darkness itself reached for her from somewhere beyond her vision.

Tia stood, unsteady but determined. It was past time to return. The two men stood also, but Daniel stayed her with a hand on her arm.

"Be wary, child. When you seek truth, you cannot be certain what you will find. You must be ready. Ready to stand and fight, and not to run."

His words, his grip, were like iron. Had he ever run from anything? Tia pulled away, but he was not finished.

"The pursuit of truth is not a course to be run or a stunt to be perfected, Tiamat. The consequences—" But here he broke off, as if he had said too much, and his eyes seemed to glisten with unshed tears.

He embraced Tia briefly, and she could almost believe it was her father's arm around her. Tears surfaced.

Daniel turned her toward Pedaiah. "Return her to the palace, son."

And Pedaiah did, without conversation. She could not read the set of his jaw. Anger? Condescension? They had not spent so much time together in her seven years with Shealtiel, but even side by side, arms nearly touching, they somehow kept distance between them, as they always had. As though they each presented some sort of danger to the other.

He left Tia at the palace entrance, and her thoughts took her all the way to her chambers.

"So you have returned?" The voice that emerged from within was impatient, strident.

Tia breezed in and flung her head scarves across the bed. "No cause for concern, Mother. I only went to the river to cool down."

Amytis sat upon a reed-rush chair, one long leg crossed over the other. "Do you think me a fool, Tiamat? I know exactly where you have been."

Tia narrowed her eyes and studied her mother. Did Amytis bluff? And why the sudden interest in her actions? She seemed to be everywhere these days, watching Tia's every move.

"You have been to see that old Jew." Amytis stood and pushed her hair over her shoulder. "Spend your time in whatever way you please, Tiamat. But do it in the palace and do it alone." She drew close and hissed in her ear, "When your new husband arrives, I would not wish for him to hear rumors of his bride's inappropriate behavior."

No, Mother. Of course not.

Chapter 12

The sun rose, scorching Babylon as its rays shot through the streets. Tia clapped for her chamber slaves, who were awake and attendant at once.

"Dress me with care this morning, Gula. Robes that cover. And a head scarf, as the Jews do."

Oiled, perfumed, and dressed, Tia left her chambers, trailed by her attendants, and wound through the palace's labyrinth of halls to the rooms set aside for the family of the Judaean king Jeconiah.

The palace bustled, with slaves rushing the corridors and a din coming from beyond the residential quarters. Was the cause what she suspected?

A flutter of something akin to nervousness at the family's door tickled her belly. Pedaiah's stern face, those dark, brooding eyes . . . She dreaded the confrontation.

But it must be done.

"They have gone to the banquet room." The little Assyrian slave's voice was amusingly high pitched, but his words thudded against the pressure in her chest. "There is to be an announcement."

She turned away, and a moment later one of her mother's slaves stalked the hall, his face set on her. "My lady"—he descended in a quick bow—"your mother requests your presence—"

She held up a hand. "I am coming."

She walked as if to her execution.

Aside from the throne room, her father's banquet hall boasted the most lavish decor of the palace, and thus of the city of Babylon. And if Babylon, then perhaps the entire kingdom or even the world. Intricate mosaic tiles, their blues and yellows polished until they gleamed, spread scenes of battles and hunts across the floor, and bas-relief sculptures lined the walls in tableaux so realistic, visitors wanted to run their hands over the bodies of man and beast to feel for beating hearts.

At the end of the large room, a long table reserved for Tia's mother, and whatever nobles she invited this morning, held the finest Babylonian dishes, and on either side two massive windows cut into the stone wall streamed light into the room, the sun's rays bordering the honored guests. White silk fabrics, hung above the windows, billowed in the morning breeze. Scattered throughout the room were smaller tables, four stools clustered around each.

The luxury struck her afresh, along with a comparison to the city streets she had navigated yesterday. Tia had lived all her life amidst such extravagance. She sometimes forgot the privileges of her life, how vile it could be elsewhere.

Tia's mother and sisters sat at the head table, but she would not allow her dread of her mother's *announcement* to sway her from her task. She searched the tables for her quarry.

There. As she had hoped, Marta and Rachel sat at a table near the back of the room. The occasion must be significant, for Pedaiah had joined them. Still one empty seat. She threaded through the maze of tables and came upon them just as Rachel said something to her brother, and Pedaiah laughed, a joyful, heartfelt laugh. The sound jolted her, strange but welcome. Had Tia thought him incapable of mirth?

Smiling innocently at the threesome, she took the fourth seat.

As one, the family looked to her, then to her mother's table at the front, as though waiting for Amytis's wrath to streak across the banquet room, a lightning strike capable of incineration.

The two women faced her, and Tia bowed her head to each, noting with concern Marta's shadowed eyes and downcast face. "How do you fare this morning, Marta?" Beside her, Pedaiah shifted his stool toward the door.

Marta and Rachel both sat silent, staring. Tia was saved from the awkward moment by two slaves descending with trays of purple dates and cool green melons and goblets of palm wine.

She had dined regularly with Shealtiel in the banquet room during their marriage, always at the head table. She had seen Marta and Rachel here rarely and could not remember Pedaiah ever being present.

The food and wine were spread before the four of them, and Tia lifted a goblet, intending to drink to Shealtiel, but something in the sentiment seemed offensive. Instead, she sipped the wine and set the cup down too hard, sloshing liquid onto her hand.

The room buzzed with conversation, and whatever announcement her mother intended must be scheduled for later. Noblemen poured in, took their places, and the musicians at the perimeter set to work on their strings and drums. A figure appeared behind Pedaiah, and the four turned, breaking the tension.

The servant girl from Daniel's house. But even as the girl's eyes took in the seating arrangement and lingered on Pedaiah, Tia saw her mistake. Not a servant at all. Her bearing, her expression, even her clothing bespoke a confidence borne of privilege. How had she not seen it yesterday?

The girl gave her a cool, empty smile. "I had not expected the princess to be joining us." The words were benign. The tone was not.

Pedaiah jumped to his feet and signaled a slave. "We will bring another stool. There is room here."

Something like shame threatened to swamp Tia, but she denied it. Absurd. The girl was a Judaean.

Pedaiah glanced at Tia as the stool was placed. "Forgive me, I have not introduced Judith. A . . . friend of the family."

The girl's eyes on Tia were anything but friendly. She pulled the stool slightly closer to Pedaiah, as though it were her rightful place.

Pedaiah seemed not to notice. "Your dedication to the Teacher is appreciated, Judith. He is aging, slowing down perhaps. I know he is grateful for your help."

She smiled at Pedaiah and slight dimples appeared. "I am happy to serve him. Though he has not slowed so much. His daily meetings have grown a bit shorter, I suppose. But he has all the fire he ever had."

Tia's face heated at this familiar exchange about topics outside her knowledge. The slaves brought crusty bread and yellow onions. She dug in, fueled by unease more than appetite. The raw onions watered her eyes.

"Besides"—Judith touched Pedaiah's arm—"it is only fitting for a woman to occupy herself with the quiet and respectable pursuits of hearth and home." She looked to Tia once more. "Wouldn't you agree, my lady?"

Tia choked on a bit of bread and reached for her wine.

Pedaiah did not turn but answered in her place. "Perhaps. But a certain boldness, an adventure-some spirit, are to be equally admired."

Tia's skin flushed under the indirect praise. Surely he did not speak of her. She swallowed the wine and glanced sideways. Judith's eyes were twin fires. "I confess myself unskilled in domestic affairs, Judith. But my mother would no doubt share your opinion."

As though Amytis had heard the comment, she stood, and a musician piped a tune garnering the crowd's attention. Tia's stomach spiraled downward and she gripped the edge of the table.

"My husband wishes he were able to attend this morning." She began with the usual lie, one she had told so many times that perhaps she believed it. "He sends his regards from his sickbed and wishes life and happiness to all of you." She raised a cup and the room joined her in drinking to their own good fortune. Tia sipped at her wine, and it went down sour.

Amytis's eyes found Tia's, but she was all good humor. "I am so pleased to make an announcement to you, our honored guests, this morning." She set her cup down. "As you know, my dear daughter Tiamat has recently lost her husband of seven years." She bowed in the direction of their table. "We all grieve with the family of Jeconiah and would not wish to deny their sorrow. But in these days of Babylon's great reach, there are always threats to our power, and we must do all we can to thwart these dangers."

There were nods all around. Tia's palms

slickened and she intertwined her fingers to keep them steady.

"It is my husband's decision that Tiamat should be married to the prince of Media, to ensure ongoing peace between our kingdoms."

The room hummed with surprise, but Tia's gaze was on Marta, who jerked her head toward Tia, openmouthed. Tia shook her head, a tiny movement, but enough to signal her disagreement. Marta's eyes narrowed and hardened.

Amytis waited for the room to quiet, her glance skimming over the room of officials and noblemen. "Zagros will arrive by the Akitu Festival next month, and we will celebrate the next generation of alliance with Media." Again she raised a cup. "Let us drink to the health of Tiamat and Zagros."

As one, the room raised their goblets. "Tiamat and Zagros."

Those at Tia's table did not move.

Amytis reclaimed her seat, and Tia leaned forward and grasped Marta's hand. "I have no part of this and do not wish it," she whispered. "My desire is unchanged, to wed Nedabiah and join our two families once more."

Marta did not respond, and her wary look told Tia little trust existed between them.

"I apologize for my mother's haste. It is in poor taste to make such an announcement so soon after Shealtiel's death."

Beside her, Pedaiah spoke, his words and expression like flint. "The seven days of mourning are over. Why should we ask you to grieve unnecessarily?"

Tia drew in a slow breath, in and out. Such biting sarcasm. Her fingers curled, longing to strike him, to remove the condescension his face betrayed, but she controlled the inappropriate impulse and spoke only to Marta. "I know not why she is in such haste."

Pedaiah shoved his dish toward the table's center, as though disgusted with the food. "She has no sons."

Tia studied his dish, then his face.

He shrugged. "A queen with three daughters and an absent husband. Is there anything more vulnerable?"

How had Tia not seen this? She watched Amytis in the front of the room, smiling at those placed nearby, a smile that touched only her lips, false as any lie she had ever told her. In that moment Tia saw something in Amytis she had never seen—fear. Amytis truly feared all threats to the throne, from without but perhaps also from within. From her place at the table with advisors and magi, she seemed surrounded by menace more than friend.

She was like a woman held over a towering ledge, clutching furiously at the air.

But I must focus on Marta. Marta would

ultimately bow to the wishes of her husband and eldest living son, but as all women she wielded the true influence in her family.

"We can make this alliance, Marta. It is best for all, even if my mother does not see it. Please, please speak to Jeconiah."

The nobles were exiting the banquet room, their curiosity sated by her mother's declaration. A figure approached, one Tia had not seen earlier.

"My congratulations, Princess." Amel's words were languorous and his engaging smile circled the table to include Marta, Rachel, and even Judith, then stopped cold at Pedaiah. Beside her, Pedaiah drew himself upright, chin lifted.

She felt heat in her fingertips. "My mother's plans are her own." She regretted her words immediately. Her rebellion would be better kept quiet for now. But she wished Amel to know that she did not intend to marry Prince Zagros.

His attention was all on her now. "I am not surprised. You are your own woman, I have seen since we met."

Tia smiled at his praise.

With a nod to the women and a glare at Pedaiah, Amel held out a hand. "May I accompany you from the hall?"

Trapped between the two men, she took his hand, too eagerly, bowed to her extended family, and smiled at Marta. "We will speak soon."

Amel placed her hand in the crook of his arm

and Tia let him escort her from the room, trailing glances from servants and nobles alike.

They strolled the hall, in what direction she cared not. He still held her hand against his arm, and she felt the warmth of his touch.

"You are the center of attention everywhere you go, Princess."

"You are thinking of my mother." She leaned against him and laughed.

He seemed delighted with her girlish response, though she wondered at it herself, a bit sickened at her silliness.

"It was not your mother Pedaiah watched with those hawklike eyes."

She slowed. "You know Pedaiah?"

His face was impassive. "We have met."

They reached the first courtyard and began to walk along bordered flower beds. "I sensed hostility."

Amel was silent, as though reluctant to speak ill of the Jew.

"Tell me, why do you dislike him?"

"Because he is an arrogant fool." He bowed his head. "Forgive my honesty. I know he is family, of a sort."

"He is nothing to me, I assure you. And I would agree with your opinion."

They stopped before a surging fountain and Amel gazed into the pool. "Before I came to the palace to train with the magi, I was in charge of one of the city furnaces, managing the slaves who fired the bricks."

Hard to imagine the smooth, sophisticated Amel in the heat of a furnace yard.

"Most of them were Jews. Pedaiah seemed to think that his people should not need to work, as though captives should hold more privilege than Babylon's own citizens. He constantly tried to undermine my authority there, to remove the Jews from their duties and set them in lives of ease."

Tia huffed. Not surprising.

"I must say"—Amel patted her hand still on his arm—"for the son of a vassal king, the man has more arrogance than the daughter of true royalty herself."

She smiled, her eyes trained on the bubbling water.

"Tiamat!"

Amel pulled away from her and they turned to her mother, striding toward her like a charging soldier.

Amel spoke a farewell low in her ear. "My lady." Then he slipped away before her mother's assault.

Amytis's words were clipped and furious, if quiet. "I have only just announced your marriage to Zagros and now find you flirting in the courtyards with an apprentice mage!" Her gaze followed Amel as he fled into a hall. "Why have you taken up with him? He was with you the other night, when Kaldu's body was discovered."

"It is nothing, Mother. I was only questioning him about the death, since Kaldu appeared to have connections with the magi."

Amytis's eyes fired at her. "And what is that to you?"

"I wish to know why Kaldu was killed."

"It is none of your concern!"

Tia studied her fury. "And is it a concern of yours? I hear that you and Kaldu spent time together. That you were with him on the night he died."

Amytis's face paled. "Enough, Tia!" She pinched her arm, fingers digging into Tia's flesh. "Enough questions, enough running about the city, enough foolishness. Palace life is not a game constructed for your amusement! You will conduct yourself with decorum until Zagros arrives, or I will have you locked up until he does."

She was sincere. No doubt of that. True anxiety licked at Tia's resolve. Her mother had the power to force her into the detestable marriage.

Perhaps it was time to silence her questions. To focus on her freedom.

But somewhere above her, her father roamed the Gardens, captive in both mind and body.

And who would champion *his* freedom?

Chapter 13

Tia leaned against the stone half wall of the rooftop garden and searched the nighttime desert for answers. She had no energy for a run. Here at the northern end of the city she could forget that all of Babylon lay below and almost believe herself alone in the vast darkness, with nothing but dark sand and sky.

She scanned the blackness above, traced the outlines of Taurus and Aries with her eye, naming them as her tutors had taught, wishing she could read their messages like a mage.

What would they tell her, if she had ears to hear? Should she cease her pursuit of truth as her mother insisted?

The night breeze played with her robes, drifting the purple fabric across her arm and raising a chill. The garden's silence pressed against her, a marked contrast with the noise and activity of the palace day. She breathed in the heavy scent of jasmine and curled her fingers around the lip of the stone wall.

"Palace life is not a game, constructed for your amusement."

Her mother's words haunted her steps through-out the day and followed her here, to the isolation of the garden. Tia rubbed at the stone wall until pieces loosened under her fingers, then picked at them and hurled them downward.

Was she nothing more than a palace pet? A mischievous cat chasing a ball of twine?

She wanted to deny it, but the thought plagued her. Though she wished to do something of importance, to have purpose, no opportunities to be anything but idle had been offered. And so, all her pursuits had been for her own amusement, as Amytis said. Tia took risks and sought thrills, but nothing was ever at stake. Oh, perhaps she chanced an injury, a physical blow. But she risked nothing of true importance. When there was a question of her privilege, her position—in this she took no chances.

Caught up in her own thoughts, she had not noticed the sound of conversation that drifted to her on the night air. A low laugh across the garden tensed her muscles.

She turned her head only slightly but saw no one, heard only muffled words. She shifted on silent feet along the length of the wall toward the voices.

"She knows nothing." A man's voice. Familiar, though Tia couldn't place it.

"If not now, she will." Another man.

"You concern yourself unnecessarily. Our secret is safe."

Shadir. The voice belonged to the old mage, her father's favorite. Did he frequent this garden as often as she? How often had he watched her come and go? Her heart pounded, and she held her body stone-still and silent.

"We are never safe." The other's voice was urgent, frightened even. "Our plan is too fragile. Too easily thwarted."

Shadir laughed again, and it seemed to Tia like the laughter of darkness. "You forget the powers that stand behind us. We cannot fail."

There was a pause, and then his companion responded with a voice uncertain and wavering. "I—I am not always convinced—"

"Stop. There is no room for doubt."

"There are so many pieces to put in place. How can you be certain it will come together?"

Shadir did not answer immediately, and she leaned toward the voices, pulse racing. Had she missed his response?

But when it came, it held chilling animosity. "I have waited a lifetime to bring him down. I will not be stopped, not by an unruly princess nor her conniving mother. This is our time."

His companion was still unknown, but whoever he was, Shadir seemed to have him convinced.

"We rely on your leadership." His tone was deferential. "And wait for the end eagerly."

Tia imagined Shadir studying the night sky as she had seen him doing the night Shealtiel died.

"Have no fear. He will be dead within the month."

The stone wall cut into her fingers. She loosened her grip and risked a breath. The men were moving away, crossing the garden to the palace door. And then they were gone, leaving her to review their cryptic conversation.

Secrets and truth. Power and death.

Tia and her mother both unfavorably mentioned.

And could the one whose death they anticipated be anyone other than her father?

Her muscles remained knotted and she forced herself to breathe, to release the fear. What was this plan? And how were they involved?

Her earlier musing returned with ferocity.

Would she live her life only to satisfy a lust for thrills? Or would she chance a venture of significance?

She will lock me up until Zagros arrives. If Tia were to pursue the truth, it must be in secret.

She would be risking her freedom, not only for the moment, but permanently, if it meant a forced marriage.

Strangely, the face that flashed in her mind's eye was an old man with bright eyes who lived a stone's throw from the palace and yet had never let himself become truly part of it.

"Question everything," Daniel had said. As he had done and would continue to do.

Tia regarded the stars once more, searching for counsel and finding only more mystery.

But in her heart, something had already

changed. She was no pet cat with a tangle of threads. No unruly princess interested only in amusement.

The game had turned deadly. And she was prepared to win.

Dark. Light.
Black, white, gray.
All I know.
Nose to wind, sniffing, sniffing. Meat! Throw it here. Here!
Pawing to meat, stones scratching skin. Devour. Not enough. Hungry, always hungry. Snuffling in dirt, more food, more food. Pawing at the roots, smell of earth. No food.
Black above, specked with white. So cold.
Grayness at the edge of black. Grows. Lightens. Water on my skin, falling on me. Colder.
She comes. I watch. Eyes soft, water there too.
She goes. Do not go.
Head lifted, lips open, teeth bared. Baying at the luminous white, disappearing.
Change. Change coming.
Urge to eat, urge to kill . . . receding.
Something more. There is something more.
Lingering fog.
Lifting fog.

Chapter 14

I prowl the night palace again, looking for the jackal. I search rooftop gardens where I watch the soft glow of the moon, and underground corridors lit by an occasional smoking torch burning low in the late watches of the night. I do not find him. My silent tread takes me to the throne room courtyard, to the low-hanging fronds that brush against my back as I pad along the path. So thirsty. The fountain bubbles and trickles and I approach, lean my head over its stone lip, and stare into the water at my reflection in the moonlight.

I have found the jackal.

Tia sucked in a ragged gasp of air and woke. Watery morning sunlight slanted across the floor of her bedchamber, striking a path across her eyes. She blinked against the intrusion, then reached a hand to the dust-sparkled beam, willing the sun to banish the terror.

I am not in my bed. The shock of finding herself the jackal in her dream surged again, like nausea, and Tia scrambled to sit upright, her eyes darting around the room. Her own bedchamber, but she was on the floor. Had she fallen and not awakened? Or did the dream have something of reality?

Before she was fully dressed, a male slave usually attendant on Amytis appeared at her door. Omarsa held the door ajar while Gula hastily wrapped Tia in a tunic.

The young man had the beautifully dark skin of Upper Egypt. The gold armbands her mother lavished on her slaves shone against his lean arms. "Your tutors await, my lady." His tone was deferential yet firm.

Tia's jaw tightened. Always she went voluntarily to her tutors. This escort was meant to ensure her attention to duty. Amytis would allow her no freedom. Bitter memories surfaced— memories of other days, perhaps weeks if childhood recollection could be trusted, spent behind locked doors. Tia would not risk open flaunting of her instruction. She would pursue the truth, but it would be done with stealth.

Amytis kept her occupied with lessons and meals from dawn until the heat of the day finally waned and the sun dropped into its nightly grave. Her tutors scolded her for inattention, and she was too preoccupied to notice her food, but when darkness overtook the palace, her time was her own and she had a plan.

As she had pondered through the day the unseen chain that linked Kaldu's death to the rooftop words of Shadir, she could find no obvious connection. But if one existed, Shadir's protégé, the young Amel-Marduk, might know of it and might be willing to share his knowledge with a princess.

She dressed for warmth, in an open woolen tunic in scarlet that accentuated her dark hair and fairer skin. Omarsa and Gula decked her in sapphires and jade and rouged her lips with scarlet pigments, and in their silent ministrations they required no explanation.

Babylon had more festivals, auspicious days, and holy days than one could count, and tonight's was minor, dedicated to the moon god Sin. Ordinarily Tia would ignore the rituals, but they provided a reason to visit Etemenanki, where she was certain to find Amel. More important, her mother never denied her in religious endeavors.

Soldiers were summoned to escort Tia through the city, and she strode through the convoluted palace halls, winding toward the grand entrance.

At the head of the massive staircase, she stood and looked over the darkening city, over the flat rooftops with their family altars and shelves of drying herbs. Colorful tunics, strung high across the streets to dry in the cooling breeze, waved and snapped like flying standards of soldiers. Torches bobbed and weaved under the wash lines as citizens made their way to temples and shrines.

Her lessons of the day returned to her, recitations she had made all her life, as if there were some danger of her forgetting. *The great and mighty Babylon, home to fifty-three temples of the great gods, fifty-five shrines of Marduk, and a thousand more for the celestial and earthly deities. The goddess Ishtar is worshipped at one hundred eighty altars, and another two hundred serve other gods.*

In Babylon, one could not stumble in the street without falling into a temple or shrine. Just as well, for as she had been taught since infancy, the demons sought always to destroy their great city, and the gods must be forever entreated to keep them safe from the demons' malevolence.

And across the city, the greatest temple of them all: Etemenanki, the House of the Platform of Heaven and Earth, rose to match and surpass the great height of the palace. Tia's chest swelled with pride at the sight of the seven tiers; the stairs that twisted round it, like a snake around a pole; and the topmost torches, already blazing against the orange-purple sky.

The wind caught at her scarlet cloak and twisted it around her ankles.

Must keep moving. It would take some time to cross the city and ascend the tower.

Indeed, by the time she and her soldiers climbed to the Platform, their breath came heavy and labored. Pride kept her own breath steady, but the trek had been arduous. The effort was required to please the gods, the priests insisted.

Tia paused at the top stair and gazed across the

plateau-like top of the tower, then below her, where the streets slanted away at odd angles, with toy houses and insect-sized people. The night wind blew cold and strong here, and a wave of dizziness swept her. She pulled her attention from the streets and focused on the temple at the center.

The Platform of Heaven and Earth was aptly named, for it was here that man first began to build with bricks in an attempt to reach the gods. Their first feeble efforts, millennia ago, had been thwarted by a sudden, bizarre confusion of language, scattering the builders across the grasses of the earth. But eventually some had returned and built again. And around this tower swelled the city and then the empire that became Tia's Babylon.

The crowd of worshippers was meager tonight, and Tia searched impatiently through priests and diviners to find the one she sought. Torches flared every kanû's length along the platform's edge and sunk into sockets in the half wall of stone, slashing yellow bands of light across dark faces.

In the center of the Platform, beside the temple built to Marduk, the massive altar commanded the attention of priest and mage. With their backs to Tia, they were an undulating sea of red robes embroidered with gold, swaying against the prayers of the kalû, the chanter-priests intoning incantations to the rhythmic beating of box drums and stringed tanbûrs. She could see nothing of the altar's surface, but masses of gray-white smoke twisted above their heads. *Impossible to identify Amel among his colleagues.* She would have to wait.

Tia slipped toward the altar, drawn by lilting chants of the kalû and the smoky sweetness in the air. Keeping back from priests at their duties, she closed her eyes and let herself be swept into the music of the night, held captive by the wind, rocked by the gentle hand of the gods.

And then he was there, beside her, gripping her elbow. Her eyes fluttered open and found his, glittering and hard like the cold stars against the black dome. Red, full lips and skin gone pale in the moonlight.

"Princess." That slight smile, amused, confident. Powerful. Tia was once again drawn into the spell that surrounded Amel-Marduk. "You have come to honor the gods?"

"What?" The sky seemed to tilt above her. She reached out to steady herself and found only Amel's arm. "Yes, yes. The gods."

He led her forward, through the clustered priests with their turbans wound high atop their heads, to the white stones of the altar, where the newly sacrificed bull still burned. An intertwine of smoke and incense filled her nose. Orange embers glowed under the flesh, and blood slanted between the white stones to a channel cut round the altar. In the darkness the blood glistened, nearly black. The charred bull's flesh crackled and hissed, and Amel reached across the embers to tear a piece of it, then turned and brought the flesh to her lips.

Tia opened her mouth and let him place it between her teeth. The heat burned her tongue and the ashy taste watered her eyes, but she chewed and swallowed, obedient to the gods, and somehow, strangely, to Amel. She angled her face to the wind and the night, and the taste of the charred flesh pricked her senses. Again Tia swayed on her feet and felt Amel's arm around her waist, his cheek nearly touching her own.

Across the altar, beyond the smoldering bull, she saw Shadir, his head bowed to another, whispering and watching. Watching her.

She turned away, ready to speak at last. To Amel, still close enough to hear her whisper, she said, "I must speak with you, alone."

Again the smile, the lifting of the perfect brows. He led her to the stone wall at the Platform's edge. The wind buffeted a nearby torch, its flame bent sideways as though reaching for Tia. The sky inclined again and she gripped the ledge to ease her light-headedness.

"You are worried, Princess."

He had that ability to see into her. "I fear there are happenings in the palace that do not bode well for my family."

Amel peered over the ledge to the streets,

wickedly far below. She kept her focus on his pale face.

"How can I help?"

The words she'd hoped to hear, but she must not be naive. "Shadir, he is your master?"

Amel's gaze came back to her, roamed her face. "He is."

"Is he—is he someone to whom I could take concerns about the kingdom? Does he fully support my father's reign?"

Amel lowered his chin, quieted his voice. "There are some who would say your father does not reign at all."

"Who? Who says this?" Her voice sounded petulant, even to her.

"You must be careful, Princess." His hushed words brought her closer, wrapped in their private exchange. "Those with ambition would use this time to further their goals."

"This time?"

The torch flame behind Amel snapped and Tia jumped. He laid a cool hand over hers on the ledge.

"The nobleman's strange death. There are rumors."

Tia pulled away a bit. Rumors were not surprising, but still the words struck against her heart.

Amel's long fingers closed over her own, comforting. "So fiercely loyal to your family, to

Babylon. This is one of the things I love about you, Princess."

Tia ignored his flattery, for now. "And Shadir? Is he ambitious?"

Confusion crossed Amel's features. "Shadir is a mage, without royal blood. What ambition could he have?"

Tia searched his eyes. Did he speak from loyalty or truthfulness? A gust of wind blew against them, leaning them toward the ledge. She looked back toward the altar, grounding herself in something solid.

"Your nephews, Tia."

"What about them?"

Amel glanced over his shoulder, a slight movement but fearful. "Your sisters' boys are of royal blood. Be wary."

She had been foolish. Pedaiah's warning about her father's lack of sons, and now Amel's words about her nephews, Labashi and Puzur, spun together, a splash of truth against a murky sky. A usurper must rid the kingdom of Nebuchadnezzar's grandsons before he could seize the throne without fear of attack by those loyal to her family. Tia breathed deeply of the night air to steady her thoughts and took in lungs full of incense and smoke.

Amel released her hand and reached into his cloak to a leather pouch hung from his belt. "I created something for you." He drew out a long cord, knotted at intervals around smooth white stones. He held one end, let it dangle and spin under the moonlight.

"It is beautiful."

He turned her toward the expanse beyond the tower and circled her neck with the cord. She lifted her hair and felt his fingers fasten the knot against her neck. Her skin tingled under his touch.

"An amulet," he whispered against her ear. "Every stone laid under the stars for a special blessing of protection."

She released her hair and turned back to him. He did not step back, and there was an intensity in his eyes Tia had not previously seen.

"Do not anger the gods, Tiamat. I would have you safe."

Though his words and his gift were tender and warm, a coldness seeped from the stones beneath Tia's feet and spread through her limbs. Off balance again, not in control. It was Amel that caused such feelings. Yet what should have angered her left her breathless. The way that the mage controlled—the quiet power he wielded—it was delicious.

He left her suddenly, stalking away toward the altar and his fellow magi, and she stumbled forward, extending a hand as if to pull him back. Tia watched him glide across the Platform and thought of a panther she had once seen during her father's hunts, all sleek and glittering eyes, powerful and beautiful.

She shook off the image. No time for such thoughts. Her two nephews, both precious little boys with dark curls and wide eyes, could even now be facing danger.

Chapter 15

Tia fled Etemenanki, her escorting soldiers' sandals slapping the streets to keep up, and crossed the city with the night wind tearing at her robes and hair streaming behind. The cool stones of the amulet at her neck did not warm with her skin, a constant reminder of Amel's protection, the touch of his hands, his words of warning.

Her sisters had married high officials in her father's court shortly before Tia wed Shealtiel. As though her parents decided to rid themselves of unmarried daughters in one sweep, perhaps with hope that sons would soon be born. Beltis and Banu were two and four years older than she, and for several years after their marriages, they each remained childless, to her mother's great horror.

Why Beltis and Banu had not been used for treaty, Tia never understood, but even her contribution was hardly the stuff of powerful alliances, with her kingdom-by-marriage little more than a trampled wasteland and her husband's father in a Babylonian prison.

Instead, her father had chosen to ensure loyalty from the powerful families within his kingdom and gave her sisters to men who had earned favor and accolades on the battlefield before returning home to wealth. Her sister Banu's husband, Nergal, in fact, was the very general who had led Babylonian troops against Judaea's final uprising and had laid waste the land and the legendary temple of its One God. They spent most of their time in the palace, though she rarely saw them.

Tia reached the Southern Palace at last, flew up the grand outer stairs, and dismissed her guards in the first courtyard. It took only a few minutes to twist through the halls to the nursery chamber. She slowed at the door and pushed it open silently.

Only one small oil lamp flickered in a wall niche, but across the room one of the boys' nurses was alert at once, rising from her chair. Tia raised a palm in silent greeting and the nurse nodded.

Tia kept her voice low. "The boys are well?"

The nurse tilted her head, her brow furrowed. "Yes, my lady."

Tia padded across the room and found Labashi and Puzur curled up in their large bed, their heads close together on the cushions. Moonlight streamed through a high window and traced a path across Labashi's cheek, and she ran light fingers through his soft curls. She held her breath at a stab of longing. Would she ever have such beautiful children herself?

The nurse drew alongside. "What is it, my lady? Is there danger?"

Perceptive woman. Tia pulled her from the bedside to the wall where the oil lamp played across her features. She was older than both of Tia's sisters but not aged and had tended the boys since infancy. True concern shone from her eyes. "You must take extra care to be watchful. I—I have heard things that leave me anxious."

The woman bit her bottom lip and nodded, but clearly she was uncertain of her own abilities.

"I will have a guard attend you for a while. Until we know the boys are safe."

Her face lightened a bit. "Thank you, my lady."

Tia squeezed her arm, took a last look at the boys, and escaped the room.

She would get no information about Shadir from Amcl. Foolish to think the protégé would speak openly against his mentor. She must return to her starting point, to those who knew Kaldu best and could tell her more of his actions, his plans, even his thoughts.

She would search out Ying, the eastern slave girl who tended the gardens and also apparently tended Kaldu.

Before an hour passed, her search ended in frustration. She roused slaves from their beds, questioned guards and soldiers, and searched the various gardens. Those who knew her all supplied one answer: Ying had disappeared. Vanished.

Runaway slaves were common in Babylon, notwithstanding their branded hands, but to run from the palace brought the harshest punishment. And because palace slaves lived better than most commoners, their flights were infrequent. No, if Ying was gone, she had run in fear or guilt. Tia thought of Kaldu's mangled body. Perhaps Ying had not run at all.

It had grown too late for more questions, but tomorrow, tomorrow Tia would seek answers in the Hall of Magi.

It is time to speak with Shadir.

Night came early at this time of year, and the palace halls fell into twilight, the torches not yet lit. Tia flowed silently through the maze of corridors like smoke pouring into open spaces, and the thrill of her secret task set her blood racing, muscles tightening like the challenge of the bull in her training room. She forced the smile from her lips and took a set of steps two at a time to reach the Hall located on the upper levels.

The magi had been entrenched in the palace since before her birth, when the Assyrians were defeated by the joint efforts of Cyaxerxes, king of Media, and her grandfather, Nabopolassar, then governor of Babylon. The two victors hacked apart the mighty Assyrian empire, and Media took the portion from its own land in the east to the Anatolian regions of the west. The remainder of Assyria, along with Babylonia and the coastal region, was united under her grandfather as the new Babylonian empire. Seven years later her father came into power and improved the city into a stunning capital. But behind all the political maneuvering and royal bloodlines, one truth remained: the magi were the king-makers. They wielded an unseen power, consulted on every decision, with the fate of kingdoms swayed by the omens they read in stars, in oil poured upon water, in entrails of sheep.

And this power radiated outward, like spokes of a cart wheel, from the Hall of Magi.

A wide corridor led to the Hall, with three stone columns creating two large arches into an ante-room, then a smaller arch into the Hall. Wide granite steps leading downward were an initiation to even reach the vaulted chamber.

Tia slowed at the inner arch, felt the weight of the room press outward against her, as though it would bar her entrance. A hot wind snatched her hair backward. Strange, given that the only windows in the chamber were cut high in the wall, for star study more than ventilation. She pushed against that wall of pressure, breached it, and stumbled into the lofty, octagonal Hall.

The high windows faced east, dark now at day's

end. A hundred oil lamps flickered along the walls of the cavernous chamber, no more effective than ten, for deep stretches of shadow swallowed the flames, and the heart of the Hall lay in darkness save one lamp that burned on a central table.

Tia wandered forward. Her last visit here had been long before her wedding. No less impressive than it had been to a child's eyes. White stones glittered against bitumen-tarred walls and ceiling, specks of incandescence on a midnight sky, patterned in the principal divisions of the zodiac. Shelves of clay tablets lined the walls, the ancient wisdom of the Chaldean race inscribed in wedge-shaped Akkadian, never to be forgotten. Heavy woods and heavier tapestries furnished the Hall, greedily absorbing light. And the smell . . . a heady blend of blood and incense, strong enough to coat the tongue.

A musician hunched in the corner, his legs and one scrawny arm wrapped around a bull's-hide drum, the other hand beating a slow rhythm. Several magi clotted together at a wooden table along the wall, heads bent over a series of old tablets. They lifted eyes to Tia as one, then shifted their gaze to the mage in the center of the Hall, whose back was to her and shoulders still curved over the table. From the heavy purple robe embroidered with gold crescent moons he could have been any of a hundred magi.

Shadir. She felt it.

He revolved to face her, his whole body moving as one rather than a glance over his shoulder. There seemed something unnatural in this, as though she was expected. The cold stars along the wall seemed to spark along the edge of her vision.

"Princess." His eyes on her were obsidian-black, empty as the vast night desert. The drum beat continued, slow and relentless.

Tia lifted her chin and strode forward. Shadir stepped back slightly at her approach.

Good. Let him be uneasy. "Greetings, Shadir. I trust you are well."

Tia had not spoken to the mage for many days, since the night Shealtiel had died and Kaldu had been killed, when Shadir had seen her return from her run.

He bowed, too low. Almost mocking. "And you, my lady. We are honored by your visit. You seek an omen, perhaps?" He lowered his chin, raised his eyebrows—a firestorm of expression for him, who seemed barely alive. "Matters of the heart?"

Tia hardened her gaze. She would not be baited. "I have more weighty subjects on my mind, Shadir. My recent change in status has pricked me to take more interest in the affairs of city and empire. My studies of language and mathematics rarely touch upon such things. I thought you would be the one to seek for enlightenment."

His eyes narrowed. Her flattery had not pierced his suspicion. Tia stepped to one side, to approach the table behind him, and Shadir shifted to block her, the same movement as when she entered. So. He had not been made uneasy by her approach. He was hiding something. Quickly, she circled the table and then studied its accoutrements.

It held the usual instruments of his dark practice. A wide and shallow clay bowl, teeming with entrails. Despite her usual lack of squeamishness, Tia's stomach knotted. Next to the entrails, sharp picks for prying secrets from the liver and terra-cotta liver models to consult for matching alterations in shape or color. The sharp smell of death hovered above the table. Shadir could be seeking answers for anything here, from auspicious weather for a hunt to the fall of a rival empire. Nothing to hide.

But when Tia lifted her eyes to his, a darkness poured over her. *More here than simple divination.* She sucked in a shaky breath and held it in her chest, feeling the need to expand further, as though Shadir's gaze tightened cords about her body. Too familiar, this oppression. A vision leaped before her mind's eye, blurry and indistinct. White, bulging eyes. Tearing flesh. A mouth open in a silent death-shriek. Her breath shallowed and she shot a steadying hand to the rough surface of the table. The drumbeat in the corner seemed to quicken in time with her breathing.

The vision cleared. Had she been given an

omen? A portent of evil to come or a glimpse of deeds already accomplished?

Shadir blinked slowly, his long lashes sweeping against his skin like the brush of spiders. Why had she noticed such a thing?

"How can I enlighten you, my lady? Certainly your tutors can give you all the history you desire."

Tia swallowed and fingered the white stones of the amulet at her neck. Shadir's gaze followed her movement and she pulled her hand away. Did he recognize Amel's gift?

"It is not the past that interests me as much as the future." The unseen cords still bound her, and she pushed away from the table and crossed to the windowed wall, using her mention of the future as an excuse to study the sky.

Shadir's sandals scuffed across the room behind her. He drew alongside, face lifted to the window. Grand as it was, the dome seemed only an extension of the Hall, as though the magi had created here a portal into the realm of the gods.

"It seems to me your mother has declared your future for you."

"The future of the *kingdom,* Shadir."

"Ah. I see."

Would that she could use one of those sharp instruments on Shadir's table to scrape knowledge from *him!*

"My father is getting older. And he has been—

unwell—for some time. It is the duty of even a daughter to think about the security of the throne." She turned from the stars and studied his profile. "Whom do you think will next sit upon it?"

Shadir's features were like glazed enamel and he spoke to the sky. "The people love your father. Love what he has brought to them. Your family holds tightly to the divine power. Despite . . ."

Despite the madness of which we never speak.

"And my nephews? Are they in danger?"

Shadir retreated to his table, fingered his instruments. Tia remained near the wall. A safe distance. The cursed musician did not cease his drumming.

"If the princess desires, I shall seek an answer from the gods."

Tia glanced at the entrails, but he shook his head. "This hepatoscopy is already dedicated. Another time, perhaps."

"And what answers do you seek tonight?"

He licked his lips, then smiled. "We have a common interest, I am told. The death of Kaldu."

Tia defied her fear and returned to his efforts with the liver. "And? Have you discovered his killer?"

Shadir swirled a pick through the viscous pile before answering. "I have seen things."

The gods curse you, mage. Say what you know.

"I have searched for the one who killed Kaldu, but the gods have given me to know

144

that before Kaldu was killed, Kaldu was killer."

Tia blinked. "I do not understand."

"Kaldu's end was retribution, the gods have said. Quick recompense for the slow death of another, at his hand."

"Whose death is on Kaldu?" Yet even as she formed the question, Tia knew its answer. With her own eyes, she had watched this slow death.

"Your husband. Shealtiel."

Kaldu killed Shealtiel. And in turn was killed himself, in revenge.

Her mind scurried across the thought, ran down several blind paths, and ended with the single truth.

Shealtiel was loved by only his family. And of that lot—mostly women, children, and prisoner—only one would seek retribution.

The hard lines of Pedaiah's face in Shealtiel's death chamber, his torn clothing and frightening anger—all this returned to her as she pulled away from Shadir's table and swept from the Hall of Magi.

Chapter 16

Babylon loved the night. Her citizens reveled in darkness, grabbed any opportunity to celebrate with music and dancing in the streets long after the sun's death. When Tia stalked from the Hall, the city was only beginning its nightly festivities. Her purpose would not wait.

She had not seen Pedaiah in the palace in days and had no reason to think him anywhere about. Her steps slowed. In her years of marriage to Shealtiel, she never knew where Pedaiah lived. Where would evening find the man? He was friendly with her father's private mage, Daniel. And that girl, Judith. Amel said Pedaiah frequented the furnace yard he once managed. None of this told her where Pedaiah would be tonight.

She thought better of chasing down possibilities and instead headed for her chambers. Omarsa and Gula stood at her arrival.

"Go and find me Pedaiah, son of Jeconiah, my husband's brother." Tia paced the room. "Bring him to me."

"Here, to your chamber, my lady?" Gula's voice, though timid, still held a note of scandal.

"To the palace." *Then where? Somewhere private.* "To my training room." No windows, Amytis had insisted. Tucked into an unseen corner of the palace.

The two still stared, a bit wide-eyed. She jerked an impatient thumb at the door. "Go."

They moved as one, as they always did, and disappeared in silence from the chamber. The door thudded behind them, and Tia was alone with her thoughts, unwelcome companions.

She turned a circle in the chamber. Where could

she occupy her restless mind and body until they returned? She snatched a heavier cloak and followed them out moments later, but she turned instead toward the west side of the palace, to a wide columned balcony that overlooked the Euphrates River. And beyond it, the western half of Babylon. The air's chill swept her as she crossed, and she tightened her cloak, digging tense fingers into the wool. She leaned her belly against the balcony wall and scanned the river.

Even at this late hour, the white masts of several ships glided past, toward the quay and the wharf district where their treasures would be unloaded and divided. The New City districts, beyond the Euphrates, were the larger of the two halves of Babylon. The Jewish district lay noticeably quieter, as though it were the youngest of the quarters, put to bed early before the adults began their merrymaking.

No, not innocent babes, these Jews. Disapproving old men, all folded arms and scowling mouths, trying to ruin everyone else's pleasure. Like Pedaiah.

She needed to move. She would go crazy standing about until he came. Better to wait in her training room.

On the way, she grabbed a torch from a wall socket. Her special room was unlit when she was absent. Inside, she knew its furnishings and arrangement well enough to scurry through the darkness, to touch her flame to each waiting brazier and bring them to life.

When the perimeter glowed, she shed her cloak and looked down at her garments. She wore red silk, one of her usual ankle-length tunics, too restrictive to run. The tight belt tied round her waist and its tasseled fringe hanging down her thigh would likely catch on her bull's horns and strangle her.

In the end, she settled for tugging against her ceiling-strung pulleys until her upper arms quivered with fatigue. Only then did Omarsa and Gula slip through the door at the far end of her training room, trailing Pedaiah. He surveyed her private chamber for the first time, and his usual haughty expression broke for a moment.

Surprised?

Her slaves disappeared and the door closed behind them, leaving the two of them very much alone. Pedaiah scanned the room, taking in her mats, the bull, the weights she lifted to strengthen her arms, and finally Tia, where she stood beside her bull, watching.

His lips parted slightly, but he did not speak. It amused her to have left him speechless. But she was too angry for mirth.

"So." She crossed the room, unwrapping the cloth from her hands, conscious of the dampness of her skin and the way the red silk clung to her. "Tonight I have learned the truth."

His eyes strayed to the red silk, then to her face. Was that a flush against his skin?

"What truth, Princess? That you have the power to rouse a man from his rest and drag him to your feet?"

Tia reached him where he stood with his back to the door. The braziers' light hardly touched them, and her height cast a shadow over his face, obscuring the white scar. He did not look like a man taken from his bed, with those piercing eyes, ever alert and watchful. So much darker than Shealtiel's. But he smelled of cook smoke, a pleasant scent of meat and spices.

"The truth about Kaldu."

A flicker of confusion crossed his strong features. "The slaughtered nobleman?"

She cringed at his term, so inhuman. "Do not pretend to know nothing of it."

He leaned forward. "You did not summon me to speak again of marrying Nedabiah?"

A pang of alarm shot through her. She had not thought of Nedabiah in too long.

At her hesitation he jumped into the breach, brandishing sharp words like weapons. "You need not bother. You will never marry Nedabiah. Regardless of my mother's wishes, or even my father's, our family will not again be wed to pagan idolaters." These last words were spat out, with all the hatred of his race behind them.

Tia's back stiffened. "Do not speak to me as

149

though you are so righteous, Pedaiah ben Jeconiah! You who would tear a man to pieces in revenge rather than give him over to courts of justice."

His brow furrowed again. "Princess, you have gone mad."

At the word that was never spoken, she took a step nearer, her hands tightening as they had around her pulleys.

Pedaiah held his palms to her, closed his eyes for a moment, and dipped his head. "My apologies, Princess. But I have no idea what you are saying."

"Kaldu. You killed him."

She was still only a breath away from him, and his gaze traveled from her eyes, to her lips and chin, then back to her eyes. Her accusation again seemed to leave him without speech.

He recovered. "Why would I kill Kaldu?"

"And then spread rumors about me to cover your guilt."

He watched her eyes, held her there, then broke the unseen hold and took a few steps aside toward her mats. "You have me at a disadvantage, Tiamat. This is all a mystery."

Her heart stuttered. Had he ever called her by name? She had always been *Princess* with that snarl of derision, even when she was fourteen, standing beside Shealtiel in the marriage ceremony and watching this brother—closer to her age but so remote.

"Do you deny that you believe your brother's death was unnatural?"

The light played shadows on his face, but still she thought his expression wavered. "I do not deny it. I have seen slow poison do its work before."

"And so you took your revenge on the man responsible, and then made people believe that I killed my own husband."

He swept down on her then, his face all fury. "You *did* kill your husband. Is that the truth you want to hear?"

He had her nearly pinned against the wall. One yell, and she could bring the blade of a dozen soldiers down on his neck. And she didn't need soldiers to release herself. But she did not move, save to jab a forefinger into his chest. "That is a lie. Kaldu killed your brother, and you murdered Kaldu."

He grabbed her hand, trapped it against his chest, and pulled her closer. "'Tell me, Tiamat"— his voice was harsh, rasping—"tell me you did not kill Shealtiel."

Tia stared at the set of his jawline, the blood pulsing at his temples, the burning intensity of his eyes. Her breath shallowed and she could only bring her voice to a whisper between them. "I did not love your brother, Pedaiah. I am sorry, I never could. But I swear to you on all the gods of Babylon"—at this his eyes danced with anger—"I swear to you on my own life. I did not kill Shealtiel."

He held her to him for a moment longer, then released her and pushed away. They both panted as though the altercation had been a physical one.

She had to ask, had to know what he thought of her. "You truly believed that I killed him?"

He studied the floor. Was it shame that kept his eyes averted? "Yes. Who else would have cause?"

She hid the twinge of hurt at his words. "If you believed this, then you would not have reason to kill Kaldu."

"And who told you that I did?" Some of the cold arrogance had returned to his voice, and she welcomed it. The other Pedaiah, the one with a furious passion in his eyes, disoriented her.

She wandered toward the other end of her chamber. She had no need of him any longer but was unwilling to see him leave.

"The mage Shadir. He had a message from the gods."

"The gods. Bah!"

I have no time for religious debate. But she had taken the word of the man at the center of a plot against her father. Had Shadir wished to convince her that Kaldu's death was unconnected to his own actions? Tia had fallen victim to his farce like a foolish child. She spun to Pedaiah, fuming. There were still unanswered questions.

"If I did not kill Shealtiel, and you did not kill Kaldu, then we still do not know who is responsible for either death."

"I have vowed to learn whose hand brought the poison to my brother's lips, Princess. But I do not understand your concern with Kaldu's death. From what I hear, he was likely killed by some wild animal and . . ."

Even across the distance between them, her face must have told a story her mouth never would. Pedaiah's words trailed and understanding dawned in his eyes.

A sudden longing swept her, the desire to share all she knew with someone, anyone. Someone she could trust.

And for all Pedaiah's haughtiness and disdain for everything Babylonian, he was a man of integrity. This she knew.

"There is more." Tia crossed back to him, lowering her voice. "I believe there are workings against my father's throne here in the palace."

She whispered all of it to him, the conversation she had overheard, the bits of information given by Kaldu's wife and by Ying, the slave who had disappeared. She released it all, like a burden she'd been carrying too long. Pedaiah listened, his face grave.

He touched her elbow. "You must be careful,

Tiamat. The diviners seek to control powers far beyond them. Powers that carry great danger."

His gentle touch brought a swell of emotion. "It is my father's danger that concerns me."

He looked past her, as though reading something in the dark recesses of her chamber. "The time of the prophecy is upon us."

Daniel's words. Tia had forgotten them with all else she had heard. A chill whispered across her neck and throat. "What does it mean?"

Pedaiah brought his gaze back to her face and shook his head. "I do not know. It is all too—too strange—to be unrelated. Shealtiel, Kaldu, Shadir. Perhaps we should ask."

Tia bit her lip, contemplating a request.

"Tomorrow?" He watched her, his own eyes uncertain. "When the sun has set? I will send word ahead to Daniel, and I will come for you."

Yes. "I will meet you at the shrine of Shamash, at the head of the Street of Marduk."

He sighed and briefly closed his eyes.

"Across the street from the shrine. On the far side."

At this, she almost saw a twitch of a smile. "On the far side, when the sun sets tomorrow."

He shifted to leave, and Tia clutched at his sleeve. He looked at her hand on his arm, and she snatched it away. "Thank you, Pedaiah."

His eyes lifted to hers, dark and unreadable. "Good night, Princess."

Pedaiah stalked the city streets, uncaring which direction he traveled, what destination he reached. His thoughts were as troubled as the poverty of the streets—they gushed like the small canals that laced the city, fouled by a city's refuse.

And yet his feet took him to Daniel's of their own accord, and he found the wise man at the edge of his rooftop, enjoying what little breeze cooled the night air.

Daniel did not turn at Pedaiah's march across his roof, but his words traveled to Pedaiah. "You are much distressed tonight, son. I feared you might kick a stray cat in your haste down there."

Pedaiah joined him at the half wall, leaned against the stones. "Where is this new heart, this new spirit, that the prophet Ezekiel assures us will come, Daniel?"

"Do you speak of the people, or of yourself?"

"The people, of course. They perform their fasts and observe the Sabbath as we instruct them, but their hearts are still tempted by idolatry. Is it not enough that our land has been taken from us? So many killed and those not dead, starving in the land? When will they learn?"

"They will learn."

Pedaiah turned his back to the city and to the wall. "But how can they, when they will not even remain separate from the idolaters!"

Daniel's gaze traveled the streets as if he could

see into each house, read the souls of each Jew. "The temptation to conform is great. They have no wish to suffer, and to conform to the manners and customs of those who hold us captive brings safety and even wealth."

"While sacrificing our distinctiveness as a people called out from the world."

"That is the danger, yes."

Pedaiah waved a fist in the air. "This is why I say that we must keep ourselves apart, always apart from them. We should not hear them, should not teach them."

"Should not marry them?"

Pedaiah closed his eyes and leaned his head back. "Why must you always come back to her?"

"Because she is never far from your thoughts."

"Even my mother wishes me to marry her, to give my brother an heir."

"How difficult it must be then, for you to remain apart, as you say."

Pedaiah eyed Daniel, searching for a note of mockery in his voice. But his mentor was truly concerned for him, he could see that. "I must remain so, Daniel. I cannot love a pagan."

Daniel's eyes softened, but it did not seem to be admiration for Pedaiah's declaration of loyalty to Yahweh. He saw more of sadness in the older man's gaze.

"You are a great leader for your people, and they have much respect for you, Pedaiah. As they should. But you have much to learn."

"Tell me, then. Tell me what I must know."

Daniel lifted his eyes to the stars, searched them as a wise man, as a mage. "When the Anointed One comes, the Prince of princes, He will come to the Jews. But not *only* for the Jews." He lowered his head and turned. "If you cannot love a pagan, Pedaiah, then you do not have the heart of God."

The words struck deep, slashed at the toughened places of his heart. But he could not understand how to both love them and despise their ways. How to make them part of his life and yet separate from it. "You also think I should marry her, then?"

Daniel smiled. "I thought we were talking about our people."

Pedaiah looked across the streets, to the walls of the palace lifting in the distance, the lofty trees of the Hanging Gardens silhouetted against the night sky. "We are."

"Tell me more of the princess, Pedaiah. My memories are all of her childhood. An energetic little one, I remember."

Pedaiah laughed. "You have no idea." But then sobered. "I worry for her. The young mage Amel-Marduk, who is attached to that evil Shadir, stalks her like prey. I fear she is taken in by his surface charms. He does not see her truly, though. She is only a useful and pretty tool in his hands."

"And you see her truly?"

"I see her better than she sees herself, I sometimes believe. Her mother has convinced her that she is unattractive and worth nothing more than what can be gained through alliances. She defies her mother in ways that are often selfish and silly, but only from ignorance. She has never lived outside the palace." He sighed, thinking of Tia's passionate declarations in her training chamber. "She has a fierce love for her father."

"And yet in all of this, you could never love a pagan?"

He turned away from the palace view, his heart hardening again, along with his words. "It is true, Tiamat could have been a woman of not only strength but also great influence." He left Daniel at the wall and headed for the steps.

"If only she had been born a Jew."

Chapter 17

Tia wrapped a cinnamon-colored scarf around her hair, its gold coins cool across her forehead, then veiled the lower half of her face. When she pulled her cloak from its hook, her ladies stood expectantly.

"I go alone." They sat.

She traveled through back corridors and unused wings, making her way toward the kitchens. She had no temple errand as an excuse and would take no chance of her mother hearing of her excursion.

Slaves still worked the kitchen complex. Tia passed through the cook room where she had inquired about Ying and found a dozen slaves still hunched over cook fires and chopping boards. Still working when the evening meal had ended. Preparation for tomorrow? Such long hours they worked. Curious glances shot in her direction, then turned away in deference.

The wide door at the back of the kitchen complex allowed for deliveries. From her favorite rooftop garden Tia had watched many cart-loads of vegetables and fruits travel through it over the years. Tonight it afforded the best means of unseen escape. A narrow alley ramped down-ward and opened onto the Processional Way, an exit only a slave or palace staff would use.

Tia stepped out of the alley and felt again the thrill of being in the city streets rather than high above, running the wall or racing her chariot.

Would Pedaiah be at the shrine as he had promised? Tia strode that direction and avoided the faces of those she passed. The streets were still crowded, the sun having only just set. Had she come too early? Would she have to wait?

She slid along the Processional Way, hugging the blue-glazed wall. Now and then a merchant's donkey got too close or a knot of men, drinking long before night fell, jostled her into the blue

159

mosaics with their yellow winged lions waiting to devour her.

The ziggurat loomed ahead, a mighty mountain in the center of the city, with its snake-wrapped stairs and torch-lit temple. There were fewer torches tonight, and if Amel was there, he would be standing against its darkened rim, watching the purple dome for its first stab of starlight. Thoughts of Amel swirled into those of Pedaiah, and Tia quickened her steps.

The length of the Processional Way, from palace to Etemenanki, was familiar—though she rarely traveled it on foot. But the rest of the city lay shrouded in mystery, an unknown world, observed from the far-off palace roof and city wall. Ahead, the Street of Marduk, a main thoroughfare, intersected the wide Processional Way.

And at the head of the street, in the deepening dark, a shrine to Shamash. The small, hexagonal stone building lay in shadow, but two torches stood at its narrow door, reaching to the tiled roof. A figure lingered across the street. Her heart raced ahead of her, and for a moment she felt danger. The last time Pedaiah found her crossing the city alone, he had called her naive. Her fingers strayed to the flimsy protection of her veil. She hurried forward, then slowed, for fear the man across from the shrine would be a stranger.

But then he turned and she saw that proud jawline. Tia rushed to him, and he must have seen her fear, for he met her midstride and caught her arms.

"What is it, Tia? Did someone follow?" His gaze shot past her, along the street.

She recovered her dignity and pulled away. "No. No, all is well. I—I only grew foolish for a moment."

He studied her face, his head tilted and eyes searching. "I would never call you foolish."

She smiled under her veil. Spoiled, perhaps. Inferior. But not foolish. "I am so rarely down in the city and never alone." She watched the busy street, the people rushing forth with lives and plans she did not understand. "All I see of it is from the palace or the Platform."

Pedaiah glanced at her home, sitting high above the city like a matched peak with the Platform. "Do not forget the city walls."

She turned on him, hands on her hips. "That is the second time you've said such a thing. Explain."

He shrugged. "I like to get a better view at times myself. The guard in the Marduk Gate tower is a friend. From the sentry tower you see more than the city. You see anyone who approaches along the top of the wall. No matter how fast she is running."

He did not look at her, but Tia saw the smirk. "And I am a joke among the guards, then? They laugh at me while huddling around their little braziers through the cold nights?"

Pedaiah faced her fully, his expression grave. "Every one of them would give his life to protect you, Princess. They watch you, yes. And they love you."

The intensity of his voice stole her breath. Not only his declaration of the soldiers' loyalty. That tiny window, that small crack once again, into a man that was perhaps not what he appeared. "Then I am honored, though I knew nothing of it."

He growled and looked away. "You know nothing of anything."

"Do not be rude! I have had Chaldean tutors since before I could speak!"

"Ha! Tutors! They keep your head in the sky and your thoughts occupied with aimless philosophy. What do they teach you of this?" He swept a hand toward the city. "Of the real world of your people, the streets where they live and work and love?"

"I—I have learned of our history, of the battles—"

He grabbed her arms and shook. "Not history, Tiamat. Now. Today. Do you know what it is like to be an ordinary citizen of Babylon? Or to be a Jew, captive here your whole life?"

She said nothing and he released her arms but took her hand. "Come, Tia. I will show you the true Babylon."

And then they were running. Leaving the crowded Processional Way and running as though he would weave her through the entire city before the moon reached its zenith. Winding through dark alleys with tiny doorways that glowed like eyes, past small, unfamiliar shrines and through well-tended gardens no bigger than her bed-chamber.

He still clutched her hand. They ran, and it was intoxicating—the night wind snatching at hair and cloak, the fringed coins of her veil jingling against her forehead, the pounding of their feet. And the freedom. The wondrous freedom. No one but Pedaiah knew her footsteps. She was lost to the world, to Amytis and her Median prince, to Shadir and his scheming magi.

There was only this night and Babylon. Her head sang with the thrill of the unknown.

Black garbage littered the alleys they ran, the smell of sewage assaulted her, and flint-eyed rats twitched furry noses at them as they passed. But there were also scents of cook fires and baking bread and the night perfume of rooftops that spilled jasmine down crumbling walls.

A donkey cart swung around a corner and rattled toward them, and Pedaiah snatched her against the wall, holding her against his chest until the snorting beast and its owner passed. Her veil fell from her face, and she laughed up at him and was shocked to see him grinning too. A wide, full smile she had never seen in all her life and did not think possible.

They both panted with the exertion, and when the cart disappeared at the end of the rutted alley, they parted hastily and continued at a walk.

"We are almost there." Pedaiah pointed. The dash through the city had not been random. The Euphrates gleamed ahead, between low-lying buildings of the wharf district. The grand bridge that spanned the river and connected the old and new halves of the city lay to their left. Tia caught the fishy scent of the river.

"Where are we going?"

"There is more to see."

At the river's edge it seemed Pedaiah had friends not only in guard towers but also at the harbor. He left her at a pier for a hurried conversation with a younger man, who glanced toward her and nodded.

Pedaiah returned, snatched a wooden oar from a pile, and extended a hand toward a small skiff bobbing at the water's edge. "He needs it delivered to the New City."

Her jaw dropped. "We are going across? On the water?"

Pedaiah lifted his chin, a challenge in his eyes. "Afraid?"

In answer, she hopped into the little boat and planted herself on a low bench.

The skiff cut across the current, directed by Pedaiah's muscled paddling, and she stopped watching him to gaze along the ripples—

diamonds against black water. She leaned over to trail her fingers through the cold Euphrates for the first time in her life. One could not feel the water from palace balconies.

The run through the city had fired Tia's blood, but it was not the effort that made her heart pound in her chest now. It was something else, something she could not describe. The sense that this was *real,* the streets, the people, the river, and that her life in the palace was only a show.

When they reached the western bank, Pedaiah pulled her from the skiff. He held her until her feet were steady on the bank, then secured the boat's leads with practiced hands while she secured her veil. They turned toward the New City. She had never been on this side of the river.

Pedaiah led. "We will walk now."

"Too tired to run?"

He shot an annoyed glance at her but saw she was teasing and, surprisingly, softened. "I want you to see more on this side. To see *my* people."

And she did see. The New City, despite its name, was burdened with far more poverty than Tia witnessed on the eastern side. They wandered through the Jewish district, where captives her father brought to Babylon spent their nights. Their days were spent at furnaces, goldsmith shops, the streets of weavers and tanners. All the best artisans of Judaea were brought to their city to help them make Babylon a dazzling jewel in the desert.

And yet, it was not dazzling here. Why did the Jews not beautify their own district when they were so skilled?

Perhaps they have neither time nor money. The thought shocked her a bit, and her intake of breath brought Pedaiah's eyes to her, but she was not ready to speak her thoughts.

In the midst of homes like hovels, filthy streets, and tattered clothing that hung on even more ragged wash lines, there was beauty, and it came from the people themselves. They smiled on the couple as they passed, and singing came from many homes—melodies at once haunting and lovely.

"It is the beginning of Shabbat," Pedaiah said as though this explained the singing.

She did not ask for more.

"Here." He slowed at a door and knocked.

They were making a visit? Tia felt some disappointment to end their private exploration.

The door swung open to reveal a short, heavy woman with ruddy cheeks.

"Pedaiah!" Her voice rang across the narrow street. "Come in, boy, come in." She yanked his arm. "And you've brought—"

A wave of something akin to horror passed over her face. Was it Tia's clearly Babylonian dress? Or was she recognized?

Pedaiah guided her through the door with a hand against her lower back. "Hannah, I must ask for your discretion, yes?"

She recovered quickly and shut the door. "Of course, of course. Come. We are about to eat."

Pedaiah smiled. "I was counting on that."

The family made room at their table, and Tia squeezed between Pedaiah and one of their four children, a boy about six, with an adorable shyness. It was a meal unlike any other she'd eaten. Foreign food, mostly breads and vegetables, heavily seasoned. A very little bit of meat, too much of which ended up in her dish. Their generosity embarrassed her. She shared a bit with the little boy beside her and was rewarded with a lovable grin. But it was the foreign talk that was strangest—not that they spoke their native tongue, for it was all her own Aramaic—but the subject of their conversation was strange to her. She ate in silence and gleaned much. Pedaiah, it seemed, was more than the son of the imprisoned Judaean king. He was something of a leader of his people.

"And when they *do* close their ears to the Babylonians, they are just as likely to listen to the false prophets as the true ones," he said. "I fear they will never learn."

Hannah scooped her bread into her stew and shrugged. "This you should expect, Pedaiah. We are a stubborn people."

He smacked his palm against the table, and the heat of his anger blazed against Tia's arm. "It was their stubbornness that brought us here. Are they not ready to go home?"

Abner, Hannah's husband, held up a hand. "This is our way, Pedaiah. Why should we not suffer?"

The meal ended too quickly. Pedaiah signaled her with his eyes. They still had questions for Daniel, and it grew late. Tia nodded.

At the door Tia gave her thanks to Hannah and Abner. The woman grasped her hand with both of hers and studied Tia, but her words were not for Tia.

"Be careful, Pedaiah. You play with fire."

Tia opened her mouth, but Pedaiah's slow shake of his head kept her silent.

They ambled toward the river. Her belly was too full to run, and her head too full to speak. Everywhere were more symptoms of hardship— doors in disrepair, children with sunken eyes. A weathered old man hobbled toward them, his twisted body leaning heavily on a bent stick. He passed and looked up at her. He was not much older than Pedaiah. Crippled and hunched from a life of servitude. A young mother sat in an open door nursing an infant. Her gaunt face followed Tia as she passed. Tia glanced at her malnourished baby, felt a rush of grief, and had to look away.

Pedaiah whispered, "Don't turn away, Tiamat. It is why we are here."

The boat they brought across was to be left on this side, so Pedaiah led her to the massive bridge that spanned the river. From its entrance Tia could not see the five piers it stood upon, though she had counted them many times from her balcony. A narrow rail, waist-high, was their only separation from a precipitous fall into black water. She ran her hand along its cold length and they walked in silence.

When it felt as though they must be halfway across, they stood against the rail and gazed upriver toward the palace. A chilly wind pressed them toward the water, and Tia's cloak flapped against her legs.

"It is such a different perspective on my home. The palace is like something from a story, blurry and indistinct, when all this is reality." So often it felt like a prison. From here, suspended between Old and New City, the square-cut notches of varying heights along the palace wall glowed with a hundred torches, and the lush greenery of the Gardens overhung the upper levels like a lavish layer of protection. "The opulence shames me."

She dropped her head, studied the water, her stomach churning like the agitated waves against the piers.

"What is it?" Pedaiah's words were almost gentle.

"How can they live like that?"

He did not answer. His presence was solid beside her, his eyes on the palace.

"I understand now why you hate me."

She heard his sharp breath. "I—I do not—"

She held up a hand to silence him, and surprisingly, it was effective. "I am a pampered, spoiled princess. I know nothing of the world beyond my luxuries. Down here"—she thrust her chin toward the Jewish district—"is another world."

Another world. She had loved and despised it, both, tonight. How could they not provide better for their people?

"It is not all misery."

"No, no, I can see that. But still, they are so—so *poor*."

His laugh was low and not derisive.

"How can I go back, pretend not to care about those who suffer?"

He leaned sideways against the rail and studied her profile. A sudden gust tangled her hair across her cheek, and Pedaiah swept it back with the barest touch of his hand.

Tia's thoughts were as tangled as her hair. Her mother's threat to toss her from the palace, from her position and her luxuries if she did not marry the prince from her homeland. How could she ever live among squalor? The inability to return to her selfish life after all she'd seen and the equal impossibility of reconciling herself to poverty held her trapped in a vise.

"You must let me marry Nedabiah." The words

spilled out, and Pedaiah's hand, still at her hair, became a fist. He turned and stepped away.

Tia moved closer and he shifted again, his face set toward the water, as hard as the rocky banks. They had been like this all night, like the ebb and flow of the water, washing against each other, then pulling away. Her palms grew slick against the rail, and her mouth was dry as desert sand.

"If I marry Nedabiah, I will be a voice for your people, Pedaiah. My mother will at first be angry, but her advisors will placate her, and she will see that I am still married to a prince, so all is well. And I will retain my position, where I can do some good . . ." Tia plucked at his sleeve. "Pedaiah, are you listening?"

He snatched his arm from her. "I am listening, Princess. But all I hear is empty wind."

She took a step back from the venom in his voice.

"You have learned nothing tonight. You are still a foolish child, chasing after baubles and fine foods, afraid of truth." His eyes were on her now, full of that familiar fury, the angry arrogance. "I do not know why I even tried."

She fought the tightness in her throat, the too-ready tears. He would not have the satisfaction of making her weep. She gathered her hair under her head covering and secured the veil across her face.

"You speak of truth, Pedaiah. Perhaps it is time

171

to cease our worthless amusements and accomplish what we intended. Pose our questions to your diviner, and see if *Belteshazzar* knows the truth."

A glance revealed the blood pounding in his temples, the twitch of his jaw muscles, the hard slash of his lips.

The closeness they'd shared had fled. It was time to return to the familiar.

Chapter 18

The moon had risen high by the time they reached Daniel's house. The lateness distressed Tia. Their excursion to the New City would leave her vulnerable to detection when she returned. But she would not go back to the palace without speaking with Daniel about his prophecies, without questioning him about Kaldu, and even her late husband.

The same doorkeeper they had last encountered met them at the door. Would they rouse the old wise man from his bed? Tia need not have worried. Even before they exited the narrow passage to the courtyard, she heard the distinct buzz of a crowd.

Pedaiah led the way and she held back, surveying the mob before allowing herself to be seen. The courtyard where they had conversed quietly with Daniel during their last visit over-flowed with Jews, mostly men and some women. Indeed, even the balcony that circled the court-yard held a crowd, their faces turned downward to the open space. Around the central figure of Daniel on a reed chair most of the men sat cross-legged, allowing those behind a better view. For a crowd so large, the conversation was not so loud, but the murmurs held an anxious intensity. What was this gathering?

Daniel's gaze lifted to the passage they exited, took in Pedaiah. He extended a palm to the space beside himself, inviting Pedaiah to his side. Was this honor given to him as a prince? Or as a teacher? Pedaiah shook his head, the movement slight. Daniel's gaze traveled to Tia and he nodded.

"Friends"—his voice carried throughout the courtyard and to the level above, and the crowd hushed at once—"I thank you for your attendance this night. We will read from the Torah first."

Their holy book. Pedaiah pulled her by the arm to the far side of the courtyard against the wall. His cold fingers burned her skin.

"He will teach for a while. We must wait."

"Did you know we would be delayed? You could have brought us earlier, avoided all that running through the city."

He left Tia at the wall without a word and threaded his way through the seated group until he reached an empty place near Daniel. Tia followed him with her eyes as he lowered himself to the stones beside the Jewish girl Judith. A flush of unwarranted anger heated her chest. She forced her attention away, to the unknown crowd.

There were readings, prayers to their One God, even singing. A letter from someone in their homeland, Jeremiah—perhaps a prophet? Much about a future redemption. She focused on little of it and spent her time examining those who gathered. Most of the men wore plain tunics and fringed head coverings, something she had never seen on the Jews who worked in the palace. The center of the group, those seated closest to Daniel, were a mix of head-covered Jews and bare-headed Babylonians with their red and gold embroidered robes.

She slid along the wall to get a better look at faces. More than one glanced at her with the same surprise she felt, though with her face veiled Tia doubted she was recognized. Her presence clearly caused anxiety. A ripple of attention passed through them, each turning their head in her direction. Was it only the presence of one of their own? Did they fear reprisal for their interest in the Jewish diviner? Some of them were palace diviners themselves, were they not?

Yet they seemed out of place. She scanned the overflowing courtyard and compared it to the Hall of Magi. All she had known of the palace diviners had told her they were a scheming, back-stabbing lot who lusted for power. Here, she sensed a united community—a common goal, a desire for truth, perhaps even a shared bitterness. She was annoyed at the delay, intrigued at the reason, and drawn to the unfamiliar.

When Daniel's teaching ended, he and Pedaiah stood and moved out of the crowd, toward a narrow doorway at the rear of the courtyard. The girl remained, but Pedaiah signaled Tia with his eyes to follow.

The room was lit only by the courtyard torches spilling shadows through the doorway, and neither man brought a lamp. Still, in the darkness Daniel examined Tia, perceived her with more accuracy than was comfortable.

"So, you have returned, Princess."

"I am looking for answers."

He smiled and inclined his head. "So much like your father."

She bristled. "My father always sought truth from his diviners, even when it was unfavorable."

Daniel turned from her and retreated into the darkness, found a chair. "Yes. But how often was the truth actually given by those who feared him?"

"You are all liars, then?"

Pedaiah drew himself up as though she'd insulted *him,* but Daniel only chuckled and held up his palm. "This is for you to decide, Princess."

She balled her hands at her sides. "You spoke of prophecies. I would hear more of them. And of what the future holds for our kingdom."

A saddened smile passed over his lips. "Come, sit."

As though summoned, a young boy appeared at the doorway with a small oil lamp. Daniel beckoned him forward and indicated a small table that also held a shallow bowl and a terracotta jug. When the boy had placed the lamp and gone, Pedaiah and Tia seated themselves beside him in reed chairs.

Tia pointed to the bowl and jug. "You will seek an answer?"

Daniel followed her extended finger and frowned, his look quizzical.

"It is for reading the oil poured on water, is it not?"

At this, Pedaiah made a little sound, like a father aggravated with his toddler's foolishness. "He is not one of your palace sorcerers, Tiamat."

"Sorcerers! We have no sorcerers at the palace. Every one of our wise men seeks the will of the gods and summons their power only for the protection of our people!"

That little snort again, but Daniel touched Pedaiah's arm. She would rather the touch had been rougher.

"My lady, the powers that your diviners summon are dark, even if their purpose for doing

176

so is not. Since the first garden, evil has always worn the mask of good."

"What is this 'first garden'? My father's Hanging Gardens?" Tia should have been at ease with this captive Jew, but his words left her fumbling over her own.

Daniel drew his chair closer, a conspiracy of three. "Not far from here at all, my lady. Where Euphrates meets Tigris, and two more rivers once flowed from a place of unimaginable beauty. The very first garden, where the One God placed the first man and first woman, and the evil one whispered to them of a good that was not good. A choice that would destroy, even as he promised it would exalt."

Tia sat wrapped in the spell of his story of the creation of the world, a story very different than the monstrous dragon Tiamat birthing the world in her death throes. After a while Pedaiah joined the story, his face lit with a joy Tia had not seen, and Daniel deferred to the younger man. Pedaiah spoke of the flood that purified the world, a story familiar to her in parts, but somehow different than the Babylonian Gilgamesh. His eyes danced over the story of the One God's desire to redeem the world, to bring One who would someday save, and His defining of a people, through whom He would speak to and save the nations.

Daniel watched Pedaiah's passionate telling with a strange amusement, but for her, all the coldness of their exchange on the bridge evaporated, and his words swept her into the history of his people. Somehow his teaching spoke to Tia's heart rather than her mind. So different than her years of study under palace tutors. He was like a wise man himself, all knowledge and eagerness and brilliant intensity. Tia could have listened for hours.

Pedaiah seemed to have run out of air. Daniel laughed and patted his arm. "She is good for you, my boy. I have been waiting years to see in you more zeal than austerity, fervor rather than arrogance."

But Daniel's words only pushed Pedaiah back, away from both of them. Tia watched as the veil of the impersonal fell over his face once more, and she wished it had not returned.

Daniel saw it too and dropped his head for a moment before smiling again on her. "But none of this is why you came, Princess."

She sighed. "No. But I thank you for the teaching."

He patted her knee, a fatherly gesture that brought unexpected tears. How long had it been since anyone had touched her with affection?

"Your father is a proud man, my lady. The first time I came before him we were both young and newly returned from Judaea, he the conqueror and newly crowned king and me the captive, training to be a scholar." Daniel smiled and lifted

178

his head to peer into the past. "He was all rashness and youth then, demanding that his wise men not only interpret his dream but tell him the dream itself, for it had fled with the morning. Yelling that he would see them all executed as charlatans if they could not produce the dream."

Tia had never heard this story and she drank it in, desperate for word of her father, even if it was stories of the past.

Daniel laughed again. "The commander of your father's guard—Arioch, if I remember correctly, a good man—began rounding up all of us who studied in the palace. I asked him why we were to be put to death, and he told me of your father's absurdity."

Tia smiled. Only a man who had become a good friend would speak thus of her father.

"I went in to the king and asked for more time, then I and my companions spent a night in prayer. Before the night's end, the One God had given me the dream and its interpretation in a vision." He shrugged as if the matter were a simple one. "I returned to your father, gave him the truth, and young as I was, he made me chief of magi from that moment."

"He always told me that the Jews' God was one of the most powerful."

At this, Daniel's face fell. "I am afraid he still has not learned the full extent of truth. I had hoped, after that business with the monstrous statue, that he had changed. But that overweening pride of his—it has brought him low. Just as the prophecy said." The longing in his voice, that of a man grieving sharply for a close friend, was like the warmth and weight of a woolen blanket on her heart.

She leaned forward and took the old man's hand. "Tell me of the prophecy, Daniel. I fear for my father and must know if there is danger."

"There is always danger, my dear"—he squeezed her fingers—"whenever there is power. But the day approaches when your father will lift his head to heaven and acknowledge what he has long refused. And his mind will be restored."

Her heart leapt within her chest. Finally! News of the end of their long exile. Her hands convulsed around Daniel's. "When? When will this happen?"

"Soon. That is all I know. The seven times have nearly passed over him now." Daniel's eyes narrowed. "But I cannot say if he will still be king when this comes to be, nor for how long he shall live after."

She would not be satisfied—she must wring every drop of knowledge from the wise man. "This danger, it is from the other magi? Those in the palace? I have heard things."

His eyes closed and Tia pressed on. "Do you know who killed Kaldu? Was my husband poisoned?"

Daniel released her hand and sat back against his chair heavily, with an air of fatigue. "This is why I no longer live at court. Always the scheming. But I know nothing of it, I am afraid."

"Please, Daniel. I must keep my father safe."

"We do not control our own lives, Princess."

She recoiled at the words as if he had slapped her. "I will control my own."

He studied her again, and she squirmed under his scrutiny. When he spoke, his words were soft and low, like a priest reading the signs. "You run on a narrow ledge, Princess. Clinging to security but longing for adventure. There is only one way to succeed in what you undertake."

She waited, her breath suspended.

"You must learn how to risk everything."

Too vague. She must have more. "Tell me how, then."

He shook his head. "This you must learn on your own." A smile at Pedaiah. "Perhaps with some help."

"Someone seeks to overthrow my father's throne. I must know who the usurper would be."

"The palace is full of secrets, my lady. It has always been so. Secrets meant to protect but with the potential to destroy. You must be very careful."

Pedaiah stood. "The hour is late, Princess. I must return you to the palace before an alarm is raised."

Tia exhaled, unsure if anything she had heard could assist her efforts. She would have to think on all of this, but it did not seem that she had learned much tonight.

At least not about the danger to her father.

Daniel gripped her hands, and she kissed him on both cheeks and followed Pedaiah from the chamber. The courtyard lay in dusky solitude, no trace of its crowd among the dark green plants and sweet-scented white jasmine. Even Judith was gone. Tia suppressed a smile at the thought of her waiting for Pedaiah to emerge from their private meeting, then leaving unsatisfied.

They were silent for the short walk back to the palace. It had been a strange night. A run *through* the city rather than around it, one that had given her more pleasure than anything she could long remember. The sight of poverty and joy inter-mingled in the Jewish quarter. Pedaiah's anger on the bridge. Daniel's cryptic warnings. How was she to feel about all that had transpired?

Pedaiah slowed long before they reached the wide staircase that swept upward to the palace entrance. "I will leave you here, Princess."

Tia understood, though the truth saddened her somehow. It would not be wise for either of them to be seen returning together. She looked into his unreadable face. "We learned little."

His eyes looked pained. "No? I had hoped you saw something new."

"That is not—I did not mean—" Tia folded her arms. "My eyes have been opened to many things this night, Pedaiah. I have much to ponder." He blinked and looked away, so she touched his arm. "I am returning to the palace a different person than I left, and I thank you for that." He would not look at her. "But I fear I am no closer to the truth about my father and the recent deaths. And this is what I must pursue."

"Then I shall leave you to it."

And he did leave, vanishing into the dark night. Tia made her weary way up the palace steps, under the arch, and then through the courtyard and hall to her chamber, anxious now for her ladies to settle her into bed.

She pushed open her chamber door and searched the gloom for Omarsa and Gula.

Instead, sitting straight-backed in a carved chair, one leg daintily crossed over the other, Tia's mother waited.

Chapter 19

Her mother's face lay half in shadow, but the sharp incline of her jaw, the dark-ringed eyes, betrayed sleeplessness, fretfulness.

Tia unwound the scarf and veil from her head and tossed her cloak across her bedding, then sat heavily to face her, to face whatever threats Amytis had come to deliver. Her ladies were absent.

Was it fatigue or was it fear that etched those lines around her mother's mouth? Amytis plucked absently at her sleeve with one hand, worrying the fabric against her wrist.

"The hour is very late." Her tone was flat, emotionless.

"Yes."

Perfect eyebrows twitched upward, the only sign that she found Tia's answer unsatisfactory. "You were running?"

"I ran. Yes."

Her eyes strayed to Tia's conventional clothing. She had dressed in one of her finest robes to meet Pedaiah.

"I do not like you outside the palace so late. You know this."

Tia ducked her head. "I am often restless."

"I know."

Tia searched her mother's sunken eyes for compassion married to understanding, but Amytis was darkness to her, one more mystery Tia could not penetrate.

Amytis lifted her chin, her drawn face wavering in the lamplight. "You must attend to your duties better."

The words were ordinary, the same she uttered frequently. Yet tonight they held more portent, even threat, and they pressed on Tia, as though words could smother.

Amytis was gone a moment later, her perfume following her on the air like a wisp of smoke.

Tia stretched upon her bed, still dressed, and pulled the bedcoverings across her chest and legs, her eyes heavy with the adventure of the night, but her mind fractured into a thousand thoughts.

The night wore on, fragments of conversation and shards of images chafing her drowsy consciousness. Tia thrashed about on her bed, still feeling the pressure of her mother's words.

Or was it the other? The strange heaviness that often assailed, especially at night. She lay unmoving, her eyes searching the darkness. She had thrown those fearsome amulets from her chamber, but were there others? Had someone left evil charms against her, hidden in her chamber to work their silent curse? Tia fingered Amel's protective charm at her throat.

But the air grew thick and she toiled to breathe, pulling in great draughts through her nose, between whispers of ineffective prayers. Was that the smell of sacrifice? Of charred flesh?

She sat upright, searching for smoke, but the smell and the heavy air dizzied her, dropped her back against the cushions.

She fell at last into a disquiet sleep, and when morning came she stumbled through her ablutions without feeling cleansed. Indeed, the day weighed as heavily as the night, and she staggered through it as one still asleep.

Time was passing, she sensed, though she was making no progress in her quest, nor doing anything to protect her father or herself from what was to come. Instead she half listened to her tutors, picked at her meals, and fell into her bed as soon as darkness descended. Some kind of stupor had wrapped her in its clutches.

At night she often woke, shaking and beating at her own limbs to rid herself of the feathery touch of scorpions scuttling across her skin. At times she smelled the sacrifice again, even tasted the blood of it in her mouth. She awoke in the center of one night to see the demon Labartu hovering over her, her lion's head looming and ass's teeth gnashing. She could hear the distant chants of the kalû priests.

And though the nights were long and fearsome, the days were little better. Everywhere she felt on her body the eyes of the palace. The harem women, usually content to lounge the garden court-yards entertained by dancers and acrobats, all seemed to watch her. Their eyes followed her as she walked, their red lips sneered, their heads swiveled slowly to trace her steps. In the banquet hall the furtive glances of the black-bearded magi skittered away when she turned on them. Their dark curls, held by gold bands, hid their eyes.

Twice Tia found herself at the end of a day with no memory of time passing. Terrifying.

Day and night blended and swirled until she lost count. Was she ill? But no fever overtook her. To be certain, one night before falling into her bed she stood before her lady Gula and asked her to place a hand upon her skin, to search her eyes for fever. But while Gula examined her, Tia's glance fell upon the amulet at the slave's neck, the face of the demon Labartu nestled in the pulsating hollow of her throat, leering at her with that wicked grin.

She stumbled backward, caught herself against the wall, and raised a shaky finger to Gula's neck. "Why do you wear Labartu?"

Gula reached for the amulet, her eyes fearful. "You know why, my lady. For protection. I have always worn it."

Not true. Gula spoke lies to frighten her. She was part of all the watching, connected to all those who wished her harm and were forever whispering curses when she passed.

Gula took a step toward her, her hand out-stretched, but Tia smacked it. "Get out!" She pointed at Omarsa. "And you. Both of you, get out of my chamber!"

They fled, but she did not truly wish to be alone. The heaviness was strongest here, in her chamber. She lurched into the hall, shut her chamber door, and moved along the corridor, her fingers tracing the length of the wall and her thoughts racing ahead.

Was it a spell? Had Gula placed a spell upon her? But no, why would she? Tia shook her head, trying to clear the stringy cobwebs of incoherence.

She must seek Shadir. Why, she did not know. Somehow this was part of him, part of her questions. Her steps led her to the Hall of Magi, but when she turned the final corner, Shadir emerged from the vaulted Hall entrance, veered away from her, and strode down the corridor, dark robes trailing.

She followed.

She wore only an ankle-length tunic, her feet were bare and soundless, and her breath controlled by months of running. Shadir moved with heavy tread through the corridors and she shadowed him easily, keeping to the wall, ready to disappear into a recessed doorway or darkened wing should he turn.

But he had no sense that Tia followed and twisted through one lengthy corridor after another, then down a narrow flight of steps without a backward glance. Where did he go at this hour?

They dropped another level in their strange race, then another until they were underground, where secret passages and chambers honeycombed the underside of the everyday workings of the palace, supporting it with sewage tunnels, storage chambers, and deep cisterns from which the Gardens were fed. Only an occasional torch against the damp walls illuminated the corridor, and Tia hurried through those patches of light, anxious to remain unseen. The dank air smelled of sulfur and earth. Still Shadir walked on, and still she followed.

But somewhere in the stretch of darkness beyond the next torch, he disappeared.

Tia slowed. Did he wait against a slick wall, ready to grab her? Her stomach cramped against her ribs, and she held her breath and moved forward, balanced on her bare toes.

A narrow doorway ahead suddenly blazed.

Tia jumped backward. No torch appeared to seek her out. Lamplight, from within a chamber. She crept forward to the dusty edge of the opening, stole a glance into the room, then pulled away.

Shadir stood within, his profile to her. She shifted so one eye cleared the door frame and braced her hands against the mildewed wall, breathing openmouthed past her desert-dry tongue.

He stood before a small table, like the one she had seen in the Hall of Magi. The same trappings of his art lay spread across the wood—clay bowls, knives, jugs of what must be oil. At his left hand a length of rope hung over the edge, and there was a figure of some sort lying on its side. She watched, entranced, as he began his rites.

It was the divine duty of every ashipu priest, given the power of divination and the wisdom of the stars, to protect king and kingdom from the demons, to seek the defense of the gods against their evil force. Shadir had been a mage for many years and knew his art. He began with a singsong chant in words foreign to her ear. Akkadian, perhaps—the language of his ancient tribe. He swayed over the table and lifted the figure, grasping it in his fist. She had seen only that it was a woman. His voice lifted, words in her own tongue now.

"Her name has been spoken. Her name has been exposed. By this I rob her of her power. By this I bring defeat."

Tia shuddered. She had heard magi use the Power of the Name against their enemies—those believed to be sorcerers and sometimes the demons themselves—but to whom did Shadir refer? She had not heard the name when he spoke it.

"I call upon Labartu to torment her. I call upon Labartu to distress her." His voice rose and fell, and she strained forward as far as she dared, trying to catch every word.

Shadir raised his clutched hand, the wood figure still strangled in his hold, and placed the other hand around it. With a snap, he rotated his hands opposite each other, as though wrenching the life from the image.

She felt the quick motion in her gut.

He dropped the figure into the terra-cotta bowl and, with muttered incantations, poured oil and touched it with flame. The bowl blazed and lit his face with an unholy glow.

She shrank back. He had only to turn his head and he would see her.

The torture and burning of a demon figure was an oft-used symbol meant to transfer destruction upon the demon that caused suffering. Yet something was not right here, something was different. What was it?

Shadir lifted the rope from the table, held it aloft by its two ends over the burning bowl for a moment, then quickly tied a knot into the rope. Then another.

As he tied the third knot, a flash of understanding swayed her on her feet.

He should be releasing the knots, not tying them afresh. *He is running the rites backward.*

It meant only one thing. Shadir was not performing his duties as a priest-mage, called to protect Babylon and its throne. He was acting *against* someone, trying to influence fate to harm someone or for personal gain.

Shadir is a sorcerer.

A low buzzing in her head terrified her, and her feet had grown roots into the floor. She must escape. But she could not. Her breath expelled from her chest and she could not get it back. She gripped the door frame with whitened fingers and willed her feet to move.

He held a branch of wood now, a thin stick, slightly bent, and with it he traced circles around his head, calling out the spell. "In my hand I hold the circle of Ea, in my hand I hold the cedarwood, the sacred weapon of Ea, in my hand I hold the branch of the cedar tree of the great rite." A circle of protection with only himself inside.

He had entangled his enemy in the rope's knots, burned a figure of the enemy in the clay bowl, and exposed her by name. Left her outside the circle. Who was she?

At last, at last Tia broke from the darkness that held her, spun away from the evil chamber, and fled.

Her feet carried her across the shadowed expanses of the corridor, past the flickering torches, their light swallowed.

Only a heartbeat from the first set of stairs, she slammed into something—*someone*.

"Pedaiah?" His name escaped her lips like a desperate plea.

"Princess?" The man moved her backward, into the light.

"Amel!" It was the second time she had collided with Shadir's mage-in-training. Her body responded with that strange comingling of fear and pull he always produced. Was he part of the dark plan?

"Princess, you are shaking."

"It is nothing. I—I was lost for a few moments. Here are the stairs. I am fine."

Behind her, she heard the one voice she dreaded. "Amel? Who do you have there?"

Tia shook her head, but Amel was peering into the darkness. "It is the princess. She was lost."

Nothing but silence returned to them. Then only two words from Shadir: "Bring her."

Her limbs flooded with hot panic. Would it seem suspicious to flee? More dangerous? Would she learn the truth if she stayed?

She let Amel lead her to Shadir's secret room and felt as though neither of them truly had a choice. Inside, the last remnants of the wood figurine had turned to embers, and only the oil lamp gave off light.

"Curious that you should be down here this night, Princess." Shadir waved a hand over his table. "I was just seeking the gods for your protection."

She licked dry lips, tried to swallow the tightness in her throat. Amel still held her by the arm, whether to comfort or detain, she could not tell.

Shadir stirred the dying fire with a sharp iron instrument. "I have been given to know that you have been plagued by the demon Labartu." He jabbed at the ash. "I sought to protect you from her evils."

Tia shuddered and again cursed her transparency. Labartu? Was that the "she" that he had burned? The one named in his incantations?

Tia had been certain that he used his power to bring evil on someone. A woman. Had only her imagination led her elsewhere? She looked to the rope—surely that would be proof—but it lay pristine across the table, unknotted.

All those watching eyes in the palace—were they nothing but false suspicion?

Amel stroked her arm now, and she saw herself through his eyes for a moment—pale and shaky, eyes wide, lips parted.

Did Shadir speak truth? Perhaps she *had* let her imaginings run away.

But beneath her questions, her uncertainty about Shadir and even Amel, there was another possibility. One that had tickled at her thoughts for some days now, since all of this strangeness began . . .

Madness ran in the family.

Chapter 20

Tia escaped Shadir, and even Amel, and ran back through underground passages, up narrow stairs, and through corridors until she fell upon her bed, alone but not comforted. The long night labored past and birthed another day, murky and gray like those preceding. She wandered the courtyards, absent from her lessons but hardly present anywhere. The fountains and towering greenery did not soothe, and the harem women, with their garish dress and spoiled manners, irritated.

A hand on her arm arrested her slow spiral through yet another courtyard.

Pedaiah. She blinked once but had no words.

His eyes took in her face like an object of study. He glanced left and right, then spoke quietly. "Princess, are you well?"

Tia shrugged. Her attention strayed to a near fountain, with an orange and white fish fluttering in its pool.

"Tia, follow me." His voice was strangely urgent.

She watched him go for a moment—his steady stride across the flagstones, his solid shoulders. He did not turn back. She followed.

The palace held many rooms for which there seemed no use. Into one of these, lit only by the gray dawn that filtered from the courtyard, she followed Pedaiah. He turned on her in the gloom, his brow furrowed.

"I have been looking for a moment to speak to you since we returned from Daniel's house, these seven days. Where have you been? Have you learned anything more of Shealtiel's death?"

Her heart slowed. "Seven days? It has been seven days?"

He grabbed her upper arms and peered into

her eyes. "What has happened, Tiamat? Has someone . . . harmed you?"

She shook her heavy head, the effort nearly too great.

"You have the look of someone hunted. Tell me—who is hunting you?"

Her lips parted and she pulled the words from somewhere. "I think Shadir is a sorcerer . . . Or perhaps . . . I am going mad." To speak the words made them closer to truth, and a chill ran through her, even under Pedaiah's warm hold. He released her at once, as though fearful he would contract this madness.

But no, his hand went to her head instead. Covered her head like a priest. The other hand he lifted above them both. His eyes closed and his chin dropped to his chest.

He spoke, so quietly Tia strained to hear, to hear the prayer he poured over her like warm oil on abraded skin. Soft words that filled the chamber.

"He that dwells in the secret place of the Most High shall rest under the shadow of the Almighty. I will say of Yahweh, He is my refuge and my fortress, my God, in Him will I trust."

Her breath expelled, her shoulders sagged.

"Deliver her, Yahweh, from the snare of the enemy, from the poison of the evil one. Cover her with Your feathers, and under Your wings let her trust. Let Your truth be her shield. Let her not be afraid of the terror by night, nor of the arrow that flies by day, nor for the plague that walks in darkness in this palace, nor for the destruction that would steal her strength."

He paused, as though emotion had choked his words. Tia studied his closed eyes, the fine lines that traced outward, and her own emotion swelled against her chest. But he was not finished.

"Yahweh, command Your angels concerning her, to guard her in all her ways. Because You love her, deliver her. Open her eyes. Show her Your name, teach her to call upon You, answer her and be with her in trouble."

Because He loved me? Who had ever loved her besides her father? Something loosened inside Tia's heart, cords she had not known were binding her. Something fearful released, taking flight like a great black bird frightened from its prey. With the release came a spreading warmth to her cold limbs and a wash of tears.

Pedaiah opened his eyes. His hand was still upon her head, but he slid it down the side of her face, then lingered there a moment to collect her tears in his palm and wipe them away.

She would have him speak again, to reassure her that his prayer would save her, but he said nothing more and a moment later was gone.

Tia stepped from the chamber, reveling in the freedom his words brought.

Her slaves, Omarsa and Gula, descended before her eyes adjusted to the courtyard light. "Your mother has summoned, my lady. She is in your chamber."

She drew in a deep breath, somehow more ready to face Amytis than in recent weeks. Omarsa and Gula followed to her chamber.

"Ah, Tiamat, good." Amytis waved her in, her attention elsewhere. Four or five female slaves bustled around the room, laying rich clothing across her bed and setting carved wooden boxes on tables. Her two sisters were also present, though their cool appraisal made it clear they had come for duty, not love.

Amytis was babbling. "The palace seamstresses have finished your bridal wardrobe, and I have brought everything for your approval. Your trunks will be packed soon, so you will be ready when Zagros arrives. Come, take a look at the robes, and then I will show you the jewels I intend to send with you. You must show all of Media that Babylon's riches are not to be surpassed."

After the solid tranquility of Pedaiah, her mother was like a fluttering, chirping bird, feathers preening. Tia crossed to the bed wordlessly and ran her hand over the smooth silks she had assembled. So much red. As though Amytis sent protection against the demons that would chase her all the way to Media.

Media. She had given much thought to another marriage, to falling victim again to a man who would only use her and not love her, but she had not spent much time on thoughts of leaving Babylon. She let a silk robe slide through her fingers and saw herself, there in the palace of Media, growing old with her husband as king, separated from her parents, from her people, from all those who were dear to her. Alone and purposeless. Her stomach tightened.

Amytis was pushing perfume jugs into her hands. "I want you to have these, Tia. The finest alabaster." She removed a stopper and waved the jug under Tia's nose, smiling. "Yes? You smell that? What prince could resist such a scent?"

"Mother, what do you know of the diviner Belteshazzar's prophecies concerning Father?"

Her mother's face went dark and she stopped up the alabaster jar with a heavy hand. "Prophecies. Bah! That old fool."

"Father trusted him completely."

"Yes, and look at your—" Amytis glanced at the busy slaves and cut her words short.

"Why were you spending time with Kaldu?"

Amytis placed the perfume jug on a table and shooed Tia's sisters and slaves from the room with long fingers until they were alone, then shut the chamber door and turned on her.

"Too many questions, Tia. You waste your time with this useless chatter. I would have you preparing for your wedding, making yourself both beautiful and wise in the way princesses have always secured the loyalty and affection of their husbands." Amytis smoothed her robes, as if thinking of her father.

Her resignation sickened Tia. "Those things did little to endear me to Shealtiel. He seemed always to feel guilty for marrying me. As though he performed all his rituals, all his obligations to his God, simply to erase that one mistake."

Amytis waved a hand. "You cannot take anything these Judaeans do as typical. I should think you had seen that by now. They are a bizarre race, with their One God."

"Father didn't think so. He once decreed no one could speak against Yahweh."

Amytis's eyebrows lifted at her use of their God's name, but then she dropped her gaze and turned away. "Your father had a strange fascination with the Jews' God, I will admit. He once told me"—her words grew soft as if in confession—"he once told me that he suspected our gods were nothing, that the Judaean One God was all there was. This was just after that great statue he built on the plain, after his insistence that everyone bow. He had seen something, something he did not wish to speak of later. But it—it affected him."

"Then why do you dismiss the prophecies of Dan—of Belteshazzar, as though they are nothing?"

She whirled. "Because they *are* nothing! They must be nothing. We must be loyal to our own gods, Tiamat. They are our only protection."

"Protection from what?"

"From the secrets." Amytis's face grew dark, removed from Tia somehow. "Secrets that were always meant to shield but can also destroy."

Her words echoed Daniel's so closely, it raised the hair on Tia's arms. She crossed the room and took her mother's hand in her own. "Tell me, Mother. Tell me. What did Kaldu have to do with these secrets? And Shadir? What do you fear?"

Amytis inhaled sharply and snatched her hand away. "I will send the slaves back to pack everything for you."

She left Tia standing beside her robe-strewn bed, staring at the luxuries of a princess. How little had changed since the day of Shealtiel's death.

Tia had vowed to keep her freedom and protect her father. But she had learned little. The Median prince was even now descending on her, and Pedaiah would never let her marry his younger brother. She was still little more than the palace pet, chasing circles around the city. Pedaiah had good reason for his disdain.

At the thought of him and his prayer over her, she swept her arms across the bed, seized the robes into a heap, and thrust them to the floor.

Whether he still hated her, Tia could not know. She only knew that when she should have been thinking of herself and her father, she could not stop thinking of this one angry Jew.

Chapter 21

The night again brought dreams, dark and fearsome.

In the way of dreams, I rise from my bed, not on two legs but as a solid piece, first hovering in gloom above the fabrics, then rising slowly, slowly, to glide across the chamber.

The chamber door opens without my hands, for my hands are also solid, wed to the substance that is my body.

The door closes heavily behind me, and I drift through the palace corridor, silent, not touching the floor beneath. Though my mother's chamber is not in this wing, I pass it anyway. Amytis will surely be sleeping. Her guard seems not to notice me.

I soar down the tiers of the Hanging Gardens, but my father is not to be seen. Or perhaps it is I who cannot be seen. At this thought my substance grows cold.

I speed through the palace, across its three courtyards, down the wide palace steps, and out into the gray night. An unnatural fog snakes through streets and curls around huddled mud-brick homes, barely visible under the heavy, moonless sky.

My solid body turns, as though I am a temple

statue spun under the hands of a priest, and I face the palace. Its varying slashes of roofline cut against the limitless gray, and at one corner a torch blazes. Behind me the Platform of Etemenanki rises like a solid partner to the palace.

But then along the roof I see a shadow move, quick and animal-like. Father? No, it is Shadir. He looks down over the ridge of the roof and shakes his fist. But here in the street I am a solid thing, far away. What harm can Shadir inflict? The wind kicks up. It chases the fog and whistles against the houses.

Shadir is sliding something along the roof, something larger than himself. I watch, impassive, as he brings it nearer the torch.

A wooden figure. Like myself. Carved as a man, with black cuts deep in its smoky-tan surface. Eyes, lips, mouth. A face I have not seen whole in many years. This is Father.

And then Shadir is dragging another figure, smaller than the first, cut with the unmistakable likeness of my mother. Shadir sets her beside the first, peers over the roof again to scowl, then snatches the torch and with a smile at me, he touches the flame to my father's face.

A fluttering throb begins in my cold heart and races through all of me. I want to shout, to scream, but no sound comes from my wooden lips.

The flames lick at my father's face, then smother him greedily. Shadir shoves the torch at my mother and she, too, is consumed by the orange death.

The sky opens and water pours down from the gods, but it does nothing to quench the flames. They crackle fiercely above the din of the downpour, turning it to an evil mist around my burning parents.

I shiver in the cold wet, try to pull my eyes from the horror but cannot.

And then they begin to call to me.

"Tiiiaaaamaaattt . . ." My father's agonized cry cuts through me. I try to reach out to him, but my arm is still part of my solid self.

A great and terrible guilt shakes my core.

More figures appear, all of them burning. My sisters. My nephews. Everyone I care for in the palace, burning, burning as I watch, helpless.

"You must go back."

I cannot turn to the whisper behind my ear, but I know the voice. Amel-Marduk. He touches my hand and it springs to life under his touch, becomes once again living flesh. I clutch at his warm hand and the life spreads up my arm, across my chest, through all of me. I look down at my humanity and see that I am dressed in beggar's rags.

Amel brings his face near my own. His flawless skin glows with the reflection of the flames, and he smells of age, of ancient things, as though he has always been. His full, red lips smile patiently. "If you love them, you will go back. You are the only one who can save them."

This guilt is real, then. It is my fault they burn. I have not done enough to save my father, have never loved my mother like I should, nor my sisters. My wooden heart has let them come to this.

The rain courses down my face in heavy rivulets like false tears. I turn from Amel to my burning family and feel the weight of decision on my shoulders of flesh.

And I awake.

Still in her bed, Tia lifted a hand and turned it before her eyes in the dim light, then put it to her face and found her skin wet. Perhaps she was not without feeling, then, if her evil dream had drawn true tears. She lay unmoving, willing her heart to slow its frantic beat, her limbs to relax. She was still in the palace, her mother and father still alive, her family sleeping somewhere under palace protection.

A dream such as this held deep meaning. Meaning that was not to be ignored. Poor man or king would seek a diviner's wisdom for a dream such as this.

There was only one diviner whom she trusted with her secrets.

She waited for dawn, and when its first rose-tipped petals bloomed at the horizon, she slid from her chamber, ran through the still-dark corridors, and escaped into the streets. The cloak she'd hastily donned beat against her legs as she ran.

Memories of the circuitous route she and Pedaiah had taken to Daniel's house last week sped her feet. She would be there before the sun had fully risen.

She did not hail a doorkeeper, did not wait to be invited into Daniel's home. Before she breached the courtyard, she heard voices. He had already begun his day.

Tia hesitated at the end of the passage from the street and searched the leafy courtyard for the old diviner. She found him standing in the center, facing her but with head bowed under a covering, a shawl of some sort. Another man's back was to her, a shawl over his head as well, tasseled and striped in blue. The second man was speaking, and her breath caught at the recognition of Pedaiah's voice.

He was praying. Again. This time the words were lost to her, spoken in his Judaean tongue. Daniel joined him, and they prayed the words in unison, their deep voices blending, old and young, kind and haughty, until she could not tell them apart.

She leaned a shoulder against the wall, and the anxiety of her rush to reach Daniel evaporated.

The courtyard lay in early morning shadows, but a warm breeze blew across her face and chased away the night terrors.

Their prayers, though she did not understand the words, seemed to her to be prayers of praise and confession, not the temple priests' demands and pleas. They rose like incense, with the scent of sweet sacrifice, from the lips of the two men.

He was a radical man, this Daniel. All these years in the upper strata of Babylonian power and still he retained the faith of his homeland. Risked everything to remain faithful to his One God. How much had he sacrificed?

Tia shifted on her feet, and the slight movement caught his attention. Prayers arrested, he lifted his eyes and smiled on her.

"Forgive me, Daniel." Tia bowed her head. "I did not intend to intrude." She did not look at Pedaiah as he turned.

"Come, child." Daniel held out his arms. "There is no better place for you than in the center of our prayers."

Her throat tightened at these words, and she crossed the courtyard on swift feet and fell into his grip. He smelled of oil and wine, as though he himself were the libation poured out to his God.

"I have had a dream, Daniel." The words were a whisper against his ear but loud enough for Pedaiah to hear. Daniel led her to a bench and sat beside her. Pedaiah stood nearby. It would be senseless to ask him to leave.

Daniel lifted her chin. "This dream has troubled you greatly."

She looked into his clear eyes, then noted how much dark hair he retained amidst the gray, his youthful physique. Odd. She had thought him old because he had always been this way even when she was a child. But this morning he seemed young to her, and she thought of her dream, of Amel and his smell of age. "How old are you, Daniel?"

He smiled and glanced at Pedaiah, as if to share his amusement. "It has been more than forty years since your father brought me to Babylon as a youth. We have aged together, he and I."

At this mention of her father, the image of his burning face blazed against her memory.

"What is it, child? Tell me your dream."

She poured it out to both of them, though she could not look at the man who stood apart, only at the one who held her hand through the telling.

When she was through, Pedaiah spoke for the first time. "And did you return to the palace with the young mage?"

She faced him finally and chewed her lip. "I—I do not know. I awoke before I made my decision."

Daniel patted her hand. "*Decision* is a fitting word, child. For that is what you will soon face."

208

"What does it mean, my dream? Does it signal madness?"

He closed his eyes and bent his head over her hand. He had no sheep's liver nor oil-on-water. Did he yet seek his One God for an answer?

When he lifted his eyes, they were clear but guarded. "There is no interpretation of this dream for you yet, Tiamat. But it will come, in time. Know only this: The mage Amel-Marduk is not a friend to you. Even now there is a war for your soul in the heavenlies. Do not let the darkness masked as light take you prisoner."

"Amel has something to do with all of this, then? The danger to my family?"

Daniel's fingers clenched around her own, uncomfortably tight. "Tiamat, a lie, no matter how beautiful, is still a lie."

It was a warning. A warning to stay away from Amel. And yet even as Tia left Daniel's home, left Pedaiah's silent watching, her mind and heart went directly to where Daniel said they should not go.

She felt again the moment of her dream when Amel's warm grasp had returned her to flesh. She wished again to feel that warmth.

She would seek out Amel.

In the night street, not far from Daniel's house, Pedaiah knocked at the door of Samuel ben Hananiah. Samuel had proven himself a loyal servant of Yahweh, training his family in the ways of the Law, and had become a friend to Pedaiah, though twice his age.

The door swung open, sliding against the dirt-packed floor, to reveal the humble but tidy interior of the small home Samuel shared with his wife and still-unmarried daughter, Judith.

Samuel grinned from the doorway, the lamp-light behind him making him look birdlike with his always-disheveled hair and angular build. "Pedaiah! We were not expecting you this night. Come in, come in." He pulled the door wider.

"I—I am sorry to come with no invitation—"

Samuel's wife appeared behind him, small and compact and smiling. "Nonsense." She called over her shoulder, "Judith!"

Pedaiah ducked into the home but needed only wait by the door for a moment. Judith appeared, a pleased look of curiosity lighting her eyes.

Her mother fanned herself with a pudgy hand. "So warm in here tonight. Why don't you two see if there is a breeze on the rooftop?"

Pedaiah hid a smile. It was no secret what was in the mind of a Jewish mother with an unmarried daughter. Judith raised her eyebrows to Pedaiah in a silent question and he nodded. She took a terra-cotta oil lamp from the table, and he followed her up the narrow stone stairs and onto the open roof. One half of the roof lay covered in drying reeds, but two chairs placed side by side faced the river, away from the palace.

Judith set the lamp down on a small table between the chairs. "You seem distressed, Pedaiah. Has something happened? Is Daniel well?"

Pedaiah dropped into a seat, glad that from a seated position very little of the city could be seen. "I have just come from him. He is well."

"But you are not." Judith pulled the other chair closer and sat, their knees nearly touching. "Will you tell me why?"

He sighed, watched the orange tip of the lamp wick, and tried to sort his thoughts.

Judith took his hand in her own warm fingers. "Pedaiah, you know that I care for you."

He nodded. Why had he come here? It was unfair to Judith.

"You can tell me anything. I'm stronger than you think."

Pedaiah studied their hands, intertwined. "In over forty years our people still have not learned the lessons of exile. I fear they never will."

Judith leaned back in her chair but did not release his hand. "Those of us born here are only now becoming leaders, Pedaiah. Perhaps this is why our future is still bound up in Babylon and will be for years to come. You must have patience."

"Patience! Bah!" He pulled away and crossed his arms. "How can they eagerly await the return to the land, prepared to forsake idolatry, when

211

everything about this pagan place is so enticing?"

"Because you will teach them to do so."

He closed his eyes against her misplaced confidence. "How can I, when I am a hypocrite myself?"

The night air swirled along the edges of the roof, ruffling the dry tips of the reeds and lifting the hair from his damp neck. Judith was silent. Did she understand his self-loathing?

At last she spoke, the tone soft and contemplative. "Perhaps Yahweh has given you this trial so you would better understand your countrymen and the temptations they face."

Pedaiah sat forward, his eyes on hers. "It is a test, then? I am to set an example?"

Judith shrugged one shoulder. "I do not know the mind of Yahweh."

"Perhaps you are right. This—this distraction— it keeps me from pushing forward with my teaching, from what I am supposed to be doing. Just as my fellow Jews are distracted by the charms of Babylon."

"Or perhaps this distraction is the very thing you are supposed to be concerned with."

Pedaiah eyed her warily. Did she truly know of what they spoke?

"I am not a fool, Pedaiah. I see the way you look at her, the way you speak of her." Judith's voice was soft, sad perhaps. "You care deeply, and that is one of the qualities that make you a wonderful man."

He dropped his eyes, rubbed at his forehead with two fingers. "I am confused, Judith."

"She is very beautiful."

Pedaiah closed his eyes again, avoiding the pain in hers. "It is not her beauty. It is what I see beyond it. Her strength, her devotion to her family."

"Does she know?"

He shook his head. "How can I tell her? When everything I've ever taught is screaming in my head to walk away, to turn my back on the palace and everyone in it?"

He waited for her answer, and in those moments Judith seemed to recede from him, though she still sat in the chair beside him. A distance, more than physical, was growing between them. Her voice came to him as from far away, resigned but not despairing.

"Pedaiah, how can you not?"

Chapter 22

In the copper blaze of a dozen braziers scattered at the palace courtyard's perimeter, the lush greenery of the atrium danced with green shadows and silvery lights. Palm trees rooted deep beneath the palace floor spread branches across the darkness of the night sky, a thousand stars piercing their fronds. Trailing vines swung from the tiered balcony that ringed the courtyard. A fertile oasis in the desert, the garden seduced all in its leafy arms and earthy smells and the pulsing rhythm of celebration.

The largest of the palace's four courtyards was often used for social gatherings in the evenings, sometimes centered around a holy day, often impromptu and spurred by bored harem wives. A large conclave of women lounged tonight.

For three days Tia had sought Amel, in banquet room and corridor. She had not dared to enter the Hall of Magi again. Now she stood at the edge of the courtyard and skimmed the crowd with her eyes, as she had done with every crowd for days. *There*. A surge of victory quickened her pulse.

Amel-Marduk sat cross-legged across the courtyard on the other side of the large circular pool in the center. He spoke with someone, and his smile was visible even from here. His upper body rocked slightly, in time with the drummers whose fingertips flew over impossibly complex rhythms on the drums between their knees.

A cluster of dancers twirled between them, blocking Tia's view of him. The women's multicolored robes spun outward with their movements, and their hand cymbals clinked in harmony with the gold beads of their veils. She waited for them to pass, then crossed, skirting the central pool along its blue and yellow mosaic tiles.

Amel's gaze connected with her own and his smile grew. He slid to one side, creating space for her. She lowered herself to the stone floor and drew her legs up, hugging her knees to her chest. "I have been looking for you."

They faced the courtyard, but Amel's voice was for her alone. His eyes went to his amulet around her neck, then back to Tia's face. "Then I am overjoyed you have found me."

In the days she had been searching for Amel, Daniel's warnings had not been utterly lost on her. This mage was Shadir's special pupil. She could not trust him entirely, and indeed should probably even suspect him of complicity in his tutor's plot. She would be on her guard.

She watched the dancers in silence for some minutes. There were perhaps a dozen of them, sometimes dancing in concert, often spreading through the crowd to please one particular cluster. The melody of lyre and flute tumbled over haunting minor notes and gave their undulating bodies a sultry, hypnotic cadence. Mixed with the brazier smoke and the perfume of the harem women, Tia's head spun with their movements. She leaned against Amel to steady herself and felt him return pressure against her arm.

"I must ask you some things, Amel."

"The night is too beautiful for questions, Princess." His voice was low, his words spoken against her hair.

She shook her head. She must hold on to her reason for coming. "You spoke once of danger to my sisters' sons. Is all my family threatened?" Tia thought of her dream, of Amel urging her back into the palace to save the figures burning on the roof. "Is there something I can do to save them?"

"I would not want you to put yourself in danger, my lady."

Tia watched him from the corner of her eye, traced his close-cropped beard along the sharp jawline, watched those long lashes lift and his dark eyes fix on her. He leaned closer, until his shoulder-length oiled curls brushed her skin.

His eyes burned. "There are some who would stop at nothing to claim, or retain, power."

In this he spoke truth, but a seed of fear took root in her heart. How involved was Amel in whatever was happening? He spoke of power and she sensed his own attraction to it. Could he have killed Kaldu himself if the noble had impeded his goals? That night, when they found Kaldu's body together, had their chance meeting not been chance at all? Had Amel *led* her to Kaldu?

"Who? Who seeks power at any cost?"

His head was still close to hers, but he glanced left and right before speaking. "Shadir. I do not know what he plans, but there is something . . ."

Her heart raced with this confirmation. Or perhaps with the nearness of Amel. His arm still brushed hers, and the skin there burned like a hundred desert suns.

The dancers circled to perform for them, and

they were silent as they strutted left, then a look tossed back over the shoulder, a backward kick, a turn and a sharp clang of the cymbals. Then right, kick, turn, *clang*. The movement was simple but effective, and she watched Amel's gaze follow them with a jealousy she ought not to feel.

The dancers spun away and she reclaimed his attention. "Tell me what you know of Shadir." She felt the eyes of those around them. They would be surprised at her intimate conversation with the mage. *Let them wonder.*

"He does not confide in me. But I hear things. Words spoken about—" At this, he seemed to change his mind. A slave passed with a tray of fruits, and Amel held up a hand, then took two large pieces of melon from the tray.

"Words spoken about what, Amel?"

He lifted one piece of the melon, its pale green flesh dripping, and placed it between her lips. "Let us think of more pleasant things, Princess."

She bit into the cool melon, tasted the sweetness filling her mouth, felt the juice trickle down her chin. Amel put the remainder of the fruit in his own mouth, then wiped her chin with the back of one finger.

She chewed and swallowed and let him speak of the stars and their movements tonight, of good omens and auspicious days. His words wrapped her in silk threads, some kind of cocoon. But what would she be when she emerged?

She whispered against his shoulder, "I must know what Shadir is planning."

Amel looked away, at something across the courtyard, but her attention was on him, on the glint of the gold band across his forehead.

"It is not Shadir's plan, I do not believe. He works under the direction of someone else."

She held her breath, sensing he would reveal it without her question.

"I think, Princess, that it all flows from one person. And that person is your mother."

Her breath left her. She followed his gaze now and found it turned on Amytis herself, whom she had not seen earlier. She sat on a reed chair, directly across the courtyard from them, alone.

And her eyes, like black stone chips, were trained on Tia.

Tia's chest heaved as though she'd been running the palace wall. For the first time, she suspected her mother of everything. Had Amytis killed Kaldu herself? Perhaps even Shealtiel, to free Tia to marry her kinsman?

Amytis returned her gaze, more fearful than defiant perhaps, but she did not look away.

What was a daughter to do when one parent set herself up against the other?

It was a question with no answer, and as the music played around them and the food and wine and dance flowed on, Tia feared she would never know.

Chapter 23

She must to do something, *anything,* to prevent her mother from carrying out a plan against her father. On the heels of Tia's angry resolve came clarity. The time for questions had ended. She had sought information from Kaldu's wife, pushed Shadir for answers, and searched out Amel more than once. She had found Daniel and had lost a slave girl. Even her mother had refused to give her the truth. No, it would take more than well-placed questions to understand what secrets clung to the palace walls.

Amytis's schedule was predictable. After the morning banquet hall cleared, she would be in the throne room, performing her husband's duties through whispered words to her favorite advisors. Never the magi. Always noblemen she had placed close. Kaldu had been one of these. Had he learned something of her secrets?

Tia stood at the rear of the throne room, her hands braced behind her against the cool blue-tiled wall. The morning breeze chilled her feet. She should have worn more than her simple bleached tunic. A host of citizens crowded the room, waiting for an audience. Some stood in clusters, muttering their complaints. Others stood apart, against the bright walls, leaning against the false columns painted red and white, as though they would be devoured by the yellow lions. Amytis was resplendent on the dais, purple-robed and heavily jeweled.

The larger vacant throne beside her paid homage to her missing husband but seemed the only place his presence was lacking. In all else, the morning court functioned as it should. As it had these seven years. She had done well, Tia would give her that. In the hands of a lesser woman, the kingdom would have been ravaged —from within or from without.

The penitents came one by one—matters of business to be decided upon, favors to be granted. Each was heard, judged, dismissed. Tia kept a careful eye on the crowd. She would not stay too long.

When the numbers dwindled, Tia slipped away, through the lofty squared entrance at the back of the room. A corridor ran the length of the throne room, then turned west and followed its perimeter. She ran on light feet, ignoring the shifting gaze of guards, heart pounding.

At the end of the second corridor lay her destination. As the room was not yet occupied by the queen, it was not yet guarded. Breathing heavily at the chance she was about to take, Tia glanced over her shoulder to ensure she was not watched, then darted into the small chamber.

Windowless and dim, save one small oil lamp

that burned on a central table. Several chairs were scattered through the space, and on the far wall, in lieu of a window, a heavy tapestry hung with a scene of the god Marduk defeating the monster Tiamat.

In spite of the risk, a smile twitched at her lips. Ironic.

Tia fingered the edge of the tapestry. Was the gap large enough to accommodate her thin frame? She wedged herself between the tapestry and the wall, unseen to the room, and settled herself in a position she could maintain with some comfort, head turned. She could be here awhile. She pressed slick palms against her fluttering belly. Would she be able to remain motionless through her mother's entire session with her advisors?

Voices approached. Too late for second thoughts. Tia lowered her arms and held her breath. Then forced herself to breathe normally. It would not do to be gulping air once the room was occupied.

Little light filtered to the back of the tapestry. Her eyes adjusted only enough to see yellow threads knotted against the dark background. The smell of dank wool enveloped her.

Then a man's voice, effeminate and grating— they were still in the hall.

". . . and there is not much we can say in response."

A snort, closer. Amytis led the way into the

room. "There is always something to say." Her mother, sharp and impatient. A brighter light surged, and Tia closed her eyes, as if the light would reveal her and she had only to cower from it to remain undetected.

"But my queen, we have been repeating the same story for seven years. How much longer—?"

"Soon, Rabi. Soon it will all be over. It must be."

The rough underside of the tapestry scratched at Tia's cheek. Did the hanging move with the rise and fall of her chest?

Another male voice, the tone stronger and more defiant than the first. "Kaldu's death, my lady—"

"I know this! Do you think me a fool?"

"I think you are an optimist. Believing you can maintain this pretense indefinitely, regardless of circumstance."

The scrape of chair legs on the stone floor. Were there only three, then? Did they sit in a tight circle, conferring with heads close together? Or did her mother fling herself across a chair, apart from the men, one leg crossed over the other, unaware that her daughter stood only a breath away? More irony, this. Amytis had wished Tia unseen all her life.

"We must maintain it, Dagan. You know this. One slip, one crack, and he will somehow find a way to slither through it."

"Perhaps my lady gives him too much credit." The softer voice again. "Perhaps he has nothing. Knows nothing."

A pause, and she could almost see her mother's hard eyes dissecting the weaker man. "He knows. Have no doubt. He knows."

"How can you be certain—?"

"Why else would he have taken the whelp under his wing? In all his years in court, have you ever known him to take a student?" Her voice rose, a wisp of hysteria creeping across the tightness.

A thread tickled at Tia's lip, and she struggled to rid herself of the annoyance and still give close attention. Did they speak of Shadir? Of Amel? Or was her own suspicion coloring her interpretation?

"My queen, do not excite yourself." Rabi's words placated but his tone seemed almost aggravated. "If he *does* know, he has made no move to reveal this knowledge."

Amytis laughed, a sardonic laugh of condescension at Rabi's naïveté. "Only a matter of time. He is waiting. For what, I do not know. But this business with Kaldu could be the start."

"The people will not respond to leadership from a mage."

Tia chewed at her lip to relieve the irritation. So it was Shadir. A trickle of sweat ran down her spine, though the room was cool. She had come for just this. *Speak on, Mother. Tell me all of your insidious plans.*

"Perhaps not. But if he has proof of the boy's claim . . ."

Dagan seemed to have all the answers. "We will destroy this proof."

"You are a fool, Dagan. Kingdoms rise and fall on rumor as much as evidence. With no king to produce, the damage will be done. And then how long do you suppose my family will survive?"

The young boys, Labashi and Puzur? Was this the danger of Amel's warning?

Neither man answered, and Amytis continued. "I will tell you. Our lives will be forfeit before the next new moon, and that boy will take my husband's throne."

"My lady, could we not clean him up a bit?" Rabi offered his timid suggestion in a shaky voice. "Ride him through the city, reassure the people—"

"Stop. Do not speak of it again. I will not have him mocked."

"Or perhaps you do not wish to see him yourself." Dagan had more courage. Tia had to agree with him. Amytis had not seen her father in seven long years.

She ignored the accusation. "We will continue with my plan. Zagros will arrive soon, and his marriage to Tiamat will purchase more time and ensure the future."

A wave of heat began at Tia's toes and surged

224

upward through her body. To hear her name and *purchase* together confirmed all she believed about her upcoming marriage. Amytis would never let her marry Nedabiah. It would be a waste of a valuable asset.

A scrape of a chair against the floor. Then two more. Her mother had stood, and her advisors had followed.

But Amytis had one more thing to say, the words delivered in the hiss of a threatened animal. "Hear me, both of you. And I swear before the gods. I do not care if that boy *is* my husband's son.

"Amel-Marduk will never sit upon the throne of Babylon."

Chapter 24

Somehow Tia held her ground until Amytis and her advisors left the chamber, taking the light with them or extinguishing it, she did not know. Stomach roiling, she stumbled into blackness, took three steps, and grabbed at the table. The rough wood splintered against her hand, but she barely noted the pain.

Amel, the son of Nebuchadnezzar? Vying for the throne, danger to her father?

Her *brother?*

In truth, while the threat to her father greatly

concerned her, it was this last that set her stomach against her, that flooded her chest with the bitter taste of revulsion. How close to her he placed himself last night! The way he spoke against her ear, pulled her into his quiet confidence. Not the affection of a brother. Something very different.

Tia leaned over the table in the darkness, braced herself with her forearms, and tried to think. Her mother's perfume still clouded the air, dizzied her.

Did Amel know he was her brother? He certainly must. Shadir's protégé.

Who was his mother? Not one of the harem women, or his birth would not have been kept secret.

Oh, Father, what choices have you made that will be our undoing?

But it was her choice, her secret feelings for Amel, that sickened her. How could she not have known, *somehow,* that he was her brother?

She needed to be away from this chamber, should one of them return.

Her stomach rebelled when she stood, and she paused and closed her eyes, hoping to quell the nausea. When she felt able, she moved forward with wooden steps, out of the room and down the corridor toward the first courtyard.

What was Shadir's plan? How did he intend to place Amel on the throne? Whom did it endanger?

And what could she do to stop it?

After the darkness of the advisory chamber, the

courtyard's harsh sunlight pained her eyes. She sought a shadowy path beneath tangled green vines that arched over plantings of bitter herbs. She could hear the fountain water spurting fitfully beyond the green veil that hid her from view.

A flash of white on the path ahead lifted her eyes.

"Pedaiah!" The word came out in a rush and matched her footsteps. She would speak with him of all she had heard. She trusted him. She reached him in a moment and clutched at the blinding white tunic across his chest. "Pedaiah, I must speak with you—"

He caught her hand and pulled it from him, his face pained. "And I, you, Princess."

She did not like the way he called her *Princess*. It was his way of distancing himself, and she needed a close advisor of her own today.

She peered through the greenery that sheltered them. Insufficient. "Come, we will speak privately."

It seemed only natural to lead him to the chamber where he had prayed to his One God over her days ago.

In the dim light she turned to unburden her heart, but he raised a hand. "I must say what I came to say."

Something about the way he shifted on his feet, or perhaps the way he seemed to labor for breath, closed her mouth.

"Tiamat, I cannot be—part of your life—any longer." His chin fell to his chest, which rose and fell too rapidly.

"I do not understand—"

"You deserve the truth." His eyes found hers again, and she saw determination strengthen him. "All these years I have stayed away. Made my home outside the palace, kept some distance."

"I have always known your feelings, Pedaiah. You were disgusted with Shealtiel's choice of marriage."

"Disgusted, yes. Outraged. Even I felt betrayed —that he betrayed our people with such a treaty."

She struggled to hold her tongue. None of this was new, so why should she argue or defend?

"But more than anything, Tia, more than my aversion, more than my anger, what kept me from the palace, what kept me from Shealtiel, was jealousy."

Her eyelids fluttered, as though to clear the blurriness of his statement.

"Tia, I have loved you since the day you married my brother."

What was this? Tia reached a shaky hand toward him, but he backed away. The beats of her heart seemed audible in the echoing chamber.

"You were nearly a child still, I know. But I watched you become—become the woman that you are, and every year my love for you grew stronger until I thought it would consume me."

"You never said . . ." Her voice was whispery, faint.

"Of course I never spoke of it! How could I? You were married to my brother!" He paced before her, and she could feel his anger. "And beyond that, you are a Babylonian!"

"Yes."

He stopped pacing and turned on her. "And that remains unchanged."

She swallowed. "Is that so important?"

"It is everything, Tia! It is why we are here, in this place." He waved a furious hand at the room, the palace, all of Babylon. "Ripped from our homeland because we let ourselves be polluted by people such as you!"

The sting of his words straightened her spine. "You have always been clear about your own superiority, Pedaiah. The superiority of your God to ours."

He rushed at her, grabbed her arms, shook her. "How can I make you understand? There is only One God! Your gods are the very demons you fear!" He released her and whirled away. Even in the half-light, his tunic shone white, as though he himself were one of the gods—distant and unreachable. She felt flawed, weak. Mortal.

But he would not like that image. Only One God, he would say, who reaches down to man.

He pounded a fist against the wall. "This is why I cannot see you anymore. Cannot run around the city with you or help you discover what secrets the palace holds." His hard-edged voice held no mercy.

"Because you fear being with me will leave you polluted."

He faced her with the simple, devastating answer. "Yes."

Tia had been a fool to think he had softened toward her, to hope for it, even. She would not show such weakness again. She drew herself up, lifted her chin. "I am sorry, Pedaiah, that I have been the source of so much grief. But clearly your detachment through the years has been for the best, as it will be in the future."

She hardened her voice, a blade thrust of condescension. "I can tell you that the disgust you feel at the thought of me is quite mutual. I would not have you, with all your arrogance and self-righteous pride, if all other princes of the earth disappeared. You are cold and unfeeling, and you believe your captors should be your servants, that the conquerors should bow to the conquered. We never shall, Pedaiah. Never. Not as a people and not this princess."

With that she pushed past him and stalked from the room with a prayer to the gods that she should never see him again.

Tia's feet carried her onward while her mind and emotions careened around a thousand shadowy corners. Down, down into the depths of the palace, then the chest-heaving climb to the seventh tier of the Gardens. The revelations of the morning took their toll. She was strangely winded when she reached the locked door, and her fingers shook so frightfully she could barely get the key into the lock.

She slipped onto the upper tier and let her gaze tumble over the knotted trees and snarl of flowering plants. Her father was not to be seen, and from their vantage points beneath, no guards would see her here. She could be alone with her thoughts.

A measure away from the door, she dropped to the paving stones beside a tangle of wild spearmint and wrapped tight arms around her drawn-up legs, hoping the constricted position would ease the disquiet in her stomach. It did not.

Below her, a pool filled slowly from the rock-cut channel, the water gurgling against a slimy sheen of algae. The odor of fertilized earth hung heavy in the air.

Amel is my brother.

Enough. She would think no more on what might have been. She had learned the truth before there was anything to regret.

The old gardener, the only one entrusted with the maintenance of the Gardens now, hobbled along one of the lower tiers, his white tunic bobbing, blurring among the plants.

Pedaiah has been in love with me.

This second revelation, following hard on the first, was no less shocking. She set her chin against her knees and remembered his hateful words. Anger. Aversion. *Polluted.*

The words were like sharp stones pelting her skin. She could not allow herself to feel, to bleed, to be destroyed by the gift he offered and then ground under his heel.

A slight breeze rustled the palm-tree branches in the air high above her, and they scratched and hissed against each other. If her father were whole, Pedaiah would be executed for such a speech.

But her father was not whole, and her mother was not innocent, and she had no one in this palace or in this world who truly cared for her.

Nor could she trust anyone. Amel had whispered to her of Shadir's plotting, of danger to her nephews, of her mother's involvement. Was any part of it true?

Kaldu's death, Shealtiel's death—were they even related? *Think, Tia.* All of it seemed muddied now. What did she know with certainty?

She forced her thoughts back over the events of the past weeks.

Shadir plotted to bring down her father. He was not in league with her mother, and had taken Amel—a son of her father—into his confidence. He must reveal Amel's parentage at the right time and put him on the throne.

In the meantime, her mother fought against this with her own plan. Marry Tia to her Median cousin. Tia saw the logic at once. The two kingdoms joined, with her at the center. Zagros and she would be sovereign over Media and Babylon both, the bond strengthened. Perhaps even more than a treaty. *"Soon it will all be over,"* Amytis had said when Rabi asked how much longer they could keep her father's condition a secret. Did she have plans against him herself? With him out of the way, would she give the entire kingdom to the Medes to ensure the perpetual safety and nobility of her own family?

A scratching sound, not too far away, alerted Tia to her father's presence. She watched in silence, unmoving, as he snuffed at the base of a palm tree. So close, yet he might as well have been fighting one of his wars in a kingdom across the earth. He lifted his head, sniffed at the wind, and brought his gaze around to fix on her. Once she would have told herself they held some recognition, but she had learned better.

Two plots, then. Interwoven, yet distinct. Both Shadir and Amytis posed a threat. Tia still did not know how Kaldu's death was related, nor if Shealtiel was truly poisoned. But what she did know called for a decision.

If her mother intended to give away Babylon to the Medes, an enormous dowry that would convince any man to marry, then Tia would have to deprive her of the means. If she had no daughter to give away in marriage, there would be no reason to harm her father.

But neither could she allow Shadir to succeed. He was evil, and any plan to put Amel on the throne could only be a bid for power himself, a way to control the kingdom for his own ends.

That night, weeks ago, when Tia had overheard Shadir on the rooftop garden, she had vowed that she would be more than a simple, pleasure-seeking princess. She tore a leaf from the stalk of mint beside her and chewed it for her stomach's sake, but the sharp tang also brought clarity.

It would take more than a vow. She saw that to truly affect change in the world, one must be willing to lose everything for the cause. Only if she believed that what she fought for—king and kingdom—were more important than her own happiness would she be able to push forward, knowing that she must sacrifice for the sake of others.

The Gardens, for all their wild freedom, were still rooted deep in the palace. Must be rooted here to thrive. She had always felt a kinship with the Gardens in that way. She, too, was a part of this place, even as she sought out excitement and freedom. Could she rip herself from the palace and survive?

Above her, a single wisp of cloud drifted across the wide-open blue sky, like a ship alone in a vast sea with no anchor. A swell of emotion she could hardly name—fear? resolve? loneliness?—pained her chest, brought her to her feet.

Her father's eyes swung back to her, alert, wary. Tia moved down the steps to the next tier. The old gardener saw her now and raised a weathered hand—in greeting or in warning?

She reached her father's crouched figure, held out a palm, and waited for him to approach. He shambled over and nudged her hand upward to his matted head. Her tears were for both of them.

"We will not let them have Babylon, Father." Tia spoke the words aloud, let them echo down over the tiers, to where the guards stood at the entrances. Three appeared below her in a moment, their hands on sheathed swords and their attention on her.

Let them see her. All of them. Let them report back to her mother and let Amytis be afraid.

Tiamat, the pampered princess, was gone.

With unknowing foresight, Amytis had chosen her name. For she would be the dragon monster.

Tiamat. Who, from her slain body, birthed a new world.

She comes. Again she comes.

All is dark when she is not here.

Sense her. Know she watches. Come out from hiding.

Let her see. Here. Here is me.

235

Do not go. Do not drop me back to where there is nothing but instinct and hunger and meat.

Closer. Closer she is coming.

Makes sounds with her mouth, and almost I understand. Grasping, grasping for the sounds and for my own sounds. Tia . . . Yes. Clutch the name. Hold on to the name.

Hand outstretched. I approach. Beautiful hand. Here, here on my head.

Warmth. Comfort. Affection.

Never leave me, child. You are my own, and I am coming back to you.

Chapter 25

Tia could not be certain that from this height the guards would recognize her.

"You there!" One of them hailed her, his shout wary.

She did not wait for them to climb the tiers to where she stood, her hand still on her father's snarl of long hair. With a quick good-bye, she turned to run upward. But that look—that look her father gave her just before she turned—she bent to him again. "Father?"

He smelled of earth and sweat and wildness, but there was something in the eyes, something different. As though her father were trapped in a deep pit, and she stood over it with a torch, with only his upraised eyes glowing in the reflection of the light, begging her for rescue. The wordless communication shook her. She took his muddy, bearded face in her two hands and whispered to him, "I will be back for you."

Then she dashed past red blooms and churning pools to the upper tier, through her hidden door, and locked it behind her long before the guards had climbed.

She took the dark stairs slowly downward to the belly of the palace. It was impossible, this plan forming in her mind. But she must accomplish it. She could not leave the palace yet, could not deprive her mother of her bargaining piece until Tia had secured her father's safety. And that safety could only be found outside the palace. But how could she remove him? And where would they go?

She was in the first courtyard before she even realized it, and Gula rushed her as though in fear for her life.

"My lady!" She paused, swallowed hard.

"Catch your breath, Gula. What has happened?"

"Your mother—the prince—"

Which prince would that be? Pedaiah? Amel-Marduk? Zagros? Tia sighed at the irony.

"The Prince of Media has sent runners. The caravan arrives within the hour. Your mother is frantic trying to find you."

So. It was to be a day of change. *Let it come.*

"I will go to my chamber to prepare, Gula. Tell Amytis she can find me there if she wishes."

Gula bowed and ran. Poor girl. She served Tia, but Amytis was her true master.

And Tia's new master would soon arrive. She took a deep breath and made her way to her chamber. The charade would continue for yet a little while. It was not time to let her mother know her plans. Let her think that she was the compliant Tiamat at last. The ruse chafed, but it was preferable to awaiting her Akitu Festival wedding day behind locked doors.

She let them bathe her and dress her in gorgeous robes, layer her with jewels, and veil her lower face, all the while wondering if this would be the last time. Would she dress herself for the rest of her life? Rather than concern, the thought shamed her. How had she not seen how spoiled she had become?

Her mother arrived and fussed over every detail of her appearance. More color for her cheeks and lips, even though they were veiled. *Much* more kohl for her eyes. Could they not wrap more jewels around her upper arms? What about that pearl anklet—where was that piece?

Tia stood unmoving in the center of her chamber, like a goddess statue being dressed for her yearly appearance to the people. Like a package of valued goods presented for trade. Like a sacrifice prepared for offering. *Just get it done.*

And let her take her father and leave this place.

A furious knock at her chamber door startled all of them. Her mother breathed a curse—or a prayer, Tia could not be sure.

Omarsa opened the door and a breathless slave boy nearly shouted, "They are coming!"

Amytis surveyed her, from the sapphires at her forehead to her onyx-encrusted sandals. "Let us hope it is enough."

Thank you, Mother.

Though the servants were all haste, they walked serenely, queen and princess, through the corridors of the palace, through the courtyards, to the grand palace entrance with the sweeping stairs down to the street. Here, at the top of the stairs, they waited for the envoy from Media to round the final corner.

They did not wait alone. It seemed the entire palace—magi, harem, and slave alike—had turned out to the see the arrival. Even the street below began to fill, as though Babylon waited for its own returning king. Tia's limbs grew hot and her jaw tight at the comparison.

Amytis was soon called away to consult on some pressing matter, pulled into a tight, whispering knot with her advisors. Tia stood alone for only a moment before a figure drew up close at her back, and an unwelcome voice spoke low in her ear.

"I have been looking for you."

She did not turn. "Hmm. I was under the impression you wished nothing more to do with me, Pedaiah."

"I have a message for you."

"Indeed? You did not say enough earlier?"

"I have spoken to my father about a marriage to Nedabiah."

At this surprise, a spark of hope did turn her head, though it was a mistake to look into those eyes, so close. Her lips nearly grazed his jaw, but he did not take his gaze from the crowded street below. "And?"

"And he forbids it."

The hope died as quickly as it was born.

"Jeconiah says the marriage to Shealtiel was a mistake he never should have made. And now he has lost his eldest son. He will not sacrifice another."

"Sacrifice? As though I were the cause of Shealtiel's death? Is that still what your family believes?" Her fists tightened against her thighs.

Pedaiah looked down on her, seemed to realize how close they stood, and stepped back. "If he was poisoned, I do not believe it was by your hand, no. But his alliance with your family undoubtedly brought about his death."

The Medians had reached the palace street, and the crowd sent up a cheer. Musicians had been pushed to the head of the caravan, and two bare-chested slaves piped merrily as the chariots ground along behind them, their wheels churning the dust into angry puffs.

"Very well." Tia had no wish to beg Pedaiah. She supposed she had given up her plan to marry Nedabiah some time ago. She had a new plan now. But the refusal, and its reasoning, still flushed her with shame and indignation. "Your precious brother shall be safe from danger. Safe from *pollution*."

From the corner of her eye she saw Pedaiah draw himself up at the word, jaw tight, the proud Pedaiah again. Here was the arrogant, detached man she had despised for so many years. She secured her veil across the lower half of her face.

The prince's gold chariot followed a cluster of loaded camels, driven by slaves with white switches. The shouts of acclaim dwindled until she could hear the snorts of the camels and the jingle of their festooned packs, all reds and golds.

Her first sight of the Median prince came a moment later. He stood in the second chariot and raised a fist to the crowd. Again, they cheered as though he were their conquering king. Tia scanned the palace entryway for her mother and saw her across the steps, fingers entwined at her waist and a pleased smile for the prince.

Zagros alighted from his chariot with a flourish, landed squarely on the street, and then swept up the stairs, trailing his entourage. Amytis held both hands to him, still smiling, and he grasped her fingers and brought each hand to his lips for a kiss. "My lady, you are like a drink of water after a long, parched journey."

Tia assessed him quickly. Tall, but not lean. He was imposing in every way, a future king to inspire confidence in his subjects. Thick lips, full nose, unnaturally large hands. Some might say good-looking, but it was the attraction of some-one with *presence* more than beauty. He was perhaps ten or fifteen years older than she, but when Amytis turned him toward her, Tia felt like a child under his powerful gaze.

"My daughter, Princess Tiamat." Amytis's voice overflowed with affection and pride, and Tia nearly laughed to hear it. She could play any situation for her own benefit.

Zagros approached, and she fleetingly looked behind her for Pedaiah, but he was gone. Zagros took his time assessing her. Did not want to purchase inferior stock, she supposed. But what-ever he saw seemed to be to his liking. Those thick lips widened into a leering grin. Amytis stood behind him. Would she have been concerned if she had seen the look he gave Tia?

"Ah, cousin, your letters did not exaggerate." He licked his lips. "She is even more than I have been imagining for all these long nights in the desert."

Tia was breathing hard now, lips tight, short, jagged breaths through her nose.

"Shall we get out of the heat?" Amytis extended a hand toward the palace. "Somewhere we can speak more privately?"

Zagros took Tia's hand, tucked it into the crook of his arm, and did not release her from his gaze. "Yes, private. Excellent."

They were soon in the advisory chamber off the throne room—the prince, Amytis, and her two close advisors. Tia eyed the tapestry, as though it might reveal her secret.

"I trust your journey was not too difficult." Amytis's words dripped with honey, and she directed a slave with a jug at the door to pour wine for all.

Zagros grabbed a cup immediately and raised it to her. "Only the length of time I had to wait to see my cousin." He glanced at Tia. "And her fine daughter."

"We must speak of the marriage." Amytis sipped at her own cup. Tia left hers untouched. "It would please me to get it done today, but the people require more pomp, I'm afraid. For them to recognize the alliance, to accept it, even welcome it, they must feel part of it. So, one week from today, at the Akitu Festival, if it pleases you, cousin, we shall complete the agreement."

Tia had a flash of imagination, of Zagros's face as he watched her race her chariot before their marriage, but she could not find amusement in the thought.

His gaze slid to her again. "I am not sure I can wait seven days."

Tia swallowed, a coldness racing into her hands and feet.

Zagros shrugged and sighed. "But as I am getting far more than I had imagined, I suppose I must."

Did he speak of her? Was she more than he expected? Or was it the kingdom her mother was handing over with her?

"Come, Rabi. Dagan." Amytis led the way from the advisory chamber. "Let us leave Tiamat and Zagros to get acquainted. Zagros, a slave will be in the corridor to show you to a private chamber." Her eyes leveled at Tia in silent warning. "Whenever you are in need of it."

With that sickening pronouncement, the three left and Zagros set his cup down on the table with a teeth-jarring thud.

He wasted no time with pleasantries and had Tia pushed against the wall a moment later. He smelled of too many days of travel and too much wine, and she realized that he had been drinking heavily long before he reached the palace.

"Now." He hooked a thick finger around the clasp of her veil. "Let us see if what is under here matches the beautiful eyes and delectable body I have already admired."

Tia pushed his massive hand away and undid the clasp. The veil fell to one side, and though it had only been a flimsy scrap of fabric, still she felt more vulnerable, exposed, without it.

He chuckled—a superior, amused laugh that set her teeth on edge. The coldness had spread to her entire body, and she had lost control of her breathing, which came in tiny, panting expulsions. She put her hands against his chest, a feeble effort to erect a barrier.

Those strange, huge hands were around her waist now, sliding upward. His eyes fluttered closed and his lips parted, and she could think of nothing but a giant rutting boar that could do whatever he pleased.

She pushed against his chest. "Not yet, Zagros. Not yet."

He opened his eyes and peered at her from under bushy eyebrows, as though surprised she had even spoken, let alone objected.

"I am not a palace concubine or one of your slave girls, Zagros." Tia pushed harder and raised her voice. "Perhaps, there in the uncivilized wilds of Media, you are unfamiliar with the etiquette necessary to wed a princess."

Her slur found its mark. His eyes narrowed.

"Here in Babylon, a princess is sacred until the day she marries." She took advantage of his hesitation to sidestep him and cross the room. She must be gone before he remembered her mother had practically tossed her to him. "I trust you will show me the proper respect for the next seven days."

His slow grin was part animosity and part animal lust. "All the sweeter when I have you then, Princess."

She gave him a quick, false smile and fled.

The encounter had shaken her, it was true. But more than anything, as she returned to her own chamber at a run, it strengthened her determination. They were leaving the palace, she and her father.

And they would not look back.

Chapter 26

Nightfall seemed elusive, as though the heavens themselves conspired to keep them trapped in daylight. Tia made the necessary arrangements— trading a bit of jade from an old bracelet for a wagon and donkey. Her purchase would be waiting in an alley behind the palace, outside a rarely used delivery door, when the sun set.

At last the western sky beyond her chamber window streaked with purple and orange, and the sun fell into the sea of clouds at the horizon. Tia leaned her forehead against the window's edge and drank in her last view of the sunset from the palace.

"Omarsa, Gula." The women shuffled behind her, ready for their final command from her, though they were unaware it was the last. "I am tired and feeling ill. I wish to be alone tonight."

"Does my lady require the asû?"

Tia smiled over her shoulder. "No, thank you, Omarsa. You—you are always good to me. Both of you." The women were silent. Did they sense the good-bye? "You may go."

When her chamber door clicked shut behind them, Tia turned to the room. The moon would be nearly full tonight, rising on the other side of the palace to reveal deeds better kept secret. She would need to move quickly, before it emerged from entangling clouds. Her heartbeat fluttered and her stomach echoed. *Focus on the task, Tia.*

She snatched a dark red bedcovering from the base of her bed and, with a flick of her wrists, snapped it outward and let the lightweight fabric settle to the floor. She must choose carefully what she would take. The load must be light enough to carry alone, substantial enough for a long journey.

Her flowing robes and silk tunics lay all over the room, draped over chairs, pooled in baskets. She moved about in silence, touching each she would leave behind. The green silk she had worn the day Labashi was born. The purple cloak on her wedding day. Three of these, the most common-looking she could find, she tossed to the center of the spread fabric.

A warmer cloak, an extra pair of ordinary sandals. Her possessions were dividing themselves into *princess* and *commoner* before her eyes, even as her heart was trying to accept the loss.

Enough clothing. Tia crossed to a side table, where she had carelessly flung a few armbands and ropes of pearl yesterday. How many provisions could these pieces buy? She crammed them both into a carved wooden box—a childhood gift from her father—and placed the box in the center of the piled clothing. Outside her chamber the drift of voices stilled her hands. She listened, focused on the tone, on the words. But the disturbance passed, continued along the corridor, and faded.

What else need she take? Tia sniffed the stopper of a jar of myrrh, then pulled it out and applied the musky perfume to her neck. One last scent of royalty before she would smell of the streets. Yes, she would leave the perfumes, the jeweled shoes, the treasures of adolescence. The vestiges of royalty were even now shedding from her. What would be revealed? Would she survive as a commoner in a new land? Would she even survive the journey?

A quick change into her running clothes and Tia was ready. She tied together the corners of the red bedcovering. Was it too heavy? It was too late to make changes.

She slipped from the room, made sure she was alone in the corridor, and hurried toward the nearest stairs, a narrow passage she never used but one that served her purpose.

A trembling began in her fingers, already fatigued from their taut grip on the improvised pouch, and traveled like a ripple of water up her arm, across her chest, through all of her. She pushed on, gained the dark stairwell, and hurtled downward to the bottom level of the palace. She peered through the open doorway. Alone. She hugged the bulging sack to her chest and crept along the stone wall to a small storage room, where a narrow delivery door gave access to a narrower alley. Good thing she had been an adventurous child, exploring every chink of the palace.

As promised, a beaten-down wooden cart stood in the murky twilight. A hitched donkey pawed at the stones with impatient swipes of one hoof. The alley smelled of garbage or perhaps sewage. Tia thrust her belongings over the wagon's side, then wedged her foot between two splintery wheel spokes and hoisted herself high enough to see the bed.

In a nondescript pile beside her sack she found a skin-scratching blanket, large enough to cover a man. Hopefully. And the rope she had requested.

Good. All was ready, then.

The spoke gave way under her foot. She grabbed the rope, clutched the cart, and fell a half step, breathing hard, then jumped down and eyed the wheel. Would it hold? She should have paid more for something better. She had been so concerned with blending into the peasantry. The cart's former owner was probably laughing over his cook fire tonight.

The clack of sandals on stones reached her from the end of the tight alley. Tia shifted away from the sound and wedged herself against the donkey's warm flank. Two voices, some laughter, and she was again alone. She patted the donkey's rump, but his long gray ears flattened, as though he were displeased and felt no camaraderie with her or her foolhardy task.

A moment later Tia was in the storage room, the coil of rope hooked over her shoulder. She threaded through the barrels of grain, reached the corridor, and headed for her next set of stairs, those that would take her to the lower levels where she could access her secret passage to the seventh tier of the Hanging Gardens.

At the top of the stairs, she yanked the key from under her clothes and jammed it into the lock for the last time. The door gave way with a creaking protest.

Inside the Gardens Tia sat for a moment in her usual place, to catch her breath, to still her heart. To prepare to meet her father.

The moon had crested the bank of low-lying clouds and from this height Tia felt almost equal with it. As though she and the moon god Sin both looked down on the king with pity. No, not pity from Sin, for his brightness would soon reveal two fugitives in the street.

She closed her eyes for one last deep breath. The rope's weight tugged on her shoulder.

When she opened her eyes, the rope lay beside her. *Strange. I did not feel it slip.*

The bitter taste of fear, a warning, stung the back of her throat. A flutter began in her chest. She looked to the moon for confirmation. The flutter roared into a stampede. Above her, the moon had shot upward, like a white spark against the night sky. How much time? How many hours had she lost?

She scrabbled at the rope with numb fingers. Her thin running clothes were damp with perspiration, though the night was cold. A chill shook her body and would not release her.

Not again. Not tonight. She needed her full wits about her tonight, if ever sanity was essential.

She clamped her lips, cutting off a foolish urge to yell for her father. The same plan. There was no need for alteration. The streets were bright with moonlight, yes. She would be more cautious.

She picked her way down the crumbling steps to the next tier, her ears alert to any sound of guard or king. Through the lofty palm fronds the moonlight spattered the stones like white blood. Shadows could hide anything. Would her father attack an intruder? Did he even know her?

She searched the sixth tier, then the fifth. The smell of rotted earth filled her nose. Her fingers cramped around the rope. The night wore on. Did he cower in a tangle of underbrush? Sleep in a hollowed recess?

By the third tier Tia was tempted to call for him, but this close to the guards, she dared not take the risk.

And then she saw him. Those white eyes, always so startling in the darkness, in the darkness of his bearded, dirt-smeared face. He sat in a human position, legs drawn up to his chest.

"Father?" Even her whisper seemed loud. His eyes flicked toward her, but there was no smile of recognition, no open arms. Just a wary animal sniffing, as always.

Tia crept across the space between them, her hand held out in the usual way, the other hand gripping the coiled rope. She was loathe to bind him like a beast but could not be certain he would follow her if she didn't.

"Father, we are leaving." Close enough now to touch his head. The moon shone off the gray streaks in his dark hair and beard.

Her heart never raced like this when she ran. Like she had run all the way to Assyria and back. She crouched to face him, held the length of rope in shaking hands, looped it over his head and down his body. *Steady, Father.* She did not take her eyes from his. *Feel how much I love you.*

She swallowed against the desert dryness in her throat. He did not move.

To secure the rope around his waist, she must have him move his drawn-up legs. She had only ever touched his head. With one hand she retained a hold on the loop of rope. With the other she pushed against his knees, lowering his legs. He was like a docile pup.

With his waist exposed, she quickly tied the rope, snug enough to hold but not constrict. Guilt over the bizarre action flooded her, sprang tears to her eyes. She blinked away the blurriness and tugged on the rope. "Come, Father. It is time to leave."

Why did he have to be all the way down here on the third tier? Would he make a sound as they climbed? Alert the guards?

She coiled the rope once around her wrist, then turned and stepped away, with only a gentle pull. The rope tightened against her hand.

Come, Father. Trust me.

The resistance released. He had moved. She risked a backward glance. He had shifted to his typical crouch, balanced on the toes of his bare feet and the knuckles of his hands. She tugged again, took a step. He followed.

That's it, Father. We will go together.

Indeed, he scrambled forward until the rope was slack in her hand and they walked side by side. She refused to entertain the analogy of a pet.

Think of him only as an old man, bent and crippled, in need of assistance.

Tia had never seen him climb steps, but he took them on all fours, and they were on the next tier. The rest of the climb was quick, save a brief stop at a bubbling pool where he lapped greedily. The action startled her. How would she care for him on the journey, or even once they reached their destination? Could he learn to drink from a cup? Eat like a human? Tia shook off the questions. They were not for tonight.

They reached the door, still ajar, and she slipped into the shadow beyond and pulled on the rope. It bit into her fingers. "Come, Father. Through the door. We must leave."

But he rocked backward on his haunches again, his arms tight around his legs. Was it the darkness beyond the door? Or simply the unknown? Tia could do nothing about either.

She pulled again. "Please, Father. Trust me. All will be well."

She could not bear to drag him through the door like a stubborn animal. She bent to him and unwrapped one hand from his self-embrace. The nails were long and clawed, the hair on the back of his hand wild and bristly. She held it in her own chilled grip and placed her other hand over it.

"It is your Tia, Father." Her whispered reminder seemed to catch his attention. He looked at their entwined hands, then at her face. "Yes, that's right. Tia has come for you. And you must follow her." She pulled gently on his hand, and he did not resist. Stepped backward and drew him again. *Yes, yes, that's it. Follow me.*

Tia still held his hand with both of hers and the rope dragged behind.

A moment later they were through the door.

Chapter 27

Tia snatched up the rope that bound her father and clutched the key that swung from her neck. One last time locking the door, with a nervous glance over her shoulder to see what he would do, now that they were in the stairwell, with only a wisp of torchlight reaching them from below. His head swung back and forth, taking in the new surroundings. He had not left the Gardens in nearly seven years. Did he feel relief or fear? Did he feel at all?

With the door secure, she ventured past him to the first step. She had seen him climb the tiers of the Gardens, but navigating downward in his unnatural position would be difficult. Could she get him to stand upright and walk down as a man?

She took another step down, her face now level with his. His gaze roamed her face, as if searching for the familiar.

"We are on the stairs, Father. We need to go

down." Tia pantomimed stepping down, as if he were a small child. How else did one communicate to someone such as he? "Can you stand?" She straightened her back, lifted her shoulders. Would he mimic?

But he only watched her, his nose twitching. She would have to use the lead tied to his body and hope he could balance his malformed body on the narrow steps.

"Come, Father." Tia turned and descended another couple of steps, pulling gently on the rope. Behind her he was silent, unmoving. The rope dug into her palm. She pulled harder. Nothing.

Back up the steps, faces equal again. Her eyes had adjusted enough to the dim torchlight to see his expression. Fear? Rage? His rough lips pulled back from his teeth, yellowed from his years of madness, even blackened in some places. Guilt stabbed her. They should have cared for him better. She should have found a way. There was a yellowing in the whites of his eyes too. Malnutrition, probably. But his wolfishness frightened her.

"Come," Tia whispered, not even certain she wanted him to obey.

The rope was not effective—she could not simply haul him down the steps, even if she did possess the strength. She wrapped a hand around his upper arm and tugged him toward her own body.

But it was too much. Whether it was her touch or her insistence that he move, he suddenly pulled back. A low rumble, too much like a growl, sounded from his chest.

"Father, you must come with me!" Tia did not release his arm. "You are in danger here. We must—"

He yanked his arm from her grasp and scrabbled backward on the platform. "Sheeggaaahhh!"

It was the first sound Tia had heard from his lips in seven years, and it frightened her more than his eyes or his fury. She set her teeth to keep from crying out.

He paced on hands and feet, back and forth like a caged animal about to be released for the hunt. Hungry, desperate for a kill. Unpredictable. Dangerous.

The first bitter taste of true fear had her grasping at the wall for a handhold.

"Kkkrrrruuaaahhh!" His bellowing noise bounced around the stairwell and echoed downward, a stone falling into the underworld.

Tia's breath was coming fast now, and she tripped up the steps and held out both hands. "Father, we must be quiet—"

He whirled on her outstretched arms and smacked them away with a clawed fist. His hand struck her mouth and she gasped at the pain, and then at the taste of her own blood.

"No!" Too loud. She had cried out in shock, but

it was too loud. "Father, no. I am trying to help!"

He backed away until his feet ran against the wall, then wedged himself into the corner and wrapped his arms around himself once more.

She crawled across the platform. Her bottom lip throbbed. She probed it with her tongue and could feel it swelling. But she did not take her clear eyes from his cloudy gaze. Somewhere, somewhere underneath the animal instincts of self-preservation, was her father.

He rocked against the wall, more penitent child than threatened beast. She crept closer, closer, until they were side by side and she drew her own legs up, mimicking him as she had wished he would her.

They sat in silence for some minutes, though she knew the darkness was flying past. She had lost time in the Gardens. Their escape had eaten up the night. And now he refused to take even the first step. How was she to get him all the way down to the lowest level of the palace, then up to the street and out the back entrance to the waiting wagon?

This close to him, Tia smelled the odor of his body, his decaying breath. The deep, familiar sadness swamped her. She leaned her forehead against her knees, willing the tears to stop for they did no good.

"We were going to see Daniel, Father. Your Belteshazzar, whom you care for. And he cares for you. He would have hidden us for a time, I know. And then I planned to take you far from here, somewhere safe from the scheming of magi and royal wives."

His chest heaved against his thighs, but he did not lash out.

She pressed the back of her head against the wall and watched him. Though his body was quiet, his gaze still roamed the platform, the dark steps beyond. It was fear that kept him from following her, but it was a fear she could not break through.

"I have tried to be brave, Father. Tried to do what you would have done." She let the tears flow now and felt them drip to her bare shoulder. "You never retreated from a risk, from danger. I never saw you frightened." His breathing seemed to slow at her voice, but she spoke more as a release than to calm him.

"I have tried to do whatever was needed to save the king, to save the kingdom. But I am frightened, Father. Things have happened—strange events—I do not know if perhaps I am going mad myself. Was this how it was for you at first? Did you feel the darkness coming and not tell any of us?"

It was out, then, if only spoken to her father's insensible ears. "They say that madness runs in families, Father. Am I more like you than anyone has even known?" The last words were only a whisper, as if she could hide the truth from even the darkness. But at this last confession, he glanced at her and she saw again that flicker of some understanding. It was gone in a moment, but in the next he surprised her. With only a slight movement, he shifted his upper body toward her, until their shoulders touched, and then his head was against hers, and he leaned on Tia with the closest thing to affection she'd felt in seven years.

Love for him pushed against her chest, threatened to shake her apart, but she would not move, would not break this blessed, tenuous connection. Instead, she closed her eyes against the tears, closed her senses against the animal smells, closed her mind against the fear. And opened her heart.

He knows me. He was her father still. Somewhere he was her father. Somehow she would free him.

But not tonight and not this way.

They remained there against the wall until her legs grew numb and she knew the daylight must approach. Loathe to leave him, she stroked his matted beard and whispered her love to him, then stood and unlocked the door.

At its opening, the beginnings of the dawn swept into the stairwell. Her father's head jerked upward, he looked to her, and then to the open door. Tia nodded.

He approached slowly, crouched beside her, held still while she untied the rope from his waist.

And then he was gone, bounding back into the Gardens like a boy released from his lessons. She closed the door, locked it tight, leaned her forehead against it, and wept.

But there was no time for self-pity. Or pity of any sort.

She reversed her trek of hours earlier, retrieved her pack from the wagon in the alley, and swatted the donkey's rump to get it moving. Where the animal would wander, she did not care. The first rays of the sun streaked across the streets of Babylon as she slipped quickly back toward her room.

But she would not return without being noticed. In the hall outside her door, her two slave women huddled and spoke in hushed tones. Gula spotted her first, and her lifted head and parted lips quieted Omarsa's chatter and turned her to Tia. Omarsa nudged Gula's arm with her fingertips. "Go," she whispered. And Gula fled past her, head down.

"My lady." Omarsa opened her chamber door and took the pack from her arms. "We were concerned. You mentioned an illness, and when we came to check on you in the night, you were not here."

Tia breezed into the chamber and tossed her hair over her shoulder. "I thank you for your concern, Omarsa, but it was unwarranted. I am fine."

"Your mother—"

Tia spun on her. "What about my mother?"

"When we couldn't find you—"

"You didn't tell her, Omarsa? Tell me you did not go running off to Amytis to report my absence."

"We were worried, my lady."

"And Gula?" Tia eyed the closed chamber door. "Where did you send her just now?"

"To assure your mother that no harm had come to you. That you had returned."

Tia cursed under her breath and snatched the pack from Omarsa. "Help me with this." Her fingers fumbled at the knot, suddenly cold and uncooperative. "And say nothing of it!"

The pack spilled open on the floor and she shoved the clothing at Omarsa. "Put these away." She placed them on a pile of tunics in a nearby basket. "Under! Under the others."

She kicked the pairs of sandals against the wall, grabbed the carved wooden box of jewels, and deposited it onto the side table.

Did she still smell of him? Tia sniffed at her shoulder but caught only the faint whiff of the myrrh she had applied, it seemed a lifetime ago.

She could hear her mother's voice in the hall as she seized the red bedcovering off the floor and tossed it to the bed. The jewel box—it sat at a strange angle on the table. She nudged it back into place, shot a warning look at Omarsa, whose wide eyes were enough to betray her, and straightened her shoulders against the coming attack.

The door flung open and her mother paused only a moment, framed by the entrance. Gula cowered behind her. Amytis took two strides into the room, clutched Tia's arms, and rotated her left and right, inspecting her like a purchase that might have been damaged. "You are well, then?"

"Fine, Mother. I am sorry you were—"

She saw Tia's clothes. "You have been running? All night? Again you are running about the city like a peasant?"

"Not all night. I woke feeling better and needed some air."

"Bah! There is air in the courtyards. Air on the rooftop gardens."

"I prefer my air untainted by greed and betrayal."

Amytis slapped her.

The open hand stung Tia's cheek and she clenched a fist rather than raise her hand to the sting.

Amytis stared her down and Tia met her gaze, aware of Omarsa and Gula backing toward the door.

"How dare you." The words escaped through Amytis's clenched teeth. "Everything I do is to keep this family safe. Everything. You have no idea the lengths I've gone to and the plots that rise up against me."

"Against you? Or against my father?"

Amytis was like a rearing cobra, hood spread

263

and ready to strike. "What do you know about any of it, little Tiamat?"

"I know that neither the throne nor my father is safe."

Amytis spun away. "If there is a threat, it is inconsequential. Pretenders rise up to make claims, fabricate a right to rule. But we never allow them to succeed."

A flicker of doubt crossed Tia's thoughts. Was Amel the pretender? Was his claim fabricated and was he not actually her brother? She fought to recall each word of the overheard conversation in the advisory chamber. "You have proof that this claim is false?"

Amytis waved her question away. "There are better ways for royalty to handle themselves than stooping to acknowledge such foolishness." Her eyes burned into Tia's. "Quietly eliminate the threat. Bolster your own political strength. These are the strategies of royalty."

She was like a rock. Like a jutting stone in the river, unmovable while everything around her rushed into foam.

"Yes, you have always been strategic."

Amytis's lips tightened. "I will not abide anyone who works against me, against the safety of my family."

Did that include Tia?

"They are my family too, Mother. I will not stand by—"

"No. You will not. You will do your part. The day of your marriage approaches." Amytis scanned her clothes with a disdainful eye. "Focus on your duty, Tia. Duty, above all else."

"But, Mother, if there is a way to prove—"

"Tiamat!" The word was like a curse on her mother's lips. But then she sighed and dropped her shoulders. "Omarsa, Gula, leave us." Gula fumbled at the door's latch and the two slipped into the corridor. Tia watched them go. "You must learn to hold your tongue, Daughter."

"If we can prove that this claim to the throne is false, if he is not truly—" Amytis's frozen look stopped Tia's gush of words.

"Of whom do you speak, Tia?"

She debated only a moment. It was time to work together, not against each other. "Amel-Marduk. If he is not truly the king's son—"

"How do you know this?" Amytis's eyebrows drew together until a deep crease formed between, a furrow that gave her the look of a lioness on the hunt. "Who told you this?" She took a step toward Tia and Tia retreated. "It was that Jew, wasn't it? Your husband's brother? He sees too much, speaks too much."

"It matters not how I know, Mother. What action will we take? I will find proof of his deceit if you will tell me—"

"You will do nothing!" She hurled herself at Tia, shook her by the shoulders. A little gasp escaped her mother's lips, a stuttering sort of inhalation that was almost a sob. "Nothing, Tia. Do you hear me? You will stay away from all of it. You're a foolish girl, and your questions will destroy all I've done to save this kingdom." Her long fingers dug into Tia's skin. "Why can you not simply do your duty and prepare yourself for marriage?"

"Because I want more for my life than to be bought and traded! I wish to—to—"

"To *what,* Tia? Say it! What is it that you wish?"

"I wish to make a difference!" Tia yanked away from her tight grasp. "To live a life of consequence, not simply of comfort. To have a cause to live for, more than power and luxury. To find something so important, I would even give my life!"

The declaration spilled from her like a newborn truth Tia had not known until she looked into its face. It left her breathless.

Her mother's expression shifted from cold amusement to something other, something almost like kinship, as though Tia's desires had resonated in her own heart, reminded her of who she once was, given her a taste again of what it was to ache for meaning.

But the link between them was too fragile to hold. Amytis turned away and left it broken.

"You need children, Tia. That is all. Marry

Zagros and have his children and you will find all that you seek."

The words were lifeless. They fell from her lips like stones, hit the floor, and made no sound.

Tia did not bother to respond.

Chapter 28

Tia found him in the palace.

When Amytis swept out of her chamber, leaving her hollowed, empty, Tia collapsed onto her bed and snatched a few hours of agitated sleep. But before the sun completed half its daily trek, she rose, remembered her mother's words, and churned through the palace corridors, intent on questioning Pedaiah.

The secrets of the palace had denied her in every direction she pushed. Fitting that she now hunted an outsider for answers. Why had Amytis assumed it was Pedaiah who told her of Amel's claim to sonship?

If she could prove Amel to be a pretender for the throne, Shadir's plan would slip through his fingers like grains of Babylonian sand. Her father would be safe from his plotting. Amytis would have no reason to ally them with the Medes, with her as the adhesive between two kingdoms. Such a simple solution, why did Amytis not work toward that end? Why, instead, did she try to sell Tia off to ensure peace?

The web of chambers belonging to the family of the deposed king Jeconiah lay in the south-western corner of the palace, level with the street. Directly under her own, two floors down. She knew the way well enough, for one of the rooms had belonged to Shealtiel, and she had been summoned there often through her seven years of marriage.

"Why can you not simply do your duty?" How could her mother spit out such an accusation? Had she not followed duty to Shealtiel's bed since she was a girl? True, he had never been cruel. Never violent. But never loving.

She intended to force Marta to point her to Pedaiah's dwelling in the city. When she shoved against the outer door of their set of chambers, a voice in singsong cadence, familiar and low, vibrated the air. Though she could not see him, somewhere Pedaiah prayed.

She hesitated. Listened. She understood none of his Judaean language, but the tenderness of the prayer, more like a song sung in the night to a sleepless child, flowed over her chafed spirit like a balm. *"He knows you, wants you to know Him."* They were not empty words. Pedaiah's heart belonged to his One God. It had not been like this with Shealtiel. Perhaps if it had . . .

"Tiamat?"

Nedabiah, the younger brother she sought to

marry, stared at her with wide eyes from across the simple chamber. A smaller version of Pedaiah, who was beside him a moment later, removing the fringed prayer cloth from his head.

The anger that had fueled her steps had seeped out of her body at Pedaiah's prayer. She fumbled for an explanation. "I—I came to speak to Marta—"

Nedabiah crossed thin arms over his chest. "She is not here."

How had she not seen how alike these two were? Did Nedabiah know her plan for him?

Pedaiah circled an arm around his young brother's shoulders. Did he think she'd come to snatch the boy? A flush of heat slithered up her neck.

"I was only coming to ask where I could find *you.*"

Pedaiah said nothing for a moment, only narrowed his eyes in that condescending way of his, too much of which had etched lines at their corners, though she could not see the creases from where she stood pressed against the door.

"What can I do for you, Princess?"

Such coldness. Was this the same man who had taken her hand and run her across the city?

She bit her lip and glanced at Nedabiah. "I would speak with you. Alone."

At this, Nedabiah's eyebrows lifted, as though a pauper had come demanding audience with the king. Yes, they were much alike, these two.

Pedaiah nodded to his brother, then inclined his head toward the deeper rooms of the complex. Nedabiah obeyed and disappeared. Pedaiah watched him go, then turned back to her, silent, waiting. He wore his customary white tunic, so plain yet always unsullied, and the purple fringe of the prayer cloth lay over his shoulders like a mantle of royalty.

In all the years she had frequented these chambers, the austerity of the decor had always been a mystery. The wide chasm of bare floor between them, the unadorned walls and simple furniture. Tia had assumed that when the Jews came from their dusty, backward villages, they brought their simple tastes with them. Could it be that like everything else about Pedaiah, this plainness was a refusal to assimilate into the Babylonian culture?

She sought a casual opening. "I did not expect to find you here."

"I am living in the palace for a time."

Her heart tripped over the statement. "Why?"

He glanced to where Nedabiah had disappeared. "To protect those I hold dear."

Ah.

"What can I do for you, Tiamat?"

Pedaiah's repeated question jarred her. "I have questions for you." A flicker of interest, perhaps even hope, flamed in his eyes. "Questions about

Amel-Marduk." Just as quickly, the flame was gone, doused with cold water. His clean-shaven jaw worked, the muscles there tense and bulging.

It was ridiculous, this conversation from two sides of the room, so she crossed to him, close enough that Nedabiah would not hear her words. Pedaiah seemed to withdraw, without ever moving his feet. How did he always accomplish this?

"I need to know more about Amel. About his days before he came to the palace to study under Shadir. You said that you knew him—"

"We were never friends, Princess."

"No, no, I did not assume you were. I only want to hear more of him."

Pedaiah sidestepped her, went to a small table, and poured water from a jug into an earthen cup. He offered her none. He was not thirsty; he was stalling.

If Pedaiah would not answer simply, Tia would provoke. "You were jealous of him, perhaps?"

His back was to her, but she heard him laugh into his cup. A laugh that signified not that she was amusing, but rather that she was a fool. "You should stay away from him, Princess. He—he is not worthy of you."

Worthy of *her?* Pedaiah had made it plain that she was only so much Babylonian dirt under his feet. The offense of his former words returned her to boldness. "I did not ask you for advice, Pedaiah. I asked you for information."

271

He slammed the cup to the table and turned on her. "And why must I be the one you interrogate?"

"Because you know more than you will say. And I must know of him. Where did he live before the palace? Who is his family? He worked at one of the furnace yards, you said."

"I did not say."

"Then—then I suppose it was Amel who told me that he saw you there."

It was Pedaiah who drew close now, close enough that she could smell fire on him, as if he had come only a moment ago from the furnace. A flash of memory, of her father's head against her own. She shifted toward him, feeling every speck of the narrow space that separated them.

"And what else did he tell you of those days?"

"That you acted as you always do, proud and arrogant and insisting that the Judaean captives not be tasked with brick-making. That you helped them shirk their duties."

The small smile again, this time close enough for her to touch him.

"Yes. Yes, I helped them escape from Amel-Marduk. From the curses that fell from his mouth, only slightly less frequent than the lashes of his whip. From the forced hours on their feet, beyond all human endurance. From the unbearable heat that sucked the life from their pores. He would have left them where they fell in the sand, kicked aside only to make space for more slaves to feed

272

his ambition." He brought his mouth to her ear, and the words were sharp with accusation. "That is your Amel-Marduk, Princess."

She gripped his arm. *Do not pull away now.* "He is not mine, Pedaiah. I—I do not—"

But he retreated, his face once again set like marble. She could believe almost that it was jealousy that fueled his bitterness, but no—no, it was a fury borne of protective instinct, a herd leader defending his pack. *What a father he would make.*

"He lived in the farmers' district." The clipped words seemed to cost him. "His mother's name was Dakina. He had no father, as I recall. I know nothing more."

Tia had been dismissed. She did not wait to be forced from the chamber.

In her own rooms once again, she paced and tried to focus on her next actions, tried to forget how Pedaiah looked when he spoke of the injustice to his people with such beautiful fury.

She would go to the farmers' district, search out Amel's mother, find the truth about his parentage. She reached for a cloak tossed over the back of a carved chair, but her hand wobbled with the effort. Her sleepless night and the clash with both Amytis and Pedaiah had left her exhausted.

Later. Later she would go. For now she'd partake of a cup of the wine kept at her bedside and a few hours of sleep.

She coiled on her bed, pulled coverings over her body, and sought peace from the peculiar sadness.

But the dreams came.

Roiling, churning dreams of Labartu and blood and fire, of night screams and daylight tortures, of pain and of death.

She awoke in darkness. Relief at the release from terror spilled over her, and a chilled breeze cooled the sweat on her forehead. She breathed against the darkness, long drags of the night air to fill her constricted lungs.

The sensibility of something amiss came slowly, too slowly.

A sticky wetness on her hands. Had she spilled her wine? Her bed, hard as stone. A coldness in her limbs. She forced her weighted lids open, took in the star-spattered sky, and shuddered.

Outdoors. Not in her chamber, not in her bed. Different this time. She had not lost only hours, but also her own movements.

Tia pulled herself to sitting, noting again the wetness of her hands.

The Gardens. How had she come to be in her father's Hanging Gardens? She held her palms to the moonlight, and in the shadows of the trees the spilled wine looked like blood.

But no, there was no wine.

She searched the undergrowth for her father. Did he watch her? Did he know how she had come to be here?

There, under a date palm, a human form with only a fragment visible to her—a leg, unclothed.

Her heart slammed against her chest. She crawled forward. Followed the length of slim leg to bare thigh, limp body. Torn robes. Deep scratches in the arms. Bloodied face.

Ying. Kaldu's missing slave girl. The same putrid mutilation.

Tia's breath huffed from her chest. She kneeled at the corpse like a penitent, lifted her bloodied hands once more, and studied the dried gore under her own nails.

The screaming began long before she realized it came from her own mouth.

Chapter 29

Tia choked on her own scream. It died a gurgling death in her throat, then fell to the pit of her belly.

She put a hand to her mouth to keep it from returning, felt the gore smear her face, and yanked the hand away.

The whites of Ying's eyes, shot through with blood trails, refracted the moonlight like shattered alabaster. Her bluish lips hung slightly open. Purple bruises stained her jaw.

Tia's own blood pounded in her fingertips, her

forehead. All her fears, conscious and unconscious, clotted together in her mind, a foul mass of self-accusation.

Ying's robe had been torn away from her splayed legs. One thigh was deeply sliced, the ripped flesh and tendons spread to reveal bone, like a split merchant's sack spilling its treasures.

The dead scream in her belly turned rancid, turned her insides rotten, turned against her and tried to rise. She skittered backward from the body and retched. Once, twice. Three times. She clutched at her distended stomach. Tears tracked her face and chilled in the night air.

Behind her an eerie moan matched the wind in the trees but came from the ground. Tia swung her heavy head and saw her father. He watched her. Saw her hover over the kill. He moaned again, like a child with a broken toy. She reached for him. Too far.

The Gardens smelled of blood and vomit, and she tasted both. A shout went up from a lower level, sharp and angry. Another shout returned, but she could make no sense of the words. Could make no sense of her own words, if any had formed. She heard the *slap slap* of soldiers' sandals. They came for her.

Her hands and stomach both were clenching, unclenching, clenching. She slid farther from Ying's body. One thought, and only one thought, pounded in rhythm with the blood in her veins.

She had been hunting a monster. *I have been hunting myself.*

What other horrors belonged to her lost hours? Kaldu?

Shealtiel?

The guards breached the tier. Her father shrank into shadows. She held out bloody, shaky hands against their attack and snatched tiny hiccups of breath.

There were three of them, or maybe ten. Her vision blurred tree and man together until she was surrounded by a forest. They clawed at her with branchlike arms.

Part of her mind slipped, like a skiff on the Euphrates, cutting smooth through water, sailing away until it fell over the dark horizon.

Not me, not me, not me.

Cruel fingers dug into her arms, lifted her to standing. Pulled her forward but she could not walk.

Dragging. They were dragging her. She wore no shoes and her heels scraped the stones. The pain shot from heel to head.

They will kill me. They will kill the monster.

In a hollow place in her mind, she saw Shadir hovering over unholy fire, the demon Labartu in his hand. Would they take her to Shadir? Let him exorcise the demon from the palace?

Father. She could not leave him.

Tia wrenched herself away from the grip of the

guards. Hot pain scorched her shoulder socket. She thrashed in their embrace and her hair clung to her mouth, stuck fast against wet blood.

"Father!"

She could not see him, could not find him, could not reach him. Not even to say farewell.

They carried her now, slung over the shoulder of one like a dead goat headed for market. Two more bound her wrists in a ferocious grip so she could not pummel the unyielding back of her captor.

She heard their conspiring whispers. What did they plan?

The corridors of the palace rushed past her, snapped at the edge of her vision like jaws, then swallowed her and pulled her down a narrow throat to her own chambers.

There was an eruption of activity. Guards scrambling, calling. Her chamber door kicked open. Voices of women—Omarsa and Gula—urging them to lay her across the bed.

She felt her body lift from the guard's shoulders, saw the eyes of Gula spin past, then the ceiling of her chamber above her, where the face of Labartu had snarled at her in her sleep, or in her madness.

Male voices faded, replaced by a strident anger she well recognized.

"What has happened?"

Amytis's cold demand for facts was met with whisperings at the door. Tia closed her eyes and tried to sink into the bedcoverings.

"Get her up. She must be bathed."

Her slave women pulled her from safety and half dragged her to the bath chamber until she found her feet and stumbled there in her own wasted strength, chased by Amytis's voice.

"What have you done now, Tiamat? You insist on ruining my plans, on destroying our chance to remain secure, to remain strong!"

Tia stood in the depressed floor and let them strip her bloody clothes.

"I cannot even begin to understand what you were doing there in the Gardens at this hour. And a dead girl?" Her voice carried all the horror, the curiosity, the fury she must have felt.

They had not heated the water. How could they have anticipated the need for so much water at this hour? The icy rush of it, dumped over her head, splashed against her naked limbs, set her shivering. She stood with mouth half open and eyes clamped shut, vibrating like a plucked harp string that sounded only ugly notes.

"Will you say nothing for yourself?" Amytis's voice scraped against her even as Omarsa and Gula tore at her skin with rough rags, scraping the blood away, away, away. In her mind she followed the blood being rinsed in rivulets from her body, dripping through the drain at her feet, coursing through the sewage arteries of the palace until it was lost in the Euphrates, as if Ying had never needed all that blood.

They were drying her now, and she wrapped her arms around herself but could not still the shaking, shivering, trembling of her body or her mind. Her teeth bounced against each other, little tapping noises like tiny demons knocking on the door of her mind.

No, she could say nothing for herself. Could not save herself or save her father or save the kingdom. She was only a mad princess. A mad, murdering princess.

Omarsa and Gula dropped a tunic over her head, cocooned her in a woolen cloak, and bundled her into her bed and still her mother hovered over her, pouring accusations colder than the water.

"You are going to see Babylon given to others who care nothing for us, Tiamat. Know that it will be your fault. You had it in your power to make an alliance that could save us all."

Tia managed to wriggle numb fingers from under her wrappings and reach for her mother's hand. Her voice, when it came, rasped against her throat. "Mother, please . . ."

Amytis yanked her hand from Tia's. "Pity? Is that what you seek? You shall have none of it from me. I have asked nothing more from you than that which I gave myself, many years ago. And you have refused."

She was gone a moment later. Tia sensed Omarsa and Gula at the inside of her door, and guards instructed to remain on the other. The old asû, Seluku, came and peered into her eyes, but she sent him away.

She was so cold, still so cold. Her eyes too weighted to remain open, yet a deep horror at falling asleep kept her struggling for consciousness. Omarsa was at her bedside, an uncharacteristically gentle hand on her brow.

"Can I get anything for you, my lady?"

There was only one thing she wanted. One thing that a small part of her mind, her heart, whispered might help, like pure water to quench a malevolent fire. Tia clutched at her arm.

"The Jew Belteshazzar. Omarsa, bring me my father's chief advisor."

Chapter 30

The hours jolted past in fits of sweaty sleep and wide-eyed wakefulness. She twisted in the bedcoverings until they imprisoned, then clawed at her bindings and gasped for freedom.

At last, at last, her chamber door sprang open and the face she longed to see peered at her through the quivering lamplight. His white hair glowed in the dim outline of the door, and worry carved lines against his forehead.

"Daniel." She spoke his name like a prayer, and perhaps it was.

He crossed the room to her bedside in a single step, it seemed.

A wave of fear lifted her and swept her into his arms. He sat at her bedside, let her cling to him, wrapped her in his tender, solid embrace.

"*Shh,* child." His warm hand cradled her head.

All the terror and the questions and the stark unknown warred in her chest and she sobbed against his shoulder, soaking his white tunic. But the tears did not purify, quenched nothing. Instead, darkness grew inside her, like a beast conceived and growing and trying to scratch its way out.

"I am going mad, Daniel." Tia cast the words against his shoulder, the sound constricted. Salty tears stung her lips.

He pulled away, turned to Omarsa and Gula huddled beside the door. "Leave us, please."

The women scurried out, as if relieved to be away from the creature she was becoming. But another form slipped in before the door closed.

She stiffened in Daniel's embrace. "Why is he here?"

Daniel laid her back against her cushions, smoothed the hair from her eyes. "I sent for Pedaiah."

He stood apart, in a pool of darkness the tiny lamp on her side table did not reach. Even in the murky light, she could trace the jagged white scar.

She turned her head from him and swiped at her wet cheeks with the back of a shaky hand, conscious of her sleep-tangled hair. "I wanted only you."

Daniel smiled, a smile one would give a child who claims she does not want any sweets.

Pedaiah shifted on his feet, still in the shadows. "Daniel insisted."

"You are both part of this." Daniel spoke to her, then glanced to Pedaiah. "Whether or not you will acknowledge that truth."

Tia clutched at his tunic, heedless of Pedaiah for a moment. "But what is *this,* Daniel? What is happening to me?"

He pried her fingers apart, encased them in his own holy hands. "There is much darkness."

"I fear the darkness is within!" Tia leaned forward, shifted so he blocked her view of Pedaiah. "Do you know do you know what has happened?"

He nodded, his expression somber. Disapproving? Tia could not be certain.

"Pedaiah, come."

They were not to have a private discussion, then. He would insist on letting Pedaiah see her as she was, know what kind of woman he fought to despise. She understood. It would make it easier for Pedaiah, easier to remain unpolluted.

"Tell me, child. What do you fear?"

She battled the vicious flush that surged through her chest, her throat, her face. *Let him hear. Let him hear everything.*

"I fear—I fear loss. The loss of everything, everyone I care about. The loss of myself, of my rational mind."

He said nothing but gave a slight nod, as if to encourage but not interrupt.

"You told me once that I could make a difference in the world, do something important. But how can that be if I am as mad as—as my father?" There were no secrets here. No words she would not speak to find answers.

Pedaiah took a hesitant step forward. "Did you kill the girl, Tia?" The words themselves were harsh, even accusing, but his tone was not. He asked the question as if he already knew the answer and wanted only to hear her denial.

Tears threatened again and she shoved them back. "I do not know." To Daniel, she said, "I have been losing myself. One moment I am thinking something, doing something, and the next moment hours have passed and I have no memory of the time. Tonight—tonight was different. When I awoke, not only had time passed but also movement. I was in the Gardens. With Ying." The name caught in Tia's throat, the vision of Ying's slashed body shook her voice. Again Tia clung to him. "Tell me, Daniel. Tell me if I am mad. If I am a murderer."

Daniel turned from her. "It is time, son."

She held her breath. What unknown plan had they conspired?

Pedaiah slid closer, his fingers twined together. But Daniel pulled the hands apart and guided his right hand to Tia's head. She bent under the weight of it, and Daniel held her hands. She felt what was coming in the holy hush that followed. Remembered the way the darkness fled when Pedaiah last prayed his heart over her. Welcomed the words that she both loved and feared, words with power to free and to heal.

Pedaiah's voice lost all its harsh arrogance when he prayed. It was a voice like music.

Contend, Yahweh, with those who contend with Tiamat.

Fight against those who fight against her.

Take up shield and armor, arise and come to her aid.

Brandish spear and javelin against those who pursue her.

Say to her, "I am your salvation."

The beast in her chest cowered and shrank. She closed her eyes and fell into the prayer.

May those who seek her life be disgraced and put to shame.

May those who plot her ruin be turned back in dismay.

May they be like chaff before the wind, while You drive them away.

May their path be dark and slippery, while You pursue them.

With every word, light scattered shadow. Evil shriveled and died.

Then her soul will rejoice in Yahweh and delight in His salvation.

Her whole being will exclaim, "Who is like You, Yahweh?"

How long, Lord, will You look on?

Rescue her from their ravages, her precious life from these lions.

Emotion swelled in her throat and she did not fight it. These tears *did* purge, or perhaps it was Pedaiah's words, or even the exquisite intensity with which he prayed.

Then she will give You thanks in the great assembly,

Among the throngs she will praise You.

Awake, and rise to her defense!

Contend for her, my God and Lord.

Did he believe his own words? Did he believe that one day she would declare his One God before her people? Once, she would have scoffed. Tonight, she was unsure of nearly everything.

But one thing she knew. The oppressive darkness had lifted from her soul. Tia looked at Pedaiah with silent gratitude. He held that familiar seriousness, but when their eyes met, connected, things were said between them without words, a lifetime of things in that single moment.

"You are not a murderer, Tiamat." Daniel's words, but her eyes were still on Pedaiah, whose lips curved upward—a slow, slight smile of reassurance.

"You are, however"—he patted her hand—"quite courageous."

Tia gave him her attention. "What has courage to do with this night's events?"

"This night, many nights. I have watched you fling yourself into this quest for truth, take great risks. Now that you have tasted loss, you are ready to hear what it truly takes to change your world."

The lamplight flickered and dimmed, as though to keep Daniel's words shrouded in more shadow.

"There are three things you must know, Tia, if you are to be the woman you desire." He held up a finger. "One. You must accept that you are a mere shadow on this earth, under the mighty hand of the One God, and He is sovereign over all."

She clung to each word, committing them to memory if not committing herself to their veracity. She would think on that later.

"Two." He ticked off his second point with another finger. "You cannot save yourself. There is no sacrifice you can make, no good you can do, that can atone before a holy God. He alone, in His great love for you, must make a way for your atonement or you will be lost."

Tia licked her lips and flexed her shoulders.

The weight of madness had lifted but these were also weighty statements.

Daniel smiled as if in sympathy. Did he know how much such humility would cost her? "And the third, Tiamat, is the true secret of an uncompromising life. When you are rooted in this atoning love, this all-consuming, never-failing love, you cannot be shaken. No loss of possessions, no hatred of man, no dark power can tear you from it. And with such strong roots, you are free to challenge the world."

Tia let out her breath and realized she had held it captive. Tempted to dismiss the Jew's words, instead she savored them, secreted them away in her heart to ponder in solitude.

Pedaiah cleared his throat.

She jolted. She had forgotten his presence.

"These lost hours, Daniel. What do you make of them?"

Daniel nodded, as if in agreement with an idea Pedaiah had not spoken. "Yes, yes, she must be cautious."

She looked between them. "Cautious? Of what?"

Daniel stood.

Tia fought the urge to pull him back.

"There are substances known, my child, to affect the mind. Such things are known to those who study the ways to induce false religious experiences."

"Priests? Magi?"

Daniel inclined his head, all the agreement he would concede. "You must watch what you eat and drink, child. Nothing from the hand of anyone but yourself. Especially at night."

Pedaiah glanced at the jug of wine and cup on her bedside table. He handed the cup to Daniel, and the older man swirled its contents and sniffed.

"Yes, it is possible."

She felt her lips part. "But that was placed by my personal slave women!"

Daniel said nothing. It was Pedaiah who answered, voice urgent, eyes pleading. "Please, Tia. Trust no one."

Ah, but did he know how much she trusted him? How she would take anything from his hand, that hand that had covered her not once, but twice, in prayers of deliverance? Tia swallowed, her throat tight, and nodded.

"It is only the beginning, Tiamat." Daniel stepped away from her bedside, and with the flickering light behind him, his shoulders appeared strong, solid. He had these roots he spoke of. A strength that had lasted forty years. He had remained a drop of pure water in a brackish pool, not absorbed or dispersed or diluted.

He spoke again, like an oracle peering into her future. "You have risked and failed. But there will be more losses to come. You must be prepared."

Chapter 31

The guards did not leave her door. Tia slept and waited for her chance to seek answers. The sun flared, then waned at her chamber window and still they did not leave. She tried to pass the time with her scrolls, but time grew short. Only a few more days until her marriage to Zagros. If she were to stop both Shadir's plot and her mother's intent, she must get proof that Amel was not her brother. She paced her chamber. Anxiety stretched her nerves taut.

True to her word, she took no food or drink from the hand of Omarsa or Gula. By evening she was weak with hunger and thirst. Had her mother made good her promise to imprison her until her marriage?

She instructed Omarsa and Gula to seek word about the death of Ying. They returned with nothing. Nothing was being spoken, even in whispers, of the strange happenings of the previous night. Power had its privileges.

Tia awoke in the center of the next night, her throat like hot sand and her tongue thick. She lay still, listened to the gentle breaths of her slave women, asleep on their nearby mats, then slipped to her chamber door and nudged it ajar. Her legs vibrated with the effort and the urgency.

No guards!

She left the door cracked, fumbled in the room for a cloak and sandals, knocked against a chair, and cursed. Her pulse raced against time. She held her breath and counted off ten quick heartbeats. Neither woman moved. She exhaled through an open mouth, wrapped her shoes in the cloak, and bolted through the door.

The corridor was cool and dark. Tia shivered against the chill and slowed to don her sandals, wrap the cloak around her shoulders, and pull its weighty hood over her head.

She dared not detour. Dawn would burst over the city soon enough, and she must be out of the palace. But as she crossed the first courtyard, the staccato beat of fountain water dragged her to the pool's edge. She plunged both hands beneath the water and even her skin seemed ravenous. Several gulping mouthfuls later, she forced herself back to her path through the greenery of the courtyard.

She took the same kitchen entrance she had slipped through to meet Pedaiah the night they had run through Babylon hand in hand. The memory scorched her, surprised her with its intensity. She clenched her fists against the pain and hurried into the night-black city.

By dawn she huddled in the farmers' district, where Pedaiah told her Amel lived with his mother before the palace. It was one of the poorer sections of the city. Mud-brick homes jostled elbows on the streets, and paltry gardens struggled to thrive, too far from the lifelines of river and canal.

She waited while the city awoke, waited for the press of crowds headed to markets, for the beggars to stir at their corners and begin their laments. The smells of the city also wakened, the night's refuse dumped, fresh morning bread baked over hot fires.

She chose her first target, a slave girl younger than herself, with an empty water jar in her arm, and gaze fixed at her feet. Tia blocked her path and she startled, lips parted. She was a pretty girl, with thick hair pulled into a knot at her neck and draped like a silk rope over her shoulder.

Tia shifted to gain height. "Where will I find Dakina, mother of the mage Amel-Marduk?"

The girl's glance ran its course over Tia's clothing.

Should have worn something less fine.

She shrugged one shoulder. "There are many Dakinas here." She pushed past Tia and hurried on.

Tia bit her lip and scanned the street. This could take all day.

Several attempts later she followed the wobbly fingered gesture of a beggar. "The Street of Enlil. The blue door." His pointing finger became an upraised palm. She never carried money. She gave him a quick smile instead, a payment he did not value from the sour hiss that followed.

Blue door. Strange, but easy to find. A heavyset doorkeeper met her, invited her into the shadows of the entryway, and left her there to announce her to the mistress of the house. No father, Pedaiah had said.

He was back in moments, moving quicker than his size would have indicated possible. "Come, come." He waved her into the home with both hands, as though frantic to get her away from the street.

Dakina stood erect in the center of her courtyard. Tia took in the home and her person in one roaming glance and found them equally displaced in the farmers' district.

Dakina was only a little younger than her father, she guessed, but her straight back and bright eyes belied her age. Her graying hair had been piled and pinned elegantly atop her head, exposing her long neck and graceful jawline.

The courtyard around her could have been transported from the palace. Blue-glazed tile walls with yellow and white mosaics echoed the throne room. The central fountain frothed even at this early hour. How was it supplied when the district seemed stripped of such amenities? The home was like a jewel lodged in the mud. The thought blazed across her mind, trailing dread. She had hoped to find a poor widow, telling tales about her son's parentage to impress her neighbors.

Dakina was no ordinary woman.

She glided toward Tia, as smooth as a cat on the hunt, and Tia saw no welcome in her eyes. A quick head bob was all the acknowledgment her status received.

"My lady, this is a surprise." Her eyes were cold, sharp. "And an honor." This last tacked on, fueled by obligation.

"Thank you. I would—speak with you—if you have a moment." The unexpected sophistication of Dakina and her home left Tia stumbling for words. Would she even deign to answer her questions?

Dakina extended a hand to chairs placed close to the fountain. Tia walked past her, head down, and lowered herself into a chair. Dakina did not sit.

This was a mistake. And yet, it was the only road open to her. She must learn the truth about Amel.

"I have met your son, several times, in the palace."

Dakina's eyes flickered, her first glimpse of softness.

Tia pushed forward. "He has been very kind to me. I think he progresses well in his training. He will no doubt be a valued advisor to the king one day."

At this Dakina smiled, but it was not the smile of a mother pleased with her son. It was the condescending, bitter smile of a woman who has been given far less than her due.

Tia licked her lips. How to proceed?

"My father relies heavily on the wisdom of his magi. He respects their knowledge."

Dakina's eyes blinked several times and her shoulders dropped a fraction.

Tia sat forward. "You—you knew my father, once?"

She watched Dakina deflate, like a banner dropped to its pole when the wind has suddenly stilled. She crossed to the chair opposite the fountain and sank into it.

"Yes. I knew your father."

"He is a good man. A good king."

Her eyes found Tia's. "Tell me. There are rumors—rumors that he is more than unwell. It has been so many years—" Her voice hitched over the words and her fingers tightened against the edge of the chair. "So many years since he has appeared among his people. Is this sickness more serious than we have been told?"

Her words, her pained look, were like a desert wind blowing away Tia's doubts. No matter what lies had been told over the years, this woman and she shared a bond. They both loved her father.

Tia abandoned the chair and sat on the stone lip of the fountain, her knees nearly touching Dakina's. "He lives, and I am very hopeful for his return to health."

Dakina pressed her hands against her abdomen and nodded. "Good. That is good."

A slave appeared, breaking the moment apart. He placed a tray of fresh, crusty bread and a jug of wine beside her on the fountain's wall. Tia's stomach roared in response. She had eaten nothing since the day before last. Did she dare trust food here? Dakina had not even known she was coming.

"Please." Dakina held a hand toward the bread. "Eat."

Tia obliged. The watered wine was cool on her lips and tongue but went down warm. She chewed the bread quickly and decided on frankness.

"Tell me how you met my father."

Dakina sat back in her chair and her eyes fluttered. A girlish flush bloomed against her cheeks. She studied Tia for several moments. "My father was a nobleman in your grandfather's court. Your father and I met while we were still very young. Before he left to conquer the world and bring back spoil."

But that had been over forty years ago. Tia calculated times and ages and came up with only more questions. "And when he returned?"

Dakina looked over her shoulder, into the past. "When he returned, nothing had changed between us."

"You had not married?"

"I could not."

Tia let this statement go, though she was unsure of its meaning. "And he did not marry for some time either."

Her attention came back to Tia. "These are memories best forgotten, Princess. Why are you here?"

Tia set her cup aside and took Dakina's hands in hers. Dakina gripped her with a warmth Tia did not expect, and the gesture brought a twinge to her heart that she could not name. "Because I wish to know the truth."

Dakina's smile was thin, watery. "The truth can bring great pain."

"And great pain can bring needed change."

She sighed and studied their clasped hands. "I loved him completely. But his father would not allow it. There was no purpose to be served in a marriage between us. Nothing gained. We were to be kept apart."

"And did you remain apart?"

"Mostly." The small smile again. "But not far enough. Later, later I was sent away. Your father was told I went to live in Assyria."

"But you were here? All these years?"

She lifted her eyes to Tia's. "I could not bear to be any farther from him."

The pang in her chest again—a mix of pity and warmth for Dakina, and jealousy that she had been Amel's mother and not her own. Tears clung to Tia's eyelashes and she blinked to release them. Dakina placed a cool hand against her cheek, and the hostility Tia felt on entering her home seemed a lifetime removed.

"Did he know?" It was the only question she cared to have answered now. "Did my father know that you carried his child?"

Dakina bore the question with dignity and only shook her head. "The mage Shadir arranged everything. This home"—she lifted a hand to the courtyard—"Amel's education. Everything we needed."

"And you never married." Tia imagined Dakina here, all these years so close to the palace, raising Amel alone, knowing he was the king's only son.

"I was overjoyed when Shadir came again after so many years, took Amel under his wing. He will give my son a chance to make something of himself. To at least live near his birthright, even if it goes unclaimed."

"But why does he not claim it?"

Dakina's eyes widened, as if she had remembered something too late. She pulled her hands from Tia's.

"What is it, Dakina?"

Her lips tightened and she shook her head. "Shadir warned me of this. I have been a fool."

"You have nothing to fear from—"

"You are his daughter!" She stood as though to dismiss Tia. "I fear for his life!"

So Shadir had convinced her that Amel's life

would be in danger if he revealed his identity. Tia thought of the knot of advisors close to her mother. Of her mother herself and her unrelenting intensity over the safety and status of her children. Of the husbands of her sisters, who no doubt hoped to find themselves or their sons on the throne one day. Dakina had good reason to fear.

Tia stood and touched her arm. "I will not share your secret, Dakina. No one will learn of it from my lips."

Dakina's breath had grown labored, as though she struggled with whether to trust. "Please, Princess. Let Amel live the life that has been given to him." She tucked an errant hair behind her ear. "He is to be married soon, he tells me." A hopeful smile. "Grandchildren for me at last."

Tia's blood thickened. "Married?"

"Yes." She nodded. "A young woman, newly widowed. Please" she clutched Tia's arm— "please do not ruin his chance for something better."

Tia patted the hand on her arm, but the action was instinctive. Her thoughts had run elsewhere and her stomach tumbled after them.

Thoughts of the palace. Of Amel-Marduk's seductive smile. Of his intended bride.

Which she feared brought her back full circle to the very place she stood.

Chapter 32

Tia stumbled from the elegant home of Dakina into the hot squalor of the farmers' district, but the heat did little to loosen the icy fingers that squeezed her heart.

Nothing was as it seemed, nor as it should be. If she was to be Amel's wife, clearly Dakina knew nothing of it.

Crowds of women headed to market and men to their work pressed against her in the street, but Tia pushed through, heeding none of the jostling shoulders and elbows, circling stubborn donkeys, stepping over refuse.

She must know the truth. The truth of Shadir's plans for Amel, and for her. And she must know whether Amel had knowledge of his birthright.

She had avoided Shadir long enough. The answers to the questions that had perplexed her for weeks were wrapped around the old mage, like the stars and moons stitched into his robes. She would find a loose thread somehow, and she would pull.

At this thought a fresh coldness weighted her chest. More secrets were yet to be revealed. What would such revelations mean for her?

She broke from the crowded main street and ducked into a narrower alley, hoping to reach the palace faster. A shuffling behind her drew her attention. The beggar that had approached earlier followed.

"I have no money for you." Tia flicked a hand to dismiss him.

He toddled closer, some deformity of leg or hip affecting his balance. His lips broke into a black-toothed grin, and an ill-worn voice singsonged from the rotted teeth. "Prrriiin-ceeesss! Here is the princess!"

A current ran along her veins, sparking from her fingers. She took a step backward.

He wobbled on, and she saw that he had only one functioning eye. The other had been scarred closed—an endless, misplaced wink.

Tia looked away from that eye but dared not turn her back to flee. "What do you want?"

His good eye pierced her, as though it saw things beyond, like an oracle with knowledge she did not possess.

"What do you want?" He repeated her words, his tone as pleasant as a merchant offering a table of luxuries, but that eye, that single watching eye, unnerved her.

He was close enough to smell now, close enough to grab her if he dared, but all he did was stare, and a fear rose in her, a fear of the unknown and of the known, of secrets and of truth, of love and of loss.

"I—I have nothing for you," she said again, and the words sounded childlike.

"Nor shall you." His scarred, puckered socket was slitted enough for her to see that one eye did roam beneath the mutilation. He raised a crusty, age-bent finger. "Nor shall you."

She waited, inhaling shallow breaths against the constriction in her chest.

"Leave truth to the gods, Princess. It is better held in their hands."

Tia's hands clutched her thighs, tightened around her robe. Her first sense had been correct. Some kind of oracle. "I cannot."

His lips closed over the black teeth and his watching eye narrowed to nearly match the one destroyed. She expected another warning, perhaps a threat. But anger merged into contempt and he turned and waddled away, the stench trailing.

Tia let go of pent-up breath, felt her shoulders loosen, and licked dry lips. His cryptic words—implying that she would have nothing if she did not cease her questions—struck at the core of her fear, humiliating as that truth might be.

There was nothing to do but resume her flight toward the palace, toward her questions and toward the answers. Though every eye of each citizen she passed seemed an echo of the eye of the beggar, and she felt that all of Babylon watched her, traced her steps toward the palace, each one with knowledge of her secrets and of secrets yet to be spilled.

She kept close to the jagged-cut walls. At each notch a compulsion to hide herself gripped her, but she pushed on, her eyes on the Gardens now, hanging above the north end of the city.

A figure fell into step beside her. The beggar? A jolt of fear and repulsion surged. She halted, tottering against imbalance, and put a hand to the wall.

Amel-Marduk slowed and faced her, leaving her pushed into a crevice, as though he had divined her urge to be hidden.

"It is early for a tour of the city, Tiamat." That half-amused smile he often wore tugged at his lips.

She swallowed, fighting the dryness of her throat and mouth. She had not seen Amel in days, not since discovering they shared a father.

He stepped closer and put a hand against the wall, pinning her into the niche. His gaze roamed her face. Did he read the confusion she felt? She avoided his gaze, studied the close-trimmed beard, the narrow shoulders. Inhaled the spicy incense.

"What has frightened you, Tia?" He ran a finger along her jawline, then touched her lips.

She felt the wrongness of it in her stomach, tasted revulsion and even anger, and yet she did nothing to stop him, nor did she want to. What was she becoming? Tia turned her head from him, fought to keep the palace in view.

He shifted and placed himself again in her line of sight. She allowed herself a glance into his dark eyes. Dark eyes with gold flecks, just like her father's. She thought of her dream, of Amel urging her to save her family.

"I must get back. They will be missing me."

"I have been missing you." His breath was warm against her cheek.

The words strummed against the tension in her chest, like fingers plucking at a strung-tight lyre. Something there might snap if she did not soon escape.

Whether Amel knew she was his sister, she did not know. But this—this fascination—must not continue.

She ducked under his arm, released herself from his cage. "I must return."

His lips drew together, a slight pout. Did he expect more from her? "I am going back myself. I will walk with you."

"No!" Tia expanded her chest against the tension, but it did not release. "No. I do not think that is wise."

"And I do not think it wise that a princess walk the streets alone."

"I can take care of myself." Tia headed for the palace but heard his voice behind her.

"This I know, Tiamat. This I know."

She swept through the morning crowds, regained the palace steps, and fled through its arched entrance, all without looking behind to see if Amel followed. And yet she knew he did follow. And with him she sensed the unknown also crept behind her, ready to overtake.

She did not stop her flight through the palace, not while this surge of energy pushed her past her own fear, toward the Hall of Magi. There could be no more avoidance. The time for truth telling had come.

She passed through the columned entry of the Hall into its otherworldly shadows and hovered at the door. Did Shadir lurk in the gloom, watching her from those star-bright eyes?

Jaundiced sunlight slashed through the slit window high in the wall and cut a line across the polished floor. Dust motes flickered in the shaft of light, twins to the braziers lit against the bituminous walls. The tar's odor watered her eyes and tightened her throat. She swallowed against the false symptoms of emotion. Shadir would find her strong.

A soft humming, a sweep of purple robe, a figure materializing from the back of the lofty Hall.

"Princess." Shadir held the final syllable too long, fashioning it into a hiss. "Another visit?" He spread his hands to the Hall. "What can I show you this morning?"

"The past. The future."

His eyebrows twitched, and a slow smile

turned his mouth, the smile of a man who has waited long for what he has just heard.

"Ah. Only this, then." He stood beside the central haruspicy table, its instruments laid ready.

Tia took a step toward him, but her legs and feet had grown heavy. "I have more questions than answers, and I would know the truth."

He tilted his head, examined her as though she were a star chart. "Are you so certain? The truth does not always bring relief."

His insight, an echo of Dakina's, caused a flutter of indecision in her chest. It was relief she sought. But would the answers instead bring pain?

She jutted her chin toward him, toward the jewel-flecked wall. "Of all people, I should think you would believe that answers to mysteries are worth any price."

Shadir clasped his hands at his waist and bowed. "You are a true Babylonian."

His pretense of respect did nothing to warm her.

"I know that you plot to take the throne from my father."

A slight movement, fingertips braced against the table. His smile did not crack, his eyes betrayed no surprise. But those steadying fingers, they gave her confidence.

"It would be better for you to keep to your amusements, Princess."

Tia advanced from the entrance, her gaze fixed on his. "Better for whom?"

He licked his lips, a quick, unconscious movement. "You have no reason to fear."

"A usurper is about to revolt against my family, and I have no cause for fear?" Tia laughed. "You must think me stupid."

Something flared behind his eyes. Contempt? Tia felt the sting of it, like a tiny whip had lashed her skin.

She tried to force her fingers to uncurl at her sides, but her body held ready, reflexes alert.

"Not stupid, Princess. Simply uninformed."

"So, inform me."

He circled his table, placing it between them. She thought to follow him around it but chose to wait. Let him have his false protection.

He wrapped his robe tighter and crossed his arms. "There has been a need for many years to put a—competent man—on the throne. You know this."

Anger surged hot in her throat, but she kept silent.

"There is one who is the perfect choice. Best for the kingdom."

"Amel-Marduk. The mage who is completely under your control."

Again the small bow. "I will admit, the boy values my advice. But he will be his own king, I assure you."

Tia laughed again, a bitter huff to inform Shadir that she knew this to be false. "And my family?"

He shrugged and rearranged the instruments on his table. "There is always some upheaval when kings transition. But no harm will come to you, Princess. You will remain in the palace, nothing will be taken from you."

"Because you intend for me to marry Amel. Become his queen."

Ah, she had surprised him. He blinked several times in succession, then looked through the window slit high in the tar-black wall. "I am impressed. I had underestimated you."

Tia circled the table and faced him, ready with one last revelation. "Hear this, Shadir. I will not marry my own brother."

Shadir's lips parted and his eyes widened. But then his face closed down again, into a sharp squint and puckered mouth.

She had spent all her knowledge now, everything that gave her an edge in this battle, and as Shadir's surprise ebbed and his anger grew, she felt a slight shift that signaled power flowing toward him, and she was afraid.

"Truly, you should keep to your games, Princess."

"I am not a child, nor a fool, Shadir." Tia spat the words at him but felt a tremor begin in her legs. "I will not be used as part of your quest for power, as if I am nothing more than a palace asset."

Shadir stroked his beard and studied her. "You

are far more than that, Tiamat. Yes, Amel-Marduk is the king's son. His only son. But his claim to the throne is still tenuous. Marriage to you will bolster that claim and will endear him to the kingdom. For they love their princesses." Kind words, served up with an ugly sweetness.

"They will not favor a brother and sister on the thrones."

Again, the smile that reshaped his face too slowly, taunting her to guess what he knew, what he would next announce, a secret too delicious not to share.

When it came, she could swear she heard the clank of heavy chains across her heart.

"Have no fear of such objections, Tiamat. For you are not the king's daughter."

Chapter 33

Shadir's words entered through her ears, bounced against the inside of her head, then plunged into her heart.

Not the king's daughter.

A cold, cold tickling in the arches of her feet skittered upward through her legs and became a chomping, gnashing monster, eating away at everything she called her own, her very identity. She grabbed for the table and clung as though it would save her from being consumed. Behind

Shadir, the Hall of Magi's star-flecked wall spiraled and blurred.

Tia found her voice, guttural and whispery. "I do not believe you." The words came from the pit of her stomach, tainted with acid.

Shadir gave a tiny shrug of one shoulder and half turned to his instruments. "Perhaps you should ask your mother."

It was his confidence that shook her, that struck like a blow to her chest and drove breath from her lungs. She could hear the *whoosh* of blood in her ears, but all else in the Hall was ghostly silence, as if the underworld had ceased its activity to listen.

"Whose daughter, then?"

Shadir inhaled and looked through the high window, as if trying to recall a time long past. He stroked his oiled beard and pursed his lips. "Let me see if I can recall. There were so many men in those days who—"

"Stop!" Tia pushed away from the table, but her hands were stuck there, in half-dried blood perhaps. The stickiness pulled at her skin and she imagined her palms torn open and raw.

Shadir laughed, a self-gratifying chuckle, and returned to arranging his instruments, still smirking. She longed to pummel the smirk from his face, but with only his words he had weakened her arms more than an hour's training.

But she could still speak, could still form objections with throbbing lips. "And why did the king not thrust her from the palace? Reject both of us?"

The square of light on the floor receded as the sun rose higher, leaving the center of the room unlit, but Shadir's gold-threaded robe seemed still to glow with an inner light. Those glistening threads held her captive, waiting for his answer.

He locked his eyes on to her own and watched her for a moment with that dead stillness of expression she had come to loathe.

"What makes you think he knows?"

Tia began to find her strength at these words. Something about his smug tone, the way he taunted her with unanswered questions.

Shadir, always with the knowledge of secrets. From Amel-Marduk's parentage to her own, from furtive plots to overthrow thrones to surreptitious spells whispered in the bowels of the palace, Shadir swathed himself in the unknown. The mysteries and questions sickened her, and she would fight back.

Tia took a step toward him, hands fisted at her sides. "Do you think I cannot stop you?"

Something behind his eyes flared in response to her challenge. "Stop me? I do not think you even understand me."

"Enlighten me, then. What is this knowledge you possess?"

He licked his lips, and she sensed he wished to tell her many things. She held her breath.

"You came to me with questions once before, Princess. Do you remember?"

"You told me Pedaiah killed Kaldu because he had poisoned my husband. None of this was truth."

"Your husband was killed to free you. I would say that makes *you* responsible for his death."

"Free me? To marry Amel?"

Shadir shrugged. "He is not the only prince who seeks your hand."

Had her mother killed Shealtiel to marry her to her cousin?

"And who killed Kaldu?"

"I would say that Kaldu knew too much. Someone had to silence his . . . eagerness to be of service."

"You? Did you rip Kaldu apart like a beast?"

"Again, you presume what you do not know."

She was getting nowhere, and he would give her nothing more, this she knew.

"I will expose your intent, Shadir. I will even expose myself if necessary." Tia drew herself up, nearly as tall as he, and took another step, narrowing the space between them. "I will tell the people I am not the king's daughter. Where will your plan to marry me to Amel be then?"

They stood with bodies nearly touching, in that grand Hall with its lofty, unseen ceilings, and she felt strong, strong enough to wield word and body against him.

But he held her there too long. No response, no flutter of fear or even concern crossing his expression. Only slack cheeks and parted lips and hollow eyes.

The room grew colder. A chill draft circled her feet like fog, swirling upward around their bodies. It whipped the brazier flames into a frenzy but seemed to douse the sunlight, and Tia touched a hand to the table again to fight the sway of her head.

He spoke at last, the words sharpened into lethal precision, cutting low against her belly. "Your objections are nothing to me, Princess. Understand that. I will have my man on the throne."

"I will tell the queen of your plot. She shall have you executed." Her voice sounded faint, childlike.

The corner of his lip twitched upward. "You have lived in the palace all your life, and still you know nothing of power, little girl. Your mother, however, is a wise woman. She knows I am only the whisper of wind before the storm that is to come."

He tipped her chin upward with his hand, a false affection that nauseated. "There is a web of power here in the palace, spread through the temples, all the way to the Tower of Etemenanki, that supports my cause. Will you untangle this entire web, little princess?"

She batted his hand away, but the dizzying

coldness threw her off balance, and she stumbled as though she'd been slapped.

He is a sorcerer. Appealing to demons, not a servant of the gods.

As though he read her thoughts, Shadir smiled. Satisfied, like he'd swallowed her whole.

But she would not be defeated without a fight. "I will do whatever I must to save the kingdom and my father."

"Yes, your father."

She would not think of that untruth. Not now. She must retain her strength, fight Shadir.

"You are not all-powerful, Shadir. You can be destroyed."

He advanced on her then, towered over her with an expression of contempt, disgust. A look one gave to a vile insect in the moment before it was crushed.

"Listen to me, Princess." The words hissed from his near-motionless lips. "They are *everywhere,* those loyal to me. Watching you. Studying you. Just as they have watched over Amel for years. Not a single action goes unreported."

She tried to back away, but he grabbed her arms and pulled her to himself.

"Everywhere you go, you are not alone. Every word you speak, it is heard." He leaned to her face, put his cold cheek against her own, and spoke into her ear. "Even your thoughts are mine."

She could not stop the spinning of the Hall. The

floor upended and the tarred walls flickered and the high and unreachable window fell to her feet. Bile rose in her throat and her legs would have failed if Shadir did not still hold her in his grip.

"Did you think you could so savagely murder the slave girl Ying and not face consequences?"

So this was part of his plan? To blackmail her?

"Do what you must, Princess." His gaze grazed her face. "But understand that I hold the very lives of your family in my hands. Your mother. Your sisters. Your young, beautiful nephews." His words battered and pounded her mind, no chance to breathe, to react. "They all belong to me."

He released her and she fell against the table. Her hand swept its surface, grasped for something solid. His knives and instruments scattered. A bowl teetered and fell, smashed to shards of blood tinged clay. She sucked air into her chest, steadied her limbs.

"It is time for you to leave, Princess."

With the simple dismissal came a release of the stranglehold on her heart and body.

He has been in control all along.

Tia clutched her stomach, still fighting queasiness, and backed away from Shadir and his table of horrors, backward through the gloom of the Hall until her heels struck the base of the steps. Shadir did not take his eyes from her.

She feared to turn, feared that he would somehow strike her dead if she showed him her back.

I must run.

She must be rid of his foul presence. With a deep breath she spun to the steps, sped upward, and fled under the columned arch of the Hall of Magi.

Chapter 34

I must run.

Tia's only cohesive thought echoed, propelled feet and body away from the Hall.

Not the king's daughter.

She would not think of it. She would hold it by her fingertips, arm outstretched, a reeking piece of filth. And she would turn away from the stench.

The corridors of the palace raced past, distorted and hazy as she ran.

She jolted around a corner and the guard in the lower east corridor snapped to a stiff salute, then trotted alongside.

"Does my lady wish to use her training chamber?"

The answer huffed from her chest on an expelled breath. "Yes. Yes, I must run."

He pushed the door open and she fell into the familiar room. Meager light from the doorway did little to chase shadows.

She stripped her robes as if they were contaminated by Shadir's words, stripped to her short tunic and even unbelted.

"Shall I retrieve a torch, my lady? Light the braziers?"

She heard the curiosity in the guard's voice but ignored it. "Yes. Light them."

He disappeared, but she would not wait.

She ran the dark circuit by memory, pounded the length of the room, turned at the shadowy corner, then turned again and sprinted back to the head of the black chamber.

I know this room better than I know my own self.

No, she would not think of that.

A musty dankness she never noticed in the light closed around her as she ran, thickening her throat. The guard returned, thrust his torch through the doorway ahead of his body, as if to ensure his safety. She passed him and kept running.

Blessed sweat seeped from her pores, a cleansing. She pushed harder, until her chest heaved and her legs trembled with the furious pace.

The six braziers sizzled and popped, their smoky oil assailing her nose at each mad intake of breath, the harsh yellow flames like six demon eyes.

And still she ran. She ran until the pain licked tongues of fire at her calves too hot to bear and then she stumbled and fell and lay panting on the floor.

Her mouth tasted of salted sweat and smoke, but the sour emptiness of her stomach intruded and she fought to keep from retching while her throbbing breaths slowed.

Amytis had lied. Lied too many times to count, but this deception was far greater than any other.

And yet she needed her mother's power, must think of king and kingdom and their protection. Only Amytis held the influence needed to stop Shadir.

Tia leaned her forehead against the cool floor mat, felt the linen wick away the dampness, felt her hair stuck fast to her skin.

She must find a way to control her destiny. She would not marry the Median prince, nor Amel, though he was not her brother.

She will not have her way. Not in this.

As her feet had carried her here from the Hall of Magi, they now directed her past her training bull, through the chamber, and into the corridor.

She would speak to Amytis.

Tia reached her chamber within minutes. No guard attended her door, meaning she was absent. Tia shoved the door open and scanned the room. A young attendant quivered at the wall, biting her lip and staring at her with wide, guileless eyes.

"Fetch my mother. Tell her I wish to speak to her at once in her chamber."

The girl's head quivered in some sort of

agreement and she scurried past to do Tia's bidding.

The room held none of its charms for Tia today. Amytis occupied these chambers, protected from truth, as though she lived encased in a cushioned shell, safe from any consequences.

The heat of her run still fired Tia's skin, lit her senses. She paced the room, unable to remain still. No words formed in advance of the confrontation. Only images. The king's arms around her on the eve of her wedding. In the Gardens, his long beard and yellowed nails scraping stones. Shadir's lifeless face, marked only by a knowing half-smile. Her mother's treacherous beauty.

Amytis arrived at last, smelling of flowers and wine, drifting into her chambers like a waft of costly incense.

She stopped inside the door, her eyes wide and lips parted. "Tiamat, by the gods, what has happened to you?" Her mother's gaze traveled the length of her.

Tia had not donned her robes before leaving the training room. She stood in her simple unbelted tunic, its light fabric clinging to her damp body the way her hair stuck to her cheeks.

"The truth has happened, Mother. The truth."

A flicker of fear in her mother's eyes. Tia saw it and a holy anger swelled like a burst dam in her chest.

Amytis turned to her attendants and inclined

her head toward the door—the slight, superior motion of a woman accustomed to having every directive obeyed.

They disappeared and Tia continued her pacing.

"Tia, settle yourself down. You are behaving like—"

"Like what? A madwoman? Has that particular trait been passed along to the next generation?"

Amytis's lips tightened, as if she tried to keep the truth from slipping through.

"Oh, but wait. How could I have inherited madness from the king?" Her voice had taken on a hot, feverish pitch.

Her mother's composure in the face of her questions angered Tia further. She noticed only a slight shift of her shoulders, a pulling back as though she braced herself for a blow.

"Yes, how could that be, Mother? *When I am not the king's daughter?*" Tia scraped the hair from her face, her eyes, exposing herself to the terrible truth. Would she shrivel in its searing light?

Amytis swallowed convulsively, the cords of her neck straining with the movement. The muscles in her jaw knotted and pulsed. She swayed on her feet and Tia thought she might fall. But then a cold light returned to her eyes and she lifted her chin.

"I did not want you to know."

"No, of course not. Why would you want your foolishness known?"

Amytis crossed to the window, a gliding motion that belied any disturbance of emotion. Did she need air? Did she feel trapped?

Tia pursued, pushed up against her back to continue her accusations, to ask the question that had burned through her since Shadir's pronouncement. Her mother's hair brushed her cheek and smelled like lavender.

"Tell me the truth, Mother. Did he know? Know what you are?"

Amytis stiffened.

"Did he know what I am, Mother?"

What did Tia wish her answer to be? That the man she had known as her father was unaware of her parentage and believed her a princess? Or that he knew and loved her still?

"He has always known." Amytis whispered the words over the city, washed in the blinding light of midday that obscured all decay.

Tia's chest collapsed against itself. "Why did he not expel you from the palace? Send us both away?"

"Because he is a proud man."

The one statement Tia knew to be truth. His pride had been legendary.

Amytis lifted her hand to her face, used an elegant fingertip to wipe the tiniest drop of moisture from the corner of her eye. "And because he loved me."

In spite of herself, Tia must also acknowledge

this truth, though she had never understood it.

She pushed away from the window, strode across her mother's lavish chamber, and turned on her. "Shadir has full knowledge of the truth, Mother. He had Shealtiel killed to marry me to the king's true heir: Amel-Marduk. He has threatened to destroy our family, down to the youngest of us, if I do not comply. You must stop him."

Amytis spun, her eyes afire. "What do you think I have been doing, Tia? Did you think I summoned my cousin from Media for your happiness?"

Tia laughed, a short burst of false mirth. "No, I never believed such a lie."

"Then let me do what I must! And you must do your part!"

Tia marched toward her, and Amytis braced her hands against the window's sill at her back. "I will not again be controlled. Nor allow you to expose the king and give his kingdom to the Medes."

Not until she spoke the words did she realize that her loyalty still lay with Nebuchadnezzar, now and always. Father or not, he had loved her as his own—more than mother or sister ever had—and she would sacrifice anything to see him safe and restored.

Amytis's eyes glittered with anger and tears she was too controlled to shed. "What *would* you allow then, *Princess Tiamat?*" The words tore at Tia, left her disgraced, humiliated. "Tell me, wise daughter, how would you suggest we save our own lives?"

Tia sniffed and rubbed at tightness in her neck. "I will announce that I am not the king's daughter. Tell the people the truth. Then Shadir will have no one to marry Amel, no one to strengthen his claim to the throne."

Amytis crossed her arms over her chest. "And you think this will put an end to Shadir's plan?"

"You must denounce him before the priests, the advisors. Have him executed."

"Hah! This is your defense?" Amytis held out empty palms. "To simply declare Shadir a traitor and be done with him?"

"You have the power. The advisors listen—"

"No, *you* listen, Tia." She drew close and seized her with those cold eyes. "You are a child, ignorant of the workings of power. You have no idea who are friends and allies, nor who seeks the destruction of our family."

Her mother's breath was hot against her face. Tia's limbs trembled at the fury, but she hardened her muscles against it. She would not show her mother fear. Her own small deceit, but why should she not be allowed some lies of her own?

"The balance of a kingdom's power is a tenuous thing. Fragile as an eggshell and just as brittle." She raised an open hand, then clenched it—a sudden, harsh movement that made Tia jump. "It can be crushed in an instant."

Tia dared not speak. Amytis must have her say.

"I cannot simply kill one of them and be assured that the threat is removed. Another will rise up and take his place."

Tia thought of the night she heard Shadir conspiring with someone on the rooftop garden. She still had no idea as to the other's identity. How many more traitors lurked behind false respect?

"I must work in other ways to secure my family's safety. That is what I have been doing. And that is your responsibility also."

Amytis grabbed Tia's arms above the elbow, squeezed stone-like fingers into her skin. "If you make that announcement, you sign a death sentence for all those you love."

Tia felt her lips part, draw more air into her compressed lungs.

"Do you not understand? If it is known that you are not his daughter, my cousin will return to Media without a bride. But Shadir will still lead his uprising, with or without you. And his first task will be to kill every member of our family, every threat to Amel's succession. Is that what you want?"

Amytis released her with a tiny shove, and Tia fought to retain her balance and her composure.

The bitter truth, layered with her mother's honeyed deceit, was enough to choke.

Tia had come to her chamber full of indignation, passionate with accusations. And somehow Amytis had twisted it all and thrown it back, as if Tia were the one whose integrity should be doubted.

"I have never been more to you than a useful coin for bartering, have I? The product of something you wished to forget, wished to hide. A living reminder. No wonder you have never loved me."

Amytis swung her dark hair over one shoulder, a fluid, feminine motion to cover her discomfort with the truth. Her face was as smooth as the plain of Dura, but if the sand were blown away, the decay and rottenness underneath would be revealed.

"You have always been a difficult child, Tia. I did my best—"

"You did what you must. Nothing more."

"Yes, I did what I must! What is wrong with that? I have watched over every member of this family for seven long years while your father has growled and drooled and scuttled through those Gardens like a senseless beast." Her eyes flared and her hands formed fists at her chest. The words cost her something, Tia could see. She never spoke of his madness. "I have kept his secret, perfected the deception, made certain that anyone who knew the truth was taken care of."

Kaldu? Ying?

"And still, you have nothing but contempt. You, who live in your own world of running and of leaping bulls, as if your only enemies were stuffed with straw!"

Hot, searing words ripped open Tia's self-deception.

It is I who have lived in a shell.

"But now you know, Tia. Now you have heard everything; you have all your answers. Only one question remains. Will you continue to play your games, seeking false thrills, or will you stand up and do your part to save your family?"

The fury that had driven her here drained away, leaving Tia hollow, emotionless. The silence lengthened between them but changed nothing. Her mouth was dry, for she had turned to sand herself, and the words emerged sticky and distasteful, but they emerged all the same.

"I will do my part."

Chapter 35

Time passed without Tia's awareness. Not the missing hours she had experienced in past weeks, but a simple, wandering lostness that carried her through the palace and through the afternoon until it was dusk and she found herself climbing the slanted steps of the Tower of Etemenanki.

Would she find what she sought on its lofty platform? What *did* she seek?

Since her agreement with her mother, Tia had felt nothing but a scraped-out hollowness where thought and emotion should reside. Could the chants and prayers of priests, the blessing of gods, fill her now?

The arduous ascent to the Tower's platform paid homage to the divine ones, showed devotion from the seeker. Tonight Tia's legs were wooden and her heart stone. Did the gods honor only those whose hearts beat with passion?

The sun had fallen into the empty horizon, and the whiplashes of purplish clouds followed like fading bruises as she climbed. Above, the torches at the platform's perimeter snapped in the dusty wind, and she could hear the drone of a growing crowd come to seek favor. With the Akitu Festival only two days away, even the most nonreligious of Babylon's citizens would remember to bring an offering, whisper a prayer.

Tia reached the platform at last and let herself be sucked into the mob, a false sense of belonging, of being wanted, pulling her toward the central altar.

The kalû chanted their rhythmic bursts of prayer like beating drums, over and over, the words pounding against her skull. She winced against the pain, blinked, and shook her head.

Magi surrounded the altar, lifted hands holding amulets to be blessed and fretting lambs dangling by thin legs and all manner of charms.

I long, also, to be somehow blessed or charmed.

Tia smelled the burnt flesh of earlier sacrifices, finished gifts to the gods that now smoldered on the altar's embers. Above her, the charred sky absorbed the smoke, drawing it away into silvery stars. The sadness pierced her again—a gleaming sharpness of starlight burrowing in her chest.

She pushed through the crowd until she reached the altar and laid her hands across its ashy stones. The coppery-red blood of the first sacrifice pooled in a basin and at the deeper edges of the altar's surface, its scent cast off with the smoke.

What am I to do?

Tia asked the question of herself; she asked the question of the gods.

Her only desires since Shealtiel's death had been freedom for herself and safety for her father. But now he was not her father. And she would give her freedom to save him and his kingdom.

Her mother did not love her, and now she knew the reason. The king's love *had* no reason —neither motive nor sanity—and as such it could do nothing.

It was true. *I am nothing more than an asset to be traded.* This was her role, her function. Her duty.

Her mother had lived a lie, and it was now her turn. Tia would leave Babylon, leave all she knew, and begin her own life of deceit in the palace of Media.

A coldness enveloped her at the altar's edge and she leaned toward its center, toward the consuming heat of its ochre flames. Someone bumped against her, priest or magi, she did not care. The kalû's chants grew frenzied, the murmur of the crowd swelled.

Everything within her reached out to the gods for wisdom and strength. "Hear my prayer." She whispered the words into the flames. "Hear my prayer."

The fire flickered and snapped, and she blinked. Did a face form in its angry depths? She gripped the dry stones of the altar wall and leaned farther. Heat flushed her skin.

A pressure grew against her chest, familiar and therefore comforting. But no, no—this was the pressure Pedaiah and Daniel had released. She had not felt it since, until this moment. The face in the flames wavered and reformed, clearer now.

Labartu! She drew back, struck with a weakness in her legs.

"What is it, Princess?" A mage appeared at her side, his words soft and kind.

"I—I see the demon Labartu—in the flames."

He laid a hand over her own. "Tell me what you see."

329

"Her lioness's head. Teeth to gnaw flesh. A great pointed cone above her." Light-headedness swept over her. "What does it mean? Am I cursed?"

"Hush, child. It is not Labartu you see but Ishtar. The goddess appears to protect you."

Was it true? She drew in a ragged breath of hope.

"You must listen if she wishes to speak."

Tia listened with all of her heart, opening herself to the goddess's wisdom, to the goddess's direction.

Her vision narrowed, constricted to that single, horrific face in the fire, and it seemed as if the torches at the edge of the Platform extinguished, and the crowd melted away, the chants faded over the desert. Only Ishtar and she remained, and Tia waited, trembling.

The mage had assured her that the goddess Ishtar appeared to her, not the demon Labartu. But in that flickering moment, gentle words spoke into her consciousness and chilled her soul.

They are one and the same.

But this was not true. The priests and magi performed their rites to appease the gods, to gain their protection from the dark powers of the demons.

They are one and the same.

The oppression bore down on her, her chest wrapped in bindings too tight to breathe.

She waited for the goddess to speak, to deny her blasphemous thought, but she did not. Was Tia unworthy of a special message? The rejected, discarded pseudo princess?

Something other than words reached out for her, slithering like tentacles. Tia's stomach wobbled and she felt an incredible thirst.

The face of the god, or perhaps demon, hissed in anger. A hate-filled, spiteful hiss like moisture sizzling in the fire.

And then she spoke. Tia did not see lips move, but the words seeped into her head.

Fear me, or serve me, it matters little.

Beneath her hands the altar stones grew wet, slimy. She heard a far-off howl from the under-world, and the reeking stench of death filled her nostrils. The odor set her gagging, even as the ferocious face of Labartu putrefied into a lascivious grin, algae-green.

Fear me. Or serve me.

Her thighs tensed and her head quivered like an aged woman. What was happening to her? She screamed, but only inside her own head, the shriek rebounding, echoing.

To whom did one pray when the gods themselves turned against you?

"Awake and rise to her defense."

"Contend for her, my God and Lord."

The taste of incense and tar, smoke and sweat and burning grain, filled her mouth.

Tia tore herself from the web of terror, slashed at the unseen bonds, covered her ears to the demanding, hateful voice.

Faintly, she heard her name called. But she was running. Running once again, from the leeching fear of the altar, toward the one person who had once set her free.

Pedaiah.

Down the Tower's zigzagging steps, across the dark city, up the palace steps.

Why had she never learned where he lived? The last time she found him in the palace, he had said he was staying there. Would he still be there tonight? Waiting to release her?

She reached the family's chamber entrance and pounded a flat palm against the wood.

"Please! Please, I must speak—"

The door *swooshed* open, held by Pedaiah, his brawny frame outlined with golden torchlight.

She fell into his arms, wrapped her own around his neck. Found no words.

Pedaiah bent, swept her up against his chest, and carried her. She buried her face in the pulse of his throat.

He laid her along a carved bench and knelt beside her, his face nearly touching her own and his palm on her forehead. She shook like a leaf in a storm under his hand.

"What is this fear, Tia? I have never seen you thus."

She chewed her lips, clutched his sleeve. "I saw something. Heard something."

"Tell me."

She spilled all of it, then. From Shadir's revelation, to her mother's betrayal, to the bewildering horror she had witnessed on the Platform.

At the end, Pedaiah raised his eyes to the heavens and whispered only, "Praise You, Yahweh."

She struggled from his hold and pulled herself upright on the bench. They were alone in the room, though several braziers burned. She saw a table laid with dishes painted like sunshine and bunches of lavender and sage. "Tell me the meaning of this vision, Pedaiah."

He still knelt before her and took her hands in his own, clutched together in her lap.

"Your eyes have been opened at last."

"But I do not understand what I have seen."

"You have seen the truth. Isn't that what you have been seeking?"

Tia slouched against the wall, tired and confused. "I do not know what is truth."

"This is what I have been trying to show you, Tia. The gods your people worship—they are nothing more than demons with different names. The powers of evil do not care if you are a sorcerer committed to destruction or a priest faithful to protect. They will control you through fear or through devotion, they care not which. Do you see that now?"

"Fear me. Or serve me." She did see it. At last she saw the wicked truth. She had thought to stave off evil by appeasing good gods, but the gods she worshipped were the very demons she feared.

Pedaiah's hands on hers were warm. "Tia, there is only One True God. And He has shown Himself to you this night."

"I have seen only terror."

"But in the terror He has shown you truth."

She pulled her hands from his. "How can I accept that everything I have been taught is false?"

"It requires faith, I know. But no more faith than what you have already given to the demons." His gaze searched her face, so intense, so earnest. She wanted to lay her hand on his cheek.

"Then the magi—they are frauds?"

He smiled, a sad smile one gives an injured child. "Some know the truth, yes. They try to control the power, to understand it, all the while knowing that it controls them. Others are simply deceived, as you have been. They believe they serve the good, when they do not."

"Shadir knows." Tia thought of his cold, dead eyes, of the way she'd seen him bent over the burning figurine in the depths of the palace. "He knows whom he serves."

"I have no doubt."

She leaned toward him and whispered, "What must I do, Pedaiah? What must I do to be free of them?"

"You must claim the True God for your own. You must accept that atonement can only come through Him."

"What if your God is no more a god than mine?"

"And what if He is?"

Tia looked away, to the table set for guests. It could not be so easy.

"Always the fighter, Tiamat. It is time to stop fighting."

A burning at her throat brought her fingers to the amulet Amel had fashioned to protect her. Did she imagine its heat? Tia yanked the cord from her neck and threw it from her.

With any vital shift in thinking, in believing, there comes a moment when one knows the peak of unbelief has been crested, and a slide into a new truth is inevitable. Even now, she was falling, falling into a different sort of belonging, being gathered in. Desired and loved. She closed her eyes and let the truth wash over her, let go of falsity and fear. A repentance, broken and cleansing, opened wide her heart. A submission to a sovereign love she had never known broke that heart into pieces. And an acceptance of grace, of love, of salvation put the pieces back together.

Joy and tranquility flooded into what had been vacant, an unfamiliar peace like sunrise. Tia opened her eyes to Pedaiah's strong and clear gaze, his knowing smile.

And then his hands were on her face and his smile only a breath away.

She pulled in a shaky breath and closed her eyes for his kiss. His fingers wrapped to the back of her neck and the kiss lingered, long enough for her blood to thrum in her ears and her breath to shallow.

When he pulled away, eyes shining, she felt as though she floated above them both, watching in amazement.

Did he know how much she loved him?

They talked then, of his homeland and his people, of Daniel and the young magi he was training in the ways of the Torah. Of this new God who had become her own.

But they must speak of the future, and in that, nothing had changed.

Tia traced the white scar on his chin with her finger. "I must marry the Mede. There is no other way."

Pedaiah's jaw tightened and his hand clenched hers. "I would take you far from here—"

"And then what? Shadir would kill my entire family and put Amel on the throne."

Pedaiah stood and paced. "For all his selfishness and immaturity, I would not think Amel cruel. He seems to care for you. How could he be part of such a plot?"

"I am not certain he knows all. I think it likely he is only a useful source of power for Shadir."

Pedaiah's words sparked a new thought, and she sat forward. "Perhaps if I spoke with Amel—perhaps we could make an agreement."

He faced her, scowling. "What sort of agreement?"

"If he will guarantee the safety of my family, I will not marry the Mede. I will marry Amel."

Storm clouds passed over Pedaiah's features.

She stood and grasped his hand. "Do you see? I can save both—my family and the kingdom! I must only get around Shadir and plead with Amel."

"It is risky, Tia. He may not keep his word."

"No, no, I will ensure it. There are too many secrets he would not wish known. I can convince him that my plan is best. A peaceful accession to the throne by the king's own son and safety for my family."

He exhaled, his gaze on their clasped hands, then slowly pulled his hand from hers. "Then I wish you the best in your new marriage, Princess."

She heard the pain in his voice, felt it in her heart. She wrapped her arms around his waist and pressed her forehead to his chest. "It is not what I want, Pedaiah. You must know this."

He stood unmoving for only a moment, then clutched her to himself like a man drowning. "Tell me you love only me, Tia."

"I love only you."

He hid his face in her hair, pressed his cheek to her head.

"It is strange how things turn out, Pedaiah."

"Hmm?" The words were muffled, his lips were against her hair now.

"I will keep the thing I believed mattered most to me—my position here in the palace, my luxuries—even though they are not rightfully mine. And I will lose the thing that truly matters—the freedom to love you."

He sucked in a breath and clasped her tighter. "How can I let this happen?"

"You must." Tia pushed away, held him at arm's length. "Pray to your God for me. That He would protect me from the dark power against me."

"He is your God now, Tia. You may speak your prayers yourself."

This truth was hard to take in—that she now had the power of the One God to break the evil that had long kept her bound.

As if he could read her thoughts, Pedaiah whispered, "To run in the paths He has marked brings freedom and glory."

She smiled, a watery, tearful smile that also held good-bye. He saw it for the ending that it was and touched her face a final time.

"Go in peace, Princess. You are loved."

She had not heard those words in seven years. They fell on her like showers across the parched plains, and she soaked them in, precious and holy.

And then she left.

Pedaiah closed the door, closed his eyes, but would never again close his heart. Not to Tia. Not even if she married Amel and became queen. He would move far from the palace, perhaps, so he did not have to see her, but he would not give up loving her, now that he had seen that it was Yahweh who had given him this love, placed him in Tia's life, then let him see the fruit it bore.

He stood at the door, forehead pressed against the wood as if it brought him closer to Tia, even as she left him behind to do what she must.

And into the empty places of his heart flooded a profound repentance, a breaking open of the hardened soil, and he fell to his knees before the door and bowed his head to the Holy One, who had patiently waited through his arrogance.

"Forgive me, Yahweh." He breathed through the storm of emotion, trying to gain control. He did not want to concern his family. But his hypocrisy overwhelmed him, and his unloving and judgmental spirit toward those the Holy One called to Himself left him broken and weeping.

"You have placed us here for judgment, but also out of mercy. To be a lamp stand to the nations, a light. And with my anger and hatred I have brought nothing but darkness."

And yet in His great mercy, Tia had seen light, had understood that Yahweh was to be her Father too. Not only Father to the Jews.

Pedaiah swiped at his face with the back of his hand and lifted his head. "Of all Your people, I should have seen how You graft the nations onto the root of Jesse." Tamar, Rahab, Ruth, Bathsheba. "My own family line—a testament to Your far-reaching grace."

He climbed to his feet, went to a wash basin, and poured water over his hands. "Forgive me, Yahweh," he whispered again, splashing his face. "Make me clean in Your sight. Give me a heart to love those whom You love."

It was a mystery, still, how to live among those who hated the One God and to love them without compromise. But it was also a truth, a calling, one he would pursue until the day he was called to his fathers.

And until then, until then he must find a way to live without Tia.

Chapter 36

Tia left pieces of herself in Pedaiah's chambers. There could be no looking back. Though a curious and newfound peace accompanied her from that hallowed ground.

She took the corridors more slowly this time, forming her plan as she walked. Tomorrow's Festival would not include the marriage her mother anticipated, but there would be a marriage.

And two men needed to understand their roles.

The Median prince Zagros had spent most of his time in the palace courtyards surrounded by beautiful servant girls, lavish spreads of food, and music for dancing. She searched for such a party, but as it was early afternoon and too soon to begin celebrations that would last into the night, Tia learned he was in his assigned chambers.

"I would speak to Prince Zagros," she said to the guard at his door, one of their own.

The guard, as young as herself, bowed his head briefly but his face twitched in indecision. "I believe the prince sleeps."

"At this hour?"

"He—he was awake most of the night, my lady."

She scowled. The embarrassed tone of the guard gave a glimpse into her promised life in the Median palace. "He will have to wake again, I am afraid. I must speak with him."

The guard pushed into the chamber, and she gave him only a moment before she followed.

Zagros was propped on one elbow on the bed, rubbing his hand over his beard. His glance fell on Tia and his eyes widened before a grin split his face, revealing wine-purpled teeth. He eyed the guard and jerked his head toward the door. And then they were alone.

Zagros did not rise from the bed.

"I had not expected to see you in my chamber

before the marriage ceremony, Princess." He patted the bedcovering, an invitation. "I am most pleased."

"Get up, Zagros. We must speak."

His grin dropped away, replaced by a wary annoyance. "Speak of what?"

"Of our marriage."

Zagros swung his legs over the side of the bed and pushed himself to standing. With a moan he half-stumbled and lashed out to grab the bed frame for balance. When he was righted, he loomed over Tia. She had forgotten their great difference in size. He reached for her, grabbed her arm, and dragged her to his chest. Ruddy cheeks bloomed above his beard and he smelled of soured wine.

"That is exactly the topic I would address." The words were slurred, soft pebbles in his mouth.

She could not show fear, despite the danger. She yanked her arm from his grip. "You have come on a fool's errand, Zagros. Been brought here through falsity and deception."

His eyes sparked, awake and alert at last. "Who has been false?"

"Your cousin. My mother, the queen. She has led you to believe this marriage would be a treaty between Media and Babylon." Tia lifted her chin, a proud defense against the humiliating words. "But I am no child of Babylon."

Zagros shook his head, as though to disagree

would be to negate the truth. "You are the king's daughter."

"I am not."

She let the words penetrate his drink-induced stupor. "My mother conceived me outside her marriage to the king."

He set his jaw and narrowed his eyes. "I do not care. The people believe—"

"If you and she force me into this marriage, I will make the truth known to all of Babylon, and word will certainly be carried to Media. You will be painted as a fool—coming all this way, laying out so much expense, all for the daughter of an unfaithful wife."

Zagros's eyes went dark. "Then who is your father?"

The question caused a strange, convulsing stricture in her chest.

I do not know.

She had been so fractured by the truth that the man she loved was not her father, she had given little thought to whose daughter she was. She fought to loosen the tightness around her heart.

"He is of no consequence. What matters now is that you and I come to an agreement."

He wobbled a bit, then sank to the bedding, an odd expression crossing his face. Fear?

Tia inhaled, ready to explain her hastily conceived plan. "You will be paid well. You must leave this night, before tomorrow's festival

343

activities begin. You will leave word that you found the king's daughter to be too—strong-willed—for your liking and did not believe she would make a proper Median queen. In this we both save face, and the people know enough of me to believe it truth."

She did not add that Amytis would also believe the lie and would berate her for it until her dying day.

"No one must know the truth, Zagros. Nor that you are leaving tonight. Especially not my mother."

It was there again, that look of desperation.

"Princess"—he broke off and sneered, then continued—"how can I return to my country with no bride? My father—"

He raked a hand through his hair, stood, and paced beside her.

He feared his father. Feared disappointing, failing him, as she did her mother. In this, they were kindred. For all his monstrous behavior, humanity lurked beneath the surface.

She held out a palm. "You will bring back treasures of Babylon. Pieces taken from the grandest temples of our enemies."

In truth, this part of her plan Tia had not yet perfected, but there would be time.

Zagros turned on her and she took a step backward. Would he attack her? Threaten violence if she did not go through with the marriage?

He seized her arms and she tensed, ready to fight.

But his voice was pleading, a syrupy sweetness. "Beautiful Tiamat, do not do this. We can continue this lie. No one must know. I will give you everything you desire in Media."

"Everything I desire, Zagros, is in Babylon."

Perhaps it was the finality of her tone, perhaps the set of her jaw, but he seemed to sense his defeat. He thrust her from him, growling curses, and stomped to the window.

Tia lingered. Was there something she could say to ensure his cooperation, his silence?

He shot a murderous look over his shoulder. "Go."

She opened her mouth, held out a hand.

"Go!" Zagros grabbed a nearby vase and heaved it at her head.

She ducked, and the vase smashed against the floor.

With a last worried huff of breath toward Zagros, she left him to his anger.

One task accomplished.

But the preparations would not be complete until she had assured herself of Amel's cooperation as well.

And her objective would be trickier with Amel, for he could not simply be threatened or bribed to play his part.

It took until evening to locate him. The palace

staff seemed to have multiplied in anticipation of tomorrow's double celebration. Her questions were treated with impatience, and her searching yielded only bustling slaves and overflowing wagons delivering colorful vegetables, freshly slaughtered meat, even bolts of exotic fabrics. She skirted merchants and servants, threading through courtyards and public chambers. She peeked into the Hall of Magi, but it was empty.

Finally, word came to her that Amel was performing duties in the Temple of Ishtar.

At last.

Without thought of escort, or her mother's disapproval, Tia took to the city streets and pushed through crowds along the Processional Way, reaching the main temple on the Street of Ishtar by the time darkness draped the city.

Temple prostitutes and male worshippers clogged the temple's grassy outer courtyard. She ignored the activity, her eyes set on the soft glow of the temple antechamber and the larger hall beyond where Ishtar's representative figure awaited.

Tia's steps slowed, arrested by new thoughts.

My first time in a temple since knowing the truth. That if Ishtar existed, she was a demon, not a goddess, and she sought to enslave.

Tia whispered an incoherent prayer to the One God. *Protection. Wisdom.* Did He hear the prayers of a Babylonian woman when she had done nothing yet for Him?

The singsong of the priestesses drew her into the temple's depths, where the overwhelming scent of incense immediately watered her eyes, thickened her throat, and shallowed her breath.

Amel, where are you?

It was more than incense that oppressed her. The familiar heaviness reminded her she had been freed.

She found him attending the goddess and her nightly ritual meal. Tia watched his narrow frame, his back to her, as he prayed over the lavish feast spread before the golden statue, then backed away and drew the curtains for her privacy. These were priests' functions, yet as a novice mage, he must learn various religious duties.

"Amel." Tia spoke quietly, but still he startled. But then his smile seemed genuine and strengthened her confidence.

"Tia." His hands were outstretched.

She went to him, her stomach warring with her heart. How many conflicting emotions had she felt for this man over these few weeks? Attraction, then revulsion at learning he was her brother. And today, now that they were no longer siblings?

Pedaiah would not be pleased to see my heart.

It shamed her, her fascination with the future king. She wished to be rid of it and voiced another broken prayer in her mind, for clarity, focus.

"Can we speak alone, Amel?"

He blinked twice, a tiny flicker of concern

creasing his brow. "Of course." He glanced at the side walls of the temple. "Here." He gestured toward a chamber door.

Inside the smallish room no torch had been lit, and only the light from the main chamber illuminated his features. It was enough to trace his beauty, so she turned away to speak.

"What is it, Tia? What is wrong?"

"Are you aware of Shadir's plan for you, Amel? For us?"

A long silence met her question. Then, "We are to be married."

It was time for plain speaking. "Tomorrow. He will announce the truth of both our fathers to the kingdom, the Median prince will leave in humiliation, and Shadir will reveal the king's . . . *condition*. Then he will put the crown on your head and marry us to appease the people."

Amel brushed her arm with his fingertips. "I have waited eagerly for the day."

"For the day of my family's annihilation."

"Why would your family—?"

She faced him, skin flushing. "Do not be foolish, Amel. Shadir cannot afford any other claims to the throne once the people know the truth about the king. My brothers-in-law, my nephews. Even my sisters, who could yet bear more grandchildren for the king. Every one of them will be dead by the end of the festival."

Tia watched his eyes. So much depended on her

accurate assessment of this man. Was he merely Shadir's unwitting tool? Or was he also greedy for the blood of royals? Could she convince him of her plan, then trust him to keep his word?

Those dark eyes with their thick lashes that beguiled her when they first met deepened with sympathy and some small outrage.

"I will not allow it!"

She searched his face for a telltale shift—too much blinking, perhaps a slant of the eyes or a nervous tic—but saw sincerity.

"You must promise me, Amel." Tia gripped his hands and spoke with all the force she could bring to bear. "I swear to you, if my family is not kept safe, I will join them in the underworld before we reach our marriage bed."

Surprise leapt across his features.

This threat was her only bargaining piece. She counted on Amel's affection, or at least his infatuation. Would he protect her family's lives to gain her as his wife?

"You must be your own king. Not Shadir's mouthpiece. You must rule Babylon from your own wisdom and courage, and not be swayed by the evil that Shadir would have you commit."

He straightened, as though the crown were being placed on his brow this very moment, then returned her hand clasp. His mouth tightened with unusual gravity and he nodded slowly. Regally.

"You have my word. From baby to gray-haired, not one of your family will be harmed."

This declaration was the best she could extract. There were no guarantees.

He released her hands, but only to place his own on each side of her head. His thumbs caressed her cheeks. "I will make you happy, Tia. You shall see." He brushed his lips against hers, the whisper of a promise.

Tia remembered her thoughts when they met. She was an unattainable princess and he a forbidden mage. Would she have smiled that first night to know that one day they would marry?

Perhaps. But as she escaped the Temple of Ishtar, through the courtyard of prostitutes, her heart thudded with a suggestion she refused to entertain.

Have I sold myself to purchase an empty promise?

Chapter 37

"There you are at last!"

Her mother's fury met Tia at the top of the palace steps under the entry arch.

Tia sighed and walked past her stormy expression. Would she forever be placating her mother's disapproval of her excursions?

"Do not turn your back on me, girl!"

Tia slowed. This was more than her usual censure.

Amytis caught up with her, pinched her above the elbow, and pulled her along in the current of her anger. "Come with me."

She marched Tia through the flowered court-yard, past its warbling fountain, to the same small, unused chamber where Pedaiah had prayed over her, so long ago. The memory of that prayer warmed her, and a peace like the court-yard fountain welled up inside her heart.

Her mother, however, was clearly not at peace. She pushed Tia into the dim chamber until Tia's back was against the wall, Amytis's black hair gleaming with near-blue highlights around her pale face. She wagged a finger before Tia's eyes.

"You will be the destruction of this family yet, Tiamat."

Tia licked her lips and waited for more.

"How *could* you? Do you know how hard I worked to create this alliance with my family in Media?"

A tiny wisp of apprehension fluttered in Tia's stomach. She studied the creases at the corners of her mother's eyes, the deepening lines around her mouth.

"But you could not be satisfied until you had your way. Zagros says he will not marry you, now that he has learned you are not the king's daughter." Her lips tightened—a narrow, pinkish slash that dared Tia to change her opinion of her rebellious daughter.

Tia had misjudged Zagros.

"Yes, he told me of your announcement. Did you think he would slink away in the night with nothing to show for his effort?"

"I promised he would be well paid—"

"He came for a bride! And there would have been no difficulty in your marrying him, regardless of your parentage. The world believes you a princess, and the treaty would rest on that belief. But now, now he will declare to the kingdom that he has discovered our betrayal. There may even be war!"

Amytis's words sputtered against Tia's face, and something more than anger was there. It was the same unexpected emotion she had seen in Zagros's expression.

Her mother was afraid.

Tia clasped her mother's hands. "All will be well, Mother, I promise. I have spoken to Amel—"

She recoiled as if Tia had struck her with this news. "Amel!"

"He cares for me, Mother. He will keep us safe."

Amytis's rage settled into something colder, more fearful. A chilling stillness that poured disdain over Tia.

"I have told him that if our family is not safe, I will take my own life."

Tia expected this bold declaration to cause some flicker of appreciation for her plan, but nothing disturbed her mother's frozen expression.

"And you believe in this you have saved us?"

"Saved both the family and the kingdom, Mother. Do you not see? You will not have to give Babylon to the Medes. The king's dynasty will continue, Babylon will be undisturbed, and our family will retain our noble position."

"All of this, on the word of the young Amel."

It was a statement, not a question, but one with complete lack of conviction, with hopelessness.

"He desires to be a good king, I know he does. He wishes to be free of the influence of Shadir, to rule from—"

But Amytis had turned away. Turned and drifted to the doorway, leaned her forehead against its frame.

Tia followed her, desperate now for Amytis to see her plan, to understand. Tia's hand trembled on her mother's arm. "It is better this way."

Amytis was speaking softly. Not to Tia, to herself. A low, chastising sort of muttering that left Tia cold.

"She was too young. Too young to see. I should have told her everything. Perhaps then . . ."

"What is it, Mother? I do not understand."

But Amytis had retreated, somewhere far from Tia. The distance in her eyes was frightening.

"Mother, speak to me. What is it you fear?"

Amytis spoke with lips nearly touching the door's edge. "I fear many things, Daughter. Many things. Most of all Shadir."

"Is he so powerful?"

"You have no idea. No idea what he is capable of, nor what he has already done. But know this, Tiamat. Amel will never break Shadir's hold on him. Whether or not he desires this, it is of no consequence. Shadir will have his way."

"Amel is ready—"

"No man is ever ready to be a king. It is a mantle too heavy for a mortal to wear, a position too close to the gods. If he is honest, he must seek a power beyond himself. Amel has found that power in Shadir. He will not let it go. Nor will Shadir release his hold on the future king."

What had she done? Tia had thought to play the hero, to sacrifice herself to save all those she loved, including her beloved Babylon. She had left them worse than they had begun. Her skin felt taut, as though apprehension and the unknown had stretched it thin.

But no, Tia could not believe Amytis knew Amel's heart. Not like she did. She must know for herself.

Before her mother could heap her with any more blame, Tia escaped the chamber.

Amytis did not follow, did not even call out.

Tia hesitated outside the chamber, on the perimeter of the courtyard. How was she to learn this truth? Simply questioning Amel would be ineffective. She could not be certain he even knew the truth himself.

In that moment of hesitation, Amel-Marduk entered through the palace arch.

Tia pulled back instinctively, into the shadowed doorway. Watched him cross the courtyard, his steps confident.

And then she followed him.

She had followed Shadir thus once, through palace corridor and down the stairs to that frightful chamber under the palace where he had performed strange incantations. Would Amel lead her into such danger?

But it would seem the Hall of Magi was his destination. Without a backward look, he slipped under its columned entrance. Tia slowed in the corridor and considered her options.

Confrontation was pointless. Neither Shadir nor Amel could be trusted. She saw that now.

Voices drifted to her from within the Hall, and she slid closer. A stone column stood close to the wall and she wedged herself into the gap. She could remain unseen here but perhaps hear conversation. She held her breath, centered on the single sense of hearing.

"She cares for her family, Shadir. I would have it no other way."

Amel's voice. Speaking of her.

Tia focused on the grayish stone column at her nose, traced spidery black cracks.

"Her family is a danger to our plans, Amel."

"I will earn their loyalty once I am king. Allow

them to remain in the palace, treat them well."

Her heart expanded at these words. Her faith in him had not been misplaced. She leaned to her right, tried to glimpse the men within the Hall, saw only slivered fragments of their faces, flickering brazier light.

"Amel. I want you to listen."

Shadir's words, hypnotically smooth, raised a chill on her arms. She watched, her face pressed against the column, one uncovered eye trained on the men.

"I have protected you from birth, have I not?"

She heard no answer from Amel, perhaps because his back was to her.

"I have trained you in all that I know, given you secrets of power, opened the heavens to you."

Shadir had drawn close to the younger mage, his face suspended a mere breath from Amel's. Why did Amel not speak, not move?

"And now it is time, Amel. It is time for us to claim what we have so long labored to gain. The kingdom you deserve. And would you have those who are not of royal blood take it from you?"

She hung on Amel's answer, waited through long moments of silence, all of her body tensed to hear the fate of her family, the outcome of her foolishness.

Amel's voice, when it fell from his lips and drifted across the Hall to her ears, was the lifeless monotone pitch of a man who obeyed and did not question.

"No one shall take it from me, Shadir. No one."

Even from her half-obstructed place behind the column, she saw Shadir's slow smile. "Good. Then we shall do what we must."

Tia circled the stone column with one arm and clutched it to her chest to keep herself upright.

Amel answered, still half alive. "We shall do what we must."

Enough. She had heard enough.

Before the silent scream in her chest had a chance at betrayal, Tia escaped from hiding and ran. Ran with one hand pressed against her throat, her teeth clenched, anything to hold back the emotion that would swamp her, leave her as half alive as Amel on the floors of the palace corridor.

You are a fool, just as Mother knew.

As always when life threatened to overwhelm, her instinct took her to the Gardens. She arrived at the top tier panting—with exertion, with fear, with her own stupidity. The lock gave way easily under her key, and she fell through the door, relieved to have made it here without shouting her frustration through the palace.

She picked her way through the darkness to her usual perch and lowered herself to the stone. The seven-tiered Gardens led downward like a staircase for the gods, leading to the city below. As if she could merely step from the lowest tier into the city streets, where families huddled around cook fires and mothers tucked their children into bed with whispered songs.

It was an illusion, however. That final step from the Garden's lip would be deadly, and from her topmost perch she felt the distance keenly between herself and the rest of the world. A strange displacement, a misbelonging.

Tia allowed the night's events to drop away for a moment. Focused on the wind's rustle of the palms, on the gurgle of water as it flowed from the lift behind her downward through the tiers. On the primal smell of earth. She longed for a connection with all that was elemental and dug her hand into the rich, reddish soil. Traced the flow of aquamarine water nearby, breathed in the clear night air. Her heart settled. Lies and secrets were an anomaly, not the truth of all that was.

"Will you hear my prayers, Yahweh? The prayers of a foolish girl?" She waited, clutched at the peace He offered. "Show me the truth."

Her father did not approach. Yes, Tia would call him *father,* now and always, for that is what he was. She saw him once or twice, rambling among the thick shrubbery farther down. Caught the glint of his eyes turned toward her. But he did not come. Had her visits become commonplace? Was it only animal curiosity that had brought him to her in times past, not some latent sense of affection? Perhaps Tia had been wrong about him, as she had been wrong about everything.

She drew her knees to her forehead, her body curled tight to ward off the chill and the truth. But the truth would not be dispelled.

I have destroyed my mother's plan to keep us safe through marriage to the Medes. Amel is Shadir's mouthpiece, Shadir's instrument of destruction, and marriage to him will also destroy our family. And the man to whom she wished to give herself could not be hers.

Zagros. Amel. Pedaiah. Three sons of kings. Three princes who would all have her. One as a means to peace, one as means to power, and the other—the other to set her free.

But he has set me free. Or rather, his God had. Free from the oppression that had blanketed her for weeks, free from the unknowing worship of demons.

For so long Tia had sought to control her own destiny. Was it possible that her destiny was safer in the hands of Pedaiah's sovereign God? Could she trust Him to keep them safe? Could she trust that even if they were not safe, they were in His hands?

It will take a mighty humbling on my part.

But what rewards for such humility? The desperate need to grasp at the false security of position and possessions, this need would be replaced by the courage to risk everything, knowing she was held in the One God's hand.

She lifted her head to the wine-dark sparkling sky and saw the truth. The full truth.

From her very birth Tia had longed to have purpose. To make a difference in her world, to have an impact. She had quenched the longing with inferior excitements and inconsequential rebellions. Because deeper than the longing lay fear. Fear that true risk would bring true loss, and without her security, she would be nothing.

But it was untrue. Without those things, she would be *more* herself.

Set free, Tia could change the world.

And freedom came only through the knowledge that she did not wield ultimate control. Someone greater, someone who *loved,* held her life in His hands.

Pedaiah's first prayer over her whispered through the Garden's cool breeze and became her own—spoken from within and without, for she could not have remembered each word.

Deliver me, Yahweh, from the snare of the enemy, from the poison of the evil one. Cover me with Your feathers, and under Your wings let me trust. Let Your truth be my shield. Let me not be afraid of the terror by night, nor of the arrow that flies by day, nor for the plague that walks in darkness, nor for the destruction that would steal my strength.

She saw the king watching her from below, those empty eyes gleaming. But the peace that rushed into the empty places of her soul was like a cool drink and a warm fire all at once. The gentle embrace of a friend, the approving smile of a father. The call to fight a battle.

Glowing with this freedom, strengthened by its promise, Tia lifted a prayer of her own. "What then, Yahweh? Tell me how to rise up and risk. Tell me how to save my family."

Let it all go.

The words were as clear as the prayer. She reached with her heart for understanding.

Her luxuries. The palace. The kingdom. Let it all go.

We must flee.

She comes again.

I watch. Watch her. Watch everywhere, that no harm will come to her. Prowl the night, listening, protecting.

She is mine to protect.

Some change is within my grasp.

My favorite places no longer satisfy.

The black roots, distasteful. The gray branches that would shield, scratch my skin.

Skin, dirt, beard. Nails. Not what they should be. Hate them.

I would be different. But I must choose.

I hear her, sounds with her mouth.

Words. They are words.

Yahweh.

I know this word.
Most High. Master.
Even kings have a Master.
Must submit.
No, no, resist.
Submit.

Chapter 38

Tia found her mother in the darkness of the rooftop garden where Kaldu's body had been found. Amytis leaned against the sandy stone wall, her back to Tia and her face to the desert. A scatter- ing of crushed yellow petals drifted at her fingertips, like jewels in the moonlight.

Tia would speak to her about what they both knew of the future.

But first she would speak of the past.

"Mother."

Amytis half turned, then resumed her gaze beyond the double city walls. *Is she weeping?*

An unfamiliar pity swept Tia to her mother's side. She joined her post at the wall and leaned her head against Amytis's shoulder.

Amytis inclined her head and her cheek grazed Tia's hair. Tia exhaled the resentment of years and soaked in this small sign of affection.

"Mother, I have been a fool, and you were right. Amel is not to be trusted, and I have interfered in your plans. Forgive me."

Her repentance had grown between the Hanging Gardens and this rooftop, and if she had expected condemnation, she found instead a woman shattered by her own secrets and lies.

"You deserved so much more, Tia. In spite of everything, you deserved more."

Tia turned Amytis to face her, studied the heavy tears sparkling on her dark lashes. "What grieves you?"

Amytis blinked, releasing a tiny shower. "I have tried, Daughter. The gods know I have tried, all these years, to give you the love you needed. But I could not, and in the end, your father—the king—loved you all the more for it, and I believed it would be enough."

Tia still held her arms and slid her hands to grasp her mother's, warm and smooth. "I understand. When you look at me, you are reminded of your mistake, and that is difficult."

Amytis tilted her head, a flicker of confusion in her eyes. "Mistake?"

Tia dropped her face, ashamed to speak of something so personal. But she was finished with secrets. "Your—unfaithfulness—to the king."

Amytis's hands convulsed on hers. Tia winced at the iron grip and lifted her head.

"Is that what he told you, Tia? That I had been

363

unfaithful?" Her eyes had turned to fire, the tears like sparks.

Tia opened her mouth to speak, but no sound emerged.

Amytis made a little noise in her throat, an angry snarl of injustice, and peered into the darkness. "Why should I be surprised? Why should I have expected Shadir to speak truth?"

"What is the truth?" *How many times have I asked that question?* And yet tonight, Tia knew she would hear it at last.

Amytis released Tia's hands and placed her fingertips along the edge of the stone wall, retreating into her own memory.

"I was not unfaithful to the king, Tia. I was— forced."

Tia fell back, heat flooding her limbs.

Who is your father? Zagros's question pounded like a drumbeat in her head.

"Raped? By whom?"

She huffed a tiny, bitter laugh. "Shadir."

Tia gripped the wall as the sky spun. "Shadir is my father?"

She would deny it. There would be some mistake.

"Yes."

"But, how—why—he has remained in the palace all these years! Why did the king not have him executed?"

"Because I lied." Amytis's lip quivered, and Tia

pulled her close, until their arms were clasped and they stood eye to eye.

"Shadir threatened me—after. Threatened your sisters, who were tiny babes at the time. He had so much power, I knew he would hurt them."

"But Father knew?"

"He discovered me. I had fought back, fought hard. There were bruises, injuries."

"What did you tell him?"

"That a slave had forced himself on me." Her breath caught on this, and the tears welled and spilled. "He had the slave executed, Tia." Sobs broke her voice. "An innocent man, killed because of my lies."

Tia pulled her mother to herself, head on her shoulder, and Amytis clutched her so fiercely Tia could feel her desperation to be forgiven seeping into her own body.

"When I learned I was with child, both of them knew. The king had left me to my chambers for weeks, so it was clear to him. I tried to lie to Shadir, but he has the knowledge of the gods, and somehow he always knew. All these years I have feared he would reveal the truth. I have lived as though he were attacking me still."

"Why did you not simply rid yourself of me?" Tia had to ask the question. Before Tia's birth her mother could have found an asû to help. After her birth it would have been the king's prerogative to expose her on the riverbanks.

Amytis paused in her confession, lifted her tear-flooded face, and Tia sensed that perhaps this had been her desire.

"I considered it. I will not lie. But only before your birth. Once I held you in my arms, it never entered my mind."

Tia smiled through her own tears.

"But as you grew, you were so—so unruly, so defiant. I feared you would turn evil, like Shadir. I did all I could to confine you, to subdue you."

Tia exhaled a little laugh. "I did not make it easy."

"No, you did not. And every bit of fire you displayed only made the king love you more." Amytis wrapped her hands around Tia's. "He was a good man, Tia. Loved me in spite of my defilement, and loved you best because of it." She touched Tia's cheek with her fingers. "He would tell me often how much you looked like me, how you were becoming so beautiful, just like your mother. Hoping to erase the knowledge of your birth."

Tia mirrored her mother's touch, tracing her own wet cheek with her hand. "I always hoped that it was true, that I was as beautiful as my mother."

"You have a beauty that shines from deep within. I see that now. The fire I feared in you, it is what makes you alive, fearless, what makes you a better woman than I shall ever be."

Her words fell on Tia like a warm anointing, and she bowed her head, breathed the scented air, and soaked in the precious words.

Her mother embraced her.

For the first time in Tia's memory, her mother wrapped warm arms around her, pulled her to herself, and held her tight. Tia circled her waist with her own arms, pressed her face into her mother's neck, and wept.

"*Sshh,* little girl." Mother whispered the words against her ear. "All will be well."

Tia collapsed into this embrace, filling with a brightness that matched the stars and a warmth that beat back the desert winds. Cocooned in the faint scent of her mother's perfume, the salted tears released the bitterness of years and replaced it with a sweet hope for the future.

When at last Tia broke away, it was with a confession of her own.

"I have not been fearless, Mother. I have risked only that which I did not fear to lose. But that has changed."

She tried to share it all with her, to tell her of Pedaiah's love and his One God, and the blessed freedom and joy that came with abandoning oneself to the sovereignty of this good God. But the words fell short of expressing this new life and seemed to deepen her mother's anxiety, not lift it.

"What is it, Mother?"

"You speak like your father." She smiled reassuringly. "The king. He had long been fascinated by the Jews' Yahweh. It took effort for me to draw him back to the worship of our Babylonian gods before they brought punishment for his disloyalty."

This was something to speak of at another time. For now, they must talk of the future. Tia leaned against the wall, studied the desert.

"Zagros leaves tonight?"

"His wagons have been loaded from the treasury, and he will slip away under cover of darkness."

"There is no bringing him back? Promises to keep the secret of my birth?"

Her mother bit her lip and shook her head. "The truth is too volatile. Now that he knows it, he would not trust us to keep it quiet."

"Shadir will force me to marry Amel tomorrow. And if he doesn't kill the family before the festival, it will not be long after."

"Yes."

Tia broached the idea formed in the Gardens. "Mother, we must take the family, take Father, and we must flee Babylon."

She was silent, her profile stony.

"Perhaps it will not be forever. But with no mad king to reveal, no princess to marry, no royal family anywhere present, Shadir will have a difficult time wresting the crown for Amel. Even if he succeeds, we will make our plans from the safety of Assyria, or perhaps Egypt, and we will come back stronger, ready to claim the throne. But first we must get everyone to safety."

Her mother inhaled deeply, her face still set toward the desert. "I am afraid."

Tia wanted to agree with her, to tell her that in this they were joined. But she could not, for in truth she felt nothing but excitement, nothing but a surety that she had at last released her grip on things that would never satisfy, to fight for what was truth.

Tia studied the bright and calming stars spread across the dark comfort of the night sky, traced their journey to the horizon of the desert, the desert that beckoned with safety and anonymity, and knew that her deepest longing was about to be realized.

She was about to change the world.

Chapter 39

They assembled after midnight in the family chambers of the imprisoned Jewish king. Somehow it seemed fitting that this group of royal rebels would find common ground with those who had survived among the treachery of Babylon for over forty years.

Tia and her mother arrived last, entering the outermost room of the chamber complex together, the queen leaning on her arm as though she had aged a decade in this one day. They joined a small crowd already waiting—Pedaiah and his mother, Marta, as well as his sister and younger brothers. Daniel smiling in welcome. Tia's sisters' two husbands had also been summoned, though they knew less of the danger they faced than anyone, perhaps. They sat in clusters on carved chairs and benches, even the woven carpet.

The chamber was lit by only a single brazier, enough warmth and light for the room, but the single light source danced grotesque shadows across the whitewashed walls behind the group, a bizarre doubling of their party.

Daniel crossed the room at once and took her mother's hands in his own, kissed her cheeks. "Your beauty is undimmed," he said, still smiling.

Her mother's lips parted, as though the compliment were unexpected. Had they been enemies when the king was whole? She tried to smile. "I— I am glad you have come. He always trusted you."

"And he loved you more than Babylon."

Another compliment, and her mother flushed with pleasure and her smile was genuine.

Daniel led Tia to a chair and she stood for a moment, suspended there at the fringes of the small crowd, their upturned faces glowing in the brazier light, a mixture of apprehension and bewilderment.

The mysteries of the past weeks had been

clarified through the last evening. Amytis had been working with Kaldu to uncover Shadir's plans, and he had been killed for the knowledge he gained. The method of the killing, along with the slave Ying's, was meant to discredit the king, to blackmail Tia. And Shealtiel—he was merely an obstacle. All of it had led them to this night, to this secret gathering of those who would not be quietly pushed aside.

Pedaiah emerged from the gloom and reached his hand to her. Tia grasped it and would not let go, all her deep longing for him poured into that handclasp. She drank in his face, his eyes, that scarred chin.

"We are leaving, Pedaiah." She whispered the words for him alone.

"I know."

What would he say if she asked him to join her? To flee Babylon, his family, his people? Her hand trembled in his and she said nothing.

"Come." He led her to the group and she curled up on the floor at her mother's feet. Somehow it did not seem that this meeting was hers to lead. Pedaiah sat cross-legged beside her, his knee brushing her thigh and his arm stretched around her back. She warmed to the familiarity but saw her mother's raised eyebrows and felt a flush creep across her skin. From across the room, Marta glared. *Does she no longer wish me as part of her family?*

It was Daniel who stood, Daniel who spoke to them all as the wise man that he was, who delivered the truth to those who had not yet heard.

"It is no longer safe in Babylon for the family of the king. The plots have grown thick and the danger imminent. We must find a way to remove you from the threat until it has been removed."

Nergal growled, "What are these threats you speak of?" His face reddened. "And why do we listen to this Jew?"

"Nergal!" Her mother's voice was razor sharp. "You would do well to listen. The king trusted Belteshazzar in all matters, as any future kings of Babylon should."

She spoke of her grandsons, but it was no secret that Nergal and Nabonidus, Tia's other sister's husband, would have accepted the crown had it been offered. Nergal settled into grumpy silence, arms folded across his burly chest.

Daniel acknowledged Nergal's outburst with a nod and an explanation. "As you know, in Babylon, the magi, above all else, consider themselves kingmakers. The mage Shadir has long conspired to put his own man on the throne. His young protégé, Amel-Marduk, is in truth the king's only son."

"What!" The news rocked both noblemen. Nergal lurched forward, hands on his knees, and Nabonidus stood and shook a fist at Daniel.

"It is a lie!"

Daniel's small smile was patient, even kindly. He looked only to her mother.

The queen nodded once. "It is the truth."

At this, Nabonidus kicked his chair and sent it sliding against the wall and Nergal cursed loudly.

"There is more." Daniel's words were soft but held authority. They all waited, hushed, as though they did not know what came next.

"Shadir wishes to amplify Amel's claim to the throne by marrying him to Tiamat, who is not the king's daughter."

No shocked outrage met this announcement, only a silence that spoke as loudly.

"Shadir plans to reveal the king's condition to the people at the festival tomorrow, and if Tia does not marry Amel—and I am afraid even if she does—Shadir will have each of the royal family executed to prevent any other bid for the throne."

Nergal stood. "He'll be in a brick furnace before dawn."

"Sit down." Her mother had regained some control. "You are a fool. Shadir has half the magi loyal to his cause."

"The problem," Daniel said, "is that we do not know which half."

"Traitors!" Nabonidus's voice was the whine of a child.

"Yes, traitors." Her mother smiled grimly. "But deadly all the same."

Nergal was unwilling to admit defeat. "We

must fight! Bring the army down on the entire class of magi. Execute them all if we cannot be sure who will stand for us."

"Your first charitable act as king, Nergal?" Amytis's calm superiority, her blatant disdain, cooled his zeal and set him back in his chair.

Nabonidus remained against the wall, pouting.

Her mother looked to Daniel, giving up leadership to the king's chief advisor, and it seemed to Tia that she gave it willingly.

The old mage nodded. "There will be a time for ferreting out traitors, Nergal. But you must act from a position of strength, not defensive desperation. And your first concern must be for your wife and son."

Nergal clenched a fist against the arm of his chair and glared at her mother. "Why is this Jew telling us how to act?"

Her answer was pointed, obvious. "Because he is the only one with any sense."

At this, her sister's husband dropped his shoulders, sighed loudly. He was difficult, but he loved his family, this much was true.

Silence stretched for several moments as they each contemplated what was to come. The brazier smoked and the oily scent filled Tia's senses.

"We must make a plan," Daniel finally said. "And there is not much time."

It was Tia's turn to join the conversation. "I have been thinking." Attention turned to her where she sat on the carpet. "I should proceed with tomorrow's events as planned. The procession, the chariot race. After the races, before winners are announced, there will be time for me to prepare for the marriage ceremony. Everyone's attention will be on the festival. We can make our escape during that time."

"The chariot races again, Tia? Must you?"

The annoyance in her mother's voice made her smile, where once she would have lashed back. "At least I have not joined the bull-leapers. Yet."

Quiet laughter around the chamber lightened the mood.

Her mother shrugged, defeated. "There will be much to do in preparation. We must have chariots packed and waiting, animals ready. The children and their mothers. And—" She broke off, a storm cloud of emotion crossing her face.

"And my father." Tia locked eyes with Nergal, Daniel, and Pedaiah. "We will take my father."

No mention was made of her peculiar relationship to the king. No need to speak of her parentage again.

"It will not be easy." Nergal was one of the few who had maintained some contact with the king over the years. "He is not easily influenced."

Tia rubbed at her eyes, burning from the late hour and the smoky air. "I will have to be there. He trusts me. But I cannot do it alone."

Her mother studied her twisted hands in her

lap, her voice barely above a whisper. "Where—how—shall we—transport him?"

Tia grasped her hand. "Leave that to others. You coordinate the rest of the women and children and all that will be needed for our journey."

"Journey to where?" It was Pedaiah's entrance into the discussion, and attention turned to him in the shadows. "Where will you go?"

"To Egypt." Amytis's voice strengthened with the change of topic. "Our relationship with Pharaoh Amasis has been strong of late. He may not exactly welcome us, but he will keep us until it is decided how we will strike back."

Tia watched Pedaiah's face. Their journey to Egypt would take them through southern Judaea. Would a glimpse of his homeland be enough to persuade him to join them? A hollow thud of fear hit her chest. Even if he did, would he stay there when they crossed to Egypt? His expression was unreadable, and he did not look toward her.

They spent another hour working out the details. There were provisions to be gathered, decisions about how many slaves to take and which ones, treasury items to secure to pay for their passage. All of it must be accomplished in a single day, under the watchful eyes of the palace magi.

They stumbled off to their own chambers, staggering their exits so as not to attract notice from any who might still be prowling the palace. Tia lingered, hoping for a private word with Pedaiah.

When at last her mother embraced her and left the chambers, and his family disappeared to deeper rooms, they were alone.

"Something has happened." He touched her hair, lifted it across her shoulder. "With your mother."

The warmth of the memory brought a smile. "Yes. The truth is a wonderful healer."

"I am glad. Glad you are reconciled. You will need each other in the days ahead."

Because she would not have him? Tia cursed her lack of courage. Why could she not voice her questions, her desires? Did she still fear to risk when the loss might be too great?

"I do not know how long we will be gone, Pedaiah."

"You may never return."

It was said as a gentle warning, but still the truth was a blow. She chewed her lip, nodding. "We may not. I must be willing to face that sacrifice to keep them safe."

"Strange to think of you crossing Judaea, where my family belongs. And my family here, where you belong."

Yes, but where will you be?

"Perhaps your family will soon be able to go home. Everything is changing."

He shook his head and set his jaw toward the window as though he could see his homeland from the tiny square opening. "The prophets have given us the word of Yahweh. Seventy years in Babylon. It will not be my generation that leads us home. Perhaps my son's."

At this, her stomach twisted, a tiny spin that affected her balance. She gripped his arm.

"Come with us, Pedaiah. You can see Judaea. We can be together."

He did not pull his gaze from the window. "Trust me, Tia, I have thought of little else all night. I have sought the wisdom of Daniel and have prayed for guidance."

"And what have you decided?" Her heartbeat hung suspended.

"I have no decision."

She breathed out the tension and turned to the door.

"Tia—" He grabbed her arm and pulled her into his embrace, his face against her hair. "My family, my people, my duty—they are all here. But you are mine as well."

She could hear the pain in his voice but could do nothing to rid him of it when her own heart was breaking. "Perhaps there are more sacrifices to be made."

She knew not what she meant by the words. For whose sacrifice did she call? The look in his eyes was unbearable, and Tia pulled away and escaped the chamber, then fled through the silent halls to her own rooms.

Only a few hours remained before daylight. Tia would spend them in her bed, trying to gain strength for what lay ahead.

Chapter 40

Their final day in Babylon dawned scorchingly hot, the strange and heavy moisture lifted at last. Omarsa roused Tia well past daybreak, concern straining her features. She had not heard Tia slip in only hours before.

"Are you well, Princess?"

How is that question to be answered? Tia nodded, then turned her head and breathed in the morning air. Where would she be when tomorrow dawned?

The palace was in full uproar this morning. Between the festival and her marriage, the corridors buzzed with the frantic activity of slaves intent on meeting expectations. The frenzy was the royal family's ally—much of their own activity might be hidden by it.

By prior agreement they did not meet together this morning, any of them. Each knew his or her assignment for the day, and less attention would be drawn if they did not interact. Somewhere outside the palace, in a stable yard nearby, six wagons and their horses were readied for a long journey, and here inside the palace, clothing and provisions were secreted out by two of the slaves they had decided to take—her nephews' nursemaid and a trusted cook who could keep them from starvation.

Tia took her morning meal in her room, then dressed and left to do her part. She wandered through the lower corridors, trying to appear relaxed, as though the muscles across her upper back were not strung tight with tension and her stomach knotted with the unknown.

She passed her older sisters in the east wing, each carrying a basket. Had she ever seen them carrying anything themselves? Tia gave them a strained smile, but they passed her with wide eyes, as though the revelations of the night had changed her into something other than their overlooked youngest sister.

She felt the eyes of the palace on her as she strolled toward the main arch. Slaves peered at her from lowered eyes, harem women stared boldly. But it was the magi and diviners clustered in courtyards and whispering in corridors that quickened her pulse with their suspicious watching, watching, always watching. She crossed the final courtyard and fought an involuntary shudder at the antagonism directed toward her back.

The city pulled Tia into its heat, but the air of frivolity common to a festival day did nothing to relieve her apprehension. She must be seen attending to her horses this morning. Lack of attention before a chariot race would be noted and perhaps passed along to those who would ask questions. She looked them over, patted heads, spoke with the stableman, but her heart was not present. He'd have them ready for tonight, but did she even care?

Back in the palace she had one more task for the day, but she delayed until the afternoon was well spent. Instead, she had Omarsa and Gula help her pack her belongings—the city still believed she would marry the Median prince tonight and be taken to her mother's homeland—and the women seemed genuinely saddened to see her leave. Though Tia had determined to take Omarsa with her when they escaped, she would not tell her until the time drew near.

Finally, there could be no more putting off, and she braced herself for one more encounter with Shadir.

My father.

Revulsion coursed through her, a wave of disbelief and anger that sickened and weakened. But she could not afford weakness. Not today.

Yahweh, give me strength to face what is next, to walk boldly into Your plan.

As expected, she found him in the Hall of Magi. But she would not enter. Not today and never again.

She waited at the columned entrance, gazing down into the chamber, waiting for him to notice her presence.

As though they were connected in some perverse way, he lifted his head from his charts and returned her attention.

"Princess." His lips seemed to hardly move. A chilled perspiration rose on her neck.

"You have won, Shadir."

"I did not realize we competed."

"I will marry Amel-Marduk as you wish. I have sent the Median prince away in the night, though it is to be kept secret until the festival."

Shadir used long fingers to push his hair from his face, but his expression remained unchanged. "You have shown wisdom, Princess."

"I will tell you again, my family is to be kept safe." A useless injunction.

He nodded, slowly, twice. As though he carefully considered her request and had acceded. "Whatever you say, Princess."

It was enough to put him off for the day. To allow them their preparations. She lifted her chin, threw him a hateful glance, and left the Hall.

The hours crawled until nightfall. It seemed impossible that with her life on the precipice of great change, she should spend the afternoon in her chambers letting Omarsa yank a comb through her hair and Gula fuss over the packing of her last few pieces of jewelry. But others were tending to the details of their journey. And to the preparation for removing the king from the Gardens. All would be ready when she would again step onto the stage of this drama, to play her final part.

Through her darkening chamber window, Tia heard the swell of the festival and left Omarsa's ministrations to stare over Babylon. Thousands took to the streets, to follow the procession of Marduk and Ishtar, their statues carefully guarded in chariots and led through the city to the Akitu House, where their ritual marriage would be performed to ensure the fertility of the kingdom. Drumbeats lifted to her window, each beat louder than the last as though the drummers climbed unseen on steps to the heavens. She could make out the piping of flutes at the head of the procession, but it was chants of people that thickened the air.

What did the One God think of all this celebration?

When the sun had disappeared at last and spreading darkness had reached the western shore of the desert, Tia turned from the window and dressed in her running clothes—the Persian trousers her mother despised, the bindings around her chest and ribs, the short belted tunic. Omarsa caged her hair with gold combs, but she would wear no veil.

Always before a run she steadied her mind, focused her thoughts on the air in her lungs, the muscles in her calves. Tonight, the chariot race called for heightened focus. Instead, her muscles trembled with what would come after.

It was time for the ultimate risk.

Head high, Tia strode through the palace corridors, trailing two guards. They reached the palace entrance, and she paused at the head of the wide stairs that led to the street, drinking in a last look at her city from this familiar perch. Below her, news of her presence lit through the crowd, and a mighty cheer arose. Tia lifted her arm in a salute, and they screamed with accolades. She was a favorite whenever she raced.

The two guards escorted her down the stairs and across the Processional Way, and the people parted before them, leaving a wide swath of stone. They reached the city wall at the Ishtar Gate, climbed the internal staircase, and Tia emerged alone on top of the wall to another shriek from the citizens.

Four chariots, two abreast on the wall, awaited the festivities, their horses harnessed and pawing the stones expectantly. She recognized her own pair of blacks pulling one of the first two chariots. She would race first against Kuri, who was favored to win. But the people would cheer for her. Once, this would have thrilled her. Tonight, she cared for only the race that would occur after this one—the rush to leave the city, the protection of her family.

Yellow torches flamed from the wall's waist-high crenellations, posted at the space of six strides, from the Ishtar Gate to the Enlil. In the streets below, the people waved pennants from here to the finish, a sea of speckled white in the torches and moonlight.

Even the fields that lay between the double walls held spectators. No one wanted to miss the princess in her final chariot race, nor the marriage that would take place after.

The participants wandered the wall, receiving anxious encouragement from their sponsors, pacing nervous circuits around their gilded chariots.

But Tia's anxiety was not race-born. The fluttering in her stomach, the clammy chill across her neck, the dryness of her mouth—all these would continue beyond the finish line, until her family fled along the desert road outside the walls.

Until I say good-bye to Pedaiah.

"Princess, you are ready?" The race master bowed, a small man with a protruding lower lip that made him look sullen.

Tia nodded and tried to smile. There would be time for thoughts of good-byes later. Or perhaps not, which might be better. Never mind that she feared she would be leaving parts of herself in Babylon tonight.

Tia climbed into the black and gold two-wheeled chariot and unlooped the reins. The wind tugged at her hair and tunic, and the horses snorted and pawed the dusty wall, as though they felt her impatience to be off. The chants of the city pounded upward, a rhythm that infected her blood, set it pounding to match. The reins felt slick in her hands, and she wrapped the leather around each palm twice.

Kuri gained his chariot, and Tia pulled her gaze from him and the city below while she pulled her thoughts from the future and from Pedaiah. She must give herself to the race now, abandon all that she was to this central purpose.

The inner wall of Babylon was wide enough for two chariots to race abreast, but only one could make the turn at the Enlil Gate and circle back, passing the other. If she were not first to the turn, the odds of pulling the lead on the sprint back to the Ishtar Gate were slim. More important, a tight race at the turn might send one of the chariots against and over the lip of the wall. Neither horse nor driver would survive such a fall.

The crowd quieted in anticipation of the start, and the moment suspended, stretched out like the city wall before her, thread-thin and taut. Once the trumpet sounded, there would be no turning back. The events of the night before her would take on life, could not be stopped.

The wind rose against her back, the stars poured silver over her head, and she raised a disjointed prayer to the One God.

Give me the only victory with meaning. The safety of my family.

The starting trumpet blasted, she flicked the reins in reflex, and the city bellowed their excitement. The horses surged and with them the blood in her veins. They were off!

Stars and torches and blazing city streamed past, a torturous tide of wind and light that threatened to sweep her from her mount. Kuri's chariot nearly kissed hers, his white horses gleaming, heaving, pounding beside her blacks. The night air tore at Tia's hair combs, stole them from her, and her hair streaked behind in wild release.

The Enlil Gate, too far to be seen, awaited. And she would arrive there first. Thoughts of escape and family fell away, replaced by the intense ache of competition—that unrelenting drive to win that had always fired her spirit.

The leather reins twitched in her hands and the horses' hooves kicked dust into her eyes. Tia watched the wall ahead, watched Kuri beside her, heard the roar of the crowd below.

Her chest bindings grew damp, then cold in the night wind. Smoky torches and salt burned her eyes.

"Hyah!" She snapped the reins over her team's backs, urging them faster. The jeweled bracelets she had donned slid along her forearms to the elbow and pinched her skin.

The pounding, pounding of hoofbeats, the

rumble of chariot wheels, the huff of animal and her own beat of breath, all combined into a heady mix that tore a shout of glory from her chest. Sweet victory, bitter defeat—it almost mattered not. All that mattered was this moment, to be alive, to be free, to run.

"To run in the paths He has marked brings freedom and glory."

Like the chariot race held on the wall. Full life, an adventure lived, but within the confines of these stones. To breach the path would be foolish, deadly. But to remain, to remain was to live gloriously.

The scream in her chest turned to laughter, a laughter that swelled in her lungs until they would burst with it, laughter that burned through all her fear like fire through chaff and left her purified. Purified and ready.

The Enlil Gate grew in the distance, like a date palm tree springing unnaturally toward the sky. Kuri still ground along beside her, eyes bulging and teeth bared.

Time to finish this.

Torches flashed past in swift succession, as though thrust from the underworld and then extinguished. She leaned into the wind, sang out encouragement to her horses, and felt the chariot pull ahead.

She reached the gate before Kuri. Braced her feet outward against the walls. Leaned into the turn. Tighter, tighter. Chariot lifting to one wheel and horses perilously close to oblivion. Shrieks of the crowd. Did they retreat from the wall in fear of horse and chariot and driver plunging over their heads?

Kuri came up hard and fast behind her turn. Her own chariot barely pulled right before his skimmed in the opposite direction. The scrape of wood jarred her courage, sent her heart clawing upward into her throat.

Headed home.

All that remained was to outpace Kuri for the thirty ashlû back to the Ishtar Gate. Her arms trembled with fatigue, but her grip remained tight.

She sensed the Hanging Gardens on her left, perched above the city walls. Did the king watch? Did he know his Tia raced this night? Or that she would come to save him soon?

The scattered shouts and general roar of the crowd coalesced into a pulsing shout. Her name —shouted from a thousand lips—raised to the heavens.

Tia-mat! Tia-mat!

Fields and city, torch and dust, stars and sky flew past and then she was there, flying at the Ishtar Gate, pulling up on the reins, screaming commands at her horses before they flung themselves into the desert.

Kuri rolled in behind her, defeated. The race master bounded to her chariot, took her hand as she stepped to the stones and to the edge of the wall, then raised her fist above her head.

Below, the city yelled their approval, brandished their colorful pennants, chanted her name.

Tia searched the wall for any who would share her joy. None of her family was present.

Only Shadir.

He stood a few paces off, arms crossed and hands invisible inside the sleeves of his cloak. He nodded once, his lips sealed and eyes unmoving.

"Congratulations, Princess. It seems the night is an auspicious one for you in many ways."

She bowed, hating herself for the humiliation. "But you must excuse me, Shadir." Tia pulled at the sweat-soaked tunic clinging to her skin. "I must prepare for the more important events of the evening."

"We await you eagerly." He spoke of Amel, though the young mage-prince was not to be seen. Did he linger at the Akitu House already, anticipating her arrival? He would have a long wait.

With a last look at Babylon from the height of its massive walls, Tia escaped to the stairs and let her guards before and aft funnel her through the city, back to the palace to say good-bye to the only life she had ever known.

Chapter 41

Tia saw none of her coconspirators upon entering the palace. The first courtyard lay in darkness. Harem women and slaves alike attended the festival and had no need for palace entertainment.

She left her escorts and hurried along the corridors, her feet ticking a frantic rhythm toward her chambers.

Omarsa and Gula met her at the door, instructed to remain to prepare her for the ceremony.

"My lady." Omarsa bowed, a slight smile twitching her lips. "You have survived another race, I see."

"Survived and triumphed, Omarsa." Tia couldn't help the bit of pride in her voice.

Gula's pale face emerged from the shadows. "How long until the ceremony?"

"Soon. There are several more races, and then the people will be expecting me at the Akitu House." Tia stripped her tunic and trousers. "I would wash first."

Her haste was no doubt logical in the minds of her women, though its reason was not what they believed. They unwound her chest bindings and led her, naked and shivering, to the bath chamber.

The women spilled two pots of warm water over her head, and the dousing ran into her eyes and splashed noisily against the floor. Back in her dressing chamber, droplets clung to her eyelashes and refracted the colors of the room into a myriad of jewels—sparkling rubies and diamonds. A room of luxury she would leave behind.

Omarsa insisted on perfumes, but when they brought the wedding robes, Tia held up a hand. "I do not need those."

Omarsa frowned. "Your mother especially chose—"

"Plans have changed." Excitement tinged her voice. They were really doing this—escaping the palace and all its secrets!

Tia tied her wet hair with a strip of fabric and pointed to one of her everyday robes across a chair, a dark linen that would blend with the shadows. Gula lifted it, a quizzical look on her brow.

"I will not be married tonight." Tia took them both in with her glance, her voice lowered. "We—the family—are leaving."

"Leaving?" Gula rubbed the palm of one hand with her thumb.

"Leaving Babylon. All of us. There is a plot afoot to murder my family, and I will take them to safety before it is accomplished."

Gula's face blanched and she reached a hand to the wall to steady herself. Did she fear that as Tia's personal slave she would be included in the massacre?

"Gula, you must carry a message for me." Better to keep her busy, to keep her mind occupied. "Go to the alley behind the northwest side of the palace. You will find wagons loaded there and some of my family. Tell my mother that I am ready for what comes next."

Gula's lip trembled. "I—I do not understand—"

"Tell her that, Gula. She will know what to do. Go!"

The girl fled from the room, and Tia turned to Omarsa, whose narrowed eyes held more suspicion and challenge than fear "You are coming with us, Omarsa. I need you on the road, and I will need you wherever our journey takes us. Gather some things and meet us in the alley. We leave within the hour."

Omarsa's face was impassive, a wall of non-expression. But then a quick nod and she bowed and left the room.

A last swift survey of her chambers. Her essential belongings had already been packed for her supposed trip to Media. Tia fingered the silk robe meant for her wedding and a wave of sadness swept over her—for what, she could not say. She dropped the robe to the bed and took to the corridors once more.

Her tunic and robe twisted around her legs as she ran, and she lifted both to increase her speed. The steps that led underground were barely lit, and her sandal slaps echoed against the stone floors. She found the bottom, raced through the three vaulted chambers, then up the spiral stairs that led to the seventh tier of the Gardens.

Tia unlocked the door with her key. *For the last time.* Never again would she leave her father caged.

The Gardens were silent. Too silent. Had the trusted guards her mother sent done their work?

She slipped to the sixth tier, then the fifth. The darkness was a solid thing here, with only the stars and moon for light, and yellow flowers, oddly muted.

"Father?" Tia whispered, afraid that guards who kept her father locked up would hear and run her off.

A terrible shriek pierced the night and drew her upright. Tiny hairs prickled her neck and a shudder ran through her.

The king appeared, gripped by two guards—her mother's men.

"Where are the others?" Her voice was hoarse, as though unused for days.

One of the two jerked his head backward toward the lowest levels. "They will not detain us."

Her father thrashed in the grasp of the younger men, his eyes huge and white and his lips drawn back over his teeth.

"Father"—Tia reached a hand to him and spoke gently—"it is Tia. All is well. Do not fear."

He eyed her carefully, still struggling. His hands were curved into claws, the nails long and yellowed. If he could have reached their necks, he would have slashed open the throats of the guards.

She slid closer, both hands held out, palms up in invitation rather than aggression. "Father, listen to my voice."

His scuffling eased.

"We are leaving here, Father. We are leaving together." Tia was close enough to touch him now, and she grasped his roughened hands in her own. He held still, his eyes searching hers with something close to recognition.

"That's it, Father. All is well." He smelled foul, rotting earth and waste, and spittle clung to his beard. She caressed his hands, whispered to him, reassured him with her eyes.

"Come with me, Father. Let me take you from here."

The guards interpreted her words as a signal and pulled to lead him upward toward her secret door. He jerked, lashed out with both arms, and struck Tia on the cheek. Her teeth dug into tender flesh and she tasted blood. She lifted a hand to her face, and the guards regained their hold on his arms. From beyond the Gardens, across the city, a mighty cheer lifted from thousands of citizens. The races were concluding.

"Bring him." Tia turned and led the way upward. They were running out of time.

···

The larger beasts come to me in my prowling, snatch at my limbs, drag me where I do not wish to go.

But then she comes. So like her mother, who never comes.

I wish to speak her name, to reach for her. But my flesh does not obey my mind, which is only now beginning to clear, like the desert air after a sandstorm. Still gritty with confusion, still hazy and indistinct.

But one thing I know. I must follow her.

They wish me to walk upright and I am out of practice. Their grip on me is painful. I allow it, cease fighting it; they bring me along behind her.

Tiamat.

Daughter.

Up, and then down. Through darkness under-ground, into moonlit darkness once more, but not my Gardens. Not my familiar Gardens.

I am returning, but I will not fully return until I submit. The Most High has called my name and He will not be denied by a mortal king.

Tia sped along the back corridor, the strange trio in her wake, to the back entrance of the palace. Here the narrow alley ran alongside, a trench between palace and city wall. No torches lit the path, but even in the gray murk she could see the series of tan wagons, hitched and waiting. The alley smelled of rancid garbage. She searched the darkness for the one she must see before leaving, but Pedaiah did not appear.

Instead, her mother's form flew toward her, her robes fluttering. At the sight of her husband, Mother drew up and sucked in a ragged breath. How long had it been since she had seen his face? Four fingers went to her lips, as though to capture breath before it left her completely. With her other hand she reached out, tentative and too far away to actually touch him. But the pity, the anguish in her eyes, it clogged Tia's throat with emotion.

"You brought him." Amytis's words were a whisper, an exhalation.

"We must get him secured." Tia spoke to the guards. They dragged him to the back of a wagon and pushed him upward onto its bed, then jumped in alongside. Tia joined them, ignoring her mother's squeak of protest. The rough wood of the wagon's dirty side scraped her leg, set it on fire. She hunkered down beside her father's huddled form, tried to connect with him through the eyes.

Where is Pedaiah? Tia had her answer, then. They both had a duty to their people. One that did not include each other. Would it be Judith who filled his life once Tia was gone?

Her mother came to stand beside Tia's place in the wagon, her long fingers curled over the side.

Still staring at her father, Tia patted her mother's cold hand, her heart numb. "We must be off. Find your place."

The walls were closing in on her. She felt the cold stone creeping closer, and a nausea borne of anxiety churned her stomach. Her mother disappeared into the darkness. Her wagon would be closer to the head of the procession, and Mother would give the order to be off.

Far ahead, Tia could hear the *snick* of the first driver, urging his wagon forward. A last look at the narrow door, where they had each emerged from the palace.

There—a shadow, a figure, familiar and beloved.

Tia kneeled at the wagon's side and reached for him. "Pedaiah!"

He ran the length of the alley, grabbed her fingers, shoved a foot into the spokes of their wagon wheel, and thrust upward until their faces were a breath apart.

"Wait!" Tia called to the driver.

Pedaiah held the wagon's side with one hand and her face with the other. He bent his lips to her cheek, her hair, her ear. "Be safe, Princess."

A low whimper came from her throat, the sound of an animal, frightened or injured. How could she leave him?

"Pedaiah . . ."

He silenced her lips with a kiss, long and heartfelt, and she heard and felt nothing but his kiss until at last she realized that there was shouting somewhere, an angry, outraged shouting.

She pulled away, breathless, and peered down the alley. Pedaiah still cradled her head with his hand, and his fingers tensed against her neck.

Gula. Pointing. Shadir, with a raised fist and a terrible fire in his eyes.

The timid Gula. Tia had underestimated her. In a flash she thought of Daniel's suggestion that she had been drugged. Had Gula been the source?

Shadir disappeared.

He cannot stop us all alone. But he would bring back guards, soldiers. In chariots, on horseback, on foot. They would give chase, they would block the city gates, and this many wagons could never escape the city unseen.

Fear shot through her, the fear that all their plans were for naught and that she would marry Amel after all and see her family murdered before the Akitu Festival ended.

"He will come for us!" Her voice shook with terror and she grabbed at Pedaiah's tunic.

He uncurled her fingers and jumped from the wagon. "You must hide."

And then he was gone, racing forward to the head of the caravan.

A moment later her wagon jerked forward to follow the others. She watched the alley, waiting to pass Pedaiah one final time, to whisper a tortured good-bye. But he did not appear.

The wagons careened through the city streets, chased by unseen horrors that were yet to come. The frantic speed strangely calmed her father, who sat with arms wrapped around his knees. He did not take his eyes from Tia, watching as she bounced along beside him, clutching the side for support.

Within minutes the wagon slowed. She rose to her knees to peer into the darkness ahead.

Daniel's house!

Her family alighted from their wagons one by one—her mother and sisters, their husbands and children. Pedaiah ushered them through the doorway, into the darkness beyond. Tia signaled the guards and pushed down the back of the wagon. They dragged the king forward and he did not protest. Pedaiah met her in the street.

"He has a secret chamber." Pedaiah's voice held urgency and he slipped his fingers through her own. "For the unseen training of magi in the ways of the One God. He will hide you there."

Tia watched the guards pull her father toward the door. "For how long? We must get out of the city."

"But not tonight. It is too dangerous. For now, you must hide. Until we have a better plan."

She exhaled, frustration and fear building in her gut. "You are certain no one knows of this chamber?"

Pedaiah led her to the door. "Many know of it —those who have been trained here. We must only pray that none of them are loyal to Shadir."

The risk was great—to remain rather than to flee—but she did not see what choice they had. She ducked into the doorway, traced her way through the passage to the courtyard, and was met by Daniel, who somehow embraced both Pedaiah and herself together.

"Come, come." He pulled them along. "Through here." Ahead, she saw a flicker of leather and tan tunics—a glimpse of the guards and her father disappearing into a darkened door.

They followed. Daniel snatched an oil lamp from a small pedestal they passed and Pedaiah guided her forward with his hand on her back.

Several steps downward, a twisting corridor with a low ceiling, a door half the height of a man, and they were inside a small chamber. Large enough for perhaps twenty persons to sit on the floor and learn from a wise man.

A dozen pairs of eyes shone in Daniel's meager lamplight, and he raised the lamp to flicker shadows onto the musty walls. Her little family group huddled in the darkness, but Daniel's attention was trained on only one of them.

Several hesitant steps brought him to stand before her father. The two met each other for the first time in seven years. She could see only her father's face. Pedaiah circled her waist with his arm and brought her closer to his side, but she barely noticed. It was her father's expression that held her captive.

Daniel reached a hand across the space that separated the two men, laid it gently on her father's shoulder, one man to another. Not a gesture of man and beast, nor servant and king. A gesture of friends.

Her father's entire body convulsed. A shudder that ran the length of him, but straightened rather than bent his spine.

His eyes fluttered and lifted to the low mud-brick ceiling.

Daniel's voice was like a benediction over him. "Say it, my friend. Say the words."

She held her breath—they all did—and watched something pass over her father's features. A clearing, a washing away, a letting go. His body sagged as though released from a fearsome grip and he brought his gaze to meet Daniel's.

And for the first time in seven years, Tia saw her father smile.

He smiled, and he licked his dry lips, and he spoke. Her father, the king, spoke to them all. Words that she would not have understood, would not have believed, in the days before she had known Pedaiah.

"The Most High lives forever. His kingdom is an eternal kingdom. His dominion endures from generation to generation."

The grip of the guards fell away from his arms, and her father stumbled forward. Daniel opened his arms and caught Nebuchadnezzar in a warm embrace.

Over Daniel's shoulder her father sought her out with his eyes, smiled on her. *"Tiamat."*

Their seven long years had ended.

I have been a proud man. A mighty king, skillful at politics, gifted in leadership, with achieve-ments beyond any dreamed of by my father or my father's father.

Yes, I have been a proud man. Believed that I alone controlled my destiny, that I held the reins of my life in my own hands and could direct its goings according to my choosing.

Once, years ago, I watched three rebels thrown into a brick furnace. I saw a god walk amongst them, saw them emerge unharmed. I knew truth that day. That the Most High God of the Jews was the One True God, and all others false.

But I denied this truth. Allowed only for the Most High to be added to our existing pantheon of gods, gave Him slight acknowledgment in my heart and in my kingdom.

And so He came to take the reins, to snatch control of mind and body until such time as I would admit the truth. I was ready now. A tranquility like the water of the Gardens poured over my soul, rushed into my heart, flooded my emotions.

And I opened my mouth and spoke the words, the words seven years in the making, seven years in the learning.

"The Most High lives forever. His kingdom is an eternal kingdom. His dominion endures from generation to generation."

My guilt and shame drained away with the words, replaced by a confidence that my wickedness had been forgiven, according to the justice and mercy of the One God.

In this, I acceded authority to Him whose power was infinitely beyond my own.

And with the accession came the one thing I could not grasp for myself.

My sanity was restored.

Chapter 42

Tia had never been plagued with shyness. But standing there in that cramped chamber, with the eyes of the king on her and surrounded by family, a tremor of uncertainty fluttered against her chest, held her back from approaching.

Her mother had insisted that the king knew of her true parentage. What if this had been a lie, like so many she had told over the years?

The king was a paradox. Regal bearing fastened

upon a beast's visage. Those in the chamber held their breath collectively, stunned with the transformation in process. Her mother hung back, as though fearful that to encounter this man who was half her husband would return him to his previous madness.

The king released the Jewish prophet, who stood aside like a proud father himself, and took a step nearer to Tia. Pedaiah's presence behind her was solid, and she reached a hand backward to grasp his warm fingers.

"Tiamat." The name was gravelly in her father's throat, a lingering reminder of the years past.

And then she was in his arms, the embrace she had longed for, his beard scratching at her neck and his tears wet on her cheek.

"You never gave up on me," he whispered.

She tried to speak, but a sob caught in her chest.

Beside them, a movement of light and dark, of the queen's pale skin and dark hair. Nebuchadnezzar released her to face his wife.

Tia had not seen Mother more beautiful than in that moment. Her wide, dark eyes fixed upon those of her husband, her full lips parted in a fusion of hope and disbelief, her delicate fingers reaching, reaching for what she had not believed possible.

Despite his filth, his crusted beard and yellowed nails, despite the smell of him and the barest scraps of clothing that hung from grimy shoulders, her father swept the queen into the passionate embrace of a younger man. Her mother's whimper of surprise became a cry of relief, of laughter, and then of joy.

Tia laid her head against Pedaiah's shoulder and drank in this reunion. He held her close, and the dark chamber seemed to lighten.

"How long?" His roughened voice took in the room, though he did not release her mother. "How long have I been senseless?"

It was Daniel who answered, his tone at once amused and instructive. "Seven times have passed over you, my king."

Nebuchadnezzar nodded to Daniel, some secret understanding passing between the men. "To whom He wills power, He gives power."

Daniel bowed, a slow dip of his head, and the king returned the gesture.

He still held her mother with one arm, but his gaze returned to Tia, confusion flitting across his features. "But who is this, Tia? Not your husband, Shealtiel? He is much changed."

She smiled, suddenly timid again. Where to begin?

"Shealtiel has gone to his fathers, my king. This—this is his younger brother, Pedaiah."

The king looked down on her mother's face. "I am surprised, wife. You were so opposed to her first marriage. I would not have thought you would give her again to the Jews."

Tia flushed. "We are not married, Father."

The confession and her use of the term *father* both shook her with confusing emotions.

Mother leaned close to the king. "Tia knows the truth, husband. All of it."

His shoulders sagged. "I would have preferred the secret be kept from you." He tilted his head, examined her. "It changes nothing, Daughter. Nothing."

She tried to smile, but the muscles of her lips quivered into something else. Though she was not his own, he loved her still. Like the One God, inviting her into His covenant.

The king's attention went to Pedaiah. "So, you have not married her, but you wish to?"

The startling question set the rest of the room buzzing, and her father seemed to realize at last that others were present. There came a flurry of greetings and embraces, of introductions to his grandchildren whom he had never met, of tears from her sisters, and nervous acknowledgment from their husbands.

Her mother drew him aside at last. "There is much to tell you, my king. The kingdom is not safe. We are in hiding, attempting to flee the city."

Even as she said the words, they all saw that everything had changed in this secret chamber. They were an exiled family with a mad king no longer.

It was time to take a stand.

Behind her, a shout of derision sounded from the narrow passageway and Tia turned in time to see a lean figure bend and enter, then straighten and survey the room.

Her would-be future husband. Amel-Marduk.

The room silenced at once. Tia stepped forward, as though she could shield them all with her body. Pedaiah shifted as well, toward her father.

Tia faced the young mage, the young *prince,* and lifted her chin. "So you have found us, Amel."

He surveyed the room full of royalty and brought his gaze back to her. "What is this, Tiamat? You are leaving Babylon?"

She hesitated and swallowed her first reply. Their uncertain future left her fumbling for an answer.

Pedaiah stepped behind her. "She will never marry you, Amel. Take the throne if you must, but you will not have Tia."

Amel looked between them, then broke into a laugh. "So this is who you would favor, Tia? The arrogant Jew?" He turned on Pedaiah. "And you? You think yourself worthy of a princess?" He jutted his chin toward Pedaiah. "Perhaps another scar, to match the first I gave you, would remind you of your place."

Pedaiah stiffened beside her, his hands forming fists and his jaw clenched.

Tia went to Amel and clutched at his sleeve. "Let us leave in peace, Amel. We leave the kingdom to you. There is no need for blood-shed. No need to tell Shadir what has become of us."

Amel snarled, an angry curl of the lip she had never seen. "Let you leave with a mad king and his successors? What's to keep you from return-ing to claim the throne?"

"Look at us." Tia spread a hand to the huddled group and risked a glance at her father. He stood half hunched, his eyes a vacant stare. Had his madness returned? But no, it was an act for Amel. His cunning had returned with his sanity. "With what army shall we claim the throne? We escape with little more than our lives. We are no threat to you."

He seemed to deliberate, and she pressed into his silence.

"If you care for me at all, Amel, do this for me. Allow me my freedom, and the lives of my family."

Her fingers tightened around his arm, and he stared down at her hand, then slowly removed its grip. His eyes, when he looked into Tia's, held an empty hostility. She had misjudged him.

"I care for you, *Princess,* because of what you can do for me here in Babylon. Out there"—he jerked his head toward the unknown—"out there you can do nothing, and hence you mean nothing to me."

Pedaiah was before her in a blur, blocking her view of Amel, pushing him back toward the door. "Go then, mage. Raise your supporters. Do what you must."

He gambled that Amel had come alone, without soldiers to take them all.

The men faced off, a breath apart, until Amel broke the hold and backed to the entrance. "You will never escape the city."

And he was gone.

Chapter 43

They did not have long.

Amel's departure left them in silence for only a few moments, until a hushed and hurried convening of ideas brought them together in the darkened chamber.

At the heart of their plan: the king's restoration and what it meant for the kingdom, and for their enemies. They would not flee into the night as though they had no king.

The two guards who had brought her father into Daniel's house were sent to retrieve the wagons. Daniel followed, then returned when the wagons were readied. Water was brought for the king to wash, and clothes to cover him.

In a strange reversal of their earlier flight, they piled into the vehicles and headed back toward the palace—the one location Shadir and his followers would not expect to find them. Tia and her parents took to a single wagon this time, with Pedaiah sitting cross-legged beside her.

"Daniel tells me you are one of his wisest scholars, Pedaiah." The king's voice was strong and sure, despite his appearance, and Tia glowed at the praise. "When this is over, I would learn more of our One God from you."

Pedaiah smiled and dipped his head, clearly embarrassed. "It would be my honor, King, to open the holy word to you. And to your daughter, who also has forsaken the gods of Babylon for the One God."

Her father's eyes lighted on her, bright and joyous. "This is true, Tia? You are also a follower of the Judaean God?"

Her mother watched between them, speechless.

"Yes, Father. Pedaiah has taught me much."

Her father glanced at Pedaiah again, and his eyebrows were raised in an obvious question. Pedaiah only nodded once, in the way of men who do not need to speak to be understood.

The king looked out over the darkened road, with the palace looming. "Then we shall have much to speak of." He pulled her mother to him, and she was pliant in his arms. "As do you and I."

They rumbled into the alley behind the palace. It could not have been more than an hour since they left. How was it possible that so much had changed?

One by one, they slipped into the palace and, by prearrangement, filtered upward to the level that would now be unguarded. It had been restricted for so many years that no one would think to search it for the fleeing royal family—the Hanging Gardens.

They assembled on the seventh tier, the entire family and Pedaiah, and to Tia, he felt like one of them already. The hydraulic lift at the summit of the Gardens churned its buckets into the topmost pool with all the regularity it ever had—as though the kingdom was not soon to be turned upside down—and the rhythmic splashes punctuated the still night air. The cheers and chants of the festival crowds seemed to belong to another place and time, so far off and faint.

Her father took command of the little band, a capable king once more. How strange, to be here in the Gardens with him, in appearance still so beastly, and yet to see his former glory pierce the façade.

His voice was low but commanding and took in each of the huddled group, family and servant alike. "Amytis tells me there are still many who are loyal to our family. This night we must separate faithful from treacherous and make an end of those who would bring destruction."

Nabonidus had been silent for most of the escape and return, but he pulled away from Tia's sister, his general's training replacing fugitive's fear. "We must be ready with force when the traitors are exposed."

Her father's countenance was grave, almost sad perhaps, at the thought of bringing military strength against those of his own kingdom. He nodded to Nabonidus. "You have men?"

Her sister's husband lifted his chin and expanded his chest. "More men than we shall need, all of them ready to die for their king."

"And you, Amytis?" His hand went to her cheek. "Do you know whom you can trust?"

Mother placed her own fingers over his hand against her face, her eyes warm. "Your advisors have become my own these last seven years. They have stood by you, and me, and helped rule the kingdom."

"I owe them my thanks, but this night will require even more of them. Go. Find those of whom you have no doubt and gather them in the advisory chamber."

He turned to Tia. "And of the young and faithful Tiamat, I must ask one more thing."

She squared her shoulders. "Anything, Father."

His lips twitched, a sad but affectionate smile that rewarded her for her seven-year vigil in the Gardens.

"Prepare for your wedding."

Chapter 44

Tia was loathe to leave her father, to leave Pedaiah, to break from the knot of familial security at all. And the task he had set her upon sickened her spirit. But they each had a part to play, and hers was vital.

The hastily constructed plan, pieced together under the stars, then broken apart and tasked to each of them, was risky. Perhaps impossible. But one look at her beautiful nephews and the image of them under the blade of Shadir was all the motivation necessary. They would save themselves and save the kingdom. There was great risk, but Tia had learned this: The One God was Most High and sovereign over all the ways of men, including hers. But the One God was also love and held her in His hands. To be held by a God of both love and power meant she could risk everything.

"Come, Tia." Mother wrapped her fingers around Tia's. Her voice was uncharacteristically soft. The time with the king had stripped her of the hard shell she had maintained since his exile. How had Tia not seen that it was mostly an act, a part she played to keep Babylon from falling victim to ruthless men?

Tia looked to Pedaiah, reached for him, and he

grasped her other hand. She stood that way, torn between duty and love, for a long moment. His eyes on her were understanding, loving. Had she ever believed him arrogant and sullen? Impossible.

Tia pulled from her mother's grip, sought his arms for a last embrace, heedful of the disapproving eyes of her family. Pedaiah wrapped her in a tight clasp and whispered against her hair.

"You must go, little Tia. But you do not go alone. Yahweh Himself is your protection, your sword, and your refuge."

Her cries escaped against his chest, and he leaned away to cup her face in his hands. "Go, Princess. Do what you must."

They left, she and her mother. Left the men they loved, unsure of the destiny that awaited them all.

On the main floor of the palace, in the first leafy courtyard, they parted company, but not before Mother also embraced her—a stiff, awkward embrace, unpracticed but with implicit promise to improve. She ran her hands through Tia's long hair, a caress Tia would have believed ridiculous only a few days ago.

"Be safe, Tia." Her voice caught on the words, and a corresponding swell of emotion choked Tia.

"And you, Mother."

It would take some time for both of them to complete their tasks. They must act in stealth but act with speed, and as they parted Tia's stomach fluttered with anxiety.

Where would Amel be by now? Still about the city, searching for the fugitives?

The palace was unnaturally silent, a counterpoint to the chaos that swept the streets of Babylon. She found only a few guards stationed at the entrances, and these with eyes trained outward in curiosity more than protection.

In response to her sandal slaps across the courtyard, they turned, immediately vigilant.

Tia kept her voice steady, in spite of the beating heart and shaking hands that could betray. "I have need of you both."

A few directives, and one of them nodded and left his post while the other still covered the palace entrance.

For her part, she slipped from the palace, down the wide stairs, and got lost in the crowds, hoping no one would notice a princess who was not where she was expected.

She reached the Temple of Ishtar within minutes and crossed the torch-lit outer court and the dusky antechamber. She would wait here for Amel, and hope that the guard she had dispatched would find enough colleagues that his task would not take long.

The temple was quiet. With the statue of the demon goddess gone—pulled in her chariot to the Akitu House for the ceremony earlier—it had seemed a safe place to rendezvous with Amel. But as Tia slid to a seated position against the stone wall of the main chamber, she felt the weight of the so-called gods of Babylon pressing against her all the same.

Yahweh is my protection. The words seemed less convincing in her mouth. *Pedaiah, I should have brought you with me*.

But that had been impossible. She must do this alone.

Only one torch in a wall socket remained lit in the deserted temple. Not a priest, a slave, nor a prostitute crossed the threshold. She was alone with the demon gods. She focused her gaze on that single flickering torch, willing its light to banish the darkness that seemed to crowd her soul.

The minutes dragged. Her limbs grew heavy and chilled, and a hopelessness stole through her—a whispering, otherworldly dread that all was lost, that this night would be her last, that not even Yahweh could save her now.

These thoughts she tried to ignore, then to push away, to hold at arm's length. But they slithered through her heart and mind like tenacious little worms, spreading their filth.

At last, at last Tia heard a sound beyond the chamber and braced her hands against the stone floor, senses alert.

"Tiamat?" Amel's harsh whisper held contempt but also inquisition.

She scrambled to standing, her cold legs shaking. "Here."

His beautiful face appeared, lit by the torch, and his elongated shadow on the chamber wall hovered over him like an unearthly presence. "Where are the rest of them?"

"Safe. Hidden. Until we have spoken."

His eyes narrowed. "What is there to speak of?"

"Our marriage."

Surprise flickered across his features, gone in an instant and replaced by a cool hardness. "You have come to your senses?"

She swallowed the harsh reply she wished to give and instead nodded. "I have changed my mind. I see now that the best thing for Babylon is a prince upon the throne and a princess at his side."

He folded his arms. "I have heard this once before."

"I—I grew frightened that you would not keep your word. Ensure the safety of my family."

Amel had long deceived her and she had been a fool. But tonight, after all that had happened, she was wiser. The slight leftward shift of his eyes, the twitch of lip and hand—these were enough for her to know the truth. He would never keep Shadir from swallowing her entire family in his ambition.

"I seek only your happiness, Tiamat."

She smiled, ready to play the part of deception

herself. "You will make a fine king. And I will be proud to rule with you."

He held out a hand and grasped her icy fingers. "Then let us join the festival and give the people the ceremony they have long awaited."

Chapter 45

They left the Temple of Ishtar together, Amel following Tia, and threaded through the streets crowded with revelers toward the Akitu House.

She called over her shoulder, "Shadir knows that our family fled and yet awaits us there?"

Amel's voice lifted above the music and shouting. "He was confident that you would . . . see the light."

Confident I would be dragged back against my will.

They approached the Akitu House and encountered guards with drawn swords who held back the people. They recognized her, if not Amel, and lifted their weapons to allow them to pass, then resumed their positions before any should follow.

The Akitu House was large enough for a small crowd of worshippers, though not as large as most of Babylon's temples. Tia passed under the lintel into its shadowy depths, and familiar oppression settled on her shoulders.

Shadir waited with two others—magi she had seen but did not know—at the back of the main stone chamber.

"Ah, Princess." His words held a sickeningly warm welcome, and no surprise, which infuriated her. Her muscles tensed, fingers curling. Ready to flee or to attack?

She squared her posture, lifted her chin, and shot venom from her eyes. "You shall have your ceremony, Shadir."

He bowed, those slack facial muscles undisturbed. "As you wish, Princess."

"But my mother insists upon an audience with those loyal to your cause. Gather them here."

His right eye twitched. Did he sense a trap?

"They are in full understanding of what shall transpire—"

"Gather them, Shadir." Tia steeled her voice. "It is our one condition of cooperation. She will appeal to them on behalf of our family. She does not trust you to honor their safety. They must hear her out."

Shadir hesitated, his body inert, watchful. When he spoke to his colleague, his voice was flat, resigned. "Send word to the others. Have them assemble here in the Akitu House at once."

The mage bowed and escaped, giving her wide berth as he passed, which pleased her greatly.

She nodded once and turned to leave. "And I shall bring my mother here."

Amel stepped in front of her, his face hard. But it was Shadir who spoke. "You should not be burdened with errands on your wedding day, Princess. I will have a slave fetch the queen, if you will but tell me where she waits?"

So. I am to be a prisoner, one way or another.

She returned her gaze to the older mage. He had pressed his fingertips together before him, and almost that cage of fingers felt as though it closed upon her heart, or perhaps her throat. She swallowed and stretched her neck, attempting to relax the threatened muscles.

"Your kind attention is appreciated, Shadir. Your slave will find her in her chambers, I am certain."

Shadir jerked his head toward the shadows, a slave appeared, head down and listening to Shadir's whispered instruction.

She prayed to Yahweh that the instruction was for her mother's retrieval, and not her execution.

And so they waited.

The magi left her to her thoughts, to stand at the entrance of the Akitu House, half hidden in the doorway, and listen to the celebrations that drifted, crescendoed, and then waned through-out the city. Would they grow impatient, waiting for the ceremony that was long overdue? It was vital that they still roamed the streets when the plan bore fruit.

Wise men filtered into the Akitu House over the next hour. Some she recognized, men she had believed loyal to her father, to her family, but whose eyes on her as they passed betrayed their enmity. Others were part of that great company kept in the palace and largely invisible to a princess who had not cared to be observant.

Finally, when the Akitu House buzzed with the voices of dozens of magi, there came a contingent of palace guards, marching in a formation that signaled her mother's presence within their ranks.

She straightened, inhaled courage. The time had come.

The guards left the queen beside Tia at the door. Mother's large eyes flicked toward hers only briefly, and only the barest of tremors betrayed her fear. She clasped her fingers for a whisper of a moment, then pushed through the crowd of enemies to reach the back of the Akitu House. Tia followed.

An elevated platform, usually reserved for the statues of Ishtar and Marduk, raised them above the heads of the men. Shadir stood beside them, as though they were a united presence, and they waited for quieted attention.

When silence filtered through the men and their upturned faces focused their hostility, Shadir spoke.

"We have long awaited this night, colleagues. The stars have told us that change must come. Until tonight, we have spoken only in whispers of this change, of our plan for the one who would replace madness with clear thinking—the clear thinking of the magi!"

His little speech was met with a cheer. If there had been any doubt as to the loyalty of the gathered group, that doubt was banished.

And with their cheers they had called for their own deaths.

From behind the group, a shout at the Akitu House door raised the hair on Tia's arms. It was the shout of warriors. Of men who faced their enemy with a rage and a passion.

Nabonidus had performed his task.

Soldiers loyal to him, loyal to her father, poured through the entrance, an invading swarm that chewed through all in its path.

The traitorous magi were largely trapped, save one narrow exit at the back of the Akitu House, which was soon scaled by soldiers.

Tia and her mother huddled at the back wall, alternately watching and hiding from the mass execution.

The magi were unarmed and untrained. Man after man was cut down before the swords of soldiers like hewn grass. Screams of fear, of hysteria, crashed off the stone walls, then ended in throaty gurgles of slit throats and punctured chests.

Her mother's body shook in Tia's arms, and Tia feared she would retch. Though unhurt, her mouth tasted the bitter blood of her enemies and her limbs trembled with fatigue as though she herself wielded a sword.

The carnage mounted, a heap of dead and dying. She could not watch but could not draw her gaze away.

How much learning, how much knowledge, is being extinguished here tonight?

Surely a light had gone out in Babylon that would never be relit.

It seemed like hours, but perhaps was only minutes, before the captain of the guard found them clutching each other in the darkness and saluted her mother.

"We have taken the Akitu House, my queen."

As though it were the enemy's stronghold. As it was.

Mother disengaged from her but still gripped her arm. She tried to speak, but the words sounded strangled in her throat. "You will be commended by the king for your good work."

The captain dipped his head, and a contriteness passed over his features. "I am afraid that we were not able to take the mage Shadir, my queen, nor the other—Amel-Marduk."

Shadir escaped? And Amel with him?

Tia's heart pounded against her chest, an angry, relentless beat that would not calm until she had seen them both apprehended.

They had been too quick. Had seen the guards

enter and from their place at the back of the Akitu House, they must have slipped through the exit before it had been sealed.

Amytis eyed her, her expression asking her silently what this news meant to the plan.

Could the master mage and his young protégé take the kingdom alone, with all support dead at their feet?

Tia did not know. She knew only that she would not be at rest with them free.

She and Shadir had unfinished business. It was time for the true beast and the product of his depravity to face each other.

"Proceed as planned," Tia whispered to her mother. "I will return."

She nodded to the captain. "Give me two of your best. I must get to the palace."

Chapter 46

Tia knew where to find him.

She could not say how she knew, nor what she would do when they faced each other.

She only followed what every part of herself— the thrill seeker she had been and the woman of purpose she was becoming—shouted that she must do.

The two soldiers assigned to her ran along-side, cutting a path through the city streets, with townspeople diving from their path in fear.

She raced up the outer palace stairs, through the arched entrance, and did not slow through the courtyards except to dismiss the soldiers. She would do this alone.

Tia ran along the palace corridor toward her destination, and her skin tingled from scalp to toe with the spark one could sometimes taste when summer lightning streaked across the desert plains. Tia did not run to escape, nor for pleasure, as she had run so many times. Tonight she ran toward the battlefront, and her only weapon was the One God whom Pedaiah insisted was both her shield and her strength.

And we shall see.

She had thought she would never step foot in the Hall of Magi again. Would she succumb to the evil presence?

But she had learned something through all the revelations of the past weeks—evil cannot always be avoided. Sometimes it must be confronted.

She paused under the heavy-columned entrance of that great Hall. It was empty save one lone figure, a purple-robed mage hastily thrusting instruments and charts into a leather pouch. The tar-black walls and mosaic floor were lit by only a few braziers. Barely enough light to make out the interior of the chamber. But Shadir knew his lair and did not hesitate in his flight.

He must have sensed her there at the head of the stairs. His gaze shot upward, toward the place where she hovered, and Tia saw fear.

The expression surprised her, emboldened her. A fiery flame of righteous anger flashed through her veins, ignited her blood.

"You will not leave Babylon alive, Shadir."

He yanked the pouch's strap over his head and one shoulder. "You trifle with power far beyond you, little princess." He made no move to approach and neither did she leave her perch.

"Your deeds are known. To my mother. To myself. To the king."

"Ha! The king has known nothing but dirt and grass these seven years."

She smiled, slow and sure as she had seen him smile so many times, and that flicker of fear crossed his features again. "No longer. Even now he prepares to speak to his people. To assure them of his strong leadership. To inform them of the treachery among his wise men that has been so utterly defeated."

His lips worked, pursing and relaxing, as though they would speak but he could find no words.

So she supplied the words herself.

"It was you who told me I was not the daughter of the king. Did you think I would not learn the name of my true father?"

He lifted his chin and shrugged one shoulder. "It is a day long past."

Since Tia had learned the truth of her parentage, one thought had plagued her: If she should face Shadir, would she feel an undeniable sympathy? With his blood running through her, would she somehow show him favor despite his wicked deeds?

But the cold fire that burned in her chest assured her she would not prove disloyal to the king. Shadir was enemy to Babylon, to her family, and to her. And she would not back down.

Tia raised a hand, pointed a finger, like an oracle delivering a prophecy. And indeed, she felt the holiness of truth as the words passed her lips. "Your life will be required of you this night, Shadir. For your treachery against my mother and against Babylon."

He huffed, straightened his pouch, and took a few steps across the patterned floor.

"Stop!" Her upraised hand was a flat wall of refusal now, refusal to let him pass.

He pulled up as though physically rebuffed.

The dark light of his demon gods built in his eyes, a chill spark that seemed to suck in the light of the room, and at the edges of her vision the braziers flickered.

"You have no power here, girl."

"I have the power of the One God, my shield and my deliverer."

Tia had expected him to scoff, to ridicule her newfound faith in the Judaean God. Instead, there was a rapid blink of the eyes, a tiny backward step.

Shadir himself knew the power of Yahweh.

With slow deliberation, he removed the leather pouch and set it upon the central table, never taking his gaze from her. The simple motion had all the marks of a man preparing for war.

So be it.

Silence weighted the Hall as they faced each other, neither with weapons forged in metals, but each with power nonetheless.

"The Babylonian gods are naught but demons, Shadir. They control you even as you seek to control them. They use you to control the people. To keep them from truth."

He sneered. "And what of it? The people have little need of truth. They seek only their own comfort, their own pleasures." His eyes narrowed. "Even princesses."

The beam of his hatred focused on her, his own child. There was more of demon than of man in him. The oppression that had followed her, plagued her, frightened her, since the night her husband died seemed to build within the Hall, to reach for her there on the steps, and pull her into itself. She descended the steps, her feet sluggish, against her will.

Her mouth went dry and she tried to swallow the tightness in her throat. "What are you doing?" Her feet took her closer to him, drawn by an invisible thread stronger than any woven cord.

Shadir watched, his face impassive.

Tia put the table between them, as it had been once before. Gripped its edges until her fingers hurt.

Had she known that it would come to this? Facing Shadir to fight for herself and her family? The One God of the Jews asserted over the many gods of the Babylonians? Somehow, she had known.

The darkness around them swelled, but she was not frightened.

The braziers flickered and went out, but she held her ground.

Only the moonlight showed her Shadir's face, Shadir's fear, as the pressure mounted around them in the unseen realms. The smell of burning reached her nostrils, watered her eyes. She did not blink.

Shadir's voice was a guttural hiss. "You have no power here." His eyes in the half-light were two white flames with a smoldering center.

Weak repetition, feeble words.

Tia agreed with his assertion. "I have no power." Then raised both hands, releasing her fearful grip on the table. "But I have Yahweh!"

With the name, a shriek tore from Shadir's throat and echoed off the tarred walls. That preternatural wind, hot and swirling, snaked into the Hall and eddied around them—an unseen sandstorm of malevolence.

She did not take her eyes from Shadir. Not when clay tablets of incantations flew from shelves and shattered on the mosaics. Not when darkness threatened to choke the air from her lungs, nor when Shadir's face vibrated with an inhuman energy. In all this, she stood her ground and let the name of Yahweh forge her protection.

And like the storms of the desert, the deviant gust at last played itself out. It had been the bluff of a defeated enemy—designed to frighten but lacking in strength.

It blew out like a snuffed candle, and with it, Shadir's support visibly collapsed inward. His expression hollowed, a thin veil of flesh upon a skeletal shell. A man without ally.

His hand clawed at the table, searching in vain for his pouch.

Tia snatched it and threw it from her. Heard it strike the wall, impossibly far away.

His eyelids fluttered, his lips twitched, every part of his face seemed to crawl with insects. She had never seem him so alive, and yet so dead.

I could kill him where he stands.

Without weapons, yet she knew it to be true.

But it was not her place to mete out retribution.

Shadir seemed to sense her deliberate withdrawal of power, as though she had opened the bars of his cage for a brief moment. He used the table to pull himself forward on stiff legs, then shot past where Tia still stood, watching.

431

Up the stairs, under the columns, purple robe billowing and chased by the Most High, Shadir fled into the night.

Words spoken over her by Pedaiah returned, and this time her heart beat with blessed agreement.

May those who seek our lives be disgraced and put to shame.

May those who plot our ruin be turned back in dismay.

May they be like chaff before the wind, while You drive them away.

May their path be dark and slippery, while You pursue them.

Yes, Yahweh would be her salvation.

Chapter 47

To return to the Akitu House was to return to a house of death. And yet this was where they must meet, all of them, with their people. This was where the future would begin.

Word of the mass slaying of the magi had ripped through the city. It seemed every Babylonian within the city walls had taken to the streets in confusion and fear, though some must also cower in their homes.

Tia pulled the hood of her robe over her head and pushed through the crowds. Would they all be there? Assembled as they had planned?

Troops still surrounded the Akitu House, weapons drawn to hold back the curious and the outraged. Tia whispered to a soldier at the outskirts of the fray and was rewarded with an escort through the massive bulk of loyal men.

Thankfully, they took to the outside steps of the Akitu House, avoiding the carnage within. The smell of death clung to the building, rising to the star-flecked sky like an unholy sacrifice to the demon gods.

Tia paused at the head of the steps, surveyed the roof, and smiled.

Her parents, arms entwined, stood in the center, and it was as if the years had dropped away. The king was bathed and shaved, his hair cut and his royal robes on his shoulders. And beyond the physical transformation, he seemed to glow with something new, a radiance that shone like truth. Surrounding him were her sisters and their husbands, their children.

And Pedaiah. He had come.

As though Tia had called his name, Pedaiah's head turned to her and he returned her smile. They savored and lengthened that moment, apart and yet together at last.

And then he held out an arm, and she ran to his embrace.

Her parents fell on her as well.

"Tia!" Her father's voice was sharp, reprimanding. "You should not have chased after Shadir!"

She patted his cheek, grinned through her tears. "And you should not have feared. The Most High is stronger than a thousand Shadirs."

He lifted his hand to hers, clasped her fingers, but then took Tia's hand and joined it with Pedaiah's.

"It is time to speak to our people."

Tia lifted her joy to Pedaiah's face and saw it reflected there. He squeezed her fingers, and they approached the lip of the Akitu House roof, a united royal family presented to the people, standing behind their king.

Her father's voice had lost none of its authority, though the people had not heard it for seven years. Below them, the masses of people within range of his words drank them in, passed them backward through the torch-lit streets that stretched before them to the far gates of Babylon. Tia looked over the people and she loved them, though she knew in many ways she was no longer part of them.

Nebuchadnezzar spoke of the magi dead under their feet with respect and yet condemnation. A plot to take the kingdom from him had been stopped this night, and the people were witness.

"My daughter Tiamat shall indeed be wed tonight," he shouted. "But not to the prince of Media as was expected. We shall keep our kingdom to ourselves yet awhile longer."

At this, smiles of amusement, of appreciation, rippled through the crowd.

"Instead, I wed my daughter Tiamat to the brother of her late husband. To Pedaiah ben Jeconiah, son of the Judaean king."

Pedaiah's arm circled her waist and they stepped to the edge of the roof to stand beside the king. The people lifted a cheer, though she guessed they cared little for her happiness and were only glad to see the kingdom retain its autonomy and strength, with no treaty marriage to the Medes.

She thought of Amel, whom the people had never known was to be her husband. Where was he now? Would he flee the city along with Shadir?

Behind them, at the announcement, a shriek lifted into the night.

They turned as one to face evil once more.

She had expected Yahweh to pursue Shadir and exact justice. She had not expected Shadir to pursue her.

Though in truth, it was impossible to know where his attack was directed—to her, to the king, even Pedaiah. He flew across the roof in a rage, his face a hideous contortion of malice, lips flecked with froth and eyes bulging. In one upraised hand he bore a dagger. He would carry one of them over the edge of the roof with that dagger embedded in flesh. Pedaiah pushed Tia behind his body and her father held out his arm, ineffectual defense.

Halfway across the roof, Shadir met the blades of four soldiers. One of them sliced so deeply into his neck that, stoic as Tia usually was at the sight of gore, she turned her head, faint with the spectacle.

Shadir went down in a heap, his robes settling around him like a blackbird's feathers coming to roost, and did not move.

They stood in silence, all of them, shocked by the suddenness of the attack and the finality of Shadir's execution.

Her father, her true father, pulled Tia to himself and kissed the top of her head.

"Not here, Tia," he said, as if they had not just witnessed such a horror. "I will not have you married here, with death all around us."

Tia smiled up at him and nodded. "There is only one place with beauty enough to erase all the ugliness of this night."

And so that very night, Pedaiah's mother, Marta, was brought, and his sister, Rachel, and younger brothers to join once more with her family. Surrounded by them all, she stood in the Hanging Gardens—that wild and untamed place with its roots deep in the palace—and married the man she loved.

Epilogue

One year later

Push, Princess! Push!"

"I have been pushing all night!"

Tia's sweat-soaked hair stuck fast to her face, and she spit to clear it from her lips.

Omarsa stood beside where Tia lay on the bed and clucked her tongue. "It has *not* been all night—"

"I don't care! It has been too long!"

"All the women of the world before you have endured this night—"

Her murderous look stopped Omarsa's flow of stupidity.

"You will bear a fine son very soon, Princess, I promise you."

"I will hold you to that promise, Omarsa!"

Indeed, it turned out that her slave was a bit wiser in the ways of childbirth than she. Within the hour Tia held her newborn son in her arms, and Pedaiah knelt at her side, his face buried against them both. Hot tears anointed them with his love. Tia laid a hand on the back of his head and knew completeness for the first time in her life.

She looked at Omarsa. "Send for any news. I will go as soon as I must."

Omarsa nodded and went to the door, then whispered a few words to a younger slave. Though Omarsa served her still, Tia had not seen Gula since the night her father retook the throne of Babylon.

They huddled together, the little family, for too short a time. The slave returned, face grim, with a message that was passed to Omarsa and then to Tia.

"He is fading, Princess. But it is too soon—"

"No. No, I must go. Pedaiah, take the baby. Omarsa, help me prepare."

In the end, Omarsa carried their baby boy and Pedaiah carried her, for she was too weak to walk and the king's chamber lay on the other side of the palace.

One year had passed since her father had emerged from the Gardens and taken his place on the throne of Babylon again. A year of joy, of prosperity. In his newfound allegiance to the One God, Nebuchadnezzar had become even greater than his former days, and the people's devotion had swelled.

Daniel's training of young magi in the ways of the One God had come out from its secretive cover into the palace itself. While most of the wise men still pursued the age-old Babylonian gods, a school of magi flourished—some

Babylonian and some Jewish—who were especially trained to seek the wisdom of Yahweh, and ever watching the stars for signs of the Messiah whom Daniel said was to come.

They reached her father's chamber and were ushered in. Pedaiah carried Tia to her father's bedside and set her carefully beside him.

Amytis touched her cheek briefly, but her attention was on the babe in Omarsa's arms.

"A son, Father. I have borne a son."

The king's lips formed a knowing smile and his weak fingers sought hers. She caught them up and kissed them.

Omarsa transferred the sleeping child to Tia's arms, and her mother came to stand beside her.

From the shadows, Daniel also stepped forward, his warm smile falling on her. She was not surprised to see him. He and her father had been inseparable for the past year.

The prophet stood at the bedside, one hand on her father's feverish brow and one hand on Tia's son, and his eyes fluttered and closed.

Tia's smile faded, replaced by the solemn awareness that their time under this great king had come to an end, on the very day of this new beginning.

Somewhere in the halls of the palace, Amel-Marduk waited for word of his accession to the throne.

Tia would not have thought this possible a year

ago, but in the days since Shadir's death and the slaying of the magi who followed him, Amel had become the king's son in a true and honorable way. Ironic that the very thing Shadir had plotted would now come to pass. But all had changed. Amel would be a good king, ruling as her father wished, and the succession would be peaceable. Already he had convinced her father to give up his grudge against the Hebrew king Jeconiah and grant him release.

Daniel's eyes opened and he drew in a deep breath as though he would speak. Tia studied his noble profile and read the intense sorrow of a man losing his close friend.

"It is an end and it is a beginning," he whispered.

A chill raced along Tia's flesh at this echo of her own thoughts.

"The hand of Yahweh has been heavy on His people in judgment for their idolatry. He has brought them to a land of idols to teach them His sovereignty, and never again will they turn to false gods." His eyes smiled a blessing over Tia, over her child, and her heart pounded in response to the prophetic words, now spoken over her baby. "When the days of the judgment are passed, this child shall lead them."

Tia's breathing shallowed, a sense of the holy falling on her.

Daniel's voice rose, a victorious, joyful sound.

"His name shall be Zerubbabel." *Born of Babylon.* "But he shall be the last prince of the captivity. And he will lead his people home."

Pedaiah's hand fell on her shoulder, and Tia could feel the fatherly pride surge from his fingers into her flesh.

She thought of all she had once feared to lose —her position as princess and the luxuries that accompanied it. She had risked it all, and in many ways she had indeed lost it all. They did not live in the palace, she and Pedaiah. They lived among their people, the followers of Yahweh. This they would continue to do while they waited for the return. Though the king still called her his daughter, she belonged to another house now, the house and lineage of David, from whom would come a Messiah to save all people.

But the loss of Babylon was nothing. She had gained all that she truly desired. And now, this new calling—to raise a prince of Israel who would lead his people back to their land—well, she had wanted to change the world, had she not?

The infant Zerubbabel opened his eyes in the same moment Nebuchadnezzar's closed for the last time, and the final sigh of death was drowned by the lusty wail of new birth.

Her father had gone to find his reward at the gates of the One God.

But here in Babylon . . .

Here in Babylon, her greatest adventure awaited.

Author's Note

The Hanging Gardens of Babylon were first included on a list of the Seven Wonders of the Ancient World by the historian Philo of Byzantium, around 250 BC. Only a few other ancient writers mention the Gardens, and their existence has never been proved.

We do know from extensive excavations in Babylon that Nebuchadnezzar was a great builder and that a structure of this reported magnitude was possible. By combining the accounts of those few historians, we can assume that if the Hanging Gardens did indeed exist, they were built for the king's Median wife on a series of lofty terraces and planted with trees and a variety of flowers. In writing *Garden of Madness*, I drew upon these historians' works as though they were fact, but it must be admitted that some scholars find the accounts suspect.

The characters within this novel are a mix of fictional and historical. Nebuchadnezzar and his wife, Amytis, are known to us from history, as are the names of the king's two sons-in-law and his son, Amel-Marduk (often translated as Evil-Merodach in Scripture).

We have the names of many Israelites of the captivity, including the king, Jeconiah (also known as Jehoiachin), and his sons and grandson

Zerubbabel, who is claimed as both the son of Pedaiah and the son of Shealtiel in Scripture. This uncertainty about Zerubbabel's father was the seed of the idea for *Garden of Madness*.

The themes of pride and divine sovereignty are weighty within the book of Daniel, and I attempted to examine them within this novel, from the perspective of the Jewish Pedaiah as well as the pagan Tiamat. While God allows free will and the consequences that follow, His sovereignty is total and ultimate, and as such it often takes us places we do not want to go and perhaps do not understand. We can spend our lives railing against His sovereignty, running from it, denying it exists, or pridefully trying to control it, but in the end the only path to true joy is to embrace it. It *is* possible to surrender and embrace God's sovereignty, and it is secure rather than frightening because God is good and because He loves us and invites us into intimate relationship with Himself through the work of Christ.

While I was not able to travel to the location of *Garden of Madness* (near present-day Baghdad) during its writing, I have accumulated some wonderful photos, video, historical notes, and virtual presentations on my website, along with my travel journals and photos from other books, and I'd love to have you join me at www.TracyHigley.com for more exploration of Babylon—no passport required!

The Story Behind the Story . . . and Beyond

In the research necessary for any historical novel, a myriad of fascinating tidbits surface. Many of these find their way into the story itself. Sadly, many do not, because to include them would be too much weight for a novel. But after finishing *Garden of Madness*, you may perhaps be inter-ested in learning more about events that occurred before and after the story's setting, and about Babylon during the time of Nebuchadnezzar.

The idea for *Garden of Madness* started with simple curiosity on my part. I had studied Babylon for previous novels, and knew the city was heavily walled and thoroughly irrigated, with little but desert beyond its walls. Where, I wondered, would those in charge of the govern-ment during Nebuchadnezzar's seven years of madness have stashed the mad king? Since the book of Daniel tells us that he regained his throne at the end of seven years, we must assume they kept track of him. Was it possible he was kept in the very Hanging Gardens he had built?

From there, other bits of the story formed themselves as I speculated that there must have been plots to take the throne during those seven years, and his family would have been fighting to retain power. I wanted to view the story from a Babylonian's point of view, and thus Tia was born. But I also wanted to see the city and palace from a Jewish perspective. In a reading of genealogies I stumbled upon the apparent discrepancy between two accounts of the father of Zerubbabel: in one place Shealtiel and in another Pedaiah. Bible scholars assume that one of these men died before Zerubbabel was conceived, and that his brother married the widow to produce an heir in his brother's name. For a novelist, that sort of fact sparks ideas! Zerubbabel did indeed lead the first wave of captives back to Israel, some thirty years after the end of my story, and he is part of the lineage of Jesus. We have no evidence that his mother was Babylonian—this is fiction of my creation—but certainly we see God grafting pagan nations into the line of David in other places.

I wish I could have explored all the wonderful events of the book of Daniel in *Garden of Madness*, but the story takes place in only a small window of that great book. Scholars and historians are never in complete agreement as to dates, but I offer these widely accepted dates in a sort of timeline for you, to help you place my story in the context of well-known biblical events:

The beginnings of Babylon can be found in Genesis 11, when man first began to build a tower to reach for the divine, and God confused their languages in judgment for their pride. That tower remained unfinished for years, but was most likely taken up again to become Etemenanki, the House of the Platform of Heaven and Earth, around which the capital city of the Babylonian empire flourished.

The empire became a world power around 1650 BC, during the reign of Hammurabi. Nebuchadnezzar ruled the "Neo-Babylonian Empire" some one thousand years later, in about 605 BC, right after the first siege against Jerusalem. The first deportation of captives from Israel to Babylon occurred at this time, and included Daniel and his three friends (whose Babylonian names were Shadrach, Meshach, and Abednego). Daniel was a "youth" at this time, and Nebuchadnezzar was about twenty-five years old. About two years later, Nebuchadnezzar dreamed of a huge statue and Daniel, still a very young man, interpreted the king's dream with prophecies that would stretch hundreds of years into the future. Daniel became the king's chief advisor.

About eight years later, in 597 BC, another round of captives was brought, including King Jeconiah (sometimes called Jehoiachin). Then in 586 BC, Jerusalem fell completely to Babylon, the Temple was destroyed, and another deportation of Jews occurred. It was probably about this time that Nebuchadnezzar built his own statue and required everyone to worship it. Another fifteen or so years passed and Nebuchadnezzar dreamed again, this time of a huge tree, cut down and stripped. Daniel sorrowfully interpreted this dream as a prophecy of Nebuchadnezzar's coming madness, and entreated him to humble himself before the Most High God. One year later, while the king was admiring his great city from his palace roof, the prophecy was fulfilled. *Garden of Madness* is set seven years after this, in the year 563 BC, about forty years after the beginning of the captivity and one year before the death of Nebuchadnezzar.

In e-mails from readers during the writing of this story, a few questions arose that I chose not to address specifically in the story, but will do so here. *Was Daniel made a eunuch when he came to Babylon?* The answer is that we do not know, but it is likely. Those in service in the palace often were. *Where was Daniel when his three friends were refusing to bow to the king's statue?* Another mystery. We must assume from the rest of Daniel's life that he did not submit. Perhaps he was not required to. *What was the status of the exiles while in Babylon?* For the most part they lived fairly comfortable lives, much like the rest of the common citizens, though with fewer rights. They worked on behalf of the city, so in some ways could be considered "slaves," but they were able to build their own houses and gardens, to marry and have families. *What were the Hanging Gardens like? How were they built, watered, and maintained?* As I mentioned in the Author's Note, we have very little information about the Hanging Gardens. I was deliberately vague within the story for this reason. But we are told that the Gardens consisted of seven tiers, and that they were watered by some sort of hydraulic system that brought water up from the Euphrates to the topmost level. Considering the wealth, beauty, and magnitude of the rest of the city, we can assume they were astounding!

The kingship did not experience much peace after Nebuchadnezzar's death. His son Amel-Marduk took the throne for only two years. (His name is sometimes translated Evil-Merodach in the Bible, simply meaning "man of Marduk.") Amel was assassinated by Nebuchadnezzar's son-in-law, Nergal-shar-usur (Nergal in my story), who held the throne for four years, died of natural causes, and left the kingship to his very young son, Labashi. Labashi reigned for nine months before being murdered, and the priests chose Nebuchadnezzar's other son-in-law, Nabonidus, as king. He ruled for some seventeen years. His son Belshazzar became co-regent with him and was on the throne when Babylon fell.

Daniel's story did not end, of course, at the

death of Nebuchadnezzar in 562 BC. He went on to be an integral part of Babylonian politics for another thirty years, until the empire fell to the Medes and Persians in 539 BC, and Daniel became an advisor to the Median king Cyrus, and then the Persian king Darius. It was during this time that jealous advisors orchestrated Daniel's sentence to the lions' den. Daniel's dreams and visions of the end times, found in Daniel 7 through 11, seem to stretch from the time of Belshazzar's co-regency until perhaps the time of his own death.

All of this is fascinating to those of us who enjoy history, and who love the tales found in the book of Daniel. But we love them for a reason. There is more at work here than scheming politics, and even more than dreams and visions and miracles. There is truth for our own lives, as we line up our own personal stories with the One True Story. We have been accustomed to seeing Babylon as evil, and certainly it was filled with darkness. But we must remember that for most of us, we are Tiamat—children of chaos who have been welcomed and grafted into God's family, out of the darkness. Even before Jesus walked the earth, God was calling all nations to Himself, and using Israel as a blessing to those nations.

And what of Daniel and his three friends, who managed to remain unpolluted in the midst of all this spiritual darkness? How did they do it?

We have scant details, but we can infer from their positions of prominence within the kingdom that they were faithful in a way that was not antagonistic, not condemning, not hate-filled. That a pagan king would keep a Jewish advisor close for forty years and then finally bow his knee to the Most High God at the end of his life speaks volumes about Daniel's witness within that dark city. Centuries before Jesus' words in Mark 12, Daniel had already learned what it meant to love God and to love others.

May we all be grateful for our inclusion in the family of God through Christ, and may we be found faithful to love and bless those in the dark world around us.

Acknowledgments

Since I began writing about the Seven Wonders of the Ancient World, I've been looking forward to exploring the Hanging Gardens. It's been an enjoyable task, writing Tia's story, and I'm grateful to each of the people who have been part of the process.

To my new fiction family at Thomas Nelson— I'm so excited to begin this journey with you! To Allen Arnold, Ami McConnell, Jodi Hughes, and the rest of the team who work hard to bring quality fiction to the world, thank you for allowing me to be part of that work. Thank you to Julee Schwarzburg for your editing, both excellent and encouraging.

Steve Laube, your persistence and guidance as an agent are so appreciated, as is your friendship.

Thank you to friends and family who have weathered the ups and downs of this book with me.

A special thank-you to my readers, whose input into this book was invaluable. So many of you participated in my website request for ideas and thoughts, and it was great fun weaving your suggestions through the book. I hope you'll find everything you are eager to experience within its pages!

As always, my husband and children stood alongside the writing, propping up my sagging confidence, listening to my rambling thoughts, and assuring me of their unconditional love. Ron, Rachel, Sarah, Jake, and Noah—we've finished another one together! I love you all.

Reading Group Guide

1. What were your first thoughts about Tiamat? What three words come to mind when you think of her character early in the story? How do you relate to her desire to make a difference and change her world?

2. Who did you first think murdered Kaldu? Why? Did you think Shealtiel's death was also a murder?

3. The tension between Tia and her mother was apparent from the start. What was your reaction to that relationship? Have you experienced similar tension with a parent? Were you able to resolve the problem?

4. What was your first impression of Pedaiah? How do people in the story react to his determination to remain unpolluted? What causes his heart to change, leading him to love all people as Yahweh does? In what ways do you struggle with the concept found in Romans 2, "living in the world but not being of the world"?

5. When Tia met Pedaiah in the city, why did he take her on a detour instead of directly to

Daniel's house? Did you share his frustration with her at the end of the excursion?

6. What did you think happened to Tia when she awoke in the Gardens covered in blood with no memory of how she got there? Did you think she had gone mad, like her father?

7. At what point do you first see a change in Tia's thinking? What did you feel when Daniel and Pedaiah visited her and prayed over her after her lost night?

8. Secrecy is a major theme throughout this story. Has someone kept a secret from you that changed your life when it was revealed? Do you think secrets are ever worthwhile?

9. *Garden of Madness* surrounds the madness of the great king Nebuchadnezzar, whom God punished for his pride and arrogance (Daniel 4). Nebuchadnezzar learned the hard way that God is sovereign. Do you struggle with pride or being obedient to a sovereign God? Has sin ever cost you something as it did Nebuchadnezzar?

10. Discuss Nebuchadnezzar's journey to humility and the sins that brought the Israelites to captivity in Babylon. What can you learn from their mistakes?

11. This story takes place in the Old Testament. In what ways do the characters allude to the New Covenant? How do you now think of the Jews in the centuries before Christ? Do you think they considered that non-Jews would one day be accepted by God?

12. Tia and Pedaiah face many obstacles to their relationship throughout the book from his apparent disdain of her to their ethnic, social, and religious differences. How do you see these issues reconciled? Do you believe two people can build a good relationship amid such differences? How?

13. The author portrays Nebuchadnezzar and Daniel as close friends. Do you think that could have been the case? Do you have a friend like Daniel who tells you truth, even when you don't want to hear it?

14. In what ways has this book edified you in your own journey of faith?

Center Point Large Print
600 Brooks Road / PO Box 1
Thorndike ME 04986-0001 USA

(207) 568-3717

US & Canada:
1 800 929-9108
www.centerpointlargeprint.com